Beatrice Beecham's Ship of Shadows

Dave Jeffery

Let the world know:
#IGotMyCLPBook!

Crystal Lake Publishing
www.CrystalLakePub.com

Other Novels by Crystal Lake Publishing

The Mourner's Cradle: A Widow's Journey by Tommy B. Smith

House of Sighs (with sequel novella) by Aaron Dries

Beyond Night by Eric S. Brown and Steven L. Shrewsbury

The Third Twin: A Dark Psychological Thriller by Darren Speegle

Aletheia: A Supernatural Thriller by J.S. Breukelaar

Beatrice Beecham's Cryptic Crypt: A Supernatural Adventure/Mystery Novel by Dave Jeffery

Where the Dead Go to Die by Mark Allan Gunnells and Aaron Dries

Sarah Killian: Serial Killer (For Hire!) by Mark Sheldon

The Final Cut by Jasper Bark

Blackwater Val by William Gorman

Pretty Little Dead Girls: A Novel of Murder and Whimsy by Mercedes M. Yardley

Nameless: The Darkness Comes by Mercedes M. Yardley

Or check out other Crystal Lake Publishing books for more Tales from the Darkest Depths.

Other Titles by Dave Jeffery

Beatrice Beecham's Cryptic Crypt

**Tales from
the Darkest
Depths**

PROLOGUE

THE GIRL STOOD on the prow of the galleon, thick ropes binding her wrists, her hands limp and white against the black material of her heavy skirts. Her mouth moved but the sound that came forth was as restrained as her limbs; hushed whispers that cracked and wavered as they passed over parched lips. Wide eyes stared out across the bay, where the rolling blue waters of the Atlantic Ocean rose and fell like the folds of a great bed sheet aired in the sweet, spring breeze.

Her position was precarious but her resolve was steadfast. The sea breeze tousled her hair—turning it into ebony tendrils—and the face beneath was as pale as candle-wax, marred only by a splash of strawberry beneath her right eye where a birthmark lay like a livid isle in the blanched skin of her cheeks. There was a smile on her lips, as though she knew things that others did not, yet there was no fear.

Behind the girl, the ship's crew were a jeering mob, faces twisted in hate, and their cries of malice rose into the air where seagulls screamed a token response. Despite the loud catcalls from his men, the ship's captain stood silently to one side, his hands clutching a leather-bound King James Bible to his breast, his eyes—cupped by heavy lids—never leaving the girl on the prow. He held up a hand as he called out to his men.

"Be silent!"

At his command, the crew stopped their din. The seagulls took the opportunity to reassert themselves, their screeches carrying out across the bay. The chime of sword steel against the brass buttons of their long coats brought melody to the scene.

The captain raised the book into the air, his heavy raiment flapping about him as the wind swept across the deck. A series of creaks accompanying the breeze's passing as rigging swayed against block and tackle. The captain closed his eyes for a few moments, drew in a breath, and let go a sigh as he caressed the Bible, taking comfort from it.

"I read from 2 Chronicles 33:6!" he called.

When he opened his eyes, they were blue steel, vivid against the unkempt brush of his black beard. He cleared his throat. As he began to speak, his voice became rhythmic, mesmerising those before him,

"And he caused his children to pass through the fire in the valley of the son of Hinnom: also he observed times, and used enchantments, and used witchcraft, and dealt with a familiar spirit, and with wizards: he wrought much evil in the sight of the LORD, to provoke him to anger."

The captain paused in his recital, and addressed the girl, who remained facing the sea, as though oblivious to his rhetoric.

"Thou shalt not suffer a witch to live," he growled. "Elizabeth Caldecott, ye shall be cast down to the water. And it shall reveal yer true nature."

The captain looked at Elizabeth's bound wrists, at the length of rope that snaked away from her bonds and joined a coil at the feet of several crewmen.

The captain continued his address. "The sea shall embrace ye into its depths as the purity of innocence. Or spew ye out, as an Apostate of evil. Only through The Lord will ye be made known to us all. Only through The Lord shall punishment be brought upon ye."

The crew muttered "amen" and crossed themselves. They were no longer consumed with rage. Instead their demeanour was that of a humbled mass, revered by the words of their captain.

"Ye know the crime of which ye are accused," the captain said to Elizabeth. "Better in the eyes of the Lord ye pronounce yer affinity with Satan, child. Denounce yer allegiance with his black heart, and lift the curse ye have bestowed upon the governor of these lands."

"If I am to die knowing the man who killed my mother is to waste away, consumed by his own jealousy, then witch or not, I shall be at peace, sir."

"If ye are an apostate, child, there will be no peace in this world or the next," the captain sneered. "Pikeman!"

A tall and burly crewman, who leaned against a long spear, stood to attention and then stepped forward.

"My captain," he said. His voice was heavy and rattled with phlegm. As he approached the girl, the shaft came down, the spearhead aiming at her back.

"Step from the forecastle, wench," the captain said. "The trial begins. If ye survive, ye shall be drawn from the water by six strong hands at the end of this rope, proven a witch, and this same rope will be used to hang ye until yer sorry soul departs this world."

The Pike-man edged forwards, the spearhead moving ominously close to the small of the girl's back. The waves slapping against the hardwood hull counted away the seconds.

"Cast yerself to the waters and be with God," the captain ordered. "Or stay yer fate with a confession, and release the curse."

But the girl did not look back, nor did she need encouragement from the spear. She lifted her head and stared out towards the open ocean, stepping off of the forecastle, and hitting the water feet first. Her skirts blossomed for a few seconds before being dragged beneath the waves.

The captain went to the side of the ship and peered into the sea, his rope men waiting for his command. After a slow count, he held up his hand. The crewmen grabbed once more at the ropes and began to haul Elizabeth back in.

By the third pull something quite strange happened. The rope in their hand slackened as though Elizabeth was somehow moving faster than they could pull. Their captain confirmed that things were amiss when he cried out, and the crew went to the side to look down into the water.

The undulating shape of Elizabeth Caldecott was now visible just below the surface. But she was not sprawled or swimming, she was upright, the top of her head breaking the surface, her raven hair lank and slapped to her pallid face like streaks of tar. To the horror of all who looked upon her, the girl continued to rise. Her shoulders cleared the ocean, then her waist, the water pouring from her in fat rivulets, until she cleared the waves and stood on the surface as though she had merely stepped into a puddle. The surf slopped about her shoes.

She lifted her head and stared at the men standing watch over her. Her eyes were no longer ice; they were the colour of brilliant jade under the bright sunlight. A terrible smile played on her lips.

"Witch!" the captain called down to her. The crew began to shout and cuss, but they did not look at her. Instead, they cast their eyes away for fear of being stuck down.

Below, Elizabeth peered at her bonds. She muttered a few phrases and the ropes became opaque before disappearing altogether. The men holding onto the cables on the deck double checked their own hands just to be sure they were not imagining it. They absently rubbed their empty palms against their britches as though they were soiled.

"Aye," Elizabeth spat at the captain above her. "I be a witch. Drawn to its dark power out of the despair only an orphaned, powerless child can know. My mother is dead! The man who robbed her of life grows fat on the profits from his labours. But no more, sir! He shall rot in his own envy. Mark these words, Captain: The Green Man will wake no more. My mother's death is avenged in this act."

"Yer mother harboured evil, the Devil's Child," the captain said firmly. "Thus she is equal with thee in her guilt. Sinners both, I decree."

"Sin?" Elizabeth laughed and it was heartfelt. "Your ship plays host to sin, Captain. Ye and thy kind have desire that turn hearts black as night. Ye hide behind The Book, yet there is no light there for thy soul. The holds of your ship are filled with ill-gotten gains. Gold from Spanish galleons blasted until no man lives, silk from the Ottoman, the blood of slaves on every fibre. Ye covet such things; harbour their value above life itself. *Hypocrite,* I say to thee. Murderer!"

"Ye shall once more face the rope," the captain said. "About your neck as we watch ye dance on the air."

"Ye will have no such pleasure, sir," the woman said. Her voice was low but they could all hear her as though she were with them on the deck. "Ye are all cursed, and all ye are connected to are cursed, both now and in times to come. Let the day become as night, and ye without guide, the darkness in each heart will succumb to the desires they harbour!"

With trepidation, the captain watched Elizabeth stretch out her arms until she became a tiny "T" shape on the vast, rippling seascape. The girl lifted her head to the heavens, eyes closed.

"Where despair and desire in the same place be, let this wretched child return to thee. A Ship of Shadows, a distant shore, a maiden's voyage forevermore."

There was a terrible sound on the air, a cannon-blast that sent everyone on deck sprawling for cover. Overhead the sky began to lose light, the nebulous clouds turning the colour of wood smoke. At the sound of the explosion, the captain had ducked but now he was on his feet and staring down at the incredible sight of the girl standing on the surface of the ocean. To his horror the writhing waters about her feet were slowly turning black, a pool of India ink that was spreading at a rate of knots.

The men on the ship were now moaning in terror. The sky was becoming so dark there was no definition, just an ebony infinity, space with no stars. And in the fading light, the men could see things moving in the shadows, things that were difficult to define, their form as undulating as the ocean about them.

The captain watched the ocean turn to black sackcloth and then the world was as shadow. He stepped back from the side of the ship and lost his footing. He landed on his backside and his Bible went spinning into the darkness.

At his cry of despair, Elizabeth mocked him, her laughter now high pitched and bitter. She stemmed its flow and stood on the black ocean, her breathing faint.

"Let there be light," she whispered.

All about the ship fierce green embers flickered with sinister beauty as the things in the shadows opened their eyes.

The witch began laughing once more but this time it was lost amongst the awful, terrified screams of the damned.

Chapter One

THE BOY RUNS *headlong across the beach. There is the sound of music on the air, The Beatles are singing a song about a walrus and an egg-man, and it drifts from the promenade above, turned tinny by the transistor radio.*

The gulls are also demanding attention, wheeling overhead as wind currents determine their path across the flat grey sky.

Then there is the ocean, it sucks and slurps on the pebbles and shale, a drawn out hiss marking its advance and retreat.

All of these things are secondary to the boy's sobs. They are the sounds of grief, the sound of loss. His heart is a stone in his chest, his throat raw with the screams of despair at the recent, awful news that has been brought to their door by a coastguard whose face was ashen with shock.

His father is dead. The man he looked up to, the man who kept him safe, made him laugh with terrible jokes, now gone claimed by the sea. The breeze hits his face, his eyes are already blurred with tears but now they are stinging with sea-salt, and he rubs at them with the heel of his palms.

He runs until his legs become weak and rubbery, the muscles slacken and give out, his knees ploughing into the shale, hands splaying and he is now on all fours, gasping for breath. He sees something on the ocean, a brief, brilliant flash, a perfect circle as though the sun has fallen into the writhing water.

Then it is gone and the tide washes into him, almost knocking him sideways. The shock of the icy water revives him. As he stands, he places his palms on the ground to push off and his right hand finds something in the shale, a piece of driftwood that he drags with him to his feet.

Written in the black wood are words. He stares at the words, trying to make sense of them.

All would eventually become clear to him, but it would not be until many years later, and by then it will be far too late.

To the locals, Alvechurch antiques faire was a familiar event. On the last Sunday of each month, the man in the Paisley waistcoat would come along to the village hall and set up his stall, thermos flask of coffee and a plastic blue sandwich box by his feet.

The man sat at his table, unaware that at that very moment, over 300 miles away, a boy was mourning the loss of his father to the ocean. This in itself was not remarkable; no one can know all things, after all. And had he known, he would have wept for the boy, for he had also lost his father when he was young. He never spoke about it, never drew attention to it, because some losses are greater than others, and some simply cannot be replaced.

He did, however, know his merchandise perfectly. It was spread out and individually priced with small, neatly handwritten labels. All about him the busy sounds of traders setting up their stalls, the joyful and polite banter echoed around the hall. There were over thirty tables in the hall, laden with trinkets and jewellery, coins and medals, pieces of furniture and gold and silverware of all shapes and sizes.

Those who attended were as diverse as the items on show. Young and old, professional and amateur, all here for one end, to court the past, to own a piece of history.

And the spoils of the past were indeed laid out on his table. Rows of military service memorabilia, from many conflicts, across centuries; medals and buttons, cap badges, regimental seals, and insignia, belt buckles, and service binoculars. The man surveyed them all as he adjusted his tiny glasses on his big nose, friendly eyes, watery with age, tufts of white hair escaping from beneath his red beret.

The man reached down for his flask, a polite cough stalled his hand and he looked up. Standing in front of his table was a large man who carried with him an air of authority, his broad shoulders squared off beneath a navy blue blazer, his paunch beneath his white shirt hanging over his belt.

"Good day, sir," the man in the blazer said in a firm yet jaunty voice. "My name is Clive."

"Good day," said the man in the Paisley waistcoat. "I'm Stephen. How may I help you?"

"I would very much like to purchase this item," Clive said.

He reached down and tapped the object on the table. It was a gold disc, constructed of three circles, like plates stacked on top of each other, the largest at the bottom.

"I see," said Stephen, vaguely.

"It is for sale, isn't it?" Clive said.

"Everything is for sale here," Stephen said with a beaming smile.

"There is no price tag," Clive said. "I feared the worse."

Stephen looked down at the disc and frowned. "Well, I guess I must have forgotten to price it up. Perhaps it is only right that you make me an offer."

Now it was Clive who appeared surprised. "Are you sure?"

"The customer is always right, as they say. And there is a feeling coming upon me that this item means for you to take it home."

"Very well," Clive said and made an offer on the spot.

After a few moments, Stephen stood and offered his hand. "It's a deal. Shall I wrap it for you?"

Clive watched the Stephen shroud the disc in tissue paper and then add a layer of bubble wrap. He then stooped to retrieve a cardboard box into which he placed the wrappings, finally sealing the lid with parcel tape.

He gave Clive the box and in return received a wad of notes. The two men bid each other good day and Stephen watched Clive disappear into the throng of visitors, the box tucked under his arm.

Stephen counted out the money and shook his head. Not because the amount was short, not because it was more money than he'd made in the past two months put together.

No, he shook his head, because, for a reason that was beyond him, he had no recollection of ever owning the object he had just sold.

Chapter Two

Beatrice Beecham checked her Smartphone and the vibrant screen told her two things. First, the timer was three minutes and ten seconds away from setting off the alarm to let her know the lamb roast would need to come out and rest before carving. Secondly, it told her there was a text message from Lucas Walker, the boy she had been dating for the past year, asking her if dinner was ready.

Beatrice turned around. "Will you stop doing that?"

"Doing what?" Lucas said. His grin made it clear that he knew exactly "what" she meant.

"Sending me texts when you're three feet away," she said.

"What can I say?" He flashed her a disarming smile. "The art of conversation died with the birth of the emoji."

She fought back a chuckle, helped by the alarm on her Smartphone bleeping urgently.

Beatrice went for a pair of *Masterchef* oven gloves on the grey, marbled work surface. "Lucas Walker, you'll never understand just how stressful it is having someone standing over you when you're trying to do something."

"Maybe I could, you know, help?" The offer lacked conviction.

"Shall I remind you of the last time you helped?" Beatrice replied. "It took three coats of paint to hide the smoke damage in here."

She opened the oven door and retrieved the roast. The air crackled with the sound of sizzling meat juices as she carefully manoeuvred the big, black baking tray onto the kitchen's work surface.

"You're really not going to let that go, are you?" he said with a faux-aggrieved tone. "I'll have you know that the incident made it to Dorsal Finn's Fire Department's YouTube Channel. Over two thousand hits, too."

"One day you may be able to explain how that could ever be thought of as a positive." She watched the hissing meat juice calm enough to cover the lamb joint with a clean tea towel.

Lucas smiled. "Well, we all have our talents."

He watched as Beatrice busied herself with the meal, the smile on his face betraying the pleasure he felt when in her company. And in the time they had been dating they had been in each other's company a lot.

This was not to say they were estranged before their relationship began in earnest. As members of the gang of inquisitive kids, known collectively as The Newshounds, Beatrice had known Lucas since she'd first moved to the town. The Beecham family had moved there when George Beecham, her jolly, rotund father, had lost his job. Along with Maureen, her mother, and Thomas, her irritant of a brother, the Beecham's had migrated to help out "Aunt" Maud

Postlethwaite to run the store where The Newshounds delivered copies of The Dorsal Finn Herald every morning and evening.

Their newspaper delivery days may have been over, but Lucas, Elmo, and Patience Userkaf remained like siblings to Beatrice. Their strength lay in the close bond their adventures had brought them.

"Your talent is detection and puzzle-solving, remember?" Beatrice said as their conversation continued. "Though being a pain in the arse does come in at a close second."

He flinched as though her words had cut him, before grinning at her once more.

"It's been kind of quiet around here lately," he said without any attempt to polish his disappointment. "I feel kind of redundant."

Beatrice was thoughtful. "I can do quiet for a little while longer."

A silence settled over them as they absorbed the comment.

Dorsal Finn was anything but quiet. Yes, on the surface, the town was the epitome of peace and serenity, a place of quaint tradition and quiet custom. The townsfolk were welcoming of outsiders, as Beatrice and her family had experienced first-hand on their arrival several years ago.

Yet Dorsal Finn's tranquil ambience was a persona— some would say a facade—that hid a darker tone to its balmy nature. Most knew of it, but it was never discussed, the way a family never discusses a relative who has brought shame to the front door. Details and events were only implied, a nod of the head or a knowing frown, a wink of an eye. These nuances spoke more than words because there was, by and large, a collective understanding.

Dorsal Finn had a Dark Heart. Things always happened, some that could be explained, but most could not. Well, not by natural means, of course. That was where The Newshounds thrived, in the shaded spaces between the normal, mysterious and the fantastic.

"I do feel bad that it makes you feel useless," Beatrice continued. "I thought that was my job." She chuckled at her own joke as she prepped to cream the potatoes.

"You're a better chef than you are a comedian, Beecham," Lucas said.

"And I can't think of anyone else who needs to keep their distance when I have sharp, pointy things in my hand, Walker." She laughed.

Almost on cue, her brother's voice came from the doorway. "Mum wants to know when dinner's ready?"

Beatrice sighed. "Note to self: when you think things can't get any worse, remember you have a younger brother."

Thomas Beecham entered the kitchen. He had a camouflage bandana wrapped around his head. A black vest top hung from his scarecrow frame, the combat fatigues he wore were two sizes too big, the material ballooning as though filled with water.

Lucas watched as Thomas entered the kitchen. "Why are you crawling on the floor there, chief?" he said as the younger boy inched forwards across the shining tiles on his stomach.

"In order to survive in the wilderness, you have to become the wilderness," Tom said.

"That means something, right?" Lucas said, wearing a puzzled frown.

"It's another one of his ridiculous fads," she said. "Endless episodes of *Claire Drill: Behind Enemy Lines.*"

"You mean the survival show?" Lucas said brightening suddenly. "I can see the appeal of that."

Claire Drill had exploded onto Prime Time TV earlier that year. An exponent of extreme and urban survival skills, the feisty presenter had captured the imagination of a generation of kids—and adult males, if the truth be told—who were mesmerised by her adventures. The "Drill" brand was steadily growing alongside her fan base, and she was currently purveyor of several books, outdoor-store endorsements and even had a signature "Urban Combat Chic" clothing range.

Beatrice turned to Lucas with pursed lips. "What you can 'see' is a woman in tight vest tops crawling through mud."

"I can't say I've ever noticed that," he said, looking up at the ceiling.

Beatrice shook her head and replied with a sour tone. "You're a terrible liar, Walker. Well, if you're into women who eat road kill and drink their own urine then don't let me hold you back."

"That would have been a selfless proposition had it not been for the drinking urine part," Lucas said, wrinkling his nose.

"She doesn't drink her own urine," Thomas protested from the floor.

"You mean she drinks *someone else's*?" Beatrice said in disgust.

Thomas looked at his sister as though she was stupid. "No, Bea. She doesn't drink urine *at all*. Anyone with any survival knowledge knows that drinking urine dehydrates the body because it's full of salt! She soaks her bandana in urine as a cooling agent in high temperatures."

"Nice," said Lucas with a queasy look on his face. "Let's hope she never gets her own brand of perfume."

Tom climbed to his feet. His trousers were dangerously close to falling down. "Claire teaches you how to make sure you can survive any given scenario. Covering every eventuality."

"Think a belt might be better, chief," Lucas said, observing Thomas' oversized fatigues as gravity took hold and they dropped to his ankles. The younger boy was now displaying a bright blue pair of Star Wars boxer shorts.

"Oh, for God's sake, Thomas!" Beatrice turned away quickly. "Will you go somewhere that's not here?"

The ringtone from Lucas' mobile phone interrupted her diatribe. Thomas used the reprieve to yank up his trousers and hurry from the kitchen.

Lucas smiled as he watched Thomas' enthusiastic exit, then pulled the phone from the work surface and answered it. An excited fizz came from the speaker.

"Hold on, Patience, I'll put you on speaker," Lucas said.

Beatrice turned when Lucas mentioned the name of her best friend. Then Patience's bright, urgent voice joined them, making Beatrice smile.

"Now listen up," Patience said. "We need to meet later today because I have some news. And I mean news of the pretty damn cool sort, if you get me? Tonight—my house—7:00 pm. Gotta go!"

"Patience, wait," Beatrice said, but the speaker went dead.

Lucas looked down at the phone in his hand. "Now there's a girl who doesn't live up to her name."

The loft hatch fell open, and a thin layer of dust took to the air. The motes turned to fireflies as they passed in front of the small, circular window.

The hatch stopped as its bracket locked into place, and extended ladders dropped to the landing below. After a few seconds, Tamsin Walker rose through a rectangular gap and delivered a small, delicate sneeze to the room.

"Bless me," she whispered before ducking down and retrieving a shoe box from the top of the steps. She carefully placed this onto the attic floor, pushing it away so as to create space for her to enter.

Her bright, purple hair was kept off her face by a red, lopsided bandana that almost covered her right eye. Standing upright, she adjusted the swatch after chuckling to herself.

She stood, her hands placed on her slight waist. Bright blue eyes scanned the space about her, a place of neat clutter, a past hoarded in corners or stacked against walls, most of it hidden beneath tartan blankets or pallid linen dust sheets.

"This is the only place I know where time stands still," she said as she stooped and picked up the shoebox.

Tamsin looked down at the beige, cardboard carton. There was the logo of a famous sports brand stamped across its surface. For as long as Lucas—her son of sixteen years—had been able to wear training shoes, he'd always worn the same brand. Once he'd bawled his eyes out in the middle of the shop because she'd suggested changing to a different trademark. Lucas was nothing if not loyal, a trait she adored in him.

She smiled at the thought of her son, her hands squeezing the carton too tightly, taking the cardboard walls slightly out of alignment. The action popped the lid and it became askew. In a startled panic, her token attempts to maintain her grip served only to tilt the carton so that several items fell onto the exposed floorboards before she could gain purchase.

Tamsin knelt down in order to retrieve the objects that had escaped, a whispered swear word somehow making her feel good and bad at the same time. She quickly collected the items, eager to put the carton back in its special place, the only way she could keep the past at bay, a past that almost had the same contrasting effect as her recent swear word.

But unlike her expletive, the predominant emotion was not so clear cut as feeling simply good and bad. Instead it was an overwhelming sense of love, and loss. It was from this she was forever trying to protect herself.

And Lucas.

She could cope with the love, it was in her nature to reciprocate such affection, but the loss of something—someone—so dear to her, was simply too much to bear for long periods.

Instead, Tamsin shared moments, and inside the box those moments became objects and those objects memories of a time where emotional harm held no sway. So this was how she protected herself, and above all, Lucas from the great burden that is loss.

Tamsin moved through the attic, the disturbed dust a lazy mist about her. She went over to a far corner that was kept in shadow by a large dressing table, its wooden surface warped with age and heat.

The wall beyond was made of dark, worn brick, and, as she knelt down, she placed the box on the floor, allowing her fingers to probe the edges of one of the bricks until it loosened. Rattling the block until she created a lip, Tamsin probed with her fingers and found purchase, pulling the brick free. She repeated this with the brick below, creating a dark recess, designed with but one purpose: keeping secrets.

Though she meant well, and despite a solid rationale based on protecting her son, Tamsin still felt a sharp pang of guilt as she pushed the carton to the gap in the wall. She consoled herself with the thought that she was keeping not only secrets, but maintaining the stability upon which life as a single parent depended so much. And, in her eyes, this outweighed everything else.

She replaced the bricks, sealing the shoebox inside its sanctuary where, in her mind, it would be safe until her need to revisit it again.

By the time she stood and made her way back to the hatch, her mind was on what she was going to prepare for dinner.

It was while she pondered on whether Lucas liked carrots or not that the face appeared in the air.

Tamsin took a step backwards, her hands going up to her mouth to stifle a scream. The face was one dimensional, a mask made up of dust motes and sunlight. The features were indistinguishable other than eyes and a mouth that moved as though manipulated by the shifting air about it. The lips parted, revealing only the room beyond the face, and when it spoke Tamsin found fear slipping away. The words were lilting, as though in song, telling her things that made perfect sense, unveiling things that she had often sought out, yearned for, and when she heard them she was both happy and sad.

Then the face dissolved and she felt woozy, as though she'd had one glass of wine too many, and she adjusted her stance in order to stay on her feet. She closed her eyes to help remain upright. When she opened them again the face was gone.

As was her memory of it ever having been there.

Emily Hannigan slapped her hands together, the material of her goalkeeper gloves producing a dull thud that she could feel but not hear.

Contrary to what hearing people might have thought, Emily did not see being deaf as a disability at all. It was merely part of who she was. She felt at home straddling both worlds—that of the deaf and the hearing—and her life felt enriched rather than alienated by the synthesis.

Nothing could have exemplified this synergy more than being out on the football field of Dorsal Finn High School. As the first team goal keeper, Emily's prowess had made sure DFHS FC was, at that moment, top of the school league table by ten clear points. With her hearing teammates, Emily was on track to take the school team to their first league title in its history.

She wasn't alone of course. Elmo was standing on the side-lines, waving her on, giving her a thumbs up, or signing encouragement whenever she looked over to him. She loved being part of The Newshounds, always enjoyed the camaraderie and support membership offered to them all.

Yet it was in Elmo's company that she found the greatest solace, his gentle demeanour was a great comfort, and his determination to learn sign language to a level beyond being merely proficient was a testament to his friendship. If she was honest, Emily hoped that they could become more than friends, but she was unsure if this was possible. He'd never shown any outward signs of seeing her more than part of The Newshounds, and when she thought about such things too much, it made her sad. So, she often cloaked her feelings, content with just being in his company.

She watched as the midfielders of Ashby-on-Sea High School FC—looking like giant, agitated wasps in their black and yellow kit—pushed forward from the halfway line. Their centre-forward, a tough girl with wild, raven-black hair, managed to send a through-ball to the left winger, who caught a DFH FC player off guard. The winger surged up the pitch until she was intercepted by a defender, but not before delivering an early, well-timed cross. The ball landed at the feet of the AOS FC striker, Millie Weatheroak, a stocky powerhouse of a girl who more than matched up to her surname.

So far Millie had scored in every game that season and Emily was determined to end this record. As Millie powered forward, the ball skilfully kept at her feet, Emily studied the play.

She watched Millie's body position, the angle of her hips, the tilt of her head—all precursors to taking the shot. Emily danced on her toes and bent her knees, ready to leap as she prepared to gauge how much spin the formidable striker intended to put on the ball.

Millie's face wore the stern mask of concentration. Her cheeks were twin sunsets and she had a sweaty sheen on her brow. Emily got ready, her eyes blinking prior to locking onto the image.

And it was during those moments when Emily blinked that Millie's face changed.

At first, it became smudged, like a picture that was slightly out of focus. Emily pawed at her eyes to remove the blur. This appeared to only make matters worse because then Millie's face appeared as a black smoke that wavered, framed by dark tendrils of mist. And not only did Millie's face become smoke, so did everyone who was facing up-field.

Emily took a step backwards, the muscles in her legs twitching with fear. When a series of bright green eyes opened in every smoke-face she saw, her legs seemed to liquefy and gave way.

Green mouths opened now, hyper-extended oval shapes as though in a silent, everlasting scream. In the bruised sky, a rusted disc hovered, its edges wavering as if seen through a great heat. Like she had been speared and tethered to the circle, Emily felt a fierce tug in her chest, and an awful yearning to reach out and become part of the object overcame her. Then great, black clouds swallowed it, and Emily gasped as its pull on her was relinquished.

The thing that had replaced Millie began speaking, its voice inside her head, thin and uncomfortable, like nails down a chalk-board.

"The object you desire is lost to you," the thing hissed. "That is the way it must be, Oracle. Only then will the forsaken lose hope."

Emily felt something whiz past her head, the breeze of its passing whipping her golden hair, causing her to turn to see the ball hitting the back of the net, and fear gave way to confusion. She faced the field, expecting the smoke-faces to be there, moving in to claim her.

Instead she saw the players of AOS FC celebrating, the team mobbing Millie, patting her on the back or giving hugs, each and every face was happy and smiling.

And back to normal.

Chapter Three

OOPER'S COVE LAY a mile to the east of Dorsal Finn's harbour. As with other areas in the town, the large cave, accessible only at low tide, had bad folklore attached to it. The place was known locally as *Coven Cove*, and its association with witchcraft was no secret amongst the older generations. They took delight—especially around Halloween—in scaring kids with talk about the coven of witches who used to frequent the area, one of whom allegedly wrote The Book of Shadows, a grimoire of great power.

The author was thought to be one Delores Mellor who, along with her four other coven members, died at the hands of the Witchfinder General in the 18th Century. Summer tourists often came to the cove, fascinated with its macabre history. For, although the true nature of the tales surrounding it was fantastic, it was also a fact that five women had actually died as a result of a witch trial, and such an event would only continue to serve to fascinate.

And, in part, the quest for such facts was exactly why three men were now moving cautiously over the smooth rocks, the surface made even more treacherous by wet, green moss and the dark streaks of seaweed left behind by the tide.

One of the men paused. He was short and wiry, his blue windbreaker appearing slightly too big for him. The strap of canvas satchel on his shoulder was pulled taut, indicating the weight of its contents. His brown eyes were shrewd and scrutinised the tablet in his hand.

"The entrance should be up ahead," he said.

"When's high tide, Mercer?"

The man standing next to Mercer was bigger. He had a high forehead and blonde hair that was shaved close to his scalp. The bushy beard appeared to compensate for the lack of hair on his head. His eyes were as blue as Mercer's windbreaker.

Mercer checked the read-out on his device. "Six hours, Professor Kane."

The last man's foot slithered from under him and he cursed as he went down hard onto his backside.

"Goddamn this place." His jowls were heavy and his neck was a pink inner tube of flesh. He wore shapeless corduroys, and a green, waxed Barbour jacket. The flat cap on his head was askew from his fall and, as he climbed unsteadily to feet, he pushed his black-framed glasses back up his hooked nose.

"It's *you*, not the place, Dr Ramsdale," Kane said. "This is the price you pay when you spend too much time in the museum."

"Fieldwork is greatly overrated," Ramsdale muttered as he found more stable footing and eased himself upright. As he moved his Barbour jacket hissed like an angry snake.

Kane chuckled. "Where's your sense of adventure,

Ramsdale? If we find our goal, even you will see the benefits of coming here."

Ramsdale was quiet for a moment as he composed himself. He allowed a small smile to surface.

"There is no denying that, Professor. Why do you think I'm here?"

"Our time is limited, gentlemen," Mercer said, his tone impatient. "Let's keep moving."

They found the cave via a blow hole at the south face of Cooper's Cove, a dark, circular inlet, several feet overhead that they accessed by using a sequence of ascending rocks that made an effective, albeit arduous, stairway. Ramsdale swore a lot as he climbed, his face becoming bright scarlet by the time they got to the fissure.

On the threshold, Mercer delved into his satchel and retrieved a heavy duty flashlight which he activated. Satisfied, Mercer led the way, the blow hole taking them steadily downwards until the ground levelled off. They found themselves on an outcrop of rock, and looking down upon a huge cavern. The roar of the sea came up to them from over the ledge.

Mercer aimed his torch down at the floor far below where the sea was a broiling entity in the basin, the dark water barely reflecting the light from his powerful beam.

"This ledge will be under water in five and a half hours," he called to them over the din.

"Then let's go and find what we came for," Kane yelled back.

Mercer handed the torch to Ramsdale. "Take this."

The doctor held the torch as though it were something he'd never seen before.

Mercer then pulled his tablet free of the satchel and activated it. At the home page, he hit an icon for one of the apps. He lifted the tablet and aimed it ahead of them, and the ledge became a sickly green image on the screen, the dark contours of the cave wall to their left contrasted starkly against shimmering green shades of the rocks.

"Okay," Mercer said to Ramsdale. "The software is working. If what we're looking for is here, we'll see it."

Ramsdale appeared puzzled. "You say that it's working but what does it do?"

"It can see things that the naked eye can't," Mercer explained. "Think of it as a nuclear microscope, then times that by about a thousand."

Kane laughed. "And then you'd still be understating its power. If this software is as effective as the bench tests, it will show us not only things from this world, but whatever lies beyond the fabric of our own."

"Remarkable," Ramsdale said.

Kane patted Mercer on his shoulder. "Yes he is, isn't he?"

Mercer moved off and the others followed. They crossed the ledge, Mercer guided by what was in the viewfinder of his tablet. The sound of the ocean accompanied them like a fierce, rowdy companion.

As they neared the other end of the outcrop, they came to a deep fissure shaped like a shark's tooth. It was so hidden in shadow, they would have never have picked it out without Mercer's software.

"Is this the place?" Kane said in awe. "Can this be as our records indicate? Can this be *The Tooth of the Beast*?"

"Let's see," Mercer said, entering the crevice.

They all passed through, the ground sloping once more, the angled roof of the passageway narrowing to the point where both Ramsdale and Kane had to stoop slightly.

"This incline is taking us below sea level," Kane observed.

"Which is why we need to make sure this is done in the timeframe, Professor," Mercer said without looking back.

"Noted," Kane said.

Pressing on, the trio moved through the subterranean landscape. In the viewfinder, the whole place appeared as though it was an image from an alien planet.

After ten minutes the passage opened up into a small circular chamber where a dark lake of seawater had been left behind by the tide. There was a chill in the air, and the rise and fall of the ocean were ever present, albeit muted; made ghostly by walls of thick gnarled rock all around them.

"This is the place," Mercer said, looking back at Kane and Ramsdale.

"Are you sure?" Kane said.

"You gave me the details from your source materials, Professor," Mercer said. "I'm the tech guy. And based on what you gave me, the tech brought us here. So I'm saying this is the place where Delores Mellor was executed and given to the ocean."

"And the grimoire?" Ramsdale said.

"Folklore suggests the book was brought here," Kane said. "To keep safe the exorcised spirit of the witch."

Ramsdale frowned. "Why not just destroy it?"

"It was not in the hands of those who put the coven to death," Ramsdale offered. "My research suggests that sympathisers kept the Book of Shadows safe until long after Mellor's execution, and then brought it here thereafter."

Ramsdale looked around him as if expecting the book to simply materialise. "Surely it should've perished. The ocean is unforgiving to metal and wood, let alone paper and leather."

"Yet here you stand, still knowing such risks, Ramsdale." Kane smiled. "Why is that if you hold such doubts?"

Ramsdale replied quickly. "The mere thought of this book still being in existence excites me beyond measure, Professor. It is an historical record that in its own right is priceless."

Kane nodded. "Of that, there is no question. Mercer's device will locate what we've come here to find. I believe it is protected from the elements by things not of this Earth."

Ramsdale pawed at his brow. "Perhaps this is where we differ in our application of evidence, Professor. The Mellor case may well be fact in that a coven of witches were tried and executed. And I accept that those who felt this unjust may have seen fit to engage in a parting ceremony that returned earthly possessions to the woman who led this coven. But I am unsure about the true relevance to the supernatural."

Kane laughed without any evidence of reproach. "And that is *your* right, Ramsdale. As a scientist, I understand the need for empirical evidence. I can only hope that Mercer is able to provide it."

Mercer took this as his cue and walked forwards, to the edge of the lake. Black water slurped against the makeshift shoreline and the technician didn't stop walking until the thick surf lapped against his boots. He scanned the lake with the tablet, studying the shifting images.

He found the writing on the far wall within a few seconds. They appeared as fire scrawled across the screen:

Beyond The Tooth of the Beast, the maiden lies
The Book of Shadows by her side,
Souls are destined to be set free
Children of the brooding sea!

"Professor!" Mercer called with excitement. Kane and Ramsdale were at his side immediately.

Kane looked down at the screen. "Dr Ramsdale, can I ask you to please aim the torch at the far wall?"

Ramsdale did as he was asked and lifted the flashlight, but all the beam revealed was jagged rocks and deep shadow.

"Where the hell are the words?" Ramsdale gaped.

They looked down at the screen and the strange writing was still clear to all. Kane delved into the inside pocket of his coat and pulled free a folded sheet of paper. He opened this out under the beam of Ramsdale's torch, revealing a scanned image of a yellowed page. The writing upon it was scrawled and spidery, and ink blotches stained some of the words. But his eyes were drawn to four specific sentences, and these sentences were the same as those written on Mercer's tablet.

"This piece of manuscript comes from archives

long since closed off from anyone but academics," Ramsdale said. "The rumour is, someone from this town sold it for some meagre gain, but we do not know when such an item came into the possession of the university, nor do we know the identity of the person who handed it over. It may have meant something before but today, here and now, such things are irrelevant. This is the resting place of Delores Mellor and her grimoire."

Kane still saw reluctance in his colleagues face. "What is it, doctor?"

"Superstition fuels everything here," Ramsdale said firmly. "To think otherwise is reckless. Especially if we find the book intact."

Despite Ramsdale's concerns, Kane laughed, the sound bouncing around the chamber.

"You really have spent too much time behind a desk, dear Ramsdale!" he said. "We are on a path to find what was lost. This is merely the first step."

"Gentlemen?" Mercer said with urgency. "Think you better take a look at this."

Kane and Ramsdale parked their disagreement and turned their attention to Mercer who was, once again, monitoring the lake via his tablet. He had angled the camera lens towards the water. The software stripped away the fluid to reveal a single image. What they all saw left them speechless.

A skeletal figure wavered beneath the water, the bones turned to shimmering lime by the tablet.

"Good Lord," Kane breathed. "Is that really her?"

"Statistically speaking, the odds are favourable," Mercer said. "We'll not know for sure until we report this to the authorities and exhume her."

Kane's response was immediate. "Let's not be too hasty. If we report this to the authorities too soon then we risk losing control of our objective. We are yet to establish if the book is with her."

Mercer looked up from the tablet. "We've found human remains. It has to be reported, Professor. You know it."

"And it will be, Mercer," Kane said gently. "But not until we return with the correct gear, and a diving team to take samples. Run tests. Confirm that this is who we think it is, and try to find the book. We will be sensitive and thorough. Once we've done that, then we will alert the authorities. They'll never know otherwise. You have my word."

"What if it's not her?" Mercer said. "What if this is someone's relative who was lost to the ocean?"

Kane nodded. "I understand your thinking here, but you said yourself that, statistically, this is the body of Delores Mellor. I do not refute that conclusion."

Ramsdale interjected. "Is this because you have lost objectivity, Professor? Perhaps you do not want this to be anyone other than your precious witch."

Mercer was suddenly animated. "Professor, look at this," he said, holding the tablet up again. The other two men looked upon the screen and saw immediately the issue that had Mercer so riled.

"The words have changed!" Kane said in amazement. The previous script was nowhere to be seen, replaced instead by new text in the same spidery writing:

Water and blood from the Amazon join,
True justice in search of an unsound crime,
Curses and blessings, one and the same,
Places are taken at the heart of the game

Kane's brow furrowed with frustration. "What does this mean?"

He was answered only by a noise to his left. The trickling sound originated from the tunnel that led them down to the chamber. The *Tooth of the Beast*, the script had called it. Ramsdale turned to face the exit and eyes widened as the trickling sound grew and a hiss came to him.

A steady stream of water descended into the chamber, pouring through the tunnel and pooling at its entrance as though meeting an invisible barrier. Then the water was pulled back into the tunnel where it disappeared into the darkness beyond the beam of Ramsdale's torch.

"Oh my God," Ramsdale breathed. "The tide! The tide is coming back in!"

"How is it possible?" Kane said at Ramsdale's shoulder. Fear was carved into his voice.

Mercer looked at the screen on his tablet. The clock was telling him something as bemusing as it was terrifying. "The screen is telling me we've been down here five and a half hours!"

"Impossible," Ramsdale said. "We've only been here half an hour!"

"We can't think about that now," Kane said. "We have to get out of here."

The cavern trembled and a distant roar told them all that they were far too late. The churning waters of the Atlantic blasted its way into the chamber as a solid wall, forcing the men backwards, into the lake, where they were submerged and tousled by the powerful current, each of them lost in their own final moments.

Mercer had been knocked unconscious and succumbed in a state of quiet oblivion. Ramsdale's heart gave out as soon as the chilled water poured into his nose and mouth, and flooded his lungs with its icy touch.

Disorientated and terrified, Kane tumbled through the darkness, his cheeks ballooning as he tried desperately to hold on to precious oxygen. His vision was fogged by the swirling waters; a savage all-embracing blackness grabbing at him like a thousand unseen hands.

Even in this state, he knew he was not alone. An object came out of the gloom—a grasping hand—making him think that one of his companions had somehow found him and was trying to haul him to safety.

Then he saw her.

She came to him, skin pale as ice, lips black and smeared into a parody of a smile. Her dark hair trailed around her almond-shaped face, like the tentacles of some hideous sea creature, the black dress pumping in a jelly-fish pulse as the tide played with the hem. Agog, Kane saw that this was not a woman; it was a girl in her mid-teens. His dimmed eyes saw the black strawberry smudge beneath the girl's right eye.

You're not Delores, his dying mind thought. *You're a child.*

She reached out to him, fingers splayed, and even though the bitter brine surged into his mouth,

Professor Kane tried to release his terror in one huge scream.

Then the girl in the water ended his horror with one single act: she spoke to him.

And her words were the language of the ocean.

Chapter Four

Elmo stood outside the gates of Dorsal Finn High School, his large frame clad in his usual black tee-shirt, blue jeans and training shoes. Deep in thought, he considered what he'd witnessed during the game.

At first, things were going as predicted, with his school team scoring early in the first half, and fellow Newshound, Emily, making two crucial saves as the opposition sought to reassert itself with an equaliser. By half time, however, the home team were two goals to nil up.

Then came the second half and things went kind of weird. Well, even Elmo knew this was a colossal understatement. By the first fifteen minutes, AOS FC had smashed four goals past Emily before she was substituted. Then Millie Weatheroak put away three more. End result: seven goals to two, and quite possibly the most humiliating defeat in a long, long time.

It was not this that had Elmo mulling things over in his quiet, considered brain, though. It was a concern for Emily. Because even before she came through the school gates and threw her kit bag angrily onto the pavement, Elmo knew things were not quite what they appeared to be.

"What happened?" he signed to her.

"Bad stuff," Emily signed back.

Elmo thought that perhaps he'd misread her signing, but Emily's reply came to him in large agitated movements to accentuate her irritation.

He responded after she'd finished. "Bad stuff? Slow down. You mean losing the game, right?"

"No," she said in exasperation. "Bad stuff made this happen!"

"Okay," Elmo said carefully. "Can you explain it?"

Emily took in air, letting it go as one long hiss. Her shoulders sagged a little as though she was deflating like a faulty inflatable at a kid's birthday party.

Explaining such things was not always easy, even to the well-meaning, open-minded boy standing before her. The problem was always where to start.

Emily had powers. Precognition, extra-sensory perception, foresight, whatever name people wanted to give to it, she had the ability to see things, and while these images were not always bad, more often than not they had very real meaning, and their interpretation was not always clear.

Despite this, and under the intent and considered gaze of Elmo, Emily explained her vision.

Patience applied her lipstick with precision and care, her slim fingers deft and unwavering even under the curious stare of Lucas, who sat opposite her on the large leather sofa dominating the Userkaf family lounge.

The room was large and L-shaped. A huge fireplace, framed by a marble surround, provided a resplendent focal point. There was a large gilded mirror over the mantelpiece, and a 52 inch TV sat in the wide, bay window. The furnishings were a blend of tan and cream, and the air was scented with a light citrus fragrance.

Exhausted from the exhilaration of cooking for her family, Beatrice sat next to Lucas, trying to resist the temptation to lie back for fear she would become too comfortable and doze off before her friend had a chance to make her announcement.

When she was done applying lipstick, Patience checked over her handiwork with a practiced pout and nodded to her reflection in the compact mirror in the palm of her hand.

"You can't perfect perfection," Beatrice said with a smile.

Patience grinned. "Ooh, I like you. You can come here again."

The girls laughed and, like the atmosphere in the room, it was light and natural.

"I have a question," Lucas said as Patience snapped the compact case shut.

"I haven't told you anything to ask a question about yet," she said, placing the mirror into her expensive-looking handbag perched on her lap. She placed the bag on the floor where it rested against the leg of a dark rosewood coffee table.

"It's an important question," Lucas pressed.

Patience sighed. "Go on."

"Why are you putting on lipstick when you're not going anywhere?"

Patience stared at him, her face stern. "You should stop talking now, Walker. Seriously. It's a small thing I'm asking but it comes with huge health benefits."

Lucas chuckled and sat back, allowing the soft brown leather cushions to envelop him.

Beatrice nudged him in the ribs. "Stop teasing my friend."

"She's my friend too," Lucas said in good-natured protest.

"That's under review," Patience said.

Beatrice giggled. She loved the playful air that always pervaded their banter. The digs and jibes were all part of who The Newshounds were, but it came from the tenet of respect. Respect was fundamental, the beating heart of their group, and a tenet that bound them together like glue; the many experiences—dangers—they had faced together during their time as the town's unofficial champions had augmented this further.

Beatrice knew she would do anything for her friends, without question or reproach, and she was absolute in her belief that this would be reciprocated by the others. It had already happened on more occasions than she cared to count.

"We did say 07:00 pm, right?" Patience said, checking a delicate gold watch on her slim wrist.

"Yeah," said Lucas.

"I'm wondering what time zone Elmo and Emily are working on," Patience said. "Because it sure isn't GMT."

"How about giving us a hint of what this is all about?" Lucas said.

Patience gave him a look that told him this was never going to happen.

Lucas shrugged his shoulders. "A guy's gotta try, right?"

"Oh, believe me, you're very trying, Walker," Patience said with a wink.

At that moment, the doorbell rang. Patience jumped up and went out into the hallway.

Patience's muted welcome came from the front door before Elmo and Emily shuffled into the lounge. As soon as Beatrice and Lucas saw the perplexed look on their faces, they knew that Patience's announcement was going to have to take a backseat for a while.

The waves pounded the beach, white surf sucking and slurping upon silky pebbles and jagged shale. The sky looked like steel and the gulls overhead wheeled in the air before diving to the surface of the incoming tide, some coming away with a wriggling, glittering fish, others not so lucky.

Thomas Beecham watched the gulls frolic as he faced the ocean. He had his hands on his slight hips, and his breathing was as heavy as the green rucksack he carried. He didn't have any issue with such discomfort. As Claire Drill said in her weekly show, *"Survival isn't for the weak-willed."*

Not that Thomas was the kind of person who thought badly of those who did not buy into such values. He was, after all, a product of parents who had a passion for social conscience and equity in all. But Thomas found that passion was infectious and he applied this to everything he held dear. As such, TV shows, movies, and comic books became more than just entertainment and ways to while away the time. He would always become not just a fan but a devotee. Not to the exclusion of other shows or movies, he simply loved them all.

He saw this sense of passion in his sister, too. Though he would never say it to Beatrice, her total commitment to the culinary arts was inspirational to him and, in many ways, reinforced his own ethic.

Thomas went to turn, his intention: To continue with his run and finish at Cooper's Cove half a mile ahead. Something caught his attention. At first, he thought that the thrashing in the sea several yards out from the shoreline was another seagull hitting the surface in search of supper. Then he saw a shape rise briefly out of the churning water.

It was a person!

In fact, it was a man, his head and shoulders breaking the surface. Then his right arm shot upright, fingers clawed as through trying to gain an impossible purchase on empty air, eyes wild with panic, locked onto Thomas.

"Help me!"

The voice that came was thick with seawater that poured from the man's bearded mouth. Thomas was stunned by the scene, his mind struggling to register the severity of the situation.

Then Claire Drill's voice was in his head. *"When it comes to taking action, there is no greater enemy than fear! Recognise it, embrace it, then we can react rather than retreat!"*

"Hang on, mister! I'm coming to get you!"

Thomas shrugged off his rucksack and charged

toward the shoreline, where he ploughed into the surf. He waded into the oncoming waves, trying to keep his footing against the tide and loose shale beneath his combat boots.

The man floundered, and when he saw Thomas, the terror on his bearded face seemed to intensify, his voice crying out with a frantic, shuddering tone.

"We made a mistake, we've set her free."

The man disappeared, yanked beneath the water by something powerful. Thomas parked his own fear and took a huge breath. He dove under water, eyes open despite the irritated sting this act evoked. The water was thick with swirling sediment and tangled seaweed, a murky mass that made things difficult to fathom.

Through this hazy soup, Thomas made out a shape. It broke free of the murk and drifted towards him on a shroud of bubbles. He reached out for it, grasped it in his hands before another powerful surge of water took him off of his feet and dumped him back onto the shoreline.

Thomas took in several gulps of air as he stood and stared out to sea. Cursing with frustration, he spent several desperate seconds looking at the water yet he saw no sign of the man he'd tried to save.

He turned and ran to his rucksack where he retrieved his mobile phone. Within seconds he was reporting the incident to the Coast Guard who told him to stay put until they arrived. Thomas delved into his pack again to prepare for the wait.

As he stood there wrapped in his aluminium anti-hypothermia blanket, Thomas used the time by checking out the electronic tablet he'd just retrieved from the ocean. The screen came to life as soon as he looked at it, the words swirling like a cheap visual effect, and he whispered them, his face pulled into a puzzled frown.

Water and blood from the Amazon join,
True justice in search of an unsound crime,
Curses and blessings, one and the same,
Places are taken at the heart of the game

The words dissolved and then a girl's face appeared; a livid red smudge beneath her right eye, and the skin of her cheeks as white as a Star Wars Stormtrooper uniform.

A voice came into his head; it was distorted, like a bad Skype connection.

"The path is not yours to make," it said. *"But it is yours to follow."*

Before Thomas could blink, the screen died, and the only sound he could hear was that of the relentless tide.

The Newshounds sat in silence. For the most part, Emily had told her story in sign, resorting to speech when she spoke about the frustrations of a sudden bout of vertigo following her vision, resulting in substitution.

Elmo sat quietly throughout, his face set in an expression of concern. When Emily began to cry angry tears, he put his big arm around her and she snuggled into him to accept his comfort for a while.

For Beatrice, this demonstrated just how fragile Emily was following the experience of the day. She was usually strong and fiercely independent, showing more resolve than any other Newshound. This filled Beatrice with a quiet anger.

"Is there any way this could be part of your vertigo?" Lucas said to Emily.

She watched his lips carefully as he spoke, then shook her head. "You get funny stuff going on: like flashing lights and prisms. This was different."

"You mean this was like your usual visions?" Lucas said. "The ones you've not had for a while?"

"For a whole year." Emily sniffed away her tears and sat up. Elmo moved his arm back to his lap where his big hands clasped together as though in prayer.

"Then we have to assume the worst," Beatrice said. "We have to assume the town is planning something."

To anyone not from Dorsal Finn, the idea of a town having a consciousness, and a malevolent will at that, would have been akin to madness. Before coming to Dorsal Finn Beatrice would have certainly thought this, such was her practical nature. But enough bizarre stuff had happened since her arrival to make her a believer. The town had a maligned heart, a Dark Heart as they called it, and they knew its intention—to be free of an eternal prison—even if they did not know its origins.

Beatrice felt Lucas take her hand. He squeezed it gently and she looked at him. The concern she saw in his eyes was disconcerting, to say the least.

"I'll be okay," she said softly.

When she saw her words did nothing to placate his anxieties, she squeezed his hand back. An understanding passed between them and he turned his head away. Beatrice knew Lucas wasn't happy about it and could understand why. The Dark Heart had designs on getting free which began and ended with Beatrice being dead.

Patience interrupted Beatrice's reverie. "Things have been quiet for some time," she said. "I knew it was too good to be true."

"We could try and look at it another way," Elmo said. "One that doesn't assume the Four Horsemen of the Apocalypse got themselves on the guest list."

"Go on, big guy," Lucas said.

"Maybe Emily's vision is an early warning," Elmo offered. "This town is sly, right? It's patient in the way it goes about making its sordid plans."

Lucas sat forward. His face appearing agitated, a twitch had taken possession of his right eye. "You saying we should just wait and see what happens?"

"Easy there, my bleach-blonde friend," Elmo smiled. "I get why you're never gonna want to put this idea on a tee shirt, but it means that we can keep an eye out for the strange stuff. Try and piece it together before we throw ourselves into the deep end. Or—"

Lucas interjected. "Or it comes for Bea?"

"It could come for any one of us," Beatrice said. Her words came out fast and trailed off as she tried to take the edge out of them. "We hurt it last time. Our friendship was our greatest weapon. It was then, and it will be now."

"At least we can finally see a positive in all of this," Emily said. "This conversation was becoming about as much fun as an undertaker's expo."

Despite the mood in the room, they all fell about laughing.

As their hilarity died away, Lucas addressed Patience. "So what's the big news?"

Patience dabbed at the corner of her eyes with a white handkerchief. "You mean apart from the potential return of some evil entity? Thinking about it now makes my announcement pretty lame."

"This is what it wants," Beatrice said. "It wants us to live in fear, change who we are. If we allow that, it wins."

They all nodded.

Beatrice looked at Patience. "So let's hear some good news."

Patience's mood lifted immediately, as though a switch had been thrown and the darkness was expelled from the room.

"Well, seeing as everyone is so *keen*, I have these for you," she said pulling something from her handbag.

They were tickets—five in total—which she passed to each of her friends.

Elmo ran his thumb across the matt-black finish, then took a detour as he traced the embossed gold letting.

You are cordially invited to attend the prestigious launch of the latest Super-yacht from Redfern Maritime Leisure Company (RMLC):
The Spirit of the Ocean
This ticket admits one guest.
Dress Code: black-tie event.
Please note this is a charity event with all proceeds going to Dorsal Finn Lifeboat Rescue Services

Elmo whistled.

"Wow, The Spirit of the Ocean is one quality product," he said. "As rare as a compliment from Edna Duffy, too."

"So, spill," Lucas said to Patience. "How did you get hold of them?"

"My father runs a holiday travel company, numpty. Have a wild guess."

Lucas thought this over. "And we got tickets because . . . ?"

"Because I *asked* him for some," she said slowly. "At first I thought of only us girls going along but I know what mischief you guys get up to if left on your own for a night. So he agreed you could come too."

"Looks like a posh do," Elmo said. "I might have to wear a clean tee shirt. The sacrifice you have to make when you're popular, I guess."

"I bet their catering team are amazing," said Beatrice. "I will have to check out the kitchens. They *must* have Rangemaster cookers, and Polar Counter Fridges, oh, and Vogue prep-tables, got to have those, and a Global knife block—seven pieces, I'd expect nothing less . . . "

Beatrice felt everyone staring at her. There was a brief silence before everyone burst out laughing, Beatrice included.

"Oh, dear Beatrice," Patience giggled. "You're hopeless when it comes to that kind of thing. What about just enjoying the party?"

Beatrice laughed. "That *is* me enjoying the party. Who knows, they may even let me help out."

"Will you stop!" Patience said, and her voice was

merry. "I insist that, for once, you enjoy yourself, as a guest."

"Okay," Beatrice said. "But I get to see the kitchens first."

They all knew this was as good a deal as they were going to get.

Gideon Codd stood in his office, staring with pale, watery eyes at the painting on the wooden-panelled wall opposite his heavy, ornate desk. The painting depicted an image of a 16th Century galleon, it's prow high, smashing through the waves, sails forced into taut 'C' shapes by the wind.

Codd's fat and immaculately manicured fingers absently stroked his white goatee beard, the residual light from a small horizontal lamp above the painting made the skin of his balding head sparkle.

He had been mayor of Dorsal Finn for over twenty years and carried the arrogance of a man of repeated electoral success. Yet everyone held this man-of-high-office in such low esteem; his continued re-election should have been considered one of the town's greatest mysteries.

The answer, however, was not magical or fantastic, it was the outcome of a very unanimous conceit, and the conceit was known in politics as 'voter apathy.' More often than not, people would consistently grumble in the run-up to polling day, and on the day promptly re-elect him because to think otherwise would take too much thought. The whole process would start again for the next three-year tenure.

Codd had never associated with words such as *fairness* and *team-work*. The concept of a group working together in order to achieve a common goal was incomprehensible in that most of his goals involved his personal gain and didn't leave much room for anyone else.

If he was to be honest with himself, an event that had a probability factor akin to winning the lottery, Codd would have admitted that he was insecure. This meant he was consumed with the desire to have something which appeared to come naturally to others. That 'something' was the ability to connect with people, make friends, and foster relationships.

When he saw how effective such things were in business, and the prestige and renown that often came along with it, he found himself becoming frustrated at how inept he was in such matters. He had established ways in which to gain wealth and power by using easy routes. He'd aligned himself with unscrupulous methods such as manipulation, deception and downright bullying.

These were perceptions that he could understand. Therefore he reinforced his sense of achievement in the use of such methods by the outcome, a position of power in local government, and the assumed trappings it brought with it, wealth, kudos and a bolstered esteem.

On occasion, his jealousy surrounding the real nuance of business—of fostering positive working relationships and inspiring others—tended to consume him and the decision-making process.

And today was one of those days. Codd was riled by Khaldun Userkaf and a deal with *Redfern Maritime Leisure Company*. An invitation to the charity launch had arrived that morning, and ever since it had been playing on the mayor's embittered mind.

The launch gala was an inspired covenant, bound to bring only good things to the Userkaf's, and the town overall. Looking at the invitation on his desk had Codd feeling the cold steel of envy pinning him to the spot. This event should have been engineered by him, not some local businessman. A quiet spite began to build and he took several breaths to steady himself.

He got himself moving, and walked across the plush carpets, heading to the rosewood drinks cabinet where he picked out a crystal decanter and poured himself a hefty measure of brandy.

"For medicinal purposes, of course," he justified to the empty room.

He drank deeply, but the jealousy did not leave him. It coursed through him like vile poison and he found the room waver as though he was going to pass out. He leaned against the wall until the sensation passed. Putting his glass down the mayor carefully ambled back to his desk and thumped down onto his chair.

He reached for the intercom on his desk. When Primrose Meadowsweet, his PA, answered, he pushed the invitation away from him as though it was diseased.

"Yes, sir?" Primrose said in the speaker.

"Get in here, Miss Meadowsweet," he said. "I need to see you."

"Very good, sir."

The intercom clicked off and, for the next few minutes, Codd found himself with only his all-consuming jealousy for company.

Lucas and Beatrice walked hand-in-hand through the quiet streets. The sun hung low in the sky, turning the sea in the bay below them to simmering fire. They stopped to take in the view. Both of them lost in their own thoughts.

"You never talk about it," Lucas said.

Ever since they had left Patience's house Beatrice had been waiting for him to raise his concerns. Beatrice put her arm around his waist and Lucas reciprocated. They held each other as the setting sun turned the sky to a deep orange.

"What is there to talk about? You know what I know," Beatrice said softly.

"Do I?"

"Of course," Beatrice said turning to look at him, her expression one of puzzled concern. "Why would you say that?"

"I'm scared," he said flatly. "Scared The Dark Heart is coming back to finish what it started. Coming back for you."

"If there is one thing I do know," Beatrice said, "it's that, for whatever reason, The Dark Heart is afraid of me. It isn't going to be reckless. I think we can be certain that's not how it does things."

Lucas was about to answer when the distant thud-thud of rotor blades came to him from the bay. They watched as the yellow bulk of the Coast Guard chopper rose lazily into the air and peeled east towards Ashby-on-Sea.

"That can't be good," Beatrice said.

"Sign of the times, maybe?" Lucas muttered.

Beatrice didn't reply.

Chapter Five

PRIMROSE MEADOWSWEET TYPED out a memo onto her PC. Her delicate fingers danced across the keys as staccato clicks filled the air. Her face was a pallid mask, and her black hair was styled into an acute shoulder-length bob.

Her desk was situated in a small, rectangular office that had a door at one end, and Gideon Codd's chambers at the other. The walls were smattered with photographs of cats. There were black cats, white cats, tortoise-shell cats, kittens with balls of wool, or peeking out from baskets and armchairs.

She had two cats back at her small cottage on the outskirts of town. Laurel and Hardy were Siamese and sole companions in her sedate and uncomplicated life. The appeal of the feline lifestyle had fascinated her from an early age. The only daughter of a civil servant and a primary school teacher, Primrose was brought up in a home that was appropriately polite and straight-laced. Her mother was prim and proper. She was not that experienced in the world outside of education. She raised her daughter as she would a pupil at the school, every activity had to have educational merit, and enjoyment was defined by learning outcomes.

Her father was strict and obsessive with paperwork. His suits were always black pinstripe, his bowler hat always bought from Christys', and when he ate dinner he drank from a glass goblet engraved with the family crest—three roses cut diagonally across a shield.

A combination of the traits of both parents, Primrose's desk was neat and tidy, pens lined in a row, her jotter aligned with the corner of the table, and inside the notebook, pages were full of her neat script. The photograph of Laurel and Hardy—named after her father's favourite comedians—was behind glass in a solid silver frame. Every time she looked at it, a small smile played on her thin lips.

Her cats made her feel content and, as always when in such a state of mind, her fingers would go to the fine gold chain around her neck, where a small oval pendant housing miniature pictures of her parents hung. She rubbed the gold-plated surface and this added another layer of warm comfort to the moment. She relished it.

With dexterity, Primrose finished up her report on the computer. Yet it wasn't professional training that had given her such skills, her mother had also been a proficient typist, sharing this with Primrose from a very early age. Even with the advent of PCs, her mother would use an old Underwood Number 5 typewriter, a machine produced in the 1900s and still working up until the point of her mother's death on her 90th birthday.

Primrose had intended to keep the machine, but its presence left her with such an acute sense of grief, she donated it to a charity store and it was sold on for a good cause.

Primrose was good with this up to a point. These days she wished she'd never got rid of it, hindsight showing her that the thought of the machine now brought only warm memories, a connection that made her feel at peace.

At one point she'd gone down to the charity store on the off-chance the Underwood would still be there, not surprised in the slightest when it wasn't, yet the regret at having so wantonly given it away almost taking her breath away. Whenever she thought of her mother, Primrose would smile, and it would be infused with rueful sadness.

This was a contrast to the smile that was currently in place as she recollected her recent discussion with the mayor who had now left his chambers to head off home.

Primrose recalled that her boss's large frame had appeared very unsteady as he'd left for his staff car, and she immediately stopped typing to jot a reminder on a Post-It note to give him a call in the morning. The way he had swayed on his feet, she had thought he'd perhaps had one glass too many of his 'medicinal' brandy. But what Codd had asked of her made her think that he was clearly not himself.

She replayed the conversation in her mind. The mayor had called her into his office, and no sooner had she stood attentively in front of his desk, he had pushed a piece of card towards her.

"I want you to attend this event," Codd said, his face was very pale, as though he'd just been given bad news.

"Very well, sir. May I ask what it is?"

"How about you read the card?" Codd said with

impatience. He pulled a cream handkerchief from his pocket and mopped his brow.

Primrose took the card from the desk and read it without expression.

Codd stopped pawing at his brow, the handkerchief hanging limply in his hand like a flag without a breeze. "Our patrons at Bramwell Hall have given sanction that the superyacht may berth and celebrate the launch party on the proviso a selection of townsfolk are included on the guest list as a gesture of goodwill."

"I see," Primrose said as though all was clear.

In fact, the situation was anything but clear. But Dorsal Finn was owned by *The Pontefracts*, town patrons for over a hundred years. They had funded and built the town, and their reach from Bramwell Hall was long. Primrose knew that Codd may hold the official title, but the true power was bestowed elsewhere. This was a premise she understood very well, her father had been a civil servant, after all.

"You are to represent this office in my absence," Codd said. Primrose saw that despite his best efforts with the handkerchief, the mayor's brow was still moist.

"Are you all right, sir?" she asked.

"What do you think?" Codd said sharply.

Primrose had merely acknowledged him with a nod. She was used to his surly manner, almost impervious to it. And, whilst daunting, treats such as representing this office at lavish events were going to be gratefully received as recompense for her unerring acceptance of Codd's sour attitude.

Yes, a night sampling a little luxury was something

that appealed to her. And now, as she thought about it, a small giggle came from her as she saved and closed her document on the PC, and pushed her chair away from her desk.

It was at that time when the low tones of a tolling bell came to her.

At first, Primrose thought she was imagining it, and then came the notion that the sound could be buoys out in the bay, their warnings carried through the open window behind her workstation. The bell came again. Primrose counted the chimes.

The bell stopped at eight chimes, the last of which rolled out as she located the direction.

It was coming from Codd's office.

Carrying a gait that was considered and austere, reinforced by the formal business suit and white blouse she wore, Primrose went to the door. She paused, waited for the bell to resume its mournful peal.

Sure enough, the sombre chimes came a few seconds later and she followed them, her steps slow, her gaze fixed as though the sound was now her world, the only thing that mattered. She pushed open the door and entered chambers, movement fluid and determined.

Primrose blinked away her fugue and found herself standing before the painting of a galleon on the high seas. The colours were vibrant, the paint glistening like wax.

Or water.

She lifted her hand, fingers reaching for the illustrated ocean. As her fingertips touched the paint, she withdrew them in surprise. The surface of the painting rippled as though she had just touched the surface of a pond. Water ran down her fingers and Primrose was consumed by a sudden desire to taste the liquid that had flowed from the painting. She placed her tongue to her palm; the sharp taste of brine filled her mouth. She gasped.

By the time Primrose's hands fell down to her sides, her mind was taken to a place that should not have existed, just like the things that waited for her.

Beatrice kissed Lucas goodnight a few hundred yards from home. He lingered, and she thought he'd changed his mind and planned to stay around for a while longer. Then he gave her a wan smile, hugged her tightly and headed off home.

As she watched him walk away, a great heaviness filled her heart—a feeling she'd not experienced in all the time they had been dating. Seeing Lucas so disillusioned made her believe she was somehow responsible. He would never admit it to her, but Beatrice sensed that Lucas needed to feel as though he could protect her from whatever forces were at play.

Beatrice loved living in Dorsal Finn. Despite the terrible thing harboured in its borders, the town was her home and she could never see herself living anywhere else. In many ways, the fact she loved the place and the people so much made her determination to protect it from whatever evil held it in its sway all the more potent.

The idea that all of this should fall to her to resolve became oppressive enough to stall her steps. She let out a small sigh and wondered if the sense of responsibility now pervading her spirit was akin to how Lucas felt about wanting to protect her.

Sometimes, when she was in the company of her friends, she would look up during the quieter moments and see them staring at her, their eyes curious, scrutinising what it was about her that had attracted the malevolence that was the Dark Heart. Beatrice didn't blame them, it was a question she often asked herself. She hated being considered in terms of the cliché, though. She wasn't *The Chosen One*, had no grand design to champion and unite a blighted world. She was just in the wrong place at the wrong time, picked out from the many good souls within the town.

Maybe the mistake she'd made was to agree to do it.

With these ambiguities rattling around her head, Beatrice continued down Crab Mill Terrace until she came to the family's shop.

When Beatrice had first arrived in the town, Postlethwaite and Beecham's News and Chocolate Emporium was Maud's small confectionary shop. Now it had branched out into groceries and canned goods, and pretty much anything else in between. Whilst many things in Dorsal Finn tended to progress at a sedate pace, the store was not as compliant. Much like her aunt Maud, it was always moving with the times.

Maud was a gregarious, fun-loving woman. She was tall and thin, with a mop of grey hair, shrewd blue eyes and a gold incisor that sparkled when she laughed. She laughed often, such was her nature. She always wore a long red cardigan and matching Doc Marten boots, but despite her effervescent demeanour, she was not flighty or inconsiderate. She was measured and kind and thoughtful, and saved her sharp tongue for those who were not any of those things, much to the chagrin of those who were on the receiving end of her ferocious wit. Maud and mirth were always synonymous in Beatrice's world.

She entered the shop, her arrival announced by a bright chime. Behind the high wooden counter, Maud stood hunched over a magazine.

"Think I'll be shuttin' up a little earlier this evenin'," Maud said as Beatrice closed the door behind her. "Trade's slower comin' than Edna Duffy gettin' a round of drinks in. Lock up that door would ye, young'un?"

"Of course," Beatrice said. She paused as she watched the old woman stretch and released a long yawn.

"Giddy goodness," Maud said. "As me years get later, me bed time seems to want to come earlier."

Beatrice smiled. "You're not that old."

Maud chuckled. "Bless ye, dear, but if there's one thing ye've never been good at its lyin'. If this weary carcass looked any older, they'd be boxin' it up and puttin' it on display in the museum."

"You're terrible," Beatrice said as she turned back to lock up the shop.

As she turned the sign so that it read 'closed' to those in the street, a shape stepped into view through the glass panel, startling Beatrice to such a degree she had to suppress a small cry of surprise.

When she saw it was her brother, Beatrice was struck by several conflicting emotions in quick succession. First, her irritation gave way to bemusement. Thomas was, after all, wrapped in a sheet of aluminium, like a turkey plucked from the oven on Christmas Day.

Then, the annoyance threatened to return as she thought her brother was back on one of his madcap obsessions with whatever TV show he was currently fixated upon.

And then all of these emotions were brushed aside when Beatrice realised Thomas was not standing outside on his own.

Behind him were two tall adults, both of them in police uniform.

Lucas walked into Gull Cottage and kicked off his training shoes in the hallway, where they rested up for the night beside his mother's Converse pumps and a lonely pair of high heeled shoes.

The sound of Tamsin singing from somewhere in the cottage made him smile. Aside from Beatrice, no other person in the world made him feel so content. No sooner had this thought dropped into his head when something stirred within in him. His heart ruffled like meadow grass in a summer breeze.

An image came to his mind, a shadowy figure—a man—with brass buttons on his uniform glittering under the lights from a kid's mobile hanging from the ceiling. The image blinked out of existence as quickly as it came, but it left Lucas perplexed.

"Ah, you're back," Tamsin said behind him.

"No, your son has been abducted by aliens and this is your replacement." Lucas chuckled.

"Well, I hope this version knows how to keep his room tidy," his mother replied. "You eaten?"

"Yes," he replied quickly. His mother meant well but her cooking was about as appetising as road kill. "But I am tired. Think I'll head up to bed."

"Oh," his mother replied. It was one word, but the mournful delivery spoke volumes.

"Or we could watch some TV together?" he offered.

"That's a great idea," she said brightly. "How about a quiz show? You know how much you love shouting out all the wrong answers?"

"I don't know they're wrong until they tell us the right answers," he said, deadpan.

"Makes *me* laugh," she said.

Lucas smiled. In truth, seeing his mother happy meant a great deal. There were times, when she was unaware he was watching her, that he could see a vague look on her face, a distance that was so far removed from her effervescent personality that he often wondered what it was she was trying to recall.

This trait was not always at the forefront of his mind, but when he came across it, Lucas thought about it intently. Perhaps it was because this concept only came within a few moments of his own fading memory of the man with shining buttons, his curiosity piqued with such intensity the words were out of his mouth before he could stop them.

"Mum, was Dad in the army?"

His mother looked at him and for a moment Lucas thought he could see suppressed panic in her eyes. Then, in an instant, it was gone, and a smile returned to her face.

"Let's go and watch those quiz shows, eh?" she said. "Hope we've not missed Tipping Point."

She turned away and went into the small lounge, where the TV announced the evening's schedule. In the hallway, Lucas looked at his mother and considered the possibility that she was losing her hearing in spectacular fashion, or that perhaps he had merely thought the question and not asked it out loud.

It crossed his mind to press on and continue the conversation in the lounge, but by the time he sat down beside her on the small cream sofa, Lucas found that the moment had passed. If he was honest with himself, the unsettling feeling in his heart made him conclude that he did not want it to return to him for a while.

Emily poked at the remnants of her dinner, the fork making intermittent squeaks as it met the surface of the dish. She saw a shadow on the table and looked up to see her mother waving her right arm to get her attention.

"You're making a horrendous noise," her mother signed.

"Sorry." Emily placed the fork on the placemat.

"You got something on your mind?" her mother asked.

Emily shook her head but avoided her mother's stare, which prompted her to thump the table with the flat of her hand to bring Emily back.

"You sure?"

Emily sighed and nodded.

What else can I do? she thought to herself. *Tell the truth?* She continued to play out divulging events that afternoon to her mother. *Well, mum, not only am I deaf but I also have the power to see things that may happen in the future, things with green eyes and no faces. Yeah, that's going to go down well. I'd be off to see the psychiatrist by the end of the sentence.*

Mrs Hannigan tapped the table again making Emily realise that she'd been neglecting to stay focused on her mother's face.

"What happened at the match today? Your father said there was an *incident.*"

Awkward, Emily thought.

"Not an incident. Just vertigo. I was substituted. No big deal."

Emily's father was the school's head teacher, so no surprise the news of her disastrous game had reached him. He tried not to interfere, treating her just as he would any other student, but even his neutrality and professionalism had its limits when it came to her.

"You're not angry you had to end the game?" her mother pressed.

"Yeah," Emily said. "But what can I do?"

Mrs Hannigan nodded and Emily thought she saw sadness in her mother's face. Then it was gone like a fleeting, irrelevant memory.

"You're right," Mrs Hannigan said. "There's nothing anyone can do. I want you to know something . . ."

"What, Mum?'

"I'm proud of you, Emily," Mrs Hannigan's eyes misted and a tear dropped onto the table top.

"Mum?" Emily said, standing and going over to her.

"Ignore me. Just silly old Mum getting all emotional."

But Emily ignored the dismissive air and hugged her mother tightly, face buried in her yellow hair.

After a few minutes, Emily stepped away. "I'm okay. I promise."

"Then so am I," Mrs Hannigan said. She allowed a small, watery smile to play across her face, her bright blue eyes now wiped free of tears.

Emily suddenly thought of something to change the dour mood in the air. She went to her handbag, made from claret and blue leather in respect of Aston Villa, her favourite football team, and rummaged around inside it. She produced the invitation that Patience had given to her, and handed it to her mother.

"Wow," she said. "I read about this in the *Dorsal Finn Herald*. It's a big deal by all accounts. So where did you get the ticket?"

Emily explained how Patience had requested them for The Newshounds.

Mrs Hannigan gave her a contented smile. "You really have some good friends."

"Yes, I do," Emily said. She scrutinised her mother's face. "You're not going to start crying again are you?"

Emily couldn't hear the laughter her comment produced, but enjoyed watching her mother's shoulders jig up and down all the same.

Patience snorted in frustration. As a sound, it was small and delicate but it demonstrated how flummoxed she was by the challenge before her. She was lying back on her bed, her long black hair pulled back into a ponytail that she preferred for sleeping, and she scrutinised the screen of her Mac Book. A notepad and pen were also close to hand on the plump, pink duvet resting across her legs.

Like all kids, Patience's bedroom was a reflection of her personality. The room was both compact and very tidy, a place where a quiet sense of order prevailed. There was a dressing table with a large ornate mirror opposite her gold framed bed, and on this table, the instruments to construct beauty were laid out, regimented and precise like the tools of a surgeon prepping for theatre.

Vanity was not a concept that Patience ever considered. In the truest sense, she was not vain at all. She did not, for instance, need to be the centre of attention, nor did she consider herself more beautiful than anyone else, though she was pretty. And far from being self-absorbed, Patience was completely giving to others, especially her close friends. If Patience ever thought she was letting someone down, it ate away at her until she could put it right, or at least try to make some inroads on a resolution.

This was perhaps why she was frustrated enough to give out the unbecoming snort to her bedroom. The image on the Mac Book was that of a picture she had taken. It was a series of strange, scrawled letters that she had found in a place known as the Cryptic Crypt. Alongside Elmo, she had found the letters whilst The Newshound tried to resolve another mystery, and periodically Patience revisited the image in order to try and make sense of it.

That Patience was a purveyor of languages was well known to the town. Some would seek her out to assist them with clarifying an issue with all types of language from any era, Agnes Clutterbuck—the town librarian—for example. Somehow she was able to learn a new language fast; she had lost count of just how many she could speak fluently, and once she had learned something it never left her. The origins of such ability were altogether unknown, and she never questioned it, she just embraced the gift.

So this made her complete inability to fathom the strange letters on the screen incredibly irritating. Under normal circumstances, she would have accessed linguist message boards for Oxford or Cambridge Universities when she was baffled with a turn of phrase, or unsure of grammatical syntax, especially with ancient languages. She was convinced that the words teasing her with their mysterious structure were indeed ancient. They were carved into the floor of a crypt that no one but a select few in Dorsal Finn knew anything about. The crypt itself was designed in a manner that clearly predated the town's existence. She recalled stone pillars and uneven floors hewn from sandstone.

She knew these words *meant something*. Yes, of course, they were meant to be understood, but Patience felt that it was far more than just making a statement or conveying language. These letters were the key to something else, something ancient that was to have a very real impact upon the present.

Patience continued to work on solving the puzzle in private, never bringing it up to the others. The incident with the Cryptic Crypt had left everyone scarred to some degree, no more so than her dear friend, Beatrice. When Patience thought about it too much, guilt nudged into her heart. So she allowed periods of time to lapse before returning to the words. Hoping at one level that fresh eyes would be the way to open the letters up to her, but more often than not, to help her cope with the subterfuge.

Her brow furrowed as she gazed at the letters as though this would magically unlock their secrets. Then she shook her head, the mysteries of the lost words were destined to evade her, a thought that made her feel both angry and sad.

Resigned that once again her goal had eluded her, Patience closed down her Mac Book and swapped the notebook for her TV remote, and within a few minutes was watching an episode of *Orange is the New Black* on Netflix.

At Crab Mill Terrace, the two police officers stood in the lounge. PC Shaw, a female officer with bobbed brown hair and dark eyes, sipped tea from a large red mug. Her male companion, PC Hope, stood easily at six foot four and made notes in a small black book. The bleeps and hiss of static from the radios pinned to Shaw and Hope's hi-visibility tabards filled the air as the Beecham family sat in solemn silence.

"Perhaps we could go over this one more time," Shaw said gently.

Thomas had changed into a pair of pyjamas with the intermittent pattern of the *Urban Survival* TV logo all over them. His face was scrunched up as he tried to recall the events on the beach.

His mother and father looked on; their faces etched

with concern. Maud was sitting in a big armchair opposite, thoughts of sleep now parked until the events of the evening ran their course. Beatrice was perched on the arm of Maud's chair, fascinated at how the evening was turning out.

"I've already done this twice," Thomas said in a grumpy tone. "What's the problem, your memory or your handwriting?"

"Now, now, Thomas," George Beecham said firmly. "There's no need to be rude."

PC Shaw held up a placating hand. "It's okay, Mr Beecham. This is quite normal behaviour for someone who's had a fright."

George nodded but his face remained unhappy. He folded his arms across his plump belly and put his ruddy face in neutral.

"We have to make sure we're clear on what actually happened, Thomas," PC Hope said smoothly. "What you told us is very serious and we have to get the report right."

This seemed to appease Thomas who nestled back in his seat on the sofa. When he spoke, his face slipped into the familiar puzzled expression he'd adopted earlier.

"Well, like I said, I was out running, in full Urban Survivor kit, none of that Lycra rubbish, and I saw this guy in the water up by Cooper's Cove. So I went into the water to go and get him."

"That's very brave," George said, softening his stance.

Thomas pushed his chest out with pride.

Maureen was careful in her response and shivered. "Yes, dear, but perhaps you could have let us know first?"

"I had to act fast, Mum. The man was in danger!"

His mother began to speak but PC Shaw interjected with a tone that seemed both firm yet cautious at the same time. "We understand your concern, Mrs Beecham. But can we please press on?"

"Of course," Maureen said. George patted his wife's arm in a show of comfort.

PC Hope addressed Thomas again. "So you went into the sea. And the man went under the water, yes?"

"He was *pulled* under the water, like that guy in the *Malibu Shark Attack* movie. One minute he was there, the next: *whoosh!* Gone."

"Then what happened?" PC Shaw said.

"I went under the water and the guy wasn't there," Thomas said. "There was just the tablet."

"You saying the guy turned into an iPad?" Beatrice just could not help herself. She'd been sitting quietly taking it all in but her words had taken flight as though she had no control over them.

"That's not what I'm saying at all," Thomas said with some petulance. "I'm saying I couldn't see him but the tablet sort of floated out of all the seaweed and stuff."

"What happened to the fella in the water?" Maud said to the police officers.

"Coast Guard has trawled that stretch of water, tide is coming in, but there's no sign of any . . . " PC Hope trailed off.

"Ye may as well call a gull a gull when it's just landed in yer lap, Officer," Maud said grimly. "Tell it as it is, that's what I'm sayin'. Ye can't find a body?"

PC Hope checked his notebook as though he needed a prompt. "Yes. That's what we're saying. Nor are there records of anyone filing a missing person report for this, or the surrounding area, in the last twenty-four hours."

"I'm guessin' ye ain't done sayin' all that needs sayin'," Maud said.

The uncomfortable silence that followed reinforced the accuracy of Maud's comment. PC Hope voiced the issue soon afterwards.

"Without a body, there's no way of confirming Thomas' story," he said.

"I'm not lying!" Thomas protested. "You think I'd make all this up?"

"Easy, son," PC Hope said. "You might have thought you'd seen someone in the water. Tide brings in all kinds of stuff from out in the bay."

"It wasn't 'stuff' it was a man!" Thomas snapped.

"What about the tablet?" Beatrice said to the room. "That proves Thomas saw something."

When she saw everyone's eyes on her, Beatrice felt heat creep up her neck.

"No, I can't believe I'm defending my brother either," she said quickly. "But he said he pulled something from the water. That proves he saw *something* right?"

PC Shaw turned to Thomas. "Thomas? Do you want to tell us more about that tablet?"

Thomas mumbled something.

"I'm sorry?" PC Shaw said. "I didn't catch that."

"I dropped it," Thomas said. "As I was coming out of the sea, it slipped out of my hands."

Beatrice looked at her brother, unease now squirming in her gut. It was Thomas' eyes that put it there. In all the times, all the arguments, they'd had in the past, she'd never witnessed what she saw there now.

Her brother *was* lying.

The mayoral Rolls Royce pulled up at the kerb and the driver, a stout man in a smart, grey uniform, got out while the engine was still running. He stepped to the back door to let Codd out.

"Thank you, Greymore," Codd said as he eased himself out onto the pavement. The driver was quietly surprised by the colour of the mayor's face. Even beneath the brim of Codd's Panama hat, his face appeared drawn. His usually rosy cheeks were grey, and his skin appeared greasy as though coated with a sweat brought on by a fever.

"Would you like me to call Doctor Foster, sir?" Greymore asked.

Codd waved his arm dismissively. "Of course not, man. I merely need a quick nap and I'll be fine."

"Very well, sir," Greymore said.

Codd left his driver puzzled on the pavement and went into his home. It was a large building, one that he had renovated using tax payer's money under the guise of a preservation order for a building of historical interest. A few hundred pounds into the back pocket of his chief counsellor had secured planning permission for the work to begin. All he had to do was place a plaque dedicated to local writer, Bevan Colchester, on the wall beside the front door. People were either too polite or too conceited to admit they had never heard of this artisan author. Which was a good thing as, in truth, Codd had completely made him up.

The building had three floors that were accessed via a large and resplendent staircase made from limestone. It stood at the centre of a wide reception hall, and it was up these stairs that Codd went without hesitation, his hands never once leaving the sweeping bannister. At the top of the stairs, a long rectangular space led off to the several rooms, including a sitting room, an office, and a library. Beyond this was another staircase that led up to the bedrooms and guestrooms. Not that Codd encouraged many guests, even those which he had any tolerance for tended to mooch around and ask too many questions.

He went into the sitting room, where there was a large sofa and twin armchairs placed at right angles to a huge stone fireplace. To the right of this was a drinks table with a soda siphon, crystal glasses, and two brandy decanters. The thought of alcohol churned his stomach and the wooziness increased as he sat down on the sofa. He lay back, removing his hat and discarding it as fatigue came over him in huge waves.

He closed his eyes and sleep took him within seconds.

The fierce envy that he'd brought back with him from the town hall followed him into the darkness.

Chapter Six

EMILY REALISED SOMETHING was wrong before she climbed out of bed. She'd instinctively reached for the bedside lamp—a cumbersome thing shaped like a football boot—and found that there was already something illuminating her bedroom.

But it wasn't her bedroom, was it?

No soccer posters or laptops and books on shelves. Instead, there was only a cramped space, thrown into uncertain shapes of brown and deep shadow by the sputtering candle on a small stand next to her cot. The walls were made up of horizontal planks of wood, the grooves where each plank joined was a dark scar that wept sea water. The whole room reeked of forest and ocean.

Her heart thudded in her chest, matching her fierce curiosity. She threw off the coarse blanket and slipped out of the cot. Beneath her feet, the floor was warm and unpleasant, as though she was not on a ship but in the belly of a great creature that had somehow swallowed her whole while she'd slept.

She stood, moving tentatively across the room towards a door with a latticed window, devoid of glass, and peered out through the tight, wooden squares.

Through the grid, she gasped as she looked upon the deck of a great ship, masts streaking up into the air, the great sails flapping lazily on a meagre breeze.

Then she saw the man sitting on the deck.

He was facing away from her so it was difficult to make out what he was actually doing. His body was hunkered down, his heavy coat pooling at his feet. Fascinated, Emily noted that his whole body was framed by a golden glow, as though something at his feet was giving off an ethereal light. Slowly, and without fear, she pulled open the door to her cabin.

The door handle was cold to the touch, it jarred in her hand as she pushed the iron bracket downwards, causing her to hesitate as she peered at the figure ahead, expecting him to stand and turn, yet nothing it seemed was going to distract him from his deeds.

Emily went through the door and took tentative steps out onto the deck. She became aware of moisture beneath her feet, seawater was making the boards as slick as the sweat on her neck and forehead. The breeze from the ocean was as breath, slight and only perceptible from the small shiver it sent through her.

She moved forward, eyes never leaving the man ahead, her steps taking her out into an arc so that her advance was measured, just in case the dynamics changed and she needed to escape. Her approach allowed her to discreetly observe the man. She saw a small wooden sea chest appear, nestled between his boots, lid open and locked in place. She allowed a small gasp to emerge when she saw the shimmering golden coins heaped inside. There were so many, in fact, that they gave off their own glow. It was this—and this alone—that was casting the watery orange light about the deck.

Emily looked past the chest and out to sea and the blackness beyond the ship was total, as though someone had put out all the stars and the sudden, crushing sense of dread almost left her unable to breathe. She felt dizzy and used a large barrel for support. The wood beneath her hands was as moist as the deck and unpleasant to touch. She moved her hand away and her palm brushed against something, causing her to look down.

There was a wizened hand resting on the barrel. She took a step backwards, heart pounding, the hand was thin and the flesh was desiccated, the fingernails, long and uneven. It was attached to a withered arm. Emily's widening eyes followed the reed-thin wrist to the forearm, a macabre curiosity taking over until she found herself staring at the ghastly grin of a skull, a buccaneer's hat pushed upright behind it like the lid of a peddle-bin. There were eyes but they were glassy, lids pulled down halfway like living room blinds on a bright summer's day.

Inexplicably, once Emily had found the body, so more emerged from the gloom, shapes of many men— the ship's crew, she assumed—scattered about the deck as though they had been there the entire time and were only now prepared to reveal themselves to her.

They were all emaciated, limbs as thin as sticks, bellies distended with starvation. Emily blinked several times. Her breathing came as stuttering gasps of fear, the confusion in her mind threatening to dull her senses. She fought it off, telling herself that she needed to keep her wits about her, that this was not the time to lose control.

Despite her revulsion she forced her feet onwards,

small steps until she was level with the man, who was now plucking a coin from the chest, seemingly unaware of her presence. Emily tried to get a better look at him but his wild hair and bushy beard hid his face.

He brought the coin up and peered at it, his fingers toying with its glittering surface, turning it one way then the other so that he scanned both sides.

Then, to Emily's horror, the man put the coin in his mouth and bit down upon it. Not only did he try to chew it, he slowly turned his head as he did so until he was looking at her. She could see that his eyes were bright with a green fire, and his mouth was bloodied and oozing, shards of shattered teeth trapped in his beard like writhing maggots in a fisherman's bait tin.

When he saw Emily, the vile apparition smiled and tilted back its chin, as it gave an exaggerated swallow. She stared, her fascination as strong as her fear and loathing at what she was witnessing. The man merely laughed long and hard as green tears fell down his cheeks like luminous mucus. When he had regained his composure he took another coin from the chest, his terrible eyes never leaving hers.

To her surprise he held the coin out to her, his smile became the leer of an animal addressing its prey.

"Eat," he said.

"That is *your* desire," she said. "We must satisfy our hunger for that which we crave above all else. Without guidance, you are trapped in your dreams forever."

The words were there without thought. It was as though someone was dropping them into her head like coins in a piggy bank.

Or gold coins down a man's throat, she thought with a shiver.

"But this belongs to you," the captain said, holding the coin for her to see. "Look. Do you not recognise it?"

Emily looked closer. The coin was made of a dull, rusted material and the edges uneven. On the surface were three, layered circles, each one smaller than the other, making it look like a target.

"It's not mine." Even as she said the words, Emily felt a yearning in her heart, and the need to reach out and snatch the disc from the man was powerful.

"Very well."

He shrugged his big shoulders and put the coin into his mouth as though it was a stick of gum. When he grinned, his teeth were mere splinters, most of them already shattered and bloody against his bloated lips. He was no longer laughing; there was despair in his eyes as he fought back sobs.

"The Green Man is my judge, child," he said as he sucked and slurped on the gold. "Soon he will be yours."

"The sentence is already passed," Emily said. "That is why you eat gold for your supper."

With a great strangled sob, the man bit down hard on the coin and the ragged remnant of an incisor flew across the deck, bounced twice, and landed between her toes.

That was when Emily woke up.

Aunt Maud shuffled into the kitchen, swathed in a red, towelled dressing gown. Her *X-Men* slippers, a gift from Thomas for a birthday she personally no longer kept, whispered over the floor tiles as she crossed the room to the fridge. Built-in under lights from the kitchen units cast a muted glow about the work surfaces, stainless-steel storage jars, and utensils giving off tiny starbursts under the halogens.

Maud pulled open the door and retrieved a carton of fruit juice, and she became aware that she was not alone. She turned to see Beatrice standing in the doorway, red hair pulled up into a loose pony-tail and a troubled expression on her face.

"We're at that time of the night where I'm a-thinkin' are ye up too late or too early," Maud said.

Beatrice came into the kitchen, her movements heavy and listless. She sat down at the breakfast bar, fingers playing with the corner of a discarded copy of Maud's *Chinwag* magazine.

Maud reached for a glass from a wooden storage cupboard. "Ye want some juice?"

"No thanks," Beatrice said.

"Ye sound like ye're luggin' the world in yer handbag, young'un," Maud said as she poured her drink. She left the carton on the counter and came to sit opposite Beatrice. "Ye and Lucas okay?"

Beatrice smiled.

"Seein' that grin when I mention that young rascal's name is proof enough," Maud said. She took a sip from her drink. "So what's eatin' ye?"

"Thomas," Beatrice said flatly.

"Well, that ain't anythin' out of the ordinary," Maud chuckled. "Ye're brother an' sister, gettin' on like Tom and Jerry most of the time. Ye'll look back on this an' laugh when ye're older. That's what me ol' mum used to say."

Maud watched as Beatrice frowned. "Or not, in this case, I'm guessin'?"

Beatrice shrugged. "Tom's always been weird. But tonight he was going for gold."

"Ye mean he was lyin'," Maud said. Her words hung in the air for a few moments before Beatrice recognised it was not a question but a statement.

"You saw it too?"

"Tom's an open book as we old uns like to say," Maud said. "He ain't lyin' without it standin' out like a penguin at a party."

"So why didn't Mum or Dad say anything? About the tablet?" Beatrice said.

Maud lifted her hands to placate her. "Yer mum an' dad will be seein' this through different glasses, me girl. Their boy just got brought home by the constable, tales of swimmin' in the ocean at high tide an' all that stuff. They're just happy he's right as rain."

Beatrice thought this over. She nodded, though her face said she didn't quite buy it.

"Now, if ye're like ol' Maud, the real focus of yer grievin' should be not what our young Tom was lyin' about," Maud said. "It's why he's doin' it."

When Emily found herself lying in bed, she realised that she was crying. Her long legs were tangled up in her Aston Villa duvet, and the restriction felt as though she was being held firm by a huge snake intent on crushing her before opening its great, elastic mouth and swallowing her whole.

She kicked the duvet to the floor and sat up, hands

going to her face, covering any potential sounds her sobs may be generating for her parents to hear. She just could not have them come in right now. They'd ask her what was wrong and, yes, she could tell them she'd had a bad dream—a terrible nightmare where a man on a galleon was so hungry he was eating golden coins—and under normal circumstances, they would have all laughed it off. But Emily had already had an incident that day, and she'd managed to stave off her mother's concerns. However, if Mrs Hannigan came into the room at that moment, she would bring with her 'The Look' and Emily was not in a strong enough position to make any more excuses.

Her mother gave her 'The Look' when she was concerned. Her face would take on an odd countenance, as though the muscles in her cheeks had been frozen in neutral, isolating and exaggerating the anxiety in her eyes, pulling her lips into a pale hyphen.

'The Look' always had a strange influence over Emily, making her feel loved but it also generated a level of vulnerability that she hated with great intensity. This conflict often left her questioning herself, her ability to cope as a Deaf sixteen-year-old in the Hearing World.

Most of the time, Emily did cope, her passion and belief in who she was, and what she could be in life, completely unfettered by her deafness. But 'The Look' stirred feelings of doubt that, on occasion, threatened such resolve, leaving her to shut off from the world around her and succumb to her enforced silence.

Even as she collected herself, pawing at the tears with the sleeve of her *onesie*, Emily knew 'The Look' was not the only reason she did not want to discuss her dream. As she brought herself to the edge of her bed, combing her golden hair with splayed fingers, there was a dawning realisation that was far worse than uncomfortable discussions and feelings of vulnerability.

It was the realisation that the terrible things she had just witnessed had not been a dream at all.

Lucas headed off to bed, a bottle of water in his hand. He'd left his mum dozing on the sofa, having nodded off an hour into a marathon game show session on TV. Lucas had tried to wake her twice so she would go up to bed, but she'd just looked at him through half-mast lids and smiled before falling back into slumber.

He climbed up to the landing, the narrow staircase creaking as his feet moved across thin, weary-looking carpets. In places, there were patches so worn, the thread came through the pile like brown atolls in a bottle-green ocean.

Lucas made for his bedroom, his territory marked out by a Saltier cross of faux "Caution, Police Crime Scene" sticker-tape. As he approached the door, his thoughts were on getting ready for bed and rereading another of his Hardy Boys novels. His pace quickened at the thought of losing himself in another mystery.

In truth, he was keen to distract himself from the ever-growing feeling of dread that lurked at the back of his mind. He could not help but feel that another, true-life mystery was writhing beneath the surface of the town, just choosing the moment where it would bubble to the surface, and reveal itself. Under normal circumstances he would relish such a concept, mysteries were his passion in life, as was the challenge of solving them.

Whenever he thought of the things happening in the town, though, his mind would beeline to Beatrice, and the need to make sure she was safe. Not that he thought he was the one who could protect her. Beatrice was, after all, more than capable of doing that all by herself. However, he certainly was the person who cared about her enough to make sure she knew he'd do anything to protect her.

He stalled on the landing.

"Lucas Walker," he said to himself. "You're trying to avoid thinking about the scary stuff by thinking about the scary stuff. How the hell is that meant to work?"

The distant sound of a bell came to him. In that moment, all other thoughts were swiped from his mind as he sought to locate the sound. The chime came again, low and mournful.

Then again.

Lucas looked up. He was standing beneath the hatch to the attic and when the next chime came, he realised it was emanating from inside the loft-space itself.

Lucas imagined the attic, trying to recall any of his old toys and items that could possibly make such a sound. The bell continued to toll and an odd sensation overcame him, a tingling ball in his sternum that compelled him to follow the pealing bell, and without any thought, he raised his hand and pulled on the small cord dangling from the loft-hatch to activate its mechanism.

The hatch dropped and the ladder slid down smoothly, landing with a dull thump. Absently he looked back down the stairs, expecting his mum to be there calling up to him to ask what was he doing at that time of night. It was not to be.

The bell sounded again, and he climbed the ladder, his desire to find the source stamping out his need for caution. He dug a hand into the pocket of his jeans and pulled free his Smartphone, activating the torch in seconds. He cast the beam into the attic.

He made a sweep of the dark space beyond, the light blanching out the far corner of the room, an old hat stand and a bureau stood to attention. As his eyes registered the items something shuddered beyond the beam. His peripheral vision said that there was someone, *something*, standing there—a hooded figure that was watching from the safety of darkness. He held his breath, extending his arm so that the beam of light could move forward and challenge the dark.

Then he saw it!

A bed sheet clumsily draped over an old, tall bookcase.

He chuckled in relief.

"For God's sake, Walker! If the Dark Heart doesn't get you then your bloody imagination will."

He climbed into the attic and listened. Mere moments passed before the bell pealed again. It remained distant, as though coming from beyond the walls. This time he counted the chimes. There were eight in total, each one with a five-second break. They made him feel sad and he pushed the unsettling feeling away.

He walked carefully into the centre of the attic, his

light creating a monochrome scene of clutter. His foot caught something and it skittered away from him, and he aimed the Smartphone after it. His quick action chanced a small object that sparkled at the touch of stark light. The object bounced against the far wall and stopped. Lucas went to it, all thoughts of hooded figures and the oppressive darkness gone from his mind. He stood over the item, his hands inexplicably trembling as he stooped to pick it up.

When his fingers touched the shimmering object, the feeling in his mind, his heart, was almost too much to bear, and at once tears fell like rain. His legs gave out and he came to his knees, the object clamped in a fist that was now clutched against his sternum as though it was the most precious thing in the world.

That was how Lucas remained for the next hour. And he would remember nothing of it.

Thomas Beecham stared across his bedroom, where his rucksack rested against his computer table. However, it was not the misshapen swatch of canvas that was the focus of his attention. It was the thought of what was stashed inside one of the pockets.

The electronic tablet.

He had intended to show the police officers the device on the beach, and again when they had referred to it as his family looked on. He regretted even mentioning the find at all because now he'd had to lie about losing it.

He couldn't articulate his reluctance to talk about it. Every time the thought about it, he got an intense feeling that he shouldn't, and something terrible might happen if he did. All of this was so overpowering it made his head spin, and put an awful churning sensation in his stomach, making him want to throw up.

This didn't mean he felt good about lying. If nothing else, Thomas had no problem being open to what he'd done. Sometimes he said things and had been sent to his room or grounded for a few days, but he would have rather have done that than make stuff up to get out of a punishment. After all, being sent to his room to read or amuse himself was not exactly any punishment at all, so why lie about such things?

So, as he sat looking at his rucksack, Thomas felt bad. How could something that felt right seem wrong? He answered his dilemma with a huge sigh and shuffled off the bed.

He approached the discarded rucksack as though he was stalking something dangerous, his footsteps light, and his movements, cautious.

He squatted, his hand hovering over the side pocket where he'd stashed the tablet whilst on the beach. His fingers were hesitant and uncertain, but after the briefest of pauses, dipped into the pocket.

The pocket was empty.

With a puzzled expression Thomas grabbed the rucksack, his trepidation now a thing of the past as he went through every pocket, nook, and cranny, dumping the contents unceremoniously onto his carpet, the frustration at not being able to find it growing with each passing second.

After several minutes it became clear that, despite his best intentions, the tablet was no longer in his possession. The question that stepped up and demanded attention came as soon as realisation dawned.

If the tablet wasn't here, then where the hell was it?

CHAPTER SEVEN

AS THE REST of the town was slowly waking up, a lone figure traipsed across the swirling grasslands of The Bluff.

Edward Chorley had cropped blonde hair, his mop of fringe hid a whirling scar where, not too long ago, he'd come off second best to a piece of driftwood brandished by a certain Beatrice Beecham. His eyes were ocean blue and glittered with mischief. His right ear poked out more than his left, as though he'd slept on it while it was folded over once too often. His nose was broad, his build stocky, but he was best known for his mean streak, which ran deep and wide.

Edward lived with his mother in a fisherman's cottage on Harbinger Street, a ten-minute walk from anywhere decent in the town, and renowned for the ever-present reek of gutted fish from the market. For Edward, there was no better place than the lighthouse on The Bluff.

To those who knew the town of old, the place was called Monument Point, named after the lowly piece of granite commemorating the crew of the clipper Charlotte Elizabeth, lost to the bay during a storm, the rumours that it was lured to its ruin by a false beacon on the shoreline. The death of the ship had seen the birth of the town. The Pontefract family had been merchants, local to the area and the Charlotte Elizabeth, the crown in their trading fleet. Her sinking was a tragedy on many fronts, but none greater than the fact they lost their son during the shipwreck.

Edward stood next to the granite and leaned a shoulder against its smooth surface. Behind him, the roar of the sea rose from the base of the cliff many feet below. The lighthouse, a thick white finger pointing into the cobalt sky, was to his right. What lay ahead made this the best place to be.

Bramwell Hall, home of the Pontefract's, could be seen as a square block of yellowed sandstone. There were small squat turrets placed at each corner and pennants were pulled horizontal by the wind.

The hall was a quarter of a mile away, accessed by roads on the other side of the bluff, though Edward had walked to it from Monument Point, crossing the steep gradient made up of wavering grassland. It usually took him an hour or so, and the route would be ultimately barred by the perimeter security fence, but Edward would feel the whole journey worth it just to look upon the place he felt was as much a part of him as anywhere else in the world.

His father had once worked for the Pontefracts, acting as solicitor for the estate before being exiled from the town based on allegations that he had conspired to bring down the family, and their alleged nefarious history. Up until the point of his father's dismissal, the Chorleys were held in esteem and enjoyed a lavish lifestyle.

All lost the day his father was sent away from the town. Now Edward stared up at the hall on the hill, yellow against green, and thought not of the past but of the future.

Monument Point should have had him consumed with grief, but instead, it motivated him, energised his belief that he was destined to return to the lofty heights of prominence that he believed the Chorley name commanded.

And he had never felt as certain of this as at that moment. The feeling had started in the early hours of that morning. He had woken from a dream in which he was staring down at the town from a great pedestal made from marble, yet the layers running through the marble were not grey, they were dark red, like veins pumping ruby blood beneath pallid skin. In the dream, he could even feel the pedestal pulsating against his hands, as though a great heart was beating beneath it. The surge of absolute power forced him awake, where he lay panting at the memory of it.

The decision to go to the bluff had been made as he'd been calming himself, in fact, the mere thought of it had left him with such a sense of weightlessness, Edward thought he wasn't actually lying on the bed at all, but floating a few inches above it. A twisting, effervescent knot in his stomach lingered as he cast his eyes over the distant building.

But there was something else from the dream that remained with Edward, a sense that opportunity to return to greatness was about to present itself.

As he began walking towards the distant hall and found the electronic tablet in the grass, the sense of opportunity became a certainty, because no sooner had Edward's hand reached down to pick it up, the screen came to life, and the girl from the water spoke.

She told him what was required of him.

Khaldun Userkaf, Patience's father and head of several local travel agencies, stood before the hallway mirror and adjusted the red carnation in the lapel of his smart, black suit. His tie was the colour of honeysuckle, his shoes as polished and shiny as fresh tarmac after spring rain.

Today was the time for being prepared, being ready. In twenty minutes he would be in the front stateroom of Bramwell Hall where, over tea and muffins, he would finalise the arrangements for the gala to celebrate the launch of *The Spirit of the Ocean*.

These were exciting times.

As he thought about the day ahead, Khaldun hummed a small, indiscernible tune. He checked himself over, and with a final bob of his head, gave himself a satisfied smile.

"And you wonder from where our darling daughter gets her preening obsession," said a voice behind him. As soon as he heard his wife, Khaldun's smile broadened. He turned around and saw Skylar standing in the hallway.

She had green eyes, and smooth skin, her hair was raven and bunched on top of her head with an ornate silver clasp, but some had still escaped and hung as tendrils about her almond-shaped face. She wore a long, blue dressing gown, edged with golden piping, and clutched a mug containing the last of her coffee.

"If we are talking about her beauty then it radiates from only one place, light of my life," Khaldun said, stepping up to her to plant a kiss on her cheek. She giggled and slapped playfully at his shoulder.

"You're as smooth as silk, Husband," she said, her grin infectious. "But your beard still tickles."

"Would you have me any other way?"

"No, I would not."

They embraced and stayed that way for a little while before Khaldun stepped free and checked over his watch. The golden face told him it was time to move.

"Duty calls."

"And as always, my husband will answer, yes?"

"As always," he said, but there was hesitancy about him.

"What's wrong?" she said as her concerned eyes searched his face.

He shook his head and attempted to laugh it off. "It's nothing. Last minute nerves, that's all."

"Nonsense! My Khaldun does not know the meaning of nerves. What is on your mind, tell me?"

Khaldun sighed. "It really is silly."

"I will be the judge once I've heard what the issue is; if you ever get around to telling me."

"I worry about how all of this looks," he said. His words were feeble, as though the weight of saying them had muted their power.

"What do you mean?"

"I have invited the world's largest super-yacht to launch here, and I'm astonished that they have agreed to do so."

"And proud too, I hope?" she added.

"Yes, in some way, I guess I am," he admitted. "But tomorrow we shall have a four-hundred-foot super-yacht weighing in at six-hundred tonnes moored out in the bay, full of people with more wealth than most in this town will ever see in their lifetime."

His response did nothing to pacify the puzzled expression on Skylar's face. In fact, her bemusement appeared to intensify.

"You never make much sense, Husband, but today you excel yourself."

He placed a hand on her shoulder. His touch was light. "I'm worried it will foster the worst things in people."

Skylar considered this as she chewed her bottom lip with delicate teeth of dazzling white. When she replied it was with a low, careful tone.

"Like most in this town, you are hardworking and, above all, put this town above everything else," she said. "This place depends on the things you bring here, tourists, the town's brand moving beyond its borders. It's how it survives. Surely being a part in keeping this town alive, making sure it survives for our children, and their children, is worth a few raised eyebrows? Besides, it is a charity event, isn't it? Surely, only good can come of it?"

"It will,' he said. "But envy can do things even to the kindest people, jealousy more so. This isn't helped by Gideon Codd, of course."

Skylar snorted with contempt, surprising her husband. "You are *not* Gideon Codd. Never suggest such a thing again."

"How can I disobey such a warning?" he grinned.

She smiled but there was sadness to it, as though she wanted to accept part of his argument but felt it would be harmful. Instead, she placed her hand over his and squeezed gently.

"You always put others before yourself, Khaldun," she said. "The people in this town know this. Patience and her friends reinforce this notion, they have saved this town too many times for those who live here to become so consumed by jealousy they will forget the good in others. Have faith in your kin, Husband."

He placed his forehead against hers. "You are right, of course," he said. "And I am now late."

He kissed her again and went to the front door. He turned as he opened it, the sunlight washing into the hallway, making the parquet flooring appear wet.

"Any requests from my meeting with the yacht's owner?" he said.

"Dinner at the captain's table for all townsfolk invited to the launch," she said.

He thought about this and then smiled. "You really are a clever and insightful woman, dear Skylar."

"And you are still late, dear husband. Now get out of here."

Skylar watched as Khaldun stepped out into the bright daylight, closing the door on her a moment later.

Beatrice toyed with her breakfast, a poor night's sleep making its mark by dulling her brain, leaving her with bleary eyes and next to no appetite. Her parents had gone to open up the shop, and Thomas was still in bed, recovering from his 'shock' of the previous night.

She was leaning on the breakfast bar, where, only hours before, she'd had a conversation with Maud about Thomas' assumed subterfuge, and this had played on her mind as it spiralled into sleep. But far from being a place to rejuvenate a tired mind, her dream world was one of confusion and anxiety and there was no doubting its source.

Something was coming.

She didn't need to define it, this had already been done in the words of both Lucas and Emily only the night before, the Dark Heart was still beating and its terrible pulse was once more permeating into the very fabric of the town. It was a premise that they had all suspected at some point, so there should not have been any surprise in it.

Beatrice knew it was not as much as *when* this would happen, it was always about *what* The Dark Heart had planned for the town, for The Newshounds.

For her.

Lucas had voiced his concerns that the Dark Heart had returned with designs on her, and as much as she tried to deny it, she could not. The entity thrived on cunning and deceit; the manipulation of others was its trademark. However, it remained in a weakened state, its true influence only effective over those who were prone to corruption.

This was what troubled her more than anything else because, as annoying as he was to her, Beatrice could not believe that her brother was destined to be a bad person.

"We're goin' to have to stop meetin' like this, young 'un."

Maud came through the kitchen. She was dressed in her familiar long, red cardigan. She went over to the kettle and filled it with water from the faucet.

Beatrice could see that the old woman's eyes were puffy from lack of sleep. As Maud rested her back against the counter opposite, she let go a sigh.

"An' I'm guessin' that ye've had about as much sleep as Ol' Maud."

The smile Beatrice gave was indeed weary and reinforced the woman's statement.

"Bad dreams," she said by way of explanation.

"Aye, but dreams all the same."

"It's hard to tell anymore."

"Well, that's what this town would have ye believe," Maud said solemnly. "A little faith in those ye know goes a long way to seein' through the fog."

"Do you think Thomas could be a bad person?" Beatrice said.

"Giddy goodness, me girl," Maud said. "If ye start thinkin' such a thing this town's already won."

Beatrice shuffled on the stool. "I know. I feel bad saying it, but the Dark Heart is trapped wherever it is trapped, right?"

"So ye told us," Maud said.

"I'm beginning to think it's coming back," Beatrice said. "Or at least whatever influence it can have over others."

"Aye," Maud said, but her tone was that of someone who hadn't quite yet grasped the point.

Beatrice pressed on. "What I mean is: what if it's weak but strong enough only to use what's already in others? Maybe an existing weakness or a flaw it can manipulate in order to get them to do bad things. To help it escape?"

Maud was quiet for a short time, her face placid but her eyes were bright with thought. "An' what makes you think that? Thomas' fibbin'?"

"Not just that," Beatrice said. She explained what Emily had told them about her vision, and throughout the tale, Maud listened intently.

"Well, I ain't able to speak for Emily," Maud said after Beatrice had finished, "but yer brother is a different kettle of fish, as me ol' ma used to say. He ain't got no bad in him, Maud would bet her red boots on that comin' out as a fact."

"But?"

"But he did tell a tale last night an' it ain't the whole story," Maud said.

"So what do we do?" Beatrice said.

"The Dark Heart prefers a windin' road, so I say we go an' see young Thomas and straighten it out."

It was an obvious way forward, but it came as no surprise to either that it was not as simple a task as it sounded.

Eccleston's Eaterie and Tea Shoppe was a place of bustle and good humour. At the centre of this was the great man himself, a character who was as renowned for his effervescent personality as he was for his poor memory for anything people ever told him.

Ernie Eccleston was in his forties, a big man with sideburns shaped like two, hairy pork chops. He wore dog-tooth trousers and a black waistcoat over a white shirt.

"I'm telling you, Harry," Ernie was saying to a man in chef whites who whisked eggs in a large stainless steel bowl, "that Stephen Finch was a police constable for over forty-five years."

"And I'm telling you, Ernie," Harry said, "Stephen was a traffic warden. The only thing that makes em similar is a bloody notebook."

"Traffic warden?" Ernie said in bemusement. "Next thing you'll be telling me he wasn't married to Paula, the vet!"

"He was married to Vanessa, and she was a physiotherapist," Harry groaned. "Ernie, I'm telling you again, you have to start writing this stuff down or you're going to eventually make me as insane as you are!"

As the two men continued their good-natured banter behind the counter, Jennifer Rice, the single waitress, meandered through the tables, her frilly hat askew on her head and her serving apron marked by a smudged, red handprint.

The tables were covered in gingham cloth, with wooden menu stands at the centre. The placemats had litho-prints of different seafood platters, the paper serviettes folded into neat triangles, their edges held down by cutlery.

At one of these tables, a girl by the name of Alison Marston adjusted her thick, black- framed glasses. This was an unconscious act because all of her attention was on the boy who had just walked into the restaurant. He was dressed in jeans and a red tee-shirt emblazoned with a Nike logo. The boy's name was James McCracken, and he was unaware that Alison was totally and utterly in love with him.

It was at times such as these, Alison hated being shy. She assumed this was because her mother and father were, by nature, quiet and timid people. Her mother worked from home as a computer analyst, her father worked as a bank clerk. Both were polite and softly spoken, and the idea of conflict was not something the Marstons would ever entertain.

Not good grounding for a sixteen-year-old daughter who was infatuated with the boy in the red tee-shirt. Alison watched James sit down at a vacant table and pluck a menu from the stand. She toyed with her hair—mousy with tight curls—and imagined having enough courage to go over and talk to him. Even the thought of it made her shudder. In his company she felt warm and cheerful; her heart physically hurt at the sight of him, butterflies tickled her belly. All of these things should have had her avoiding him at all costs, but the thought of not seeing him for a day left her empty.

For all of her anxieties, Alison was happy with coming to Ecclestone's to be in James' company from afar. Sometimes she thought this might have seemed weird to people had they known she arranged things in such a way. They may have even considered her to be some kind of *stalker*. But Alison had looked up that word and she did not fit the description. There was no way she could ever hurt James. And, even though it pierced her heart to say it, if he found anyone else then she would walk away and leave him to be happy. She loved him *that* much.

A tiny bell announced that someone else had entered the restaurant. Reluctantly, Alison's eyes flitted towards the entrance and she saw Erica Ross, a tall, slim girl from her class. Alison liked Erica, she was a popular girl but always involved Alison in the conversations she had and, at one time, invited Alison for a birthday sleepover.

Erica waved at Alison and gave her a big smile as she navigated through the tables.

"Hi Ali," Erica said as she passed by. "How're you doing?"

"Hi," Alison replied. "Nervous about the exam results. You?"

"Well, we've done all we can, right?" Erica said, her smile broadening. "Besides, it's summer, time for having fun! Can you excuse me? Promise I'll see you later."

Alison had a response ready but it fell away from her mind when she saw Erica walking toward the back of the restaurant, towards James' table. Alison's heart felt as though it was filling with iced water. James stood up at Erica's approach, and then he kissed her! *On the lips!*

Erica sat next to James and they held hands, both of them laughing at a small, inaudible comment he'd made. Erica tossed her hair back in an exaggerated manner and placed a hand on James' knee. He stroked her cheek with the back of his hand.

Alison felt sick, her stomach rebelling against both the sight of James and Erica's tryst, and the sudden overpowering smells coming from the kitchen. The pain she felt in her chest was almost unbearable. She sidled out from behind her table just as Jenny Rice came up to her.

"Can I take your order, dear?" Jenny said.

"I'm not hungry," Alison managed before heading for the door. She stepped outside as Erica's voice climbed over the kitchen din.

"See you later, Ali!"

Alison Marston stepped out into the street, pretending not to hear her friend. Her whole body was in shock. On autopilot, she steered away from Eccleston's Eaterie and down to the promenade, where she leant on the white railings and stared out to sea.

Tears fell, hot against her cheeks, bitter as she licked them away from her lips; a world of loneliness threatened to swallow her whole. Then the usual rallying of the psyche, her mother's soft voice telling her that the world is what it is, that everyone had to make their way with the lot they had been given. The James' and the Erica's of the world were just meant to be together, beautiful people drawn to their own.

It would take her some time to heal, she knew this, but Alison would let her pain be her guide for a while, allow it to cleanse her, make her stronger for the future. Tomorrow she would be accepting of what was, the way life is.

Alison sniffed away her tears and looked across the beach. Then she saw something jutting out of the shale, a back triangle, something buried in the pebbles. The object seemed odd, out of place. Before she knew it she was walking down the steps that led to the beach, her grief forgotten for the moment.

She crossed the shale, the crunch underfoot in contrast to the hiss of the ocean hitting the shoreline twenty metres away. When she looked down at the electronic tablet her face pulled into a puzzled frown.

By the time she had stooped to pick up the device, Alison's frown had fallen away and she appeared distracted, her head tilted to one side as though listening to something on the wind. Sure enough, words came to her, haunting and faint. And as they came, she didn't feel afraid, she felt appeased.

"Nemo Me Impune Lacessit." The voice mingled with the breeze, making her shiver with delight.

Then she looked at the tablet and screen. In an instant, her view of what was right and wrong became very different.

Lucas was woken by the sound of his cell phone vibrating on his bedside table. He reached for it with one hand, as the other rubbed the sleep away from his eyes. In his head, he mentally ticked through his mental calendar and sighed at the realisation that it was early enough to still be in the summer holidays not to worry too much about exam results.

He dragged his insistent cell phone to his ear as he stared up at the ceiling.

"Dorsal Finn Chinese restaurant, how can I help you?"

"You should bring a needle and thread when you come over, Walker," Patience said in his ear. "My sides have split wide open."

"Patience Userkaf, what can I do for you at—" He checked the time on his cell. "Oh, man, Patti! Don't you ever sleep?"

"Daylight is the time for being awake," Patience said. "Are you allergic to garlic by any chance? Enquiring minds wonder."

"Think I'll keep the needle and thread, joker," he smiled to himself. "So what's happening?"

Patience sounded incredibly excited. "My father is going to meet with the owners of *The Spirit of the Ocean* up at Bramwell Hall, and as soon as he returns he'll be able to give us the itinerary for the launch party."

"That sounds cool," Lucas said as he examined something underneath his fingernails.

"Cool?" Patience said in exasperation. "That's so—" she trailed off as she sought out a word.

"Cool?" Lucas offered.

"No not 'cool.' Well, yes it is cool but not just cool," she said with frustration.

"You know you're not really making much sense right now, right?" Lucas said.

"I knew I should've told Beatrice and Emily first," Patience said. "Boys are just useless when it comes to exciting stuff."

"So how come you *didn't* tell Bea first?"

"No answer," she said.

"She's probably sleeping, like the rest of us vampires," Lucas chuckled.

"I'll give her a call later," Patience said. "And don't you tell her the news until I have. Got that, Walker?"

"Not a word, Scout's Honour." "You hated being in the scouts," she said sceptically. "I'm going now," Patience said. "Just keep the news zipped. Or I'm coming round there with a stake and not the kind that goes with French fries. Got me?"

The cell went dead and Lucas filled the room with the sound of his laughter.

While Lucas was holed up in bed, Elmo walked through the town, clearing his head of sleep. He loved this time of the day, where the night yielded to the dawn, the way the light played on the surface of the ocean, and the quiet solemnity of streets devoid of people.

He'd watched the coming daylight from the promenade and then decided to walk back home, where his parents would be making sausage sandwiches and hot mugs of tea. His stomach growled at the thought, spurring him on.

Elmo hummed a few bars from a Metallica track as he crossed the street, taking care not to lose his footing on the wet cobblestones. The dawn had brought with it a summer squall and a light drizzle threatened to settle in for the morning. He turned up the collar of his leather trench coat, but neither hunger nor rain made him hasten his pace.

As usual, his stroll took him past Patience's house, and he considered the meeting The Newshounds had held there only the night before. It often troubled him when there was friction in the group. But this was how the mysterious entity like the Dark Heart impacted on the day-to-day relationships of the group.

At one time he would have been quick to play things down, or make light of it. These days this was not his first *port of call*, as old people liked to say. Now he was a little older, Elmo had found that listening and considering everyone's viewpoint was an important element to resolving problems, especially in a group like The Newshounds.

Everyone was respectful of each other, he would easily go as far to say they all loved each other, but sometimes it was the intense emotional ties, akin to close family, that would sometimes create heated debates that Elmo felt it was his job to police. He was very good at it, the others often told him as much. While others would become riled by events, Elmo would merely listen and weigh up the arguments, and take the sting out of any potential conflict with a few careful words of observation. Lucas suggested that he should invest in a blue beret, the kind the UN peacekeepers wore in war zones.

He looked up at the steel sky where the clouds were beginning to break, letting in shafts of sunlight that turned patches of ocean to brilliant flame. He loved living in Dorsal Finn, despite its issues.

"Issues?" He chuckled. "The king of understatement, that's what you are, Elmo."

The next corner took him left, away from the seafront and towards Patience's large house. It was an impressive place to live, with a large front lawn, edged by waist-height flagstone walls. Unlike the other cottages in Pinfield Heights, the Userkaf's residence was a detached three storey house, daubed annually with white paint, and stretched back deep, way beyond the footprint of the homes on either side of it.

Elmo looked up at the house in a way he'd done many times before, but this time something tickled his stomach as he looked at the building. He couldn't recall that it had looked so big compared to every other house around it. For the briefest of moments, he even considered if it was fair that Patience should live in a house that was better than everyone else's in her street.

Pausing mid-step, he almost tripped up the kerb. Such a thought seemed to have come out of nowhere and he chastised himself for thinking such a thing, even if it was fleeting.

He quickened his pace, as though the very act would put both the Usekaf's abode, and the horrible thought, behind him.

Thomas sat in his chair at the breakfast bar where, not hours before, Beatrice and Maud had discussed his lie. He was, of course, oblivious to this fact and ate his cereal with gusto, his hunger almost insatiable. He'd left the cereal carton on the counter and reached for a second helping.

He paused when he saw the figures standing in the kitchen doorway. Beatrice and Maud were staring at him with an intensity that made him squirm in his chair.

He tipped the carton, refilling his bowl.

Maud gave him a grin. "Seems ye have hollow legs."

Thomas added more milk. "Got to make sure I've got enough carbs on board. Fatigue is the silent killer."

Beatrice walked up to the counter and placed her hands on the grey surface, she looked down at Thomas, and her face was blotched with simmering rage. "Some things are far more dangerous."

A puzzled frown appeared on Thomas' face. "What can be more dangerous than death?"

Beatrice sat down opposite her brother, her eyes not leaving his for one second. "In a town like this? Try *dishonesty*."

She let the words hang in the air, as though doing so would help her brother decipher its meaning. If this was the case then Thomas was hiding it well. He stared back at her, the bewilderment looking at home in his eyes.

Maud stepped into the kitchen. "What yer sister is tryin' to say is ye can tell us anythin', an' we'll not be gettin' snippy with ye. Ye know that, don't ye?"

Maud stood behind Beatrice and placed her hand

on the girl's shoulders, the long fingers looked like aged twigs. She squeezed gently, and Beatrice sensed the message in the action. It said, *go easy, young'un. Ye don't want to scare yer brother into stayin' quiet.*

Inside her head, Beatrice counted to ten, slowly. Then she did it again.

"Thomas, we know you found something on the beach."

"The tablet." Thomas said the words with such ease, Beatrice was about to press on before they registered.

She leaned forwards. "Yes. The tablet."

Thomas looked up at her. She saw hopelessness in his eyes and it made her feel empty to the pit of her stomach. Beatrice composed herself and patted Thomas' hand.

"So where is it?" she said gently.

Thomas' eyes stayed on Beatrice. "I don't have it."

Beatrice sat upright, eyebrows arching in annoyance. "This is the kind of thing I'm talking about," she said. "Being dishonest means no one will ever trust you. Is that what you want?"

Thomas shook his head in frustration. "I *had* it, but now I don't."

"That's what you told the police," Beatrice said.

"But it's the truth—" He paused when he saw disbelief on his sister's face. "I mean, I told a fib when I said I lost it on the beach. And yeah, I brought it back here. Or I thought I did."

Maud shuffled on the spot, her boots squeaking on the tiling like mice in the larder.

"What are ye tellin' us, young'un?"

"The tablet's gone," Thomas said. "It's like . . . It's like . . . "

Beatrice's anger was beginning to boil over. "For God's sake, Thomas! Spit it out."

Thomas looked at them both, and the confusion in his eyes made it clear to Beatrice and Maud there was only truth in the words that followed.

"It's like I dreamed the whole thing," he whispered.

"Even after dreams, ye can sometimes recall em," Maud coaxed. "They may be smudged but ye can still make em out if ye put yer mind to it."

Thomas seemed to stare off beyond Maud and Beatrice, his eyes vacant as if in a trance.

"I remember words," he said. "They appeared on the screen before the girl showed up."

"A girl was on the beach?" Beatrice pressed.

"On the *screen*," Thomas replied. He described what he saw as a fascinated Beatrice and Maud listened. "The words came first though."

Beatrice went over to a memory pad attached to the fridge by a magnet shaped as a dolphin and ripped off a sheet. She returned to Thomas and slapped the pad and the pen on the counter in front of him.

"Write them down," she said.

Without complaint, Thomas did as he was asked. The look in his sister's eye made clear to do otherwise would have ended *very* badly.

Alison Marston pushed her plate away from her, the breakfast sandwich untouched.

Her mother frowned. "What is the matter with you, dear? A bacon toastie is your favourite."

She avoided her mother's concerned gaze by toying

with her phone. She stared intently at the screen but her concentration was dedicated to the incessant voice that had not left her head since finding the tablet on the beach.

When she had come home she'd gone straight to her bedroom to be alone with the device and gazed once more upon the image of a beautiful teenage girl with a strawberry birthmark beneath her right eye. Then a moment of panic when she realised the device was no longer in her bag.

Despair had made its presence known but the quiet, insistent voice of her newfound friend had come to her, soothing her with the ways in which she could help Alison restore self-respect, and be with the one person she wanted above all others, James McCracken.

At first, Alison had feared she was going mad, hearing voices that really should not have been there, but the words spoken to her provided comfort and, above all, hope. If she wanted to achieve her goal in life, her heart's desire, then all she needed to do was listen to the girl in her head. And her belief in the voice and the words it uttered shaped the person who now sat at the breakfast table refusing her favourite start to the day.

"I do worry that you're not eating enough, Ali," her mother said. "There's barely anything of you as it is. I swear if you tripped over you'd float rather than fall."

Her mother chuckled as she turned away to pour some tea into a large yellow pot. The girl in Alison's head wondered if her mother's laugh would sound different if she stepped up behind her and drew the blade of a bread knife across her throat.

Alison smirked. "You're so naughty."

Mrs Marston turned and gave her a wink. "I'm only kidding, dear."

Her mother's misinterpretation of the comment made Alison laugh.

"That's more like the girl I love," Mrs Marston said without turning around.

At the breadboard, she buttered her toast. "So what have you got planned for the day? I thought we could go into Ashby and do some shopping; maybe have a drink at that nice little coffee shop you like?"

Alison glowered at her mother's back. "I'm busy for most of today."

"Really?" Mrs Marston said.

"I'm working on a summer project with Erica. We're meeting up tonight to go through the notes we put together today." The lie was smooth enough for her mother not to even question it.

"Erica is a lovely young lady, and a good friend, too."

Alison said nothing.

"What's the project about?" her mother pressed.

"History," Alison said with effort. "We have to discuss a quote. *Nemo Me Impune Lacessit.*"

"Gosh," her mother said. "What does that mean?"

Alison looked at her mother's back with cold eyes. "None shall injure me with impunity."

Her mother began creating space on the table so she could sit and eat. "Sounds fascinating," she said absently as she took Alison's sandwich away and discarded it into a red pedal bin. "You're clearly looking forward to getting on with it."

Alison scowled behind her mother's back. "Yes. I can't wait."

"Well, I guess I'd better let you get on with it. Let me know if you need anything."

But when no answer was forthcoming Alison's mother turned around to find that her daughter was already gone.

Chapter Eight

KHALDUN PULLED HIS car up at the wrought iron gates. Through the thick, black railings, the yellow gravel of Bramwell Hall's driveway could be seen like a jaundiced river snaking through well-kept hedges and lawns.

He dropped his window and hit the intercom, a small grilled box with a large white button. There was a burst of static, and then a soft-yet-firm male voice came through the grill.

"Pontefract residence. May I ask who is calling?"

Khaldun introduced himself.

"Very good, sir," said the voice. "Can you please park at the front of the house."

There was a clunk, then a click, and Khaldun watched as the huge gates opened inwards, accompanied by a series of rattles and squeaks. It took a minute to drive up to the hall. The building loomed from behind a line of oak trees, its squared corner turrets making the most of its heritage with added pennants. There was a large circle in front of the main entrance, and in the centre of it, a stone fountain shaped in the image of a great fish rising from sculpted gouts of water, sent an incessant, arcing cascade from its mouth and into a raised stone plinth at its base.

There were three cars already parked at the front of the house, the Pontefract blue Bentley with the number plate PoNT oN3, a red Lamborghini, and a small green hatchback that appeared almost humble next to its companions. It was beside the hatchback that Khaldun parked, before climbing out and heading for the main entrance.

He was greeted on the steps by an elderly man, slightly stooped and dressed in a smart black suit. Albert Smythe had not only served the Pontefract family for over forty years, he was also the beau of one Maud Postlethwaite.

Albert was a proud and stoic man, fiercely loyal to those he held in esteem, and his pale blue eyes had seen perhaps too much of the horrors of war, yet his mind had been made sharp by such experiences, his principles shaped by them.

"Morning, Albert," Khaldun said.

"Morning, sir," Albert said with a polite smile.

Khaldun chuckled. "The formality always throws me."

"Indeed," Albert said. "I'm afraid it comes with the bow tie and gloves. Please come in. Lord Pontefract is in the state room with his other guests."

Khaldun looked at the row of vehicles. "I'm not seeing the mayoral car?"

Albert nodded. "Mayor Codd has taken ill, sir. He has sent Miss Meadowsweet as his representative."

Without another word, Albert ascended the steps, and Khaldun followed.

They walked into Bramwell Hall, through an

archway of stone, and crossed a reception area with high ceilings from which sparkling candelabra hung like giant, glass cocoons. Ahead, a broad staircase rose to a wide landing, where two suits of armour stood as though mechanised sentinels dared anyone without permission to ascend. The landing peeled to the right, where it disappeared from view.

The men went left, Albert walking slightly ahead, leading the way as though Khaldun was unfamiliar with the route. He'd been here several times, but could never get used to the etiquette of the place. It came with the history of the building—the family—who lived there, and he knew that with heritage came tradition.

So he followed Albert as they crossed the reception hall, floors of black and white tiling making Khaldun feel like a chess piece waiting to be sacrificed. Oddly, the simile made him feel uncomfortable and he cursed the awful sense of foreboding that he had not been able to shake since leaving home that morning.

The door to the state-room was deceptive. The simple rectangle of polished birch led newcomers into a false sense of normalcy before opening out into a wide room, twice the size of the reception hall, where carpets were deep blue with a gold fleur-de-lis motif, and a large boardroom table, waxed and shimmering even under the muted light from a large, leaded window to Khaldun's left as he entered.

"Mr Khaldun Userkaf, my Lord," Albert announced to the four other people sitting at the huge table.

Albert stood to one side allowing Khaldun to pass by.

"Very good. Thank you, Albert," said Lord Pontefract. He was sitting at the head of the table, a brochure laid out before him like a placemat at dinner. "Do come and join us, Khaldun."

"Thank you, Dominic," Khaldun said and made for the table where everyone stood up to greet him.

Pontefract was in his forties, trim and dressed in a suit of brown tweed, despite the stuffy heat in the room. His hair was yellow-white, thick and foppish against his brow, and a pair of golden, wire-framed glasses outlined his large ocean-blue eyes.

"Allow me to introduce, at least in person, the man who has made this all possible," Dominic said to his existing guests.

The two men with Dominic were of a similar height—around five feet, ten inches—although one was in better shape than the other.

One man, dressed in the smart, white uniform, was slim and smiled warmly from a mouth framed by a clipped white beard. On the occasional table next to him was a naval cap. He stepped up to Khaldun and shook his hand.

"Good morning, I'm Melville Craig, captain of *The Spirit of the Ocean*."

Khaldun returned Melville's smile. "Pleased to meet you, captain."

"Melville, please."

"Of course."

Melville extended his arm to introduce his colleague. The man wore a blue blazer, and white trousers, and his paunch was large, his clean-shaven cheeks ruddy. His hair was gull-grey and thin enough in places for the pink of his scalp to show through.

"This is Clive Redfern owner of my boat." Melville chuckled.

Clive clasped Khaldun's hand in his and pumped it twice. It was a businessman's greeting, and it put Khaldun at ease.

"Thank you for your proposal, Khaldun," Clive said. "A launch for our flagship super-yacht in Dorsal Finn was inspired."

Khaldun flushed a little. "Thank you for accepting the invitation."

Dominic laughed, and the sound was flamboyant and commanding. "And do not be getting ideas, dear Clive. The Pontefract fleet is still master of these waters."

Clive joined in the laughter. "It's a big ocean, Dominic—room for all. Besides, our services are very different. Your cargo ships provide the means for purveyors of commerce to make money. I provide the means by which they spend it."

Clive and Dominic guffawed loudly, leaving the others to merely look on, their gracious smiles remaining in situ.

A small, polite cough interrupted them, and Dominic turned to see Primrose walking up to Khaldun.

"Miss Meadowsweet, please forgive me," Dominic said with a degree of seriousness. "I fear that without Albert to remind me, my manners are never quite as sharp."

Primrose giggled and finished formalities by offering her hand, and Khaldun bent and kissed the back of it as Dominic continued.

"I believe you may already know, Miss Meadowsweet? She's representing Mayor Codd today and will be doing so at the event itself seeing as he is quite ill. I would never doubt this excuse as this must be a first in the history of his term in office. Mayor Codd and social occasions with free food and beverage are like wasps to sugar water."

They all chuckled.

"But I am sure Miss Meadowsweet will be a worthy representative," Dominic enthused. "As I myself cannot attend, due to an event in London, we have chosen a worthy agent to promote our interests. There has always been a *Meadowsweet* in this town."

"I will do my best, Lord Pontefract," she said timidly and toyed with her pendant, coyly. Though, for a second, Khaldun thought he could see something in her eyes, something that was gone as fast as he figured out what it was: contempt. It left him somewhat startled and it did not help that Primrose was now looking at him with those piercing eyes, and a small smile flitted across her face.

"I'm sure you will," Dominic said, unaware of the exchange. "Shall we get to it?"

Everyone took their seats back at the table. Khaldun made a point of avoiding looking at Primrose directly but he thought he could feel her eyes upon him. He forced himself to focus on the job at hand and the genial nature of Melville and Clive helped him to achieve this as the morning progressed.

An hour into the meeting, Albert arrived with tea and coffee, served with biscuits and cake laid out on a fine silver platter. He laid the tray down on a dainty serving table, and to the surprise of all, Primrose stood and went to it.

"Shall I pour, gentlemen?" she said.

Her actions made it difficult for anyone to refuse

as she was already busying herself setting the fine bone china cups onto their delicate saucers.

Dominic chuckled. 'If you insist, Miss Meadowsweet. Though I do feel Albert here is fearful you may put him out of service.'

"Very good, my Lord." Albert's smile was as courteous as always.

"Not my intention, at all, Albert," Primrose said. "I'm sure you have far grander matters to attend."

"Indeed, Miss," Albert said before turning to Dominic. "Will that be all, sir?"

"I believe so," Dominic said as he watched Primrose organise their drinks. Everyone smiled at the comment.

Only four of them meant it.

Ouside the walls of Bramwell Hall, and hidden in a cluster of bushes, Edward watched a delivery van pass through the gates, his eyes unblinking, like a rodent mesmerised by a cobra's deadly gaze.

While he crouched, his body still, his mind was fiercely calculating the distance from his covert lair to the gate, and the pace at which the gate was closing.

The decision that he could make it inside the gates before they sealed was instant. The reason for such a thing was that he knew he would get through those gates in time because something needed him to succeed. Beyond the gates, a plan was being hatched and Edward was integral to it. And as always he would not question the rights or wrongs of it because, to Edward, there was no such thing *as* right or wrong, there was only getting whatever you could and getting even.

If things went the way he had been promised, Edward was guaranteed to have both.

Aunt Maud and her good friend, librarian Agnes Clutterbuck, were sitting on the terrace of the Salty Seadog Inn. They had just finished the House Special, a burgeoning dish known as 'The Trawler-man's Platter', a tray of locally caught seafood, coated in a seasoned crumb and loaded onto an oval, silver tray.

Agnes sat back in her chair and took a sip from her half-pint glass of Cinder's Cider. "Good heavens," she said patting her stomach. "This dish doesn't get any smaller even as you're trying to eat it."

Maud chuckled. "Aye, Agnes. An' we make sure we give it a damn good goin' over, that's for sure."

The two women had known each other since they were children, playing on the beaches and dunes as WWII bombers and fighter planes courted each other high in the sky.

Agnes had been proprietor at the town library for most of her life. In fact, most townsfolk could not remember a time when Agnes hadn't been the town librarian. She was a slim, wiry woman with a thin nose and grey hair that always seemed to be pulled up into a bun. A small, blue bookies pen was rammed behind her left ear. Rain or shine, she wore a mauve body warmer, but Agnes was known for her malfunctioning hearing aid, an archaic device that often picked up more than the conversations of those about her.

Rumour had it that on more than one occasion she had heard astronauts fart on the International Space Station.

The wind coming off of the sea ruffled the edges of the plastic, gingham tablecloths. Agnes secured a corner with a spare placemat.

"So what is it you have to tell me, Maud?"

"Giddy goodness, Agnes Clutterbuck! Can't ol' Maud ask her best friend in the whole world out for dinner when time takes her fancy?"

Agnes smiled but her eyes were serious. "Don't go playing the fool. We only ever have The Trawler-man's Platter when there's thinking to be done. So what is it you want to *think* about?"

Maud's shoulder's sagged now that her ruse had been ousted. "Ye're seein' through Maud like she ain't there at all. It's true I got things on me mind, but I ain't sure if they amount to much at this point."

"Well, how about you tell me and then we can decide?"

So Maud told her about Thomas and the lie, and now the enigma of the missing tablet. When Maud had finished, Agnes sat back in her chair, toying with the hem of the plastic tablecloth.

"Aw, come on. Tell me what ye're thinkin'."

Agnes shook her head. "This might be a child's flight of fancy, Maud. Thomas is prone to such things, and who can expect a youngster not to lie once in a while? Good grief, we've told a fair few *porkers* over the years."

Maud absently pushed a breaded cod nugget around on her plate with a finger.

"Aye, that we have. But he was sure as cockles that

he saw a drownin' man an' that tablet. Even went into the sea to save him. That's more than fancy, I'm thinkin'. An' Beatrice isn't far behind me in that kind of thinkin' neither."

"So what's your plan, Maud?"

"It ain't rocket science, but it is magic, and this town is in the middle of it all, as usual."

Agnes was thoughtful for a few seconds. "Well, it has been quiet around here for a while. The Devil makes work for idle thumbs, as they say."

"An' some kind of devil holds sway over this place, for sure," Maud said in a sour tone.

"It does make you wonder what it truly wants, what its purpose is in the grand scheme of things," Agnes pondered.

Maud was thoughtful as she spoke. "We know what it'll do to get to its own ends. Seems it'll walk for as far as the world lets it an' it'll sour anythin' it touches along the way. Nothin' good will ever come of it bein' free of whatever prison holds it."

Agnes dipped into the pocket of her body-warmer and pulled out a small notebook with a red cover. The words AGNES' BRAIN had been written in the librarian's neat script. She pulled the blue pen from behind her ear and licked the tip as though it was a pencil.

"So I guess we have to accept that Thomas is telling the truth, and if so, what has he told us that we can use?"

"He told us of a girl he saw on the tablet, no more than Beatrice's age by all accounts. She had a surly demeanour an' a strawberry birthmark under her right eye. Young Thomas said she had a thick dress with a square neck an' an apron, an' white bonnet." Maud looked down at her glass of flat beer. "He said somethin' about some writin', too. A riddle, the kind this town likes to leave behind for others to find."

"From Thomas' description, the clothing is 16th Century. The square neck sounds like a *kirtle* and the bonnet, a *coif*. Peasant garb, in fact. Interesting about the birthmark, seems quite strange. It may be mentioned in some of the books I have at the library. An online search might pull something up too. I'm guessing The Newshounds are already on this though?"

Maud didn't answer and Agnes filled in the blanks. "Are you saying they're not involved in this, Maud?"

"Ol' Maud may be way off the skillet with this one, Agnes, but I'm thinkin' those kids are needin' some respite from the madness of this town. Maybe we old uns can do some diggin' an' see what we get at the end of the shovel."

"This isn't like you," Agnes said. "You'd be the first person to get them on board."

"Maybe I'm needin' to protect 'em a little, find 'em somethin' that'll give 'em a head start, so they ain't walkin' into danger without knowin' it?"

"As a good friend you know I'm bound to tell you I think this is a mistake. They won't thank us for it, Maud."

"Maybe not. But ol' Maud is puttin' down her red boots on this one, Agnes. At least until we find out who this girl is an' how she's able to be scarin' young Thomas into lyin'."

Agnes sighed. "With all the bad things that go on in this town, I often ask why do we stay here."

Maud's reply was cautious as her thoughts gained momentum. "Mebbe all of us have a place in it, for moments just like this."

"But it attracts such bad things, bad people. Neither of us are from here. Yes, we've stayed all of our lives but we were never born here."

"But we were accepted," Maud said. "That's as good *as is* in Maud's book."

"Does that mean we're bad people at heart?" Agnes frowned.

"I ain't speakin' for Maud but there's no bad in Agnes Clutterbuck."

"Yet here we are," Agnes said. "Good people in a bad town, and still none the wiser for how that can be."

"There'll be a reason an' a reckonin' one day," Maud said. "Mebbe now ain't the time to go seekin' it out. Who knows, it might come knockin' on our door all by itself."

Agnes was about to respond when her words were cut short by a drawn-out wail that came to them from across the town. The women craned their necks, looking out towards the bluff, where the main road out of Dorsal Finn would take people to Bramwell Hall, and then beyond to the next largest town of Ashby-on-Sea, several miles away. They watched the flashing lights, hidden on occasion by the swirling brush of trees, but they could make out at least three emergency vehicles, moving at speed.

Agnes sighed. "Seems some poor soul is in trouble, I do hope everything is okay. I wonder if it's anyone we know?"

Maud remained silent, pensive. She found she was clutching the edge of the table, as though to let go of it would have her spinning off of the face of the Earth.

With this thought came another sensation, a feeling that she—and everyone she knew—had become like the emergency vehicles racing out of town, charging headlong towards something terrible.

Albert Smythe walked through the dense woodland that skirted Bramwell Hall. He had shrugged off his jacket and brogues, and now wore a dark blue windcheater and walking boots. In his hands, he carried a large flask, with a red and black tartan pattern, and a small brown paper bag.

Albert was a short man with a healthy paunch, his balding head was shiny and the stubborn white hair that remained was kept clipped and neat. Although he was of diminished stature he carried the poise of stoicism, and his step was sprightly, his eyes keen, both traits he attributed to his service in the army as a young man.

Being able to take time out during the day was always a novelty, and on such occasions Pontefract's loyal manservant took full advantage of it, leaving one of the footmen to cover should anything unseen happen while he was taking a twenty-minute break.

When he had such gaps in his busy schedule, Albert would always head for 'The Stump', the last remnants of an ancient oak that had to be felled several years ago, having become too dangerous after a terrible gale had almost uprooted it.

Albert came to the clearing and there he found Dennis Hodges, the large groundsman sitting on a small foldaway camping chair. Opposite was another chair and in the middle was 'The Stump', its gnarled surface only just visible beneath a square of hessian cloth. On this makeshift table, Dennis had laid out chunks of bread, butter in greaseproof paper and pots of jam.

Dennis was a big man, his shoulders broad, his weathered face hidden behind a thick, albeit trimmed, black beard. His hair was pulled back off his brow and secured into a pony-tail that was streaked with grey.

"Hey, Dennis," Albert called. "I got tea and some pretty hefty muffins from the scullery."

"And they'll be as welcome as ye, matey," Dennis said with a broad grin. "Let it not be said that us fellas don't know how to do elevenses."

Albert put the flask and paper bag on the table. "*Elevenses*? Why, Dennis Hodges, we'll make a gentleman out of you yet."

Dennis watched Albert sit down on the camping chair. "I ain't out to be anythin' other than what I already am, Albert. Ye know that better than any man in this 'ere town."

Albert acknowledged this with a nod. Dennis was right, of course. They had known each other for many years, though their paths had never really crossed until their association with The Newshounds, and Maud.

Albert had been going out with Maud for several years, and both he and Dennis had helped The Newshounds out on several cases. During this time they had grown to trust and respect each other, a position that had only strengthened since they began working together.

"How come ye got some time off from the Master's biddin'?"

Albert poured the tea out into two lids he'd unscrewed from the flask. Steam rose lazily into the air. "His Lordship has a business meeting and Primrose Meadowsweet offered to take on beverage duties."

Dennis took a bite out of his chunk of bread. Crumbs speckled his beard as he reached for his tea. "She's got a stern way about her, has that lass, but her bark's worse than her bite."

"Either way I guess I owe her for the opportunity to share this repast with you, sir," Albert said raising his plastic cup in a mock toast.

Dennis mirrored him. "I'll drink t' that, fella."

The two men laughed heartily, unaware that they were being watched by hateful eyes.

Khaldun climbed into his car, his head full of thoughts, heart thumping with excitement. The meeting had gone well, the conversation and the hot drinks flowing equally, and the allure of further deals should the launch go without hitch.

It had been a great day's work. When he got home he planned to take his wife and wonderful daughter out to celebrate. There was, after all, nothing quite like sharing success with the people you love most in the world.

The gates of Bramwell Hall opened with their usual, sedate pace, setting him free as he pulled the car out onto the access road. He followed its meandering route until the junction for the coastal road appeared ahead. Khaldun indicated right, pulling out onto the road, where he was confronted by an incredible sight in the distance.

A swirling cloud hovered over the expanse of ocean to his left, its shape oscillating in the air, as though the cloud were impervious to the breeze coming in from the east. His eyes tried to adjust, his foot easing off of the accelerator as his focus shifted. He leaned forward, squinting at the maelstrom through the windshield, mildly irritated by a sudden ache behind his eyes as he strained to make out any detail in the nebulous mass.

Tendrils seemed to reach out, looping for a moment before fusing with the cloud once more, the fluid movement giving the impression that the whole structure was pulsating like a giant, black heart, each chamber throbbing against the deep blue sky. The sight was unsettling and, just as Khaldun found his own heart begin to beat with fear, he let go a sigh as he realised the mass wasn't some dark omen, it was a flock of seagulls cavorting on the coastline.

He laughed nervously and chastised himself under his breath. "Your imagination is getting worse the older you get, you old fool."

He increased pressure on the accelerator and moved towards the cloud, the gulls were now swirling high over the road and a part of him still felt uncertain as the car approached them. The Userkaf's had been in Dorsal Finn for over thirty years. Not once could Khaldun recall gulls behaving in such a fashion, but he shook his head to be free of the errant thought. Finding out new things was what gave life meaning and today he had found out that seagulls flocked together just the same way as starlings would over an inland city.

A huge thump on the roof of the car startled him

enough to have him swerving on the road. The vehicle went left, dangerously close to the metal crash barrier separating the road from the sheer cliff-face beyond. He corrected his steering, cursing aloud as he got the car back on track.

Another dull thump hit the windshield and the vista ahead was turned into a web of cracks, Khaldun could see exactly what was happening, though his mind refused to believe it.

The gulls were dive-bombing the car!

Just as this realisation came to him, a seabird smashed into the vehicle's bonnet, it was a huge beast, and seemingly impervious to the impact and the sway of the car. It had left a crater in the bodywork and stood staring at Khaldun through the ruined window.

In his panic, Khaldun thought he must have been going mad because, for a moment, he could have sworn the gull's eyes were no longer black, but twin points of burning green flame. The gull's head bobbed and then swung side to side on its lean neck. It was gauging things, weighing up infinite possibilities Khaldun would never comprehend.

With a flurry of wings, the gull ploughed into the windshield, the pane already weakened, it caved in. With the bird's head now inside the car, it forced its way through, oblivious to the terrible damage the passage incurred upon its body. The entry point was framed with blood and feathers, its beak and claws now tearing mercilessly as Khaldun's hands, which he lifted off of the wheel to protect his face, his screams bleeding into the cries of the gull, his feet pushing down as he forced himself backwards, and away from the onslaught.

The car accelerated, out of control, the gulls wheeling overhead now engulfing it *en masse*. The car went right, slewing across the road and into the embankment, the collision altering its trajectory, bouncing it back onto the road with the hideous sound of scraping metal on tarmac. The chassis gave out and the road was littered with the smashed bodies of gulls that had not survived the impact.

The wounds on his hands were streaks of fire, skin stripped away by the savage assault, but Khaldun fought back. His right hand found the gull's neck, holding it firm as he shoved the bird away from him, slamming it into the steering wheel. The wings beat at his face and chest, but he held on, his hand squeezing, and squeezing until he felt something give against his palm.

Instantly the bird flopped into his lap.

Any thoughts of triumph were short-lived as Khaldun realised the car was engulfed in a mass of writhing gulls, their eyes so green, the illumination turned the interior of the car to jade.

Without warning the gulls powered away from the car, the daylight now dazzling, but Khaldun could still see with instant horror that his car was heading straight for the crash barrier. He slammed on the breaks, the squeal of tyres a lost voice in the screaming din from the gulls outside.

Despite his manoeuvre, he hit the barrier fast and hard. From overhead, the screaming gulls watched the outcome with interest.

Edward moved through the grounds of Bramwell Hall. He knew the place well, the early part of his childhood had been spent with Stewart, his older brother, exploring the estate, with its acres of woodlands, secret gardens and lurking stone statues.

That was before his solicitor father had been banished from the town. Before that bitch Beatrice Beecham. He felt a cold anger rising in him as he thought of his father's fall from grace. He stopped by the thick trunk of an oak tree and looked at letters carved in the gnarled, ancient bark.

EC + SC.

He smiled as he traced his fingers over the rugged letters. His time would come. Edward felt this with an odd sense of certainty.

A noise came from behind him. He turned calmly to see Primrose standing at the borderline of the carefully cultivated hedges. She gestured for him to come over to her. He nodded and they both snuck in behind the hedge.

"We were meant to meet off-site. You're not meant to be roaming around the grounds," Primrose said curtly. "Dennis Hodges might've caught you, and where would that leave us?"

Edward scowled back at her. "Relax. Dennis Hodges is way in the woods stuffing his face with Pontefract's butler."

Primrose's gaze was firm, unwavering. "You know Hodges and Smythe are both in cahoots with The Newshounds, Edward. You were brought on board for your passion for our purpose, and that requires you to be *discreet*. Patient."

Edward shuffled on the spot in frustration.

"Patient? The Newshounds took everything from my family. I want to get even. No, not even. I want to destroy them all."

Primrose nodded and her response was muted, sympathetic. "I understand what it means to crave vengeance, Edward, but if you truly want this then you are going to have to accept it is going to take time."

Edward thought this over. "Yeah. Okay," he said. "But don't expect me to be happy about it."

Primrose chuckled and the sound was thick as though she had a throat full of dirt.

"Of course, but we do expect you to be committed to playing your part."

Edward nodded. "Just tell me what I have to do."

Primrose cocked her head to one side, listening to something on the breeze. "I believe *she* has already told you what is required of you. You have the tablet, don't you?"

Edward patted the pocket of his jacket. "I got it, but I don't get *her*. She told me to come here, to see you. That's all I got."

Primrose nodded as though this made perfect sense. "She is a mystery, but that is what it is to be great."

Edward yawned. "Whatever. Just tell me when this is all going to kick off."

Primrose looked at him and there was darkness in her eyes that, for a few seconds, made Edward feel unsettled. "Be patient, Edward. We meet an ally later at the harbour. The time will come soon."

This time it was Edward who scowled. "Not soon enough."

Beatrice paced backwards and forwards on the promenade, her arms crossed tightly against the brisk wind coming in off the ocean. Behind her, the surf was churning white foam as it heaved onto the beach. Her stomach was rolling with equal vigour, especially when Emily had contacted her that morning via Whatsapp, and explained the events of last night, and her 'dream' of a captain who was eating gold coins.

"There's something going on," she said. "This town is up to something for sure."

From his viewing bench, Lucas watched Beatrice strut in front of him. His girlfriend was walking with such energy he was becoming dizzy trying to keep track of her.

"Maybe Tom just had one of his moments, y'know?" he said cautiously.

Beatrice stopped and turned her head to look at him. "Moments?" Her gaze was stern, her hair whipping in the air like Medusa's serpent locks.

Lucas shuffled in his seat. "Well, he does fantasise a lot, right? Maybe he just—"

Beatrice interjected. "Fantasised about finding an iPad in the ocean?"

"Now that you said it, in that really sarcastic tone, I'm not so sure anymore."

Beatrice continued to pace back and forth, her voice edged with frustration. 'Even if Thomas did misinterpret things, now we have Emily's dream-that-might-not-be-a-dream. What could it be, a vision, or another portent? If only we had some clue as to what all of this means!"

She stopped again and, once more, Lucas found himself the subject of her attentive stare. "You're the one who enjoys solving mysteries. Can't you figure it out?"

"Well, I looked at the poem and none of it made any sense," he said. "There's no link between the river Amazon and blood sacrifice, not even the Mayan people—pretty big on blood-letting in the name of their gods—would kill anyone in its waters. The reference to *true justice* and *unsound crimes*, that could mean anything from breaking the law without realising it, or a simple case of injustice. But an injustice committed when, or where? It's *needle-in-a-haystack* stuff, and that's on a good day!"

"It does talk about pieces being placed in a game, right?" she said, the tone of her words was small and brittle, almost helpless.

Lucas stood up and went over to her. He carefully placed a hand on her shoulder and looked deeply into her fierce blue eyes. "This town doesn't give up its secrets easily, Bea. You know that better than anyone. It's going to be a waiting game, as always. We sort of agreed as much yesterday."

Beatrice stepped forward and embraced him, her cheek resting against his neck.

"You're right." The words were muted, resigned. "I'm sorry. This stuff is getting to me today, and I don't know why."

Lucas smiled, enjoying the embrace. His eyes were fixed on the ocean, the morning sun spangling the water. There was something about the oscillating sparkle of the tide, he seemed to recall something recently that had a similar dazzling allure, but for the life of him, he could not recall where he had seen it.

Then the notion was gone, lost to the vagaries of his mind.

"You still with me, Walker?"

Lucas snapped out of his fugue. "Yeah, sorry, Bea. Just enjoying the moment."

Beatrice snuggled against him. "Good answer. You're shaping up well. I might keep you."

The insistent theme tune of Jamie's Kitchen rang out, spoiling the moment. Beatrice reached for her phone and no sooner had she activated it when the buzz of a frantic voice came from the speaker.

"Patience, slow down, what's happened?"

Buzz-buzz.

Lucas watched Beatrice's face drain of colour. "Oh, my God. We're coming. Now."

Lucas looked on with concern. "What's happened? Bea?"

But Beatrice was already running. "Come on!" she yelled as she passed him.

Lucas followed her, bemused. 'Where the hell are we going?'

"The hospital!" she yelled without turning back. "Call the others."

Chapter Nine

BEATRICE ARRIVED AT Ashby-on-Sea General Hospital forty minutes later. She had run home, Lucas struggling to keep up with her, lungs aching with exertion. Through gasps and wheezes, she'd explained to her concerned father what a distraught Patience had told her on the phone. Without hesitation, George had told Beatrice and Lucas to follow him to the car, and they set off, collecting Elmo and Emily on the way out of town.

In the car, Beatrice, Emily, and Lucas sat in the back. Elmo kept company with George, who drove with a grim countenance. No one spoke for the entire journey, but heads and hearts raced, the fear and anguish The Newshounds felt for their friend binding them all together.

George parked as The Newshounds bustled into the reception area. The footsteps landed heavily, and the squeak of training shoes on the linoleum echoed loudly through the corridors. A security guard told them to slow down, muttering something about the place being a hospital, not a playground, and Beatrice was ushered away by Lucas before she retorted with an expletive.

They got to the desk and the middle-aged receptionist regarded them with unbridled disdain, her mouth pursed, watery eyes glinting behind frameless glasses perched on a reedy nose.

"Can I help you, *young people*?"

"Our friend is here," Beatrice gasped.

"Friend?"

"Patience," Elmo said.

"Your friend is a patient here?"

Beatrice sighed heavily. "No, her name is Patience. Patience Userkaf."

The woman's brow furrowed. "And she's a patient here?"

"Oh my God!" Beatrice gasped. "If you had any less of a brain you'd be standing in a field waiting for Dorothy and Toto to show up."

The receptionist's pencil-thin eyebrows arched with anger just as a small voice came to them. They all turned and saw Patience walking towards them.

She looked uncharacteristically dishevelled, her hair hung limply about her shoulders, her clothing was creased, but it was her eyes that left the most impression on Beatrice. Patience's jade eyes were red-rimmed and puffy, dark streaks of mascara left twin tracks on her cheeks.

"Oh, Beatrice," Patience began and fell into her friend's arms, the sobs hot and terrible against Beatrice's shoulder. Emily stepped up and placed comforting arms about them both, and the three girls wept as Lucas and Elmo stared at the sight, their faces appearing as helpless as they actually felt.

At the harbour, the gulls cried out and the waves lapped lazily at the grey stone walls. Those boats already anchored bobbed in time with the tide, the small thuds of bright blue mooring lines against the jetties adding to the hushed voice of the ocean.

Alison sat on the breakwater, the electronic tablet in her hand. The image of the girl with the strawberry birthmark spoke to her from the screen, saying things that made Alison think deeply, bad things that made her giggle with embarrassment.

But she liked her new friend. She was a wonderful companion with whom Alison could pass the time until Erica came.

She had contacted her love-rival as soon as she'd left her house. The ruse had been pretty simple: the girl in the tablet had made it easier. Love was a fragile thing in the early stages, a small doubt here, an uncertainty there, was sometimes all it took to rock the love-boat. So Alison had punched five words into her Smartphone screen and sent the message to Erica.

The words said: I KNOW SOMETHING ABOUT JAMES.

A brief exchange on messenger and viola! The meeting was set. Timing was everything, of course, the girl on the screen was very insistent about it. The event about to take place was to be as precise as it was terrible. When Alison thought about it too much, it made her hesitant.

The voice from the tablet was lilting yet firm. "Stop that, Alison."

Alison looked sheepish, as though she'd been caught daydreaming in class. "What do you mean?"

"You know what I mean. You're thinking too much. You doubt the value in what needs to be done."

"Not . . . Really . . . "

"Perhaps I was wrong. I thought you understood. *Nemo Me Impune Lacessit*, Alison. None shall injure me with impunity."

"What does that mean?"

"You will know soon enough. When you have done what is needed, I shall tell you."

Alison looked down at the face on the screen, the girl was smiling and her eyes were green fire.

"Do you promise?" Alison whispered.

"In matters such as these, I always keep my word. Soon you will be my sister. And you shall be loved like no other."

Alison felt a surge of joy that almost seared her heart with its heat. She sighed deeply.

"Alison, are you okay?"

Alice's attention had been so focused on the words of her newfound friend. She should have been startled as Erica's words of concern seemed to come out of nowhere. Instead, she looked up, a smile slipping easily across her face, as she packed the tablet away into the purple canvas bag at her feet.

"I'm okay," Alison said standing to greet the taller girl. "I'm glad you came."

Erica nodded but her face was one of suppressed concern. "What did you mean by your text?"

Alison stepped up to the edge of the breakwater. Below her the waves beat against the hem, sending a fine mist into the air.

"It's beautiful here, isn't it?" she said without looked back.

Erica was suddenly beside her. The confusion was now morphing into irritation, made clear in the tone of her voice. "Will you *please* tell me what you meant by your message?"

Alison relished the desperation in Erica's voice. "James is in love with me."

Erica laughed. It was a short, sharp sound. She stifled it with a hand. "Look, Alison, I understand why you'd want to think that, I mean *Jimmy* is a dream, right? But we're kind of an item. He already loves me. He told me yesterday."

This time it was Alison who chuckled, thick and callous. A thing a human should not be able to make. Erica stepped away from her.

"I'm going to leave now. I have to be somewhere."

Alison turned, her black glasses framing eyes that were vibrant with malevolence.

"Yes, you do have to be somewhere, child. You are special. You have to be in the embrace of the ocean. Your end will give rise to a new beginning."

With this ominous statement still registering in Erica's mind, Alison shoved her hard in the chest, the blow winding her and the momentum taking her backwards, over the edge of the harbour wall. She fell from sight and Alison went to her knees and inched forwards until she peered down into the waters far below.

Erica's face was a diminishing white blur as it sank beneath the waves, eye sockets dark as soot against the alabaster skin, mouth open as she tried to make a last ghastly, yet silent scream. A hand shot from the water, desperately scrabbling to try and gain purchase on stone slimy with seaweed and lichen.

"The sea is a possessive lover," Alison said in a voice that did not belong to her. "Once it holds you in its embrace, it will never let go. Succumb, child, be free of the woes of this world, enter the realm beyond, a sacrifice and a champion you shall be. Remembered for all time."

With these words, Erica disappeared from view, claimed by the sea as a smiling Alison looked on.

In a waiting area near to the Intensive Care Unit (ICU), The Newshounds sat comforting Patience. She leaned against Beatrice, head resting lightly upon her friend's shoulder, eyes blank and staring at the stark white flooring. When she wasn't fixated on the floor, she stared at the entrance to the ICU, twin doors of brown wood with a STAFF ONLY sign stencilled across them.

Patience spoke in monotone, her grief turning her into an automaton, devoid of emotion.

"They found the car halfway down the cliff. It's a miracle it got caught on an outcrop, but the car was banged up pretty badly. So was Dad. They've got him on life support, covered in tubes and machines; you can barely see him beneath all the plastic and metal." A tear fell into her lap, and she made no attempt to wipe it away.

George was sitting opposite. His face etched with sympathy. "They'll be doing all they can, love. This is the best place for him. And he's brawny fellow. I remember that time when we had the town fete, and he was on our tug-of-war team, pulled that rope across the line as if there was no-one on the other end. Strong as an ox is your dad."

A small smile appeared on Patience's lips for the briefest of moments, and then it was gone. "Yes. We can only pray now."

A heavy silence descended on the scene. Lucas and Elmo stood leaning against a wall and Emily sat beside Beatrice, her face a mask of concern as she studied her grief-stricken friends.

"Do they know how it happened?" Lucas said softly.

Patience shook her head. "They just said he lost control of the car."

Emily scoffed in disbelief. "Figured that out all on their own did they?"

Patience sniffed. "If he recovers we'll have more of an idea."

Beatrice squeezed her friend's hand. "Not 'if—*when* he recovers."

Patience did not reply, she continued her vigil of staring at the floor. Just as the oppressive silence threatened to return, the main doors to the waiting area opened. Three people stepped through, their strides purposive and urgent.

Leading the trio was a tall, slim middle-aged man in a smart black suit and matching three-quarter coat. He had a silver-grey beard, and the lenses in his round-rimmed glasses had a yellow tint that matched his tie. He appeared both suave and professional, his stride confident, and his companion having to work hard to keep pace.

Beatrice recognised Primrose Meadowsweet but

knew little of her, and tried hard to think that just because the woman worked as Codd's aide didn't mean she would have an attitude that was as equally repugnant.

Beatrice failed to convince herself completely.

The man in the black suit stopped and addressed them all in a voice that was soft yet authoritative. "Good day. My name is Detective Jonas Cotteridge and I need to speak with Mrs Skylar Userkaf?"

Patience looked up at Cotteridge. "That's my mum." She indicated towards the entrance to the ICU. "She's in with my father."

"Ah, yes," Cotteridge said with a small yet sympathetic smile. "And it is this very matter that I seek to discuss with your mother, my dear."

"She's quite upset at the moment, officer," George said.

"*Detective*," Cotteridge reminded him without moving his gaze from Patience.

Primrose stepped up. "And I do believe that none of this is any of your business, Mr Beecham."

Beatrice stood up, startling all, including Cotteridge who took a step backwards. "It has everything to do with us! Patience and her family are our friends and they are all suffering right now."

To everyone's surprise, including Primrose, Cotteridge nodded in understanding. "Yes, of course, I understand this, Miss Beecham."

Beatrice frowned. "How do you know who I am?"

Cotteridge laughed despite its incongruity. "Let's just say that *I'm informed*, up to a point. But I am a detective, and I'm more than capable of getting to the bottom of things all by myself. Stories are exactly that, tales to be told. The skill is to determine what is and isn't true; what is and isn't *fact*."

"Why do you need to speak to my mother?" Patience said.

"I need to check out a story that I have just been told by your father's doctors," Cotteridge said. "But that is a conversation that I need to have with your mother, my dear. Then we can see where we go from there."

Although Cotteridge ended these words with a smile, Beatrice noticed that the warmth didn't quite reach his eyes.

The Spirit of the Ocean sliced through the calm waters, her passing forming a hem of foam that sloshed and gurgled against her brilliant, white keel. Just as the hull cut through the water, so her prow—a sleek curve rising over thirty feet out of the sea—cut through the air, the brass rails a glittering crown even in the mackerel grey sky overhead.

Today had shown that a day in the life as a captain at Redfern Maritime Leisure Company (RMLC) was a varied affair. This morning he had been at Bramwell Hall, hobnobbing with the aristocracy, and a forty-minute chopper-ride later, he was back with his new vessel, heading out to sea, course set for Dorsal Finn.

From his place on the bridge, Melville surveyed the deck laid out below him. He sat back in his seat, the leather comfortable against his thickset-yet-trim frame. The computer guidance screens embedded in his console splashed green and blue light onto his face.

As he took in the view through the panoramic window, Melville allowed a moment of pride to consume him, his chest expanded against the white tunic. In his large hands, he cradled a cup of tea which quietly clinked against a bone china saucer as he stirred the dark steaming liquid, a slice of lemon swirling lazily. His eyes remained insightful, never leaving the seascape ahead.

The Spirit of the Ocean was an incredible boat. The hull was made of steel and the superstructure, aluminium. The twin Caterpillar engines could cruise at thirteen knots and climb to a maximum speed of fifteen should the need arise. It had eight cabins, with a capacity to sleep up to fifteen people, served by a crew of twenty. She flew under the flag of the Cayman Islands as RMLC had a base there—for tax purposes, Melville suspected. There were three decks, one fore, one aft, and the top deck where passengers could drink cocktails and watch the stars.

There was a cinema, a boardroom, a gala room complete with a full bar for those who enjoyed a party, and a state-of-the-art gym where they could try to recover from the same party the day after. Every piece of furniture was handmade, every fixture and fitting made from the best materials, by the best craftsmen. There was no expense spared, this was the nature of this floating statement to success.

Not only was this boat magnificent, it also belonged to him. Not on paper, of course, the owner was indeed Clive Redfern, but fiscal matters held no sway once a boat left dry dock. As soon as the hull was in the water, it was the captain who took command of a vessel's destiny, because if not, the ocean certainly would.

His knew this all too well because his father had been claimed by the sea when Melville was fourteen years of age. He'd been born and raised in the nearby town of Ashby-on-Sea and, on one afternoon, a squall had blown up as his father's boat, a thirty-footer named Mary Rose, was caught on its way back from the fishing grounds.

Even though he was an experienced seaman, Melville's father had been caught out as he steered the boat hard to stern as a rogue wave threatened to capsize the Mary Rose, but it had been too late. The wave broke too early and smashed into the boat like a wall, splitting the vessel in two, and dragged boat and crew beneath the churning waters.

The family was devastated but the community swamped them with warmth and affection, a stark contrast to the ocean that had taken so much from them all. For a young Melville it would have been easy to succumb to his grief, or retreat from the sea, make a life away from the coast, in the towns and cities inland. Yet it was his mother that had put things into perspective for them.

"The sea has given more to this family than it's taken," she'd said as they considered their futures. "This home and our community will look after us as we recover from the heartbreak of these times."

So it was. Melville grew and learned in school during the week, and crewed for local fishermen in the summer, where the storms were few and easily plotted. By the time his mother died, he was an experienced crewman, with a solid education and a yearning to do something with both.

One day, as he stood on the deck gutting fish and

packing them in ice for market, fate brought an incredible sight. He'd been wiping his brow on the sleeve of his jumper and as he dropped his arm he saw a huge yacht moving across the bay. The sunlight was turning its hull to a ghostly white, and the sight—the beauty—of it held him firm for well over a minute as his eyes tracked its course. In that one moment, Melville knew exactly what he wanted to do, what he *needed* to do, and that was to get himself onto one of those vessels.

He had no idea how he'd go about it, but once the decision had been made on his way back into port, he went to the library to find out all he could about yachts and what he had to do to make a career out of serving on one.

He started out as a steward, and while the money was good, he was drawn to those working the decks, and quickly migrated to deckhand, via several courses. His aptitude and seafaring experience brought him opportunities to climb the rungs, accumulating experiences, and he eventually found his way into Clive Redfern's prestigious company. Even at the interview— Redfern insisted on vetting all of his employees—the two men, despite their different standings, had gelled, and time had only firmed that bond. Melville had been first officer on Redfern's own yacht, and the promise of his own commission had been made during those times. And Redfern was nothing if not a man of his word. So here Melville was, with his own boat, and a feeling of contentment that was intoxicating.

A voice came to him, pulling him from his thoughts. "I have the manifest for you to sign, Skipper."

Melville nodded absently and swivelled his chair to face his first officer.

Trevor Braid was a stocky man with dark eyes and ebony skin. The men had known each other for some time, and when not on duty they were firm friends. There was no competition between them; Trevor was easy-going but a stickler for routine, making him the perfect first officer.

There was another man on the bridge, their navigator, Roy Barker. In all his time at sea, Melville had never come across a man that optimised contradiction. Barker was an expert, intuitive navigator, but his attitude was beyond poor.

Barker was skinny but tough; his dark eyes were a place that schooled malice and contempt. His humour was dour and spiteful, yet sly. Surly comments were made just out of earshot, and his bullying never in front of witnesses. The other crew avoided him, Trevor and Melville tolerated him because of his ability. Melville just needed him to do his job, and that's what the helmsman would do, nothing more and nothing less. That was enough for the captain. Sometimes Melville would consider how a man could be so sour, and at one point had considered sitting Barker down to discuss such things with him, but the moments never came, and Melville always seemed to be able to find other things in need of his attention.

Trevor handed Melville a tablet, its screen bright and etched with a list of items in a grid of blue lines. Melville held the device at arm's-length before he scrutinised it, his eyes squinting and his chin tilted back.

Trevor frowned. "Are you really going to try to read that without your glasses?"

Melville chuckled, pulling a black, oval case from

his trouser pocket and retrieved his gold-framed spectacles. He revisited the manifest briefly and then nodded.

"Very good, Number One," he said handing the tablet back to Trevor.

"Just in case those glasses of yours need replacing, or at least until you learn how to magnify the font on this piece of equipment, I'll go through the itinerary," Trevor said tapping the screen. "We moor at Dorsal Finn harbour, take on provisions ahead of the guests arriving at eight-thirty tomorrow night."

"Very good," Melville said. "Usual things?"

"Aye. Catering provisions, bar stocks and the like. Our head chef has arranged for pick up from local sources, to demonstrate support for the town economy."

Melville smiled. "A nice touch. Hearts and minds, eh?"

It had been pretty early on in his career that Melville had encountered the jealousies that came with being associated with great wealth. He had returned to Ashby-on-Sea after his mother's death and met with a few of his friends who had remained in the town.

There had been a downturn in the neighbourhood fishing industry and local fishermen were seeing hard times. One night in the local pub, he'd found the friendly atmosphere change when he mentioned that he was crewing on a superyacht for a billionaire from the financial sector.

Where he'd once stared at warm, friendly faces, he found them brooding, and no one would look at him. Someone mentioned that banks had foreclosed on their boat and that they were no longer able to support their family. Tension replaced joviality until another of his friends made light of it. The moment had remained with him, and in some way made him cautious whenever he returned home, even after the economy had picked up, and those who were once downtrodden were now making their way in the world.

Knowing such emotions had certain people doing things out of character. It made perfect sense to allow certain local representatives on board in order to recognise the town playing host. But as limited tickets to the launch gala applied only to the few, a grand gesture had been needed to demonstrate to those not attending that the company was grateful. So it was that Dorsal Finn's plethora of local merchants had been approached to provide the ingredients integral to the event.

"What time will we be taking on the supplies?" Melville asked.

"Noon tomorrow," Trevor replied as he absently scanned the screens on the console. "We're three miles out."

Melville stood up. "I want to go and freshen up before we dock. You have the bridge, Number One."

"Sure, Skipper."

Trevor sat down in the chair Melville had vacated, and the captain made his way to the exit, a set of sliding doors that opened electronically with a small hiss. He went through and followed a long narrow corridor, the floor covered with hard-wearing royal blue carpets speckled with a gold fleur-de-lis motif.

Seventy yards down the corridor, Melville came to the door of his quarters. The highly polished rosewood had a brass plaque with his name embossed into it.

Instead of a handle, there was only a black oval screen upon which Melville placed his thumb, and the lock clicked, the panel now flashing green as the door opened inwards under its own volition.

The captain's cabin was spacious and ornate, the ceilings white and the walls made up of oak panelling. It was dominated by a large bed, draped in a dark blue duvet, with white linen turned down halfway.

A large desk featured on the far wall, facing an oval window, and upon the desk, there was a ledger and a copy of one of his father's favourite books, Herman Melville's *Moby Dick*. The cover was weathered, the pages yellowed. It had been in his family for over seventy years and with it came only good memories of a time gone by.

There were other books too, encyclopaedias on naval history and famous seamen, a vast history condensed into one small space.

He stepped over to the small bar and poured himself a tumbler of sparkling water. He took the glass to the desk where he sat down and sipped from his drink as he looked down at the books.

His eyes went to the two items above his desk: display cases made of glass and framed with gold. Clive was as much a fanatic of maritime memorabilia as Melville. The whole yacht was embellished with artefacts from all over the world, and many places in time. The insurance on some of the pieces beggared belief, and Melville had cautioned his friend about, in effect, turning the yacht into a floating museum. Clive wouldn't hear anything of it, of course. The name of the game was opulence, and Redfern was a master at providing it.

Inside one of the display cases was a small compass, its surface mottled and tarnished with age, and below this, an extended telescope rested on a blue velvet cushion.

The second case wasn't bolted to the wall, it was held loosely in place on brackets, a temporary arrangement until Melville allowed Clive to transfer it to the boardroom, where it would have pride of place overseeing the huge, rosewood table.

The case was occupied by a single item. It was a rectangular piece of weathered driftwood, but carved neatly into the surface were two words, and Melville's eyes were always drawn to them whenever he sat at his desk.

When he looked upon the words they always seemed to leave him mesmerised, and he fancied that on occasions he could hear a sound of thunder and voices raised in alarm. It seemed an age since he'd found the piece on the beach, and often he would consider it with a mixture of awe and grief, the memory that his father had died the same day not dulled by the passage of time.

He took another swig from the glass and allowed his eyes to trace the words in the wood. Unknown to him, he found himself whispering the words as he read them.

The Raven.

Nursing staff kindly found a visitors room for Cotteridge and the Userkaf's to talk in private. Patience and Skylar sat on a long sofa, the detective opposite on a heavy chair made of some smooth, dark material that shone under the fluorescent lights.

Skylar had insisted that her daughter remain for the discussion and Cotteridge, impassive as always, agreed.

The detective watched Skylar's pained and worried face intently. He dug a small box from the pocket of his coat. He popped the lid and tilted it towards Patience and Skylar.

"Peppermint?"

They both shook their heads and he delicately retrieved a sweet and popped it into his mouth, closing his eyes as he savoured the taste.

He replaced the box back into his coat and leaned forwards, elbows on his knees, hands clasped in front of him as though offering someone a leg up.

"Mrs Userkaf, can I start by saying thank you for agreeing to see me at this terrible time? I understand how difficult this must be for you both."

Skylar supported his statement with a nod as she gently blew her nose into a tissue. "Thank you, officer."

Cotteridge smiled. "*Detective*. Now, I best start by asking about your husband's state of mind this morning before he left for Bramwell Hall."

Skylar's response was considered. "He was in good spirits, and looking forward to the pre-launch meeting."

Cotteridge crunched on the peppermint. "This would be the launch of *The Spirit of the Ocean*, tomorrow evening?"

"Yes," Skylar confirmed.

"A big event for the town," Cotteridge offered. "From what I can gather, your husband was instrumental in securing the deal?"

"Yes. He was very proud of his achievement."

"I see. So I would imagine he would be quiet jovial, buoyant one might say?"

Patience squirmed in her seat as exasperation began to make its presence known on her face. "What does this have to do with my father's accident?"

Cotteridge sat back in his seat, a big grin on his face. "The young have all the time in the world, yet they need all of the answers immediately. That is what I love about kids; they keep us oldies on our toes."

Patience put frustration on hold and allowed bemusement some airtime. "It was a simple question."

The detective's mouth became a dash in his white beard. "I hate to be cliché, Miss Userkaf, but the answer is not quite the case. Perhaps I may ask you a question?"

Skylar interjected. "What is this about, detective?"

The smile returned as Cotteridge held up a hand. "Please indulge me. I merely want to ask Patience here if she can tell me what the word 'accident' means."

Patience's response was delivered with an affronted air. Such things were beneath her. "The word 'accident' is a noun, meaning an unfortunate or unforeseen event that usually ends with damage or injury. It can also mean something that happens by chance."

Cotteridge threw his arms wide. "There we have it. The Oxford English Dictionary could not have done the word more justice. The important element in both meanings is that of *intent*, was it truly a random act of chance or," he leaned forward again, "was it something that could have been altogether *avoided*?"

The Userkafs stared back at Cotteridge as they

digested his words. Skylar's perfect eyebrows steeped a little. "What are you implying? That my husband deliberately drove his car off a cliff?"

The detective frowned as though he was actually mulling the statement over. "This is a little delicate. I understand all too well. Yet it is protocol for medical staff to disclose any suspicions they may have when a patient is admitted under certain circumstances, Road Traffic Collisions, for example. Especially where there are serious consequences, and no witnesses."

Patience responded firmly. "We get that, but what has this got to do with—"

"Does your husband drink, Mrs Userkaf?"

The question silenced Patience like a slap to the face. The Userkaf women looked at each other before Skylar responded. Her words were basted with contempt.

"Our faith prohibits the partaking of alcohol."

"Even if in 'good spirits' as you say? Caught up with the moment, a toast to a major achievement?"

Skylar's expression was stern. "No."

Patience reached out and placed a supporting hand on her mother's arm.

Cotteridge's face remained neutral. "Your husband was found with alcohol in his bloodstream. Can you account for that?"

Skylar stood up so quickly it startled Patience to the point where she let out a small squeak of surprise.

"This conversation is over," Skylar said. "Come on, Daughter."

From his seat, Cotteridge watched them leave, his face expressionless. As the door to the visitor's room closed, he reached for his pack of peppermints.

Chapter Ten

LISON STOOD ON the breakwater, her gaze fixed on the undulating horizon. Erica had been claimed by the sea only thirty minutes ago, and yet Alison still felt an unending sense of peace.

For a few seconds after she had watched Erica's frightened face sink beneath the water, something inside her mind cried out in horror, but with a dizzying sense of immediacy the thoughts had been shut out, like a heavy cell door on a prisoner's desperate scream. Replacing the scream had been this state of pensive emotional equilibrium, excitement building in her stomach as though waiting for a moment to arrive, but not knowing what it would bring.

On the horizon she saw a large shape, it glimmered white even in the dull light. The ship was heading towards the port and her eyes were mesmerised by it.

Her new friend was in her head again, an insistent whisper informing her that she need not be afraid because allies were coming to her aid.

No sooner had she formed a question in her mind, when Alison heard the sound of footsteps approaching from behind her. She turned around, part of her reluctant to lose sight of the ship as it cruised towards her.

She found herself looking at a youth she knew as Edward Chorley, and Mayor Codd's aide, Primrose Meadowsweet. They walked towards her, Primrose tall and thin, Edward short and stocky, the odd couple separated by age but united in their cause, and the smiles on their faces.

Alison found this smile infectious and grinned as they stepped up close to her. Edward peered over the side of the harbour wall before he spoke.

"You really pushed Erica in there?"

Alison nodded, the grin remaining in place but her eyes were fixed, robotic. Then she pulled her face into a contorted mask of anguish.

"She slipped. There was nothing I could do to save her. She was simply too heavy to pull out on my own. It's my fault."

But no sooner had she said these words her demeanour changed and she began laughing, the sound cruel and laced with malice.

Primrose giggled. "Yes, Alison. Very good. You are a natural actor, and thus a natural liar."

"Are you two here to help me?" Alison said.

Primrose stared at the girl, her eyes cold. "No. We are here to help *her*."

Edward responded, his tone surly. "Be useful to know what the hell it is she wants. Might help this make sense."

Primrose allowed her own impatience to show through, although her focus was directed squarely at her younger counterpart. "If she tells all, then she shows her hand, and then that very hand can be tethered before it can strike."

"What's that supposed to mean?" Edward snapped.

"You're talking the same riddles as that bitch on the screen."

Primrose snarled and the sound was unearthly. She walked up to Edward and slapped him so hard across the face the blow had him staggering backwards for a few steps, almost sending him over the edge of the sea wall. Alison giggled as Edward fought to regain his balance.

"Are you crazy?" he snapped at Primrose when he'd found his footing. Instinctively he came forward, his fists clenched but he stopped as though meeting an invisible wall.

Primrose's face seemed to be oscillating, as though many fingers were moving under the skin of her neck and cheeks. Her lips juddered and turned black, water began to gush from her mouth and fell as a dank and dirty cataract down her blouse. The cracking of bones was loud on the air, making even Edward wince, and before their eyes, Primrose's features changed into those of the girl on the screen.

Alison fell to her knees with a cry of awe, and Edward found himself stepping away, anger now swapped with anxiety.

"You do well to recoil from me, dog," the borrowed lips said. "Respect is what I demand, and you will incur great pains should you choose to disregard this injunction."

Edward's anger was held in check, no mean feat for a youth who was fuelled by his rage at the world.

Where his immediate emotion had been shock and fear, he now felt the incredible surge of fury at being struck. His right cheek was on fire and throbbed, but the pain was distant as he watched the undulating face in fascination.

"If we don't know what you want, we can't help you," he said through gritted teeth.

The thing wearing Primrose Meadowsweet appeared to think this over for a short time. "There is irony on this day, boy," it said turning to face the ship heading towards the harbour. "My object of desire now comes to me."

Edward stared at the oncoming vessel. "A boat?"

"Objects of desire are different for everyone," she said. "Their power and influence cannot be underestimated. Alison's deed has started a great event, and as with all things that bring change, sacrifices need to be made."

Primrose looked down at Alison who was still on her knees, forehead placed on the ground in worship of the effigy standing before her.

"Rise, child," Primrose said. "You have proven your loyalty. You have nothing to fear."

Alison climbed slowly to her feet, joining Primrose and Edward as they watched *The Spirit of the Ocean* clear the breakwater. No sooner had the huge ship crossed the threshold when something incredible happened.

The waters in the harbour began to move as though their consistency had become as treacle. For the briefest of seconds, the churning sea appeared to take on a pulsating green hue. The high sides of the vessel wavered, the very air about it rippling like the surface on a pond disturbed by the delicate limbs of a dragonfly cooling itself in the heat of summer.

Then the moment was gone, normality returning in the wink of an eye. The crewmen on the deck continued their duties regardless, making it clear to the trio on the sea wall that only they were privy to the subtle change great sacrifice could bring.

Sat at his desk, Melville saw the glass of water shudder. Seconds later he felt the floor beneath his feet vibrate.

In an instant he reached for his COMMS unit—a bulky beige phone—bolted to the wall by his desk, and clicked it on.

His voice was firm as he spoke. "Report, Number One."

But Trevor's reply was infused with surprise. "Say again, Skipper?"

"What was that shimmy?"

A pause. Seconds passed by. "Erm, that's a negative on that, Skipper. We entered the harbour, cleared the breakwater. Nothing on the sensors, and certainly no proximity alarm."

Melville looked at the glass and saw no sign of disturbance. He shook his head and squinted as though this would make things appear different.

Trevor's voice came to him, concerned. "You okay, Skipper?"

"Yes. Must've been daydreaming," he replied. "I'm coming up to the bridge."

"Right you are," Trevor said, although his voice remained hesitant.

Melville clicked off the COMMS unit and readied himself to leave his quarters. Yes, he needed to keep active, the voice of his mother dropped into his head. *The devil makes work for idle thumbs*, it said.

He left the room, the door closing at his heels, the

incident with the glass and vibrating floors now forgotten as he made his way back to the bridge.

Back in Melville's quarters, the oppressive silence that came with an empty room was tainted with a small, yet insistent sound.

On the desk, the glass began to shiver once more, the water within becoming infused with a green tint. Above the tumbler, the wooden plaque trembled with such vigour it beat against the confines of the display case. Without warning the lettering began to ooze black, viscous fluid. It pooled upon the velvet cushion where the plaque rested. The goo seeped into the material, then through it, until it fell as long sinews of ebony onto the desk. From there it moved like a living thing, crawling towards the window, black tendrils in search of the light.

The entity passed through the window and rolled down the hull until it made contact with the sea where it lost its properties, turning to a slick that spread on the surface, an oiled eddy that powered beneath the waves under its own volition. Down it went, where things long-lost waited to receive it; darkness becoming one with darkness.

The doors to the waiting room opened with a squeak and a squelch, the fast, heavy footfalls as the Userkafs entered, making it clear to Beatrice something was wrong.

Patience and Skylar approached The Newshounds who, up until that point, had remained seated in the waiting area, spending most of that time chatting quietly.

George had made a few attempts to engage with Primrose but the woman appeared to be content with staring at a vending machine in the corner of the waiting area, her eyes almost trance-like.

Beatrice had also noticed this, and it was only when she looked upon Primrose the first time, the woman's dark eyes met hers, and Beatrice found a small shudder pass through her, forcing her to quickly turn away.

As intense as this was, her attention was immediately drawn towards the arrival of her friend.

It was Patience's mother who spoke first. "Can you believe the nerve of the man?" Her face was flushed with anger.

George went to her. "What is it, Skylar?"

Patience answered instead. "That police officer accused Dad of being a drunk driver."

Primrose stood upright. "Did you say drunk?"

Skylar was quick to interject. "He was not drunk."

"An accusation all the same, Mrs Userkaf. Oh dear. This is most irregular."

Despite the concern on Primrose's face, Beatrice thought she saw something else, a sense of enjoyment.

"May I speak with you both," Primrose said to Skylar and Patience as she ushered them to the furthest corner of the waiting room where the exchange continued as a series of whispers, most of the conversation monopolised by the young woman.

Beatrice heard a sound to her left and turned.

Primrose Meadowsweet was leaning with her back against the wall, flanked by a fire extinguisher. Confused, Beatrice looked back to the Userkafs and there was Primrose again, still engaged with them.

The world about her appeared to slow to a stop. All those in the waiting room became statues from another place, another time. She turned back to the Primrose leaning against the wall, unsettled and unsure. In her mind, words came to Beatrice, spoken in a girl's voice but it oozed with a cold malevolence.

"Water and blood from the Amazon join,
True justice in search of an unsound crime,
Curses and blessings, one and the same,
Places are taken at the heart of the game."

She recognised the words as those Thomas had jotted down in the kitchen and at once a great anxiety threatened to take hold of her heart.

Something else caught her attention. A flickering silver light bounced off the wall, and Beatrice's eyes followed it for a few seconds before tracking its source. Lucas was standing, hands in pockets, an effigy frozen by whatever powers were at work. On his chest, the shimmering light sent out spangled beams towards her, the intensity almost too bright to behold.

Beatrice blinked several times, the imprint from the light remained behind her closed lids, but at the heart of those impressions was a dark image, the shape of something not only within the light, but its source. She heard a creaking sound and turned back to Primrose as about her the world took on a green hue, and Beatrice was overcome with a sensation that left her swooning.

In the jade haze, Primrose's features appeared to momentarily change, her eyes becoming dark as tar, the strawberry blotch standing vividly against the milk-white skin of her right cheek, making her look like a bloodied corpse pulled from the cold, cold ocean. Dark blue lips opened and seawater gushed from her mouth, soaking a dark dress made from wool and starched linen. A gurgling scream accompanied the cascade, as thick water slapped into the tiles.

Just as the screech built to a crescendo, it ended and Beatrice was back in the waiting room, all signs of the terrible images now gone.

She looked over towards Patience and her mother who appeared angry and distraught. They were venting this out on Primrose who was not focusing on anything other than Beatrice.

It was only as she saw the hint of a smile on the woman's otherwise stern face, Beatrice realised this had been no hallucination or vision.

Something sinister had paid her a visit, and Primrose had been its messenger.

Beatrice watched as Patience paced the car park, hands clasped to her head, face cast up to the slate sky. As Primrose had spoken to them, Beatrice had witnessed a change in the demeanour of both Patience and her mother. Skylar merely looked forlorn and put her face into her hands. Patience, on the other hand, had shouted angrily at Primrose, adding some uncharacteristic expletives before storming off in the direction of the exit.

Patience had moved at pace through the hospital corridors, even the pleading calls from her mother had not been able to stall her, and Beatrice and the others had followed.

Now Patience bristled with agitation. "This is all wrong! How could they do this to us?"

"Want to let us know what's going on, Patti?" Lucas said.

"What's going on is our language expert and fashion guru is totally pissed," Elmo muttered.

"Damn right I'm pissed," Patience said firmly, but they all saw the tears in her eyes. Beatrice went to her and held her tightly. In those moments, Patience wept freely, unabashed and wanton.

Emily gingerly stepped up to them and offered a crumpled tissue. Patience took it and blew her nose with a loud snort. Beatrice sensed that the anger was falling away from her friend, and she stepped to one side, keeping an arm around Patience's shoulder, and looked into her eyes.

"Tell us what's going on."

Slowly Patience muttered a response. "Primrose says we can't attend the launch because it'll reflect badly on the town."

"And they're letting Mayor Codd on board?' Lucas said. "Now that's double-standards if ever you needed an example."

"Codd's sick," Patience replied. "Primrose is going instead."

Beatrice flinched. "That figures."

"Why'd you say that?" Patience said from behind her tissue.

"I saw something while we were in the waiting room," Beatrice said. "And Primrose was part of it all."

She explained the details of her vision, and this time it was Lucas who came forward.

"So are we saying this isn't the Dark Heart at all?" he said, sounding relieved.

"We don't know for sure," Beatrice replied. "This town has many ways of getting under your skin."

"And nothing is ever left to chance either," Lucas said. "Patti and her family are now off that boat. Which means *we're* off of that boat, right?"

Patience nodded.

Lucas cast his arms wide in a grand gesture. "Is it me or is that a little too convenient? Makes me wonder what's on that boat we're not meant to see."

Elmo rubbed at his chin. "So what do we do, Bro?"

Lucas thought this over. "We find a way to make sure we get on that damn boat," he said.

"We could sneak on?" Emily said. "Pretend to be, I don't know, staff or something?"

Elmo smiled but it was weak. "I think we fall short by about ten years, but it was a pretty cool idea."

"You mean it sucked?" Emily signed.

"Pretty much," Elmo signed back.

Beatrice held up a hand to get everyone's attention. "Getting on the boat is one thing. Before we do anything we need to know what it is we're walking into when we do get there."

Patience dabbed at her eyes with the limp tissue. "What do you mean?"

"If we're being kept off the boat and Primrose is meant to be getting on there, then there must be a reason. We need to find what the connection is between the boat and this town."

"But the boat is brand new," Patience said.

Lucas snapped his finger as a thought came to him.

"If not the boat then the people on it, the crew or some of the guests, maybe?"

"We can do some research on the boat and the crew," Elmo said.

"I can find out who is meant to be on the guest list," Patience said. "My father said he had already received it. I'll email it to you."

Beatrice squeezed Patience's shoulder. "Is your dad going to be okay?"

"I don't know," Patience said. "I have to stay here with mum. In case anything . . . happens."

The look on her face was one of hopelessness and it was in danger of becoming contagious. Tears brimmed in Patience's eyes once more, and although her sobs were silent, The Newshounds felt every single one.

Agnes punched the keys on the PC, the clicks where her fingers made contact with the keyboard almost rhythmic in the heavy silence of the library. Her gold half-moon glasses were, as always when working, perched on the end of her thin nose, their gold chain hanging from each arm and looping behind the librarian's head. To her left, Maud sat scrutinising the monitor, the screen splashing hard white light onto her face.

The computer was not the only thing on the desk. Several heavy books lay either stacked or covers thrown wide, propped open with a stapling machine, paperweights, and any other items helpful in keeping their place.

Maud stretched her back, hoping to remove the dull ache that had taken residence there. "Giddy goodness. This is like tryin' to find a needle in a haystack an' ye can't even find the farm an' get started."

Agnes chuckled. "Research takes time, Maud. We're scratting around in the dark because you want to keep this to ourselves. That means it's just you, me, and educated guesswork."

Maud was pensive. "Aye, as Ol' Maud is the one wantin' to go solo, I guess I'd better not moan about how the tune's playin' out."

Their focus returned to the screen, Agnes taking the mouse and using the central wheel to scroll down the internet search pages. "Problem is we have no reference point to all of this," she said. "We don't know who this girl is or what she did."

Maud rubbed at her chin, eyes scrutinising the screen. 'Well, we know this town ain't natural. What say we assume this girl ain't either?"

Agnes arched her eyebrows. "Interesting. Go on."

"Girl. Magic. Birthmark," Maud replied.

"A witch perhaps?" Agnes offered. "Thomas mentioned the girl he saw had clothing from olden times. There was a spike in witch trials in the late 16th and early 17th centuries so we can add those in to try and narrow it down?"

Maud shrugged. "Ye're the boss of this here contraption, Agnes."

Agnes typed Maud's keywords and the terms "16th and 17th Century." In an instant, a list of websites dedicated to witchcraft came up and the librarian scrutinised the descriptions. She clicked onto one website and began reading the introductory blurb before doing a site search for the term *birthmark.*

"Birthmarks were certainly taken as signs of witchcraft," Agnes said.

"Bein' a woman was enough of a bleedin' sign to some quarters," Maud sighed.

"This is true," Agnes replied. "The Witches' Mark—or Devil's Mark as it was also known—could be anything from a wart or mole to any raised blemish on the skin, a birthmark for example. It was meant to represent the physical acknowledgement of a witch's servitude to the Devil."

Maud appeared grim. "As sad an' perversely interestin' all this is, it ain't clearin' any of the fog around this mystery of ours."

"I agree," Agnes said. "It doesn't help that witchcraft was by design secretive, its practice kept in families for fear of reproach, and also many localised accounts of the witch trials have been doctored to propagate the authenticity of the Witch-finders of the time. We don't know what is fact or fiction. Then there's the location—knowing where this girl was from might give us a starting point."

"Maybe she was from these parts. Dorsal Finn has had its share of witches and warlocks, eh?" Maud offered.

Agnes tapped her blue biro against her chin. "Cooper's Cove has history, Delores Mellor is well known to local folklore after all. But the murder of her and her coven was much later than 16th or 17th Century. Still, we have to start somewhere."

"Ain't no better startin' point than where ye are right now," Maud mused.

Agnes conceded and hit the backwards arrow icon on the screen, pulling up the original internet search. She added Dorsal Finn to the keywords and hit *send*.

Though they didn't realise it, Maud and Agnes held their breath.

As the screen refreshed, another list came up. The women both allowed their shoulder to sag. The folklore of Delores Mellor came up, old ground that the women knew too well from a life in the town. To outsiders, it was nothing more than folklore. These women knew differently, though. The Newshounds had come across Delores' influence and her grimoire, The Book of Shadows, had been destroyed in the process.

"Well that's nothin' but a damp squib," Maud said.

Agnes was about to speak when she suddenly laughed aloud. "What a silly old sausage I am," she exclaimed to her friend.

"Ye're statin' the obvious again, me dear."

"Dorsal Finn would not have *existed* back then," Agnes said. "This town has only been on the map for two hundred years, remember?"

Maud cast her eyes to the ceiling. "We old uns need puttin' out to grass, make no mistake. Where do we go from here?"

Agnes bookmarked her search in the 'favourites' tab in the browser. She stood up and pointed to a place where a large oak table sat in a corner with two small book cases met at right angles.

"Local history section, of course," she said with a wink.

Maud chuckled. "Ye're smarter than a stingin' nettle, Agnes Clutterbuck."

With that, the two women went in search of a town's past.

The drive back from the hospital was a sombre affair. In the backseat, Beatrice sat with Lucas, her head resting on his shoulder, and on occasion she caught her father's eyes flitting to her in the driver's mirror. The concern in his eyes echoed her own feelings of frustration and confusion.

As the car arrived on the outskirts of Dorsal Finn, Beatrice asked her father to pull over.

"You okay, love?" George asked as he parked the vehicle on a patch of ground cut into the embankment.

"Yeah, Dad," Beatrice said. "We just need some fresh air, that's all."

"We do?" asked Lucas.

"Yes," said Beatrice, nudging him. "We'll walk back into town."

"We will?" said Elmo.

Emily looked baffled and Beatrice apologised and signed her intentions. Emily responded by nodding and opened the car door, the wind tossing her hair about almost immediately.

"Decision made," Lucas said as he followed Emily out.

The four of them watched the car continue down the hill. Below them, Dorsal Finn lay innocuous, the waters in the crescent-shaped bay a writhing mass of shimmering light. To their right was a grassy outcrop that ultimately led to Monument Point. Several hundred yards away, the lighthouse stood proud against the grey sky. All around them the wind whipped the grass and tugged at their clothes.

Elmo looked up at the sky where thick clouds rolled in from the ocean.

"Nice evening for getting wet," he mused.

"Sorry," Beatrice said. "We need to work out where we go from here."

"Down the hill," Elmo grinned. "In the rain."

Giggling, Emily slapped his arm. "You big joker!"

"You say 'big', I say cuddly," Elmo said, patting his stomach with exaggerated enthusiasm.

Emily gave him a big hug and they all laughed, for the moment the sound taking the oppression out of an emotional day.

Lucas called out to them. "Would you look at that?"

They turned to look in the direction of the bay and saw a large angular shape cruising towards the harbour. Even at this distance, they could all appreciate the size of the vessel.

"*The Spirit of the Ocean*, I assume?" Elmo said.

Lucas whistled in admiration. "Must admit, looks pretty impressive. Now, all we have to do is figure a way to get on it."

Beatrice recognised the expression settling upon Lucas' face. His mind was working hard, trying to fathom a means to solve the problem.

It was Emily who spoke next, she signed at the same time. They all turned to face her.

"We need to be logical," Emily signed. "Think it through."

Elmo pointed at Lucas. "You mean, as in using our brain? That's gonna hurt, right?"

Emily rolled her eyes. "I take back the 'Joker' accolade. That was pretty bad."

He winked at her. "Must try harder. It's about the only thing I remember off my report cards."

"We could always sneak onto the boat," Lucas suggested. "Create a diversion and use that to go under the radar?"

Elmo frowned. "It's a big boat but it's not like an ocean liner. We'd be spotted straight away."

Beatrice observed another issue. "There are going to be wealthy people, and celebrities on board, so security is also going to be tight. If we're found then we'll be arrested, and that would end any chance of finding out what's going on before it starts."

They all considered this for a few moments.

It was Emily who answered first. "Then we have to get on the boat with a justifiable reason even though we've got zero chance of being invited, and no real reason to be there. Not too difficult, then."

Frustrated, Beatrice looked down at the yacht as it entered the harbour. "We've got twenty-four hours to think of something, otherwise Primrose is going onto that boat, and we'll have no way of finding out what she's up to."

Only the wind provided any response, its woeful sound echoing the misery they all felt in their hearts.

Thomas was lost in his own world as he walked down the promenade. Other than being with The Newshounds up on the bluff, his favourite place in the town was a bench facing the sea. There were plenty of benches, but there was one in particular to which he was always drawn because it was not the seat itself but the view it afforded.

The bench was currently unoccupied, and he felt

his heart lift a little at the sight of its wrought-iron frame, painted bright red, and the slats a deep umber. He sat down on the hard surface, his combat trousers bunching up.

From this vantage point, Thomas would often sit and look out upon the ocean, and in his vista, he would be able to see the large humped shape of Seer's Rock and the distant, bright orange buoy marking the fifty-metre line to the shore.

And if he timed it right, Thomas would get to hear the automated toll of the bell as it drifted across the bay, a sound that left him filled with both wonder and sadness, because the low peals had a melancholy tone. He found it fitting considering how he was feeling at that moment.

After his discussions with Beatrice and Maud, he needed some time to think about things. The puzzle of how and why the tablet had disappeared—or its current whereabouts—weighed heavy on him.

At first, the sense of loss was so powerful Thomas thought he could finally appreciate how Gollum felt when he'd lost The One Ring. But the intensity of that loss had waned, and he was left doubting his own memories of what had happened on the beach, and the man in the water.

He checked his heavy duty combat watch and smiled. His timing was perfect, a few minutes until the buoy would toll.

Thomas used these moments to settle back in his seat and took in the sea breeze. This pensive moment was interrupted by the toot of a car horn that irritated him instantly.

He turned to see a lime green VW Beetle pulling up

next to the kerb. The driver had dropped the window and was leaning over to call out to him.

"Excuse me, could you tell me where to find a decent parking place near the harbour?"

Thomas was about to give a curt response when two things happened. The buoy started to toll, making him even more vexed, but then he saw who had asked him the question, and found himself lost for words.

"Sorry to disturb you," the driver said.

"Don't worry about it," Thomas said.

From the shade of the vehicle, Claire Drill gave him a radiant smile.

Thomas' world changed. Forgotten were the incredible view and the sound of the bell. He was consumed by the unexpected and unbelievable sight of his hero in a VW Beetle.

And because of this, he failed to observe that the buoy had not tolled six times.

It had struck eight.

Chapter Eleven

I**N THE LIBRARY,** Maud and Agnes were hunched over a large book. Its cover was a battered ring binder, and the pages were a mishmash of handwritten pages, photocopies, and typed sheets. Agnes had pulled the book from a drawer in the nearby desk, and Maud had watched with fascination as her friend carefully transferred the tome to the desk, the cover moving as though the pages were alive. Agnes was barely able to keep the contents secured within the binding.

"Giddy goodness, Agnes, that book doesn't seem to want to come to our aid without a fight," Maud said.

"Happen so," Agnes chuckled. "Maybe I should split the pages into a few volumes, but it just doesn't seem right separating them. History belongs in one place."

"So what's the story in these here pages?' Maud said as Agnes turned the sheets, the act creating thick crinkling sounds about them.

Agnes rubbed at her nose.

"I can't lay any kind of claim to it," she said. "I put the book together, added to it over time, but the original pages came with the library. Before that, heaven knows their origin. I swear Freddie Mayberry, the librarian before me, was as old as the two of us added together! All he'd say is it was my duty to add to its content, not to question it."

Maud pawed a potential sneeze away from her nose. "A wise man. Not many of those buggers around these days, 'cept for my Albert. An' I'll be keepin' that thought to meself, for sure."

The two women giggled, and the sound was light in the oppressive atmosphere. Their focus shifted to the pages, as they moved through time. The content ranged from typed script to handwritten accounts of local life. Then it went back further, the information talking of events of which neither of them had knowledge or reference. They became at the mercy of narratives, the authors of which were long since gone.

It was a few hours later before Agnes came across a passage that was to add some hope to their investigation.

"Look at this," Agnes said peering down at an extract.

Maud rubbed at her eyes, her fingers probing under her large framed glasses, pushing the lenses up to her forehead.

"I'm strugglin' to see the end of me nose, let alone some squiggly writin'," she said.

Agnes smiled warmly but her eyes remained on the book. "It's not writing. It's a newspaper cutting."

Pushing away her tiredness, Maud looked at the respective page that Agnes was tapping at.

Sure enough, a black and white newspaper clipping, yellowed with age, showed a young boy holding up a piece of driftwood before the camera. He wore a big, awkward grin, and behind him was a view of the ocean.

And on the driftwood were two words.
"The Raven."

Thomas fumbled with the strap of his survival pack. He had it resting on his knees, the canvas material obscuring his view through the windshield before him.

"Are you sure you don't want to put that on the backseat?" Claire said. "It might be better if you want to show me the way if you could actually see where you're going?"

Thomas thought this over. The rucksack was a source of comfort, something behind which he could hide. Ever since Claire had pulled up he'd been tongue-tied. In all of the times he had been passionate about TV shows, and their respective stars, he had not once met one in the flesh.

Now, Claire was sitting behind the wheel, no longer a star on the screen but very real and insistent. She wore a pair of blue jeans and a red blouse, her hair swept up into a bulky brown clip, and dark strands waving lazily about her slim, pale neck. She had a warm smile and her emerald eyes sparkled with humour.

"So what do you say?" she prompted. "Want to lose the survival pack to the backseat for a while?"

Thomas nodded and threw the pack behind him.

"Now, first of all, we need some introductions," she said offering her hand to shake. "I'm Claire, though I guess you already know that?"

Thomas looked at her hand for a few seconds as though he'd forgotten introductory etiquette. Then he held it and pumped it a few times.

"Thomas Beecham," he muttered.

"Do you prefer Thomas or Tom?"

"I don't mind," he said. At that moment he could not have cared less if she'd called him a cucumber.

She smiled again. It was warm and genuine. "Well, Tom it is," she said.

Thomas settled down a little. There was something about Claire's nature that made him feel at ease. A little like talking to his mother. This feeling of familiarity was fast becoming a ready replacement for the comfort he took from the rucksack he'd just discarded.

"So what are you doing here?" Thomas asked.

"Got an invite to the launch gala," she replied. "*The Spirit of the Ocean*?"

"The boat," Thomas confirmed with a sigh. Claire spotted his gloomy response immediately. "It's just docked."

"Is there a problem with the boat?" she said.

"We had tickets to go to the party, but they stopped us going," he said with a flat tone. Thomas briefly thought about mentioning he hadn't actually been invited but it didn't seem of any real significance given the current circumstances.

Claire was thoughtful. "Something you did?"

Thomas could not believe how at ease he felt after meeting this woman for the first time. He had no qualms about continuing the conversation. He'd convinced himself that Claire wasn't a stranger; he'd watched her countless times on TV. She was tough and supportive in those shows, and he wasn't seeing anything to the contrary out here in the real world.

Without thought, he gave her a potted history of how their gala tickets had been rescinded.

"So now no one can go. Everyone is pretty miffed about it all." He stared ahead through the windshield where the evening light was now beginning to fade.

"Well, I'll tell you what, Tom," Claire said starting the engine. "If you can get me to a good place to stay, I might be able to sort out this little problem of yours. What do you say?"

Thomas could 'say' nothing, of course, because once again, Claire Drill had left him speechless.

Late in the evening, Beatrice was preparing a small supper consisting of a beef taco, with chopped spring onions, and coriander with a spiced guacamole pouring sauce. For some reason, whenever she was troubled she tended to eat late, and the spicier the meal, the better.

She was sitting at the breakfast bar reading through text messages from Patience, her heart heavy and the desire to be with her dearest friend blunting her appetite. The thought of Patience and her mother holding vigil over Khaldun's broken body was suddenly making her nauseous, and she pushed the taco away from her after only a few mouthfuls

It was at times like these, where she was at her lowest ebb, that Thomas had the innate ability to appear and irritate. That moment was to be no exception.

Her brother came into the kitchen from the parlour; impeded by his canvas survival pack that managed to knock a picture of a seascape askew as he passed.

His speech was rapid, an unwelcome contrast to Beatrice's melancholy.

"Bea, you'll never believe what just happened!"

"Aliens came and want to take you back to their planet—and you said yes?"

Thomas' face was thoughtful. "No, but that would be cool, too." He shook his head as if to resume focus. "What *happened* is I met Claire Drill!"

Beatrice put her head on the breakfast bar. She found the cool material comforting against her brow. She feared that if Thomas continued for much longer she may have to repeat the process at speed, several times.

"Thomas, now isn't a good time for me. Can you come back in, say, thirty years?"

Thomas continued, unabashed. "Claire is such a wonderful person. She's not like she is on TV, I mean, she's still nice on TV but in real life she's *really* nice and doesn't smell of urine at all. Mind you, thinking about it, she wasn't wearing a bandana."

"That sounds so wrong on so many levels," Beatrice said to the breakfast bar.

"So I showed her the way to the harbour, you know, where *The Spirit of the Ocean* is? And then I showed her to Tardebigge's Bed and Breakfast."

"She's staying at Tardebigge's?" Beatrice said with sudden interest. "I thought she was loaded?"

"Yes," Thomas enthused, "something about not being interested in fame and fortune. Says she wants to keep things real."

Beatrice sat upright, an action that was as much ignored by her brother as her head-on-the-table-in-abject-misery position. He pulled a glass from the overhead cupboard and pressed it under the water dispenser embedded in the door of the fridge-freezer. The water gushed into the glass, Thomas' rate of speech just slightly ahead on pace.

"Thing is, Bea, she's going to the launch tomorrow and I sort of explained that we were meant to go but now we can't, because of Patience's dad and all that stuff."

Beatrice's mouth hung open. She closed it with a click before speaking again. "You told a TV personality about Patience's dad?"

Thomas nodded and took a sip of water, swallowed. Only excitement registered in him. "Yeah, and I said we were all disappointed and because I helped her out she said she'd help me. I thought she meant help me get on the boat via paragliding onto it or zip-wire, but she meant she'd put two of us on her guest list."

Beatrice was not quite sure how to feel. Disbelief that her brother had absolutely no concept of sensitivity and confidentiality was at odds with a potential means to legitimately gain access to *The Spirit of the Ocean's* launch gala, and, by default, find out what Primrose was up to and stop her.

Unaware of her inner-conflict, Thomas continued. "Only two of us, though. I'm going because I got the invite. So you coming along too?"

Beatrice response came as fast as the decision was made. "Yes."

Agnes and Maud were looking intently at the monitor

screen, where a crude lithograph of a galleon took prominence, the sea reduced to several undulating, thick black lines.

The image had come up when Agnes had typed in 'Raven, ship, 16th Century, 17th Century, galleon, Dorsal Finn, Ashby-on-Sea' into the browser and the current picture had flagged in the 'images' section on the internet.

After clicking onto it, Agnes was able to navigate to the site, where a brief description of the vessel gave them their first inkling that they were looking in the right place.

The Raven:
Owners: Dennis Smith & Sons
Class: Galleon
Tonnage: 2,000
Guns: 10 Demi-culverin Cannons
Sank (circa 1587)

History:
It is alleged The Raven was believed lost at sea with all hands during a storm in circa 1588 off the coast of what is now known as Ashby-on-Sea.

The Raven was lost whilst conducting witch trials. A local girl, Elizabeth Caldecott aged sixteen, was reported executed during the trials, which saw over twenty others put to death as part of the great witch hunt of 1588. Folklore suggests that the ship's demise was a curse evoked by Elizabeth Caldecott as she drowned during the ordeal.

This assertion into folklore was perhaps reinforced by uncorroborated reports of an unknown local fisherman who reported boarding The Raven several days later when she reappeared—as he was out on open water. The mythology is that he found all the crew starved to death and the ship's captain and primary witch hunter, Jackson Crane alone and insane, eating the contents of the ship's gold store. Terrified, the fisherman left the vessel, and as he made for shore it was alleged he looked back and saw no sign of the vessel. He told his wife and sons upon his return home, and was considered mad, and was incarcerated.

"So this here tale goes back some time," Maud said after considering the information. "But we got that startin' point ye were after. Elizabeth Caldecott was a witch, an' that boat was cursed good an' proper."

Agnes' eyes remained on the script. 'Elizabeth Caldecott, eh? Let's see where that takes us.'

Maud was brooding beside her. "To no place good, I suspect."

As always in such matters, Maud turned out to be quite right.

Beatrice's Smartphone rang out shortly after her discussion with Thomas had concluded. As always, her heart lifted when she heard the warm, mischievous voice of Maud coming through the speaker grill.

"Ye need to be stayin' up past yer bedtime, me girl," Maud said. "I got some info for ye."

"I didn't realise you were onto something?" Beatrice said, bewildered.

There was a pause as Maud thought her response through. "Mebbe we old uns have been up to no good on yer behalf. An' it seems that we did the right thing for once."

With that, Maud signed off, leaving Beatrice to ponder on the implications of such a statement.

She waited for Maud to return from the library, using the time to consider the recent turn of events that would see her having to work with her brother in order to establish just what was going on in Dorsal Finn, and what *The Spirit of the Ocean* had to do with it all.

It was not lost on her that she would have to endure the tiresome antics of her brother for the whole evening, but was hoping she could use this to keep watch on the errant Primrose.

Beatrice headed for the lounge, a compact space with big, shapeless sofas and chairs, and a bulky TV. Her parents had gone to bed, her father to read his latest detective novel, and her mum to scour the online shopping stores for bargains that would usually arrive by courier the next day, only to be returned to store a few days later as they "never look like they do in the photo."

Maud whistling a non-tune interrupted Beatrice's thoughts as the old woman entered the lounge. Beatrice stood and gave her a big hug.

"Easy there, young'un," Maud giggled. "These old bones pop an' snap enough on their own."

Beatrice chuckled, "You're not old. Just well-worn."

"An' ye're a smooth talker, Lady Jane," Maud smiled sitting down in her big armchair. "Ye'll go far in this life."

They sat in silence, comfortable with the stillness it brought. It was Beatrice who broke it.

"So what have you been up to?"

"Investigatin', of course," Maud said with a wink.

"I assume you had a partner in crime?"

Maud gave her a grin. "Let's just say, Agnes Clutterbuck may have been nearby when discoveries were made, puttin' books on shelves an' all of that."

"That figures," Beatrice replied. "So what did you find out?"

"All in good time, young'un," Maud said. "First, I got a tale to tell."

"About the boat?"

"Not a boat, but a ship," Maud said. "An' the terrible things they say happened to it."

Claire unpacked her things from a small pull-along hold-all that she had placed on the bed. Her room at Tardebigge's Bed and Breakfast was quaint, with walls of stark, uneven white plaster and thick wooden struts.

In the case was a make-up bag, a change of underwear, and two brushes—one for her hair and one for her teeth. Her dress for the gala was hanging in a clothing bag in the heavy, oak wardrobe.

She liked to travel light, a habit formed at a relatively young age, fourteen to be precise, when she had run away from foster care after enduring it for three terrible years due to her parents' deaths in a car wreck.

It wasn't that she had poor experiences with foster care; she was hurting after the death of her parents, people helped with that, good and kind people. Yet, they could not prevent her true nature, the wanderlust that had been in her blood long before the death of her mum and dad.

From an early age, she'd thrived outdoors. She'd go camping with her parents; both were teachers and encouraged activities that kept her away from the TV. Ironic then that she would grow up to be such a celebrity because of her show. But *Behind Enemy Lines* was a product of her outdoor pursuits growing up. Brownies, Guides, and bronze and silver D of E before she finally found a place working in the outdoor leisure industry. After lying about her age she gained employment at adventure centres, first in England and then Europe, before heading to more exotic locations such as Nepal, Peru, and Dubai. Her passion and effervescent personality shone through, attracting praise from all who attended her sessions.

And, while taking a group of TV producers on a team-building weekend, white water rafting in the Amazon, Claire met a production team who specialised in survival shows.

By the end of the weekend, she was on a plane to London. A few days later she had signed a six-episode deal for the show that would ultimately become a global sensation, making Claire Drill a household name.

She transferred her meagre belongings to the small

yet spotless bathroom. It was a place of shining chrome and white tiles, making her think of dentists and surgeries.

Standing in the mirror, she unclipped the hair clip and allowed her locks to fall over her shoulders. So many people had told her how much she looked like her mother, and the photograph she carried in her purse pretty much reinforced this edict.

Claire shook her head and sighed, her mind in danger of going to places she really did not want to go, places that made the memories of dead parents come alive, biting deep into her mood. Her eyes misted with tears, and she swore at her reflection.

"What the hell is wrong with you, girl?" she asked herself. "This isn't the time to be thinking about them."

She was thinking about them, though, her beautiful mother, and her proud, handsome father. Long gone but never forgotten, not totally, they visited at moments like these, when she was most contented. The sensation these recollections brought were bittersweet.

She hoped that they were proud of her achievements. She believed her drive to do them justice was the key to her success.

As she looked into the mirror she imagined that she could see them both. Her father's tall and broad physique, eyes bright blue, hair thick and wiry, her mother standing beside him, a lot shorter, hair jet black and cut into a bob. Claire realised she was smiling.

Her mother reached out to her, palm up as though waiting to take her daughter's hand in hers. Claire found herself lifting an arm, fingers splayed, and placing her own palm against the mirror.

The light in the bathroom appeared to dim a little though she was only vaguely aware of it, her eyes were locked on the images standing behind her, the fluorescent tube over the bathroom mirror began to flicker, strobing her reflection, and the once happy smiling faces of her parents were now twisted in fear, mouths agape, becoming black holes as their cries of anguish went unheard.

Claire's hands went up to her face, the instinct to turn around strong, but her feet were fixed in place, as though set into cement.

Despite their gaping mouths, her father's voice came to her.

"The Oracle must seek out that which is lost," he said, and the sound was undulating as though it contained many layers—many voices—all speaking at once.

"You're not real," she whispered, but tears coursed down her cheeks all the same.

But her father's mouth remained wide, that awful, silent scream continuing regardless of the voice still reverberating around in her skull.

"Water and blood from the Amazon join!"

The strobe-effect was starting to affect her, she felt nauseous and a great pain began to settle behind her eyes. She squeezed her lids shut, to fight back the mounting agony inside her head, but also to shut out the image of her parents.

It was the hideous scream that filled the room that had her eyelids snapping open again. Her parents were no longer behind her, instead there were countless staggering shapes, and the bathroom was no longer there, instead it was the deck of a galleon, and the men were all screaming, thin, wasted screams, and as Claire looked upon them she could see their faces were emaciated, skeletons with only vellum-thin flesh on their cheeks, eye sockets sunken. The eyes were still bright and burning with desire.

Then the light in the bathroom ceased to stutter, and the image was gone, her parents, the ghastly sailors and the cursed ship. Claire heard the scream continue for a few more seconds before she realised the sound was coming from her.

Maud took a sip from a huge mug that had the image of Homer Simpson playing guitar on it. On a small occasional table there was a plate piled with Beatrice's home baked chocolate chip cookies, a particular favourite of Maud's.

She helped herself to another cookie. "Ye're spoilin' ol' Maud this evenin', young'un."

Beatrice giggled as she watched Maud take in another cookie, the old woman smacking her lips when she'd finished.

Maud sat back in her chair, cupping her mug in both hands, her face becoming grave as she prepared to tell her tale. Beatrice perched on the sofa opposite, leaning forward in anticipation.

"Me an' Agnes dug deep an' uncovered a sorry tale, make no mistake," Maud said quietly. "The ship was called The Raven. A galleon that sank off the coast of Ashby-on-Sea in 1588. Captain was a fella by the name of Jackson Crane. A God-fearin' man, like many around them times. Maybe that explains why folk did what they did, but havin' a reason don't make everythin' ye do in life right."

Beatrice frowned. "What do you mean?"

"Crane an' his crew were conductin' witch trials on their ship at the time of the sinkin'," Maud explained. "Local folk said it was a witch's curse that turned night to day and terrible screamin' could be heard comin' from The Raven before she disappeared in a storm."

Maud took another sip of her tea. "They put a sixteen-year-ol' girl in the water that day, Elizabeth Caldecott. Agnes put her name in her computer an' the name of that cursed ship. She got some more accounts; most maritime historians say it's just flights of fancy, that The Raven sank in poor weather. An' we'd say the same too if we didn't live in this town of ours, right?"

Beatrice nodded slowly. Yes, only Dorsal Finn could change your view of the world.

Maud continued. "So we looked up the Caldecott girl an' found out somethin' pretty interestin' about Elizabeth. Somethin' that brought her to the attention of the witch hunt of those times."

"And what was that?" Beatrice breathed.

"She had a birthmark below her right eye," Maud said. "A red strawberry-shaped thing they called Satan's Tear."

Beatrice was suddenly back in the waiting room of Ashby general hospital, looking upon the wavering face of Primrose, and the strawberry blotch on her cheek, confirming that Elizabeth Caldecott, a 16th Century witch, was back amongst the living. She relayed her thoughts to Maud who looked on in consternation until she'd finished.

"Well, that is explainin' a few things. An' I got more for ye if ye're ready for the whole bagful?"

Beatrice nodded.

"This tale don't get any less sorry for the tellin'," Maud said. "We went back into Elizabeth's life, found out why she got herself onto that boat in the first place. It's sketchy but we got the gist of it."

Maud wriggled in her seat as she made herself comfortable.

"Seems Elizabeth's dad died when she was young. Her mother, widowed but respected in their village, found herself on the receivin' end of the advances of the village governor. But she was in love an' betrothed to a woodsman, who had taken Elizabeth in as his own. By all accounts, the governor gets consumed with jealousy an' has the woodsman arrested for poachin' on his land. A trumped-up charge for sure, but the magistrate promises to spare her lover's life an' send him to gaol if she marries the governor instead. Seems the mother agreed to do exactly that until Elizabeth is out walkin' one night an' sees the governor's men burying a body in the woods. Turns out to be the woodsman who has been executed, an' the magistrate has turned the deal bad. When Elizabeth tells her mum, she confronted the governor he gives her a shove an' she goes down hard, bangin' her head on a gatepost, an' she's killed outright. Elizabeth sees it all an' she goes an' hexes that magistrate an' he just falls into a sleep, not eatin' or drinkin'—just wastin' away. The villagers get scared that Elizabeth is goin' to hex them an' all, so they get Crane an' his cronies to put her on trial. An' they drown her hopin' to break the curse on the governor."

Beatrice sat in amazement. Such stories were always fascinating, but the possibility that these things were more fact than fiction in Dorsal Finn added to their potency.

"So what does this all mean?" she said.

"I ain't done yet," Maud said. "Me an' Agnes have got ourselves a little theory goin'. We found out about The Raven because of another story. Seems a young lad from Ashby-on-Sea found part of the shipwreck, the name plaque for The Raven washed up on the beach. An' that lad was none other than Melville Craig, captain of that boat in our harbour."

Beatrice felt her jaw go slack in surprise. "That can't be a coincidence. Craig must have something to do with this."

"In more ways than one," Maud said. "Because not only did that fella find the plaque, he's got another connection to this miserable tale."

Beatrice could barely wait to listen to Maud's revelation.

"It seems Craig's mother was from a sea-farin' family of long standin'," Maud said. "No surprise there, seein' everyone around these parts can make such a claim, but the real eye- opener is when we found out her maiden name in the Ashby-on-Sea marriage records."

Beatrice sat fascinated. "And what was her maiden name?"

Maud leaned forward so far it appeared as though she was about to stand up. "It was Crane," she whispered. "Meanin' that our Melville Craig is a blood relative of the captain that put Elizabeth Caldecott to death."

Chapter Twelve

THE DAY OF the gala started out with the sun bright and brilliant. All day long, sightseers came to look upon the great yacht as it lay moored in the harbour, access to it manned by several burly security staff in high visibility jackets, and a portable access barrier consisting of a long, flat pole—striped in yellow and black—at the end of the jetty.

Delivery vans pulled up in the dock and fresh, local produce was loaded onto pallets before being carried via gurney to the vessel's loading bay.

From across the harbour, Primrose, Alison, and Edward watched proceedings.

"Please don't scowl, Edward," Primrose said. Her tone made sure it was clear this was not a request. "We are trying to blend into the moment."

Edward tried to put his face in neutral and ended up looking as though he had a severe case of wind. "Well, if you wanted people not to notice, maybe you shouldn't be standing with two kids," he griped.

Primrose nodded. "Subterfuge is an art, Edward. Those about us may not realise it but they are internalising our presence. When we attend the gala later this evening, it will be as natural as the coming of the night."

Alison giggled. "I guess magic has a part to play too, Primrose?"

"Most certainly," Primrose said with a small grin. "It is already working away in the background, biding its time, and all thanks to your great deed yesterday, Alison."

The younger girl puffed out her chest with pride.

Edward looked at the two girls and frowned. "How long do you think it will be before the police come looking for Erica?"

Primrose shook her head in disapproval. "Edward, you disappoint me. Do you not think I have already *taken care* of such a thing?"

Edward appeared surprised. "How?"

"Let us just say that, to the people who know the Ross family, they have all taken a little trip to visit exotic places. They will be gone for the foreseeable future it seems. Certainly long enough for us to complete our goal."

Edward seized the moment as Primrose's word hung in the air. "What is our goal, exactly?"

"Your goal is to stop being irritating, Edward. Do you think you can do that?"

When Primrose spoke, the intensity in her voice had Edward visibly shaking.

"Well?" she said.

"Yes, I can."

"Good," she smirked.

Edward turned to face the bustle of the harbour and, for the first time he could remember, wished he was no longer in this accursed town.

"So the plan is that Thomas and I will accompany Claire onto the yacht, and when people are distracted by the party, I can follow Primrose and hopefully find out what she's up to. If things go sour, maybe I can stop her before she can succeed," Beatrice said carefully in the lounge of Crab Mill cottage.

She'd called the meeting first thing to maximise their limited time until the gala later that evening.

The sullen faces of Lucas, Elmo and Emily stared back at Beatrice from across the lounge. There did not appear to be any end to the silence.

"I can see this idea has gone down like a mug of sick," Beatrice muttered.

Beatrice had tried to take the sting out of residual admonishment in the others by telling them what Maud and Agnes had found out about the witch, and how this whole sorry tale came to be. Sadly, it only made the concerns of the others worse, especially after knowing of Beatrice's recent vision of Primrose being possessed by an incarnation of Elizabeth.

Elmo rubbed his chin with a thumb. "On the upside, we don't have to deal with a corrupt, malignant entity bent on taking over the world. The downside is that we have to stop a 16th Century witch from getting revenge on the captain of a superyacht. Is it me or do the choices always suck in this town?"

Emily spoke next. She emphasised her words with an occasional sign. "What do we do if something happens to you on the boat? How do we make sure you're okay?"

Beatrice smiled. "I know it seems like a stupid idea, but—"

"It's not stupid, it's crazy," Emily interrupted. "You'll be on your own. Anything could happen. I thought that Newshounds stuck together."

"If there is any other way of getting on that boat then I'd love to hear it," Beatrice said. "I don't want to do this, but we're out of options, and the opportunity is here."

Beatrice was hoping Lucas would say something. His silence was getting to her more than if he had been shouting and cussing. She knew him so well, could see the frustration and apprehension in his eyes. However, she also recalled her vision in the waiting room of Ashby general hospital, the ominous light that threatened to engulf Lucas, and her thoughts were at once protective. She didn't know what it meant so hadn't said anything to him—things were chaotic enough without adding to the mix.

As it was, Lucas merely looked down at his thumbs which he twiddled rhythmically, occasionally glancing up at Beatrice, face now parked in neutral.

"Elmo?" Emily said. "Haven't you got anything to say?"

"Sure," he replied. "But it won't make any difference. Beatrice has that 'don't screw with me' face in place, it's best just to go with it."

Emily gave out an exasperated snort of disbelief. "What about you, Lucas? Surely you don't support this madness?"

Lucas stopped messing with his thumbs, and looked up at Emily. "No matter where she is, Bea will never be alone," he said with a small smile.

For Beatrice, Lucas' face seemed to cloud with a maturity she'd never seen before and, for a few seconds, her feelings for him became all-consuming, a powerful surge of love that left her quite breathless.

"What the hell is that supposed to mean?" Emily said to Elmo, who shrugged.

Ignoring them both, Lucas offered his hand and said, "Let's go for a walk, Bea."

Lucas and Beatrice walked hand in hand through town, both enjoying the sense of peace afforded by each other's company. They had left the meeting behind them, Emily and Elmo had headed off to plan a way of supporting Beatrice when she got onto the yacht.

The streets were dotted with occasional pedestrians who tipped them a nod, or offered a casual, friendly greeting. Beatrice felt Lucas' thumb stroking hers.

"Why is it I can never be mad at you," he said quietly.

"Not ever?"

He paused for thought. "Not for long."

"Maybe it's because I'm always right?"

"I think you do everything for the right reason."

"And you say all the right things."

They laughed. Beatrice slipped her arm about his waist and they continued walking with her head resting against his, enjoying the contact.

"What did you mean that I'll never be alone?" Beatrice asked after a few minutes.

Lucas slowed his pace and they both eventually stopped, and faced each other.

"I should be scared you're getting on that boat," Lucas said. "But part of me knows that you're going to be okay. You don't need the rest of us there to keep you safe."

Beatrice looked into his eyes and saw only sincerity. For a second she was confounded by where his comments came from but then she realised what he meant.

The Light.

For many years, Beatrice had found her mind slipping into a quasi-daydream in which she would consult with her five favourite celebrity chefs. She called it her *Culinary Council*, headed by her all-time favourite chef, Jamie Oliver. With Jamie were Raymond Blanc, Gary Rhodes, Mario Batali, and Gordon Ramsay.

Their counsel was sought in times of confusion, of despair and, in her mind's eye, she would have discussions and find resolution, often acting upon the decisions that were made in those few seconds.

For a long time Beatrice had never questioned this process, it was as part of her as the fiery red hair on her head. As she got older she began to consider these episodes as her own problem-solving process, that she was finding the answers from deep within herself, and that the Culinary Council was a mere manifestation of this process. She was comfortable with this as a concept.

But then came *The Light.*

As clichéd as it seemed to Beatrice, she'd first encountered the entities she had come to refer to as

'The Light', at her darkest hour. The five orbs had come to her when she had been close to death, trapped inside a cave surging with seawater, deceived and desperate, almost giving up hope.

Then *The Light* had been with her, and with it came the realisation it had always been with her, guiding her, making her who she was, who she was meant to be, *The Bringer of Joy, The Incorruptible Heart*, antithesis of the terrible darkness that lay at the heart of the town. Realisation, then, that the Culinary Council was a device, an analogy so The Light could connect in a way only a young mind could understand, without fear or recourse.

Now things were different. Since coming to Dorsal Finn, Beatrice had grown up, *The Light* was now presenting in a way she now needed to understand.

"I haven't seen The Light for some time," she winked.

"You know how corny that sounds, right?" Lucas appeared thoughtful. "I guess you haven't needed to, and this is why I know you're safe."

"You think it only comes when I'm in danger?" Beatrice had never considered this as a concept. It made sense now that she thought it over.

"Or when it feels that you need help," he said.

"And this is why you're not worried?"

Lucas reached up and brushed a strand of copper hair from her cheek. "I'm worried, Bea. Don't think I'm not. I can't explain it. I just don't want—"

He stopped, his gaze dropping down to the ground for a few seconds.

"What?" she said with a quiet insistence. "What is it?"

He looked back and to her surprise, there were bright tears in his eyes. "I don't want you to think that I don't care."

"Oh, Lucas," she said, pulling him close. "I'd never think that, I promise."

He hugged her back, face buried into her, and Beatrice could feel his tears seeping through her jacket and onto the bare skin of her shoulder. Her heart was a mix of great love and quiet despair. This place, this town, even in its darkest times brought with it incongruence, in emotions, in moments, nothing was ever without contrast.

After a few minutes, Lucas stepped away from her and sniffed. "Y'know, for a moment there I was in danger of embarrassing myself." He gave her a weak smile.

"I can remember Maud saying: 'There's more shame in scowlin' than cryin'", and she's right, as always."

"A bit like you, then?" Lucas laughed.

"What can I say? Her influence over me is total."

They continued their walk, heading down to the harbour, where *The Spirit of the Ocean* made ready for whatever fate—and Elizabeth Caldecott—held in store for it.

Detective Cotteridge stood on the harbour, hands deep in the pockets of his long, black coat. He was sucking on a peppermint and watching the distant crowds gather in the fading light. The huge yacht dominated the view ahead, the infrastructure of the vessel bristling with activity, people dropping off supplies on the jetty, crew busy with polishing and prepping the decks. He appreciated the quiet order on display; it spoke of an event that was completely under control.

His cell phone buzzed in his pocket, and he answered it straight away.

"Cotteridge."

A female voice came to him. It was brisk, factual. "PC Brookes, here, sir. Got a missing person's report coming in for your area."

"My area, but not my case," Cotteridge said squinting as another car pulled into the harbour parking zone.

"Might be linked, sir," Brookes said.

"How so?"

"Seems the person missing is related to someone on *The Spirit of the Ocean.*"

"Really? Please give me the details," he said as he pulled out his notebook.

There, as he continued to take in the scene ahead, Cotteridge considered getting changed now that he had cause to attend the gala. He had a good few hours, after all. By the time he'd finished writing in his notebook he'd decided it was better to remain in his work attire.

First impressions and all that.

He made his way to his car, parked up on the kerb only a short walk away. One of the joys of being a policeman was that you didn't have to worry about getting a ticket. He often joked that this was the only reason he'd joined.

In reality he was always meant for a career in law enforcement. From an early age he'd been fascinated by the nuances of crime, what made people do the things they did, how they were dealt with and the procedures involved in bringing someone to justice.

That wasn't to say that he'd been encouraged. His father had been in prison more times than he'd been out of it, mainly for petty crimes, but for a young Cotteridge his dad had been so absent as a parent, he'd barely known him growing up. He was a shadowy figure who came and went, never around long enough for any kind of connection to be made.

Instead he was raised by his mother, a quiet woman with a strong sense of purpose, and that purpose was taking care of her son. Cotteridge could see the damage a life of crime had done to his mother over time, the angry voices whenever his father showed up, the quiet sobbing in the parlour when the police came and took him away. When he saw the impact on his mother, Cotteridge learned to hate his father, a fact that had not changed even after his father's death.

Throughout this upheaval, his mother was the constant, and she supported him in his decision to join the police, his desire to help others, and strong ethic from the outset.

At first he thought about forensic police work, Scene of Crime Officers always seemed to have a cool job, going over the crime scenes collecting evidence and using this to support the investigation. However, the thought of getting out there and being face to face with criminals, trying to understand them in a way that he never understood his father, was never far away.

His move through the ranks was progressive, his

dedication clear to all. As a beat officer he saw the impact of crime on families of victims, first hand. After that he became interested in how to catch criminals, making sure there was evidence to keep them away from future victims and, if he was honest with himself, the families they were destroying in their own lives, their sons and daughters, wives or partners.

He'd now been a detective for over twenty years, his disrupted upbringing, and his time as a beat officer, now distant memories but their injunction no less powerful.

Then, of course, there were the cases. When a new case came his way, it yielded a surge of excitement, even after his many years in the force. The incredible feeling came to him again as he climbed into his car, and closed the door behind him.

He clicked on the interior light, his intention to check the glove box and retrieve his battery-operated shaver, a device that was essential for stakeouts. As he reached for the handle, he saw movement on the dashboard and his eyes darted to it.

The spider was small, barely a few centimetres in diameter, but Cotteridge sucked in air and spontaneously pushed himself back in his seat, his actions making the whole car shake. Cotteridge never took his eyes off the creature as it took a pause from its travels, oblivious as to its influence on the world about it. Cotteridge reached behind him, his fingers probing until he recognised the familiar shape of a clipboard. He grabbed it and within seconds was pounding the dashboard, and the poor creature, in a frenzied blur of plastic and ruffling paper.

He looked at the underside of the clipboard and

gave out a satisfied sigh at what he saw smeared there. He dropped his window and scraped the remains out onto the cobblestones by smacking the board on the sill and then wiping what was left off with a tissue, another vital item stowed in the glove box.

Wiping his brow on the sleeve of his coat, Cotteridge settled back in his seat and allowed peace to gradually work its magic on him. The tension in his muscles began to dissipate, his breathing returning to it's slow, yet steady rhythm, and a sense of amity settled upon him.

Only when he was back to normality could he appraise the obvious.

If there was something he hated more than his father, it was bloody spiders.

On the night of the gala, it was agreed that Elmo and Emily would meet up at 06:00 pm and set up an operations room at Lucas' house. This consisted of mobile phones, laptops and Lucas' PC, set up in Lucas' bedroom.

Beatrice and Thomas' Smartphones were to be activated, and then stream live footage of the proceedings throughout the evening, as well as keeping everyone assured that both were safe. It was the only way that Emily and Elmo could be convinced to stop worrying about Beatrice once she was on board. Elmo even had the local coastguard on speed dial, should things go awry, though none of them had any idea what they would say if such a call had to be made. Coastguards were well versed in responding to most perils of the sea, but Elmo wasn't sure if witch's curses featured in their training manual.

It had also crossed their minds to get in touch with Melville Craig and send out a warning, but even with what they knew about their town, the only thing they foresaw coming from this was Beatrice being banned from the gala because she'd gone mad. Through Claire Drill's offer of an invite, luck had paid them a visit, and there was no way Beatrice was going to sabotage herself at this late stage.

"Okay," Lucas said as he sat down on his bed. "Beatrice can you read me, over?"

Beatrice's irritated voice came back to him. "Lucas I haven't left the house yet. I think I'm pretty safe until I actually get on the damn boat."

"Just testing the equipment," he said in a sulky tone.

"It's a Smartphone," Beatrice replied. "It works every other time you call me."

"It's because he's missing you already," said Emily who was following the conversation on her speech-to-text device.

"I'm going to be gone for four hours tops," Beatrice said.

"Can I point out *that* comment was Emily's assessment of events and not mine," Lucas said. "Though, I might miss you if you're not back by this time next week."

"Funny guy," Beatrice said. "Will Patience be involved too?"

Elmo responded after a pause. "She's still at the hospital."

"No change with her dad," Beatrice said, sadly. "We spoke earlier. It's all a mess."

"I know adults say it all the time, and it seems pretty lame, but he's in the right place," Lucas said.

"It's not lame," Beatrice said.

"The boy can do no wrong." Elmo's comment lightened the mood threatening to settle over them.

"I have to go," Beatrice said. "Seems Thomas' date has called to say she's on her way."

"Claire Drill collecting Thomas Beecham from his house," Elmo said in disbelief. "How's he taking that?"

Thomas' distant "whoop" of delight that came from the speaker answered Elmo's question before Beatrice got a chance.

Maureen clasped her hands to her chest and let out a long sigh of amazement. On Beatrice's bed was a dress. Quite possibly the finest dress Beatrice's mother had seen in many years. It was emerald green and had small, paste gemstones sewn into the bodice, the halter neck was decorated with fine needlework that matched the hem.

"That is exquisite," Maureen said.

"Seems a little fussy," Beatrice sniffed nonchalantly.

"Nonsense," Maureen chided. "It's about time we made our wonderful daughter realise just how beautiful she is."

"You know you're saying this out loud, right?"

Maureen laughed. "Yes, and I would say it to anyone because it is true. Now, try it on and give me a call when you're ready."

Beatrice watched her mother leave the room, eyes

flitting to the dress as soon as the door closed. Resigned, she went over to the box, running her fingers over the silk material, enjoying the smoothness of its touch.

She looked at herself in the oval mirror on the wall. Her wiry frame clad in a creased, green tee-shirt and blue jeans with faded patches on the knees, and wondered when she would become interested in wearing nice clothes to go out in. Her lack of awareness in fashion was a thing that Patience simply could not fathom.

Beatrice smiled at the thought of her friend, but it was tinged with sadness. Patience had sent her the dress, of course. There was a note that had come with it:

Good luck and don't spill anything on it! Love, P xx

This had made Beatrice laugh furiously. Only Patience would send Beatrice a cocktail dress when they had no idea what they were walking into on *The Spirit of the Ocean*. She reached in and pulled the dress from the box. Underneath was a pair of matching shoes.

"Oh, no," Beatrice said as she looked down at the patent leather. "Heels."

The harbour was teeming with people. They all stood, following the contours of the jetties, their expectant faces watching the proceedings that were going on around the huge vessel. Even the light rain had not deterred their vigil. Umbrellas and raincoats, cagoules and waterproofs, were all on show.

The security staff signalled the drivers of the large black cars with tinted glass to park up so they could discreetly drop off guests by the barriers, where a large canopy had been erected on the jetty leading to the yacht, the awning stretching the length of the breakwater until it met the steps that lead up to the main decks high above.

Occasionally flashes of light could be seen from beyond the barrier as memories of the evening were captured for posterity, and the odd celebrity magazine, of course. These were accompanied by the 'Ooh's' and 'Ah's' of the distant, gaping crowd.

Through the throng, Primrose weaved her way towards the barriers. She held a large black umbrella which protected her dogtooth patterned coat from the misty rain drifting from overhead. Her hair was fixed high on top of her head with a pin fashioned into the shape of a white rose.

She cleared the crowd, and headed for the canvas stockade. The security staff stood before her, their faces deadpan, bored even. One of them stepped forward, a bald man with a thick neck, clipboard in hand.

"Name, please," he said.

She told him and he scanned down the guest-list attached to the clipboard. After a few seconds he nodded and took a step to one side. 'Enjoy your evening, Miss Meadowsweet.'

"Oh, I intend to," she said with a smile that, for some reason, made the man shudder.

Primrose walked towards the boat, made magical by the spotlights and multi-coloured garlands garnishing her decks, a sight that was breath-taking to anyone who wasn't currently possessed by a 16th Century witch.

At that moment, Primrose could feel many things going on inside her, going on *around* her, the pulse of distant music, the expectant laughter and squeals of excitement of those walking up the gangway to the vessel.

But she was not truly interested in these things, things that were wholesome and jovial. She was interested in waves of emotion coming from the distant crowds who had come out to stand in the rain, and watch those who lived very different lives compared to their own mundane existence. She knew that the crowd could only hope for excitement by proxy, longing, wishing to be a name on the security guard's clipboard, to sample just one evening of life as a celebrity, to step on the pedestal—be *someone.*

Lurking beneath those hopes and dreams was the real source of her interest, the envy, the *Green-Eyed Monster* given form. The energy these negative emotions gave off almost stalled her in her tracks, but she moved forwards, joining a small queue at the foot of the gangway. The fuel for her escapade, her purpose here this evening, was primed and ready for ignition. The time would come soon enough, and when it did a great injustice would be made right, a terrible deed annulled by the potency of cold, naked retribution.

A young man she recognised from a reality TV show, where people spoke with outlandish Essex accents and drank lots of champagne, turned to look at her, and gave her a wink.

"Promises to be quite an evening, dunnit?" he said and gave her a veneered smile that bordered on a leer. He gave off a smell of sweet cologne.

"Oh, it certainly does," she smiled back, eyes as cold as the rain.

Chapter Thirteen

"**You really didn't** have to do this, Mrs Beecham," Claire said on the doorstep. She was clutching a rather large bouquet of flowers that Thomas had thrust at her as soon as the front door opened.

"It's the least we could do for being so generous," Maureen said. "Though, perhaps you could've waited until Claire had stepped in through the door, Thomas."

Beatrice stood looking at Claire from the kitchen. There was no doubt in her mind that the TV presenter was beautiful. She wore a wine red, fitted dress that stopped just above her knees and a cream shawl covered her shoulders which matched the colour of her high-heeled shoes. Around her pale, slim neck was a delicate gold necklace that ended in a teardrop pendant.

Claire's eyes found Beatrice and she gave out a warm smile. "You must be Tom's sister," she said. "He's told me a lot about you."

Beatrice returned the smile. "Well, I guess you'll have to make up your own mind," she said, hoping it didn't come across as awkward as she felt.

"Oh, I'm sure all of the things he's told me are perfectly true," Claire said. Beatrice thought she caught something in the woman's tone. Was it snide? She cursed herself for being sensitive, and instead stepped forward and held out her hands.

"Maybe I can take those flowers and put them in water for you until later?" she said.

"You will do no such thing, young lady," Maureen said, stepping up and relieving Claire of the bouquet. "Not in that wonderful dress of yours."

Maureen took the flowers from Claire, and the corridor was suddenly alive with the crackle and crunch of cellophane as she manhandled the bouquet into the kitchen.

Thomas stepped up to Claire and offered his hand in a greeting. He was dressed in a dinner suit that Maud had somehow retrieved from one of the many rooms in Crab Mill Terrace. His hair was combed back out of his face and even Beatrice thought he looked remarkably presentable, if you ignored the faint aroma of mothballs emanating from his newly acquired suit.

"I've been told that I should—"

"Thomas," George's voice of caution said from somewhere in the kitchen.

"I would like to thank you for expending—"

"Extending," his father's disembodied voice said.

"—*extending* your incite—"

"Invite," George corrected.

"—*invite* to the gala. It is our honour to accept your kind offer," Thomas said.

Beatrice was somewhat bemused by how her brother's face contorted as he battled for concentration. It was a little like watching a bulldog chewing a toffee.

"You're most welcome," Claire said. She jabbed a thumb towards the front door. "Shall we go?

Beatrice followed Claire and Thomas to the long, black car parked outside. A tall man in a smart grey uniform and matching cap stood almost to attention at the back quarter, door thrown wide and waiting.

The interior of the car was huge with two long seats facing each other and small cabinets built into the doors. Beatrice settled back in her seat, Claire and Thomas opposite, her brother fidgeting with his shirt collar.

"What's the matter with you?" Beatrice hissed. "Can't you keep still for thirty seconds?"

"I'm itchy," he complained. "It's like I'm sharing this shirt with an ants' nest."

"I slept on an ants' nest once," Claire mused. "In Papua New Guinea. Not good."

"Papua New Guinea or the ants' nest?" Beatrice said.

"Definitely the ants. The country was amazing. I climbed Mount Wilhelm a few years ago. The views of the rainforests from the summit were incredible."

"Munu," Beatrice said.

Thomas gasped. "Beatrice, there's no need to swear. Claire was only telling us where she'd been."

Beatrice shook her head in disbelief. "Munu is a traditional dish of Papua New Guinea. Roast pork, sweet potato, rice and greens. Cooked on dried earth."

Claire looked pleasantly surprised. "Wow. You know about that?"

Beatrice shrugged. "I've cooked it a few times."

Claire seemed impressed. "You cooked it? Not many kids would even know about it."

"I'm not a kid," Beatrice cautioned.

Claire held up a hand. "No. Of course, you're not."

Beatrice wasn't quite sure if she believed that the woman's response was sincere. She saw that look again on Claire's face. A kind of distance she could not place.

Thomas stopped squirming and became suddenly enthused by the discussion.

"Yeah, Beatrice cooks, and I suppose she's okay at it, but it's nothing like you do in the wild, Claire."

Beatrice sat seething. "*Okay* at it?"

Thomas continued unabated. "I mean, like when you caught those scorpions in the Sahara Desert and cooked them over that zippo lighter, and ate them from a stick, that's what I call a chef!"

"Cooking scorpions, eating them from a stick?" Beatrice muttered.

Thomas became concerned when he looked over at Beatrice. She'd gone quite red in the face and her right eye was twitching.

Claire interjected tactfully. "That's not quite the same as cooking something like Munu, Tom."

Beatrice eyeballed Thomas. "You should listen to Claire. It may be your only chance of getting to this party alive."

Claire laughed and the sound filled the car with its brightness.

Edward looked out of the window and down onto the harbour. His breath misted the glass, turning his image into a ghastly mask of contempt.

"Don't know why we don't get to be on the boat," he hissed, flecks of spit speckling the pane. "Instead I have to babysit *you*."

"You're not babysitting anyone," Alison smiled from the chair behind him. She flicked through a book of nursery bedtime stories, plucked from the shelf above her. "Although, judging by your sulky attitude, the reading material in here is probably more to your taste than mine."

They were in a small bedroom of an empty cottage. Primrose had somehow known that the owners were not at home. Overseas, Alison assumed, by some of the materials they'd found lying around. There had been a month's worth of mail by the front door for starters.

"Funny girl," Edward sneered.

Alison went on, unfazed. She held up a small square of paper. There was writing scrawled across it.

"Besides, we'll only have to wait for her signal," she said. "Then we have to go to pay the person at this address a visit, and do what we've been ordered to do."

"I don't take orders," Edward snapped.

"Then Primrose will come back and kill you," Alison said simply, her face not dropping her smile. "Maybe that's what you want, but I don't."

Edward turned away from the window, his eyes clouded with malice. There was also fear there.

"You know that whatever that thing is, it isn't Primrose, right?" he said.

"Of course," Alison said, her voice lilting.

"Aren't you wondering *what* it is?" he asked.

"No," Alison replied. "All that matters is she's my friend."

Edward turned back to the window and recommenced his observations of events below. The rain was turning the spotlights to spangled flame, etching the figures of the crowd of onlookers in vivid yellows.

"Sooner or later you'll learn that there's no such thing as friends," he said to the glass. "There's only survival."

Alison did not pause in a response. "Primrose is both."

Clive Redfern sipped a glass of ice-cold champagne, enjoying the bitter, dry taste on his tongue. He stood in the centre of the boardroom, a huge rosewood table sat in the middle flanked by several high-backed leather chairs, and each finished with the Redfern Maritime Leisure Company insignia.

He took in a breath, relaxed for a few seconds, and then exhaled slowly and deeply, his eyes scanned the room that would have been more at home in a city skyscraper. This was his favourite place on the yacht, and for good reason. It typified the market—the clientele—that his company sought to serve, corporate business owners, huge conglomerates that would ultimately purchase boats like *The Spirit of the Ocean*, so that they could schmooze up to investors and reward shareholders. This was where the true money lay these days, and he was expert in being able to spot it.

Redfern's ability to make money was nothing new. He came from a wealthy family who had been doing such a thing for many centuries. His ancestors had started out as tea merchants that ultimately used their trade networks in the 19th Century to build corporate empires.

Consequently the Redfern name was associated

with the sea long before he'd been born, and his great-grandfather had owned a fleet of ferries and cabin cruisers which he had passed on to Redfern's father, and from this small leisure armada, the current company was expanded until, on his father's death, Redfern was CEO of a huge fleet of cruisers and two ocean liners.

The Spirit of the Ocean was, in comparison to the larger vessels, very conservative in its scope, but it was exactly what corporations requested, commissioning his company to either build or lease them for incredible fees. Despite the design and building costs, this was still small bucks compared to the profits his clients were making each year.

He brought the champagne flute up to his lips again when the door to the boardroom slid open, and Melville walked in, his ruddy face held in a beaming smile.

Redfern raised his glass in salute as the captain approached. "Good turn out, I see."

"What TV celebrity would turn down a free promotional opportunity on one of the best superyachts on the ocean?" Melville chuckled at his rhetoric.

Redfern indicated a serving stand where a champagne bottle nestled in a bucket of ice. "Can I tempt you with a celebratory glass, Captain?"

"And breach maritime law before we get out of the harbour?" Melville laughed. "That would be a great start to the evening. Why don't you invite an albatross on board and be done with it?"

"You're a stickler for the rules, sir," Redfern said. "That is why you're working for me."

"Meaning, you only want people who toe the line?" Melville gave Redfern a wink.

"Meaning I only want the best," Redfern scoffed. "Nothing left to chance and that is how successful businesses endure in these uncertain fiscal times."

Melville drifted to the windows and looked out. The rain spattered the panes, the ocean beyond the harbour entrance rose and fell, but the wind was light.

"Sometimes I wonder how we work so well together," Melville said.

Redfern joined him by the window and watched the rise and fall of the waves. "Maybe because we're in tune, like the rhythm of the tide against the breakwater?"

"Perhaps," Melville said. "Or it's because you pay good wages."

Redfern laughed fiercely. "Yes. There's that, too."

The two men shared their mirth. After it subsided, Redfern put his hand on the captain's shoulder.

"We share something else, too, my friend," Redfern said, suddenly serious. "Our taste in maritime antiquity."

Melville smiled but his eyes glittered with bemusement. "I know this already."

"What you do not know is that I have made a special gift for you, Captain," Redfern winked and pointed to the wooden plaque, now transferred and standing proud on the wall behind the head of the boardroom table. "A little something to match your keepsake."

Now Melville was intrigued. "Do tell."

"Later, on the top deck, I shall reveal a portal that houses another trinket from The Raven. Do not ask how I came by it, or how I have managed to keep it from you until now. Let's just say it is my gift to a fine gentleman and his fine vessel. When our guests have gone, I shall take you to it."

Melville rubbed at his chin. "Would you pique my interest further by telling me what it is?"

"Let us just say that such an item kept 16th Century ships on the straight and narrow," Redfern said with a conspiratorial smile.

Melville gasped. "Are you talking about an astrolabe?"

Redfern frowned. "Now you've spoiled the surprise."

"I'm more agog at how you came by the navigation device of The Raven," Melville said.

Redfern took a sip from his champagne flute, wilfully keeping the captain in suspense. "If the truth be known, I found it," he finally admitted.

"Irony that as two men we happened across items from a ship long since lost," Melville said quietly. "Some would call it an ill omen."

"Only those who believe in such nonsense," Redfern scoffed. "I prefer to call it good fortune, something that was meant to be, like us here, tonight."

"So how did you find it?"

"An antiques faire in Alvechurch, Worcestershire, of all places. Now that is irony, my friend: finding maritime navigation equipment 300 miles inland. The price was good, too. I did feel a small amount of guilt. I think I was more aware of the history surrounding the piece than the poor fellow who sold it to me. When I recognised the Smith and Sons insignia on the surface, and a raven silhouette, I knew its origin straight away. The same way I knew I would bring it to this boat, and stow it secretly behind a floor portal in the top deck."

Taken aback, Melville gave a small bow. "Thank you, Clive. I'm honoured. I will have to seek it out later, when the guests have disembarked, of course."

"Now then, sir," Redfern said stoutly, shrugging off the gratuity. "Let's make this a night that our guests will never forget."

From that point on, this is exactly what happened.

But not quite in the way Redfern and Melville had envisaged.

Chapter Fourteen

THE BALLROOM WAS a place of glass mirrors and tall, elegant pillars etched in gold leaf, interspersed with rich redwood and parquet flooring that was so highly polished it appeared slickened with grease. From chandeliers fashioned into images of glass gulls, light poured down upon the guests below. The whole room glittered like a magical prize.

The gala was in full swing. There was over thirty celebrity guests, most of which Beatrice did not recognise. She only knew they held some prestige when either Claire or Thomas pointed them out.

Despite her earlier reservations, Beatrice found Claire quite personable, she was always making jokes, and found the attention she gained from other celebrities amusing.

"They're looking into my eyes but can only see themselves," she laughed after an encounter with a muscle-bound man with a high, bronzed forehead, and heavy Geordie accent. The guy had spent several seconds asking her about her latest show, and several minutes talking about himself as he preened his eyebrows in a nearby mirror.

"Don't you think people might feel the same when they meet you?" Beatrice said.

Claire grinned. "Most likely. My shows are somewhat different to the rest of reality TV."

Beatrice was genuinely interested. "So, what makes it different? Eating bugs?"

"I think it might be that I don't do this stuff because I want to be on TV. I do this stuff because I want to do this stuff. The easiest way to describe it to you would be to compare it more to a TV cookery show."

"I can understand that," Beatrice said taking a sip of her fruit punch. She nodded her head in approval of her drink. Although she would've loved to see the head chef and the galley, with matters pressing, this no longer featured on her itinerary.

Her new plan was simple enough. She would attempt to surreptitiously keep Primrose in view, and wait for her to make her move. Beatrice suspected that as the evening went on Codd's PA would attempt to slip away from the crowds and make her move on Melville Craig.

Beatrice scanned the room, and could see Primrose talking to a short, elderly woman who was clearly wearing a blonde wig. Primrose looked directly at Beatrice, and the sedentary smile returned.

She knows, Beatrice thought. *It's like she can see into my mind.*

The unnerving sensation that came with this thought was secondary to the anxiety her next observation brought.

She knows and she doesn't care.

Beatrice felt a chill pass through her, and she was relieved when Primrose finally peeled her eyes away from her and went back to the conversation with the woman in the wig.

This sense of relief was short-lived when, to her left, a familiar voice came to her over the hubbub. She sighed and turned to see the local town busybody, Edna Duffy and her sidekick, Dorothy Arnold, heading towards them.

To say Edna was cantankerous and objectionable was a little like saying the Antarctic was a bit chilly, or a thousand miles was a bit of a walk. Edna was small of frame, her eyes pale and shrewd, and her head bobbed and twitched as though trying to avoid invisible missiles. Thomas had once said the old woman looked like a velociraptor from the *Jurassic Park* movies and, for once, Beatrice could not argue with the comparison. Despite the grandeur of the event going on about her, Edna still wore a blue raincoat and floral headscarf, and her weathered shopping bag was draped over her arm.

Dorothy followed on behind, her stoop almost reflective of her subservient nature in the shadow of her long-standing friend. Dorothy was a small woman, with reed-thin limbs, and a heavy head of white hair, which she currently wore in a bun. Her skin was wrinkled like a crumpled tissue, and dotted with liver spots. Beatrice often felt sorry for her, being Edna's friend came at a cost, meaning no one else really wanted to be anywhere near her.

"Well, this shindig is very over the top, don't you think?" Edna said. "Most of the people here haven't brought the faces they were born with." She eyed Claire, scanning the young woman's face as though it was her next meal.

"I read they *inject* stuff into their faces," Dorothy said looking around her.

"What?" Edna said.

"A substance called *Buttocks*," Dorothy whispered.

"They inject stuff into their buttocks?" Edna appeared drawn with disdain. "The world has gone mad, and we are its witness."

Claire looked at Beatrice, eyes glistening with suppressed mirth. Beatrice had to look away in case she began to giggle.

"No Maud or Agnes with you?" Edna queried.

"No." Though Beatrice really wished they both were there. Dealing with Edna Duffy by herself was a tedious affair best left to adults.

"No friends either." Edna peered into Beatrice's face. "I heard Khaldun Userkaf was caught drunk-driving. He was lucky not to be killed, or certainly lucky not to have killed someone else. I can imagine it's quite an embarrassment for the family."

Beatrice felt the anger rise within her. She responded through pursed lips. "It's all a misunderstanding. He was not drunk. He is in hospital, and very ill."

"Hangovers can do that," Edna said dismissively. "Not seeing Mayor Codd here either. It's most unusual not to have that particular hog with its nose in the trough. It really is quite a bizarre event. I'm beginning to wish we hadn't come, Dorothy."

"I'm sure you're not alone in thinking that," Claire said pointedly.

If Edna grasped the sleight, she did not acknowledge it. Instead she continued to peruse the room, occasionally taking a sip from her glass of orange juice.

"I've never seen so much mutton dressed as lamb,"

Edna whinged. "What is it people see in this bunch of misfits?"

"It's just entertainment," Claire said. "Escapism."

"And what do people want to escape from?" Dorothy said.

"The day to day things," Claire offered.

Edna appeared genuinely bemused. "So to escape the mundane they watch people who have everything?"

She hated to admit it, but Beatrice thought Edna had a point.

Claire countered swiftly.

"It's about prestige," she said. "Ordinary people watching ordinary people becoming famous. It inspires them."

"Inspires them to do what?" Beatrice asked.

"To try and achieve what it is they desire in life," a voice said behind them.

They all turned as Clive Redfern approached. He wore a smart tuxedo with a white bowtie, and his face pulled into a warm smile.

"Who might you be?" Edna said in her usual abrasive tone.

"Clive Redfern," he said. "Builder of this wonderful vessel, and your host this evening," he continued, his cordial demeanour not missing a beat.

"It's beautifully made," Claire said.

"The craftsmanship is second to none, Miss Drill," he said tipping her a nod of courtesy. "A true Object of Desire."

"Fool's Gold, more like," Edna sniffed.

"Oh, come, come, Mrs Duffy," he said with a smooth tone. "Have you not had something which you'd love to acquire?"

Beatrice shuffled with embarrassment. She knew Edna was a sourpuss but this was in part down to a great loss she'd suffered many years before, the death of her son in a boating accident when he was a child. Her grief had slowly turned to bitterness. For a second Beatrice thought she saw Edna's eyes mist over, but the moment passed, and coldness came to them.

"I don't yearn for what I can't have," she said. "Like I say, this is Fool's Gold and nothing less."

Despite the hard edge to Edna's voice, Beatrice thought this was a brave lie.

Redfern acknowledged Edna by touching his forelock.

"Very well, but I know many who do have such desires," he said. "When I was a boy I used to love sailing toy boats. While my father built the real thing, I revelled in the detail of miniature ships, and still do, even after all these years. They represent my passion, you see? I have quite a collection, and when I look upon them I'm overcome by such an incredible sense of peace it's difficult to part from them."

Claire began nodding in agreement. "Travel is my thing, if you hadn't already guessed. But I'd love to shift focus." She pointed upwards.

Thomas looked puzzled. "The ceiling?"

"Space, you idiot," Beatrice muttered.

"To go up there—be amongst the stars—that must be an incredible feeling," Claire breathed. Beatrice could see a distant look in the woman's eyes, as though she was already there in the Heavens.

Then Claire came back to earth and looked at Thomas. "What about you, Tom?"

He thought it over. "Think I'd want a complete

boxed set of *Behind Enemy Lines*. Signed would be great."

Beatrice cringed at her brother's nerve. "Thomas, for God's sake."

Claire and Redfern, however, laughed.

"I like a man who grabs opportunity where he sees it," Redfern said, shaking Thomas' hand. "You'd make a good entrepreneur, young man!"

He could try being a better brother first, Beatrice thought.

"What about you, Beatrice?" Redfern asked. "What inspires you?"

"Oh, that would be Lucas Walker," Thomas interjected. "I mean, they're glued to each other's faces most of the time."

"That is not true," Beatrice said as her cheeks and neck began to take on heat.

"Best tell your face that before it turns the colour of beetroot," Dorothy said.

Back in his cabin, Melville adjusted his smart blue tie, and took a breath.

"Moment of truth," he said to the empty boardroom. He knew Clive had gone down to the party, accepting that the comfort of such occasions didn't come naturally to his captain. Melville had used the time to compose himself, enjoying the silence the soundproofing in the boardroom provided. He intended to head for the bridge to check in on Trevor. He pushed down his mind's accusation that he was doing this to delay attending the gala.

The knock on the door disturbed his reverie. He went to it and pulled it open, surprised to see an unfamiliar face.

"Captain Craig?' Cotteridge said with a small smile. He held his ID card before Melville's eyes. "DC Cotteridge. May I have a quiet word?"

"Is it important?" Melville tried to keep his voice soft, but only just succeeded.

"I'm afraid it is."

"Then walk with me," Melville said, stepping out of the boardroom. "I have to check the bridge before heading downstairs."

Cotteridge was reticent. "Very well, Captain, but I may have some troubling news for you. It's about your Uncle."

"My uncle?"

"Yes. It appears he's gone missing while on an archaeological expedition in this very town. The university hasn't seen him for a few days, but I should warn you to prepare yourself," he paused as he looked upon Melville's blanched face. "Local police reports suggest a man fitting your uncle's description was seen underwater yesterday. We fear the worst, I'm afraid."

Melville appeared dumbfounded and Cotteridge put a comforting arm on the man's shoulder.

"I understand this is a shock, Captain," Cotteridge said.

Melville gave a small nod.

"I should say so, Detective," he said slowly. "Because as far as I know, I haven't got an uncle."

In Ashby-on-Sea General Hospital, mother and daughter watched Khaldun lying in an intensive care bed, blankets covering its bulk, pillows propping up his head, tubes secured to his mouth with surgical tape.

It was a pitiful sight, and both Patience and Skylar had shared many tears since Detective Cotteridge had left them. Primrose had mercilessly ousted them from the very event Khaldun had orchestrated for the good of the town.

The tears were not the only thing that they shared. They were united in their belief that something was seriously wrong with any person who could consider Khaldun as anything other than a committed and honourable human being. He was not reckless, not wanton, and only had the best interests of others in his heart. There was absolutely no doubt in their minds that accusations of him drinking and driving at the time of the accident were complete rubbish.

Patience looked over at her mother who was asleep, snuggled up on a large chair covered with a blanket. Outside the window, darkness had fallen over the town. Patience could not help but feel this reflected in the pain in her heart.

She shifted position in the chair, reaching down into her bag to retrieve her iPad. She could not sleep, despite the weariness she felt. Instead she thought she would look over the strange writing whose meaning continued to elude her.

Accessing the screen, she opened the file. There, the image of the enigmatic text came to the screen, washing her face with its mystery. For a second she thought about the launch gala that would by now be in full flow, and Beatrice and Lucas would be there amongst the festivities. She imagined how the dress she'd arranged to be delivered to Beatrice looked on her best friend.

To her surprise, a pang of jealousy grabbed at her heart, an overwhelming sense of unfairness when she thought of how hard her father had worked to make this event happen, only to find the Userkafs barred from attending.

But then she thought about the danger her friend was facing on the behalf of them all, using it to throw off the sensation, cursing herself for being so disloyal to Beatrice, allowing guilt to browbeat jealousy into submission.

Once again she looked at the bizarre writing on her screen:

Out of the corner of her eye something flickered and she looked up. The tiny, rectangular image of her iPad was reflected on the glass panel of her father's heart monitor, his steady pulse bleeping, a small heart-shaped icon flashing in tandem.

Patience saw something else on the iPad reflection. She saw that the script on the screen appeared to have a form she could suddenly recognise.

She carefully stood up, keen to not wake her mother but her excitement at going over to the monitor almost making her clumsy. She held the iPad in front of her, screen facing the monitor, the reflection in the panel growing as she approached. Suddenly she could see the very words that had been hiding in plain sight all the time.

> *If you wish to evoke this curse,*
>
> *Speak these words when in reverse*

As she recognised them she spoke them, her lips trying them on for size, her brow furrowing with interest.

"If you wish to evoke this curse, speak these words when in reverse."

The tablet in her hand sputtered, the white light suddenly blinking between black and a sickly green hue. Even as the device dissolved to nothing in her hand, Patience knew that she'd unwittingly made a huge mistake, and she voiced it in a hushed whisper.

"Oh, Shih-Tzu."

The glass panels in the room doors and the windows began to dim until there was nothing left but blackness. Patience went to the doors, pulling them open, expecting to see the corridor and waiting area stretched out in the gloom.

She gasped when she saw that there was nothing beyond the door but a void of absolute shadow. A dank breeze came to her and its smell made her nose wrinkle with distaste.

Stepping back, she allowed the door to swing shut.

Turning to her parents, she noticed that her mother was still asleep. She went over and tried to shake Skylar awake, but her mother remained unresponsive save for a small sigh, her head lolling as Patience increased the vigour to such a degree the blanket fell from her legs and onto the floor.

After several seconds of frenetic shaking and calling out to Skylar, Patience grabbed her cell phone and tried to ring Beatrice.

She hit the speed dial but the only sound that came to her was the hideous, pitiful sound of hundreds of voices wailing and moaning.

"That's either the weirdest on-hold tone in the world, or things really have turned bad."

She hit Lucas' number and, again, another alien sound came to her, this time the rustle of a great winds and the roar of the ocean.

Panicking now, she tried Elmo's cell. A flat tone of an automated "caller not available" message came to her and, while she thought it an improvement on screaming voices and raging oceans, it still left her feeling ominous.

"Where is everyone?" she said to the room. She finally pulled up Emily's number and sent her a text message.

Need to talk. Think something bad just happened.

Patience leaned back against the wall. The distant bleep of her father's regulator gave some sense of skewed normality to events, but there was no escaping the awful sensation of loss that coursed through her.

Her phone buzzed in her hand and she checked the screen. It was Emily's phone number but it was an incoming call. Puzzled, Patience responded and suddenly Elmo was on the line.

By the end of the call, any feelings of fear for Beatrice had been magnified beyond measure.

Beatrice glared at Thomas but the embarrassment she felt was fuelled by the truth of his words. Lucas *was* her world. But hearing it said aloud in front of people she didn't really know well was emotionally excruciating.

She was surprised when Claire put an arm around her shoulders.

"Beatrice, I think I saw someone I'd love for you to meet," she said.

Beatrice allowed Claire to steer her into the crowd of people. After a few yards, she felt Claire nudge her towards the port doors which slid open, allowing them onto the aft deck.

As they stepped through, Beatrice found herself underneath a short awning, the rain drifting down as a mist beyond its reach, the floodlights turning raindrops into a spangled curtain, and the breeze from the open ocean brought welcome relief to her burning face.

"Thanks for getting me out of there," Beatrice said, while looking at the ocean.

Claire smiled. "It was rather stuffy. You certainly needed some air."

A gust of wind turned their exposed skin to goose bumps, yet it was only Beatrice who appeared to shiver. She wrapped her arms around herself.

"The air certainly *is* fresh," Beatrice chuckled.

"The best," Claire said. "A little like this boy of yours, I suspect?"

Beatrice sighed, and this time there was no discomfort when she mentioned his name.

"Lucas is pretty amazing," she admitted. "Though I'd deny saying it if you told him."

"Playing it cool?" Claire observed. "Like it. So, what is it about him that makes him so special?"

Beatrice answered without thought. "I can be who I am around him, and he listens, not just pretends to listen. You know what I mean?"

"Oh, yes," Claire said moving a strand of hair that the wind wanted to whip into her face. "Some of us have spent a long time looking for someone like that. People who listen make you feel truly alive."

"Who said that?" Beatrice asked.

"Me. Just now."

They both giggled.

"You ready to go back in?" Claire said.

"Yes."

They turned towards the doors, and that was when all the lights went out.

The screaming started soon after.

Primrose watched Beatrice and the woman with raven hair leave the room. Her jade eyes were intense yet icy, her face impartial as she listened to the inane self-adulation the woman in the blonde wig had been spouting for the past twenty minutes.

Once Beatrice was no longer in sight, Primrose moved. The woman in the wig was still talking even as she walked away without saying a word, heading off to a set of doors that led to a short run of chrome and lacquered wooden steps taking her up to the next level. She came to an oval door, stepping through as it parted to give her access, and she moved deftly down the corridor beyond.

She was no more familiar with the layout of the yacht than any other guest, but on the air she found guidance. Hushed whispers urged her onwards, their tone insistent, impatient, driving her onwards as though she had no volition of her own. These voices were infused at once with fear and anger and pain but they spoke as one, their words blending, pleading for her to hurry, hurry, hurry.

Primrose's heart was beating furiously, a small bird fluttering against her sternum, and the sense of exultation threatened to have her keeling over on the spot. She fought off the sensation, her hands using the smooth, shining walls for support, her breathing becoming deep and regular as she recovered.

She walked on through the corridor. There were several doors running along the left wall. To the right were oval windows, their glass panes streaked with sea spray. Beyond the glass, the last vestiges of daylight were manifested by a thin white line on the shifting horizon, the storm swallowing it within moments.

Realisation came to her. Darkness was coming, and she was to be part of it, but rather than baulk at the idea, she embraced it, made it as much a part of her as her new companion who now inhabited her skin.

Primrose came to a large set of heavy wooden doors. There was a brass plaque on one of them, the boardroom. The voices on the air said that she needed to be inside, she needed to be inside *right now*, because someone would soon be coming, someone who knew she was up to no good. Most of all, it would be someone who had the power to stop her achieving her ends.

She looked down at the keypad and a quiet despair settled over her. What was the code?

She took a breath and allowed the tingling sensation to grow within her. It travelled from her chest, radiating out, into her shoulder, down her arms until it coursed through her fingers, and she felt her hands lifting, watching them as though they belonged to someone else. She laughed at the thought because at that moment they *did* belong to someone else. As her fingers touched the keypad, a green light crackled from them and buckled the metal with a small hiss, the doors flying inwards as though kicked open with great force.

On the threshold, Primrose nodded as though this was to be expected, and then stepped into the room. She scanned the walls. The display cases reflected the flickering green fire still emanating from her fingers. Listening she could hear a small, demanding noise within the room. It was a steady tapping, as though someone was beating tiny hands against glass.

With the sound came the voices, rising in pitch. She turned her head to the right and at the far end of the huge table, a display case housing the name plaque for The Raven was shivering under an invisible touch. She went to it, caution thrown aside, her determination to place her illuminated hands upon the object behind the glass. This was the only thing that meant anything anymore.

She neared the display case and the surface of the glass became opaque, rippling as it turned to water.

The piece of wood passed through this skein and fell at her feet, and the water followed it, falling as a cataract that sprayed her legs and soaked her dress.

Rather than jump back, Primrose went to her knees, the water on the sodden carpet pooling beneath her as she reached for the plaque. More green flames flickered from her fingers and a great light erupted as flame and wood connected. The light blossomed and Primrose's mouth opened wide as she squeezed her eyes shut.

Green light bubbled over her lips and even though her eyes were scrunched closed, the same radiance oozed down her cheeks as rivulets of fire. The pain was so great it made her cry out, and in that moment both natural and unnatural entities realised both had been duped but for one end.

Primrose surfaced only to be lost once again to an infinite limbo, where cries of the damned reverberated all around her. Terrified and in despair, she walked amongst them, feeling their desperate touch. Soon her cries were merging with the horde, and the last thing she recalled was not her life and things lost but the Underwood typewriter that belonged to the mother.

In the boardroom, the light vanished as abruptly as it came, and Primrose collapsed, both it seemed, having served their purpose.

Edward and Alison remained in their procured bedroom, peering out on the crowd in the harbour. Edward's face was grim, yet joy danced brightly in his eyes. The crowd hadn't dispersed with the departure of the yacht. Instead they gazed upon it in the distance, standing as rigid as penguins on a frozen ledge. More townsfolk were joining them by the second, drifting through streets jaundiced by lamplight. It was the strangest of sights but the green orbs of light that bobbed like fireflies in the skulls of all those who were present marked this to be just the start of a very strange evening indeed.

"Jealousy is a powerful weapon," Alison whispered.

Edward suspected these were borrowed words but he agreed with them. Part of him was as jealous of his companion's connection with the thing inside Primrose as the people out in the harbour were of those attending the gala.

There was also fear lurking there, and this was often fierce fuel for his behaviour. Not that he either cared or consulted with such things, but he was *aware* of it. His fear came from the fact that Alison seemed more than just an ally to Primrose. Edward suspected that they were fused on some deeper level, the way Primrose was connected to her host.

When he thought about it, he felt excluded from things. The more he considered this, the more he realised that perhaps this was by design.

Alison chuckled beside him, and he turned to meet her stare. Just like those in the harbour, her eyes had turned to green fire behind her glasses.

"Primrose?" he guessed.

Alison shook her head and tittered as though enjoying the game.

"Elizabeth?"

Alison lifted a finger and wagged it before him. The movement left jagged slashes of light in the air.

"The time for witches and their gullible servants has passed," Alison said, and in her voice there was nothing but malice and power. "Behold the nature of your Master."

Edward's mind was filled with terrible images, images of death and destruction, with creatures sculpted in forms that he could not fathom, impossible things, deadly things, and inside his mind they crawled like thousands of tiny spiders across his brain, through his brain, burrowing into the cavities, making the inside of his skull itch.

Edward tried to push these images away, but the thing oozing through his mind spoke to him, and its tone was one of mock-surprise.

"Do you deny that you have not sought this? Did you not dream of such things and place yourself at the helm of the designs of World's End?"

Edward managed to stomp on his fear and confusion, his cold hatred seemingly at home in the maelstrom going on in his head.

"Yeah, I dreamt it. What's the point of being in control when all you really are is a slave?"

A thick laughter echoed around him. "You are wise in the most wicked of ways, boy. There will be a place for you in the new order. Perhaps you will serve me better with a free mind, we shall see."

"You saying if I work with you, I don't get possessed?"

"You are indeed perceptive," the thing said. "I have seen inside your mind. It craves the things I can give, and the means by which great things are gained. Such a mind in a human is an asset."

Edward looked over at Alison who appeared to be frozen in time. "What about her?"

"She is the servant of a minion, and her place in things is now lost. She is doomed to live as a slave to my ends, the price that is paid for naivety."

Edward nodded as though this all made sense. He leered at the frigid face a few feet away from him.

"Not so big now, are you?" he sneered.

The thing in his mind cackled. "That's the spirit. Now, come, you must go."

"Where to?" Edward said.

"The address on the paper in the girl's pocket," the thing said.

"And what do we do when we get there?" Edward replied.

"We begin the plan for chaos."

Chapter Fifteen

In Lucas' bedroom, Emily was sitting in a big armchair, finishing off her fourth jumbo cookie, eyes transfixed on the nautical map on the screen of her laptop. She chewed thoughtfully as a ship-shaped cursor—indicating *The Spirit of the Ocean*—blinked lazily on the coastline.

Across the room, Elmo and Lucas were sitting on the bed eating pistachio nuts from a bag. The shells were in a bowl, a myriad of tiny, gaping mouths that evidenced just how many had been gorged in the time Beatrice had been on the boat.

The two boys were facing Emily so she could lip read them, and also signed when relaying any important information Elmo found on the ship or its owners.

So far, Elmo had found out the background of Redfern's company and a biography of the current owner. One of the things that had caught Elmo's attention was the mention of the owner's penchant for maritime antiquities, and his inclination to display these in most of the vessels that his company built.

"Got an idea," Elmo said then paused as he saw Emily was looking down at her laptop.

He picked up a discarded pistachio shell and bounced it off Emily's shoulder to get her attention. This earned him half a cookie to his forehead, and he fell backwards as though mortally wounded, making Emily laugh.

"So what you got for us?" Lucas said as he salvaged the food haul when Elmo sat upright. There was a tone in his voice, a level of suppressed impatience.

Elmo put a hand on Lucas' shoulder. "Don't worry, mate. Beatrice is going to be okay."

Lucas nodded, though his eyes were bright with anxiety. "I just wanted to be there, y'know? To make sure?"

Emily signed over to him. "Beatrice is tough. More likely she'd need to be protecting you!"

Lucas laughed. "I wish I could say you're wrong," he said. Turning to Elmo, Lucas continued, "Go on big guy, what's your idea?"

Elmo pointed at Redfern's biography that remained on-screen. "Redfern collects pieces of maritime history," he said. "Puts them on display in the ships he builds, right?"

"Okay," Lucas acknowledged.

"From what Maud and Agnes found out about The Raven, and the captain's links to Melville Craig, what if the plaque he found is on *The Spirit of the Ocean*? And what if Elizabeth needs to get to it for some reason?"

Emily frowned. "But why?"

Elmo shrugged. "That's the big question, isn't it?"

"Maybe not," Lucas said. "Yes, she has the power to control Primrose, but what if getting a piece of The Raven gives her more than just the ability to possess someone?"

"I'm pretty impressed by the ability to 'just' possess someone, if I'm honest," Elmo said thoughtfully. "What else is there?"

Lucas looked squarely at Emily and Elmo, his eyes haunted with understanding. "Maybe to get even, she has to really come back," he whispered.

"We need to tell Beatrice," Emily said.

Lucas went for his phone but before his hand could reach it, Emily cried out in horror.

She stood up, her eyes rolling back into her eye sockets until only the whites were on show, her arms rigid at her sides as her whole body jittered as if undergoing a great shock.

Elmo leapt up and went to her aid, but as he neared, a pulse of white light sent him reeling backwards onto the bed, scattering electronic devices and food packages across the room.

He tried to get back up but he was pushed away from Emily's convulsing form by pressure on his chest, as though some invisible palm was barring his attempts to advance.

He watched her helplessly, partly terrified, partly ashamed that he was unable to help his friend.

Then, without warning, Emily collapsed, her knees buckling, sending her sideways where her head connected with the corner of the arm of the chair with a heavy thud. Elmo clambered over the duvet and saw her inert form sprawled at the foot of the bed, her face pale, and a small gash on her temple.

Crawling towards her, Elmo gingerly checked her over, putting an ear to her mouth, and gave a sigh as he felt her breath against his cheek. He brought himself upright to see if Lucas was okay and got the second shock of the evening.

No matter how many times Elmo blinked at the room around him, it did not change the most obvious of facts.

Lucas Walker was gone.

Thomas stomped up to the bar, his face stern as he quietly muttered to himself. It was just like his sister to steal the limelight. One minute he was enjoying the company of the one-and-only Claire Drill, the next moment Beatrice had sloped off taking his hero with her.

He wasn't impressed. Not in the slightest. In fact, he could feel the simmer of jealousy building up in his guts with such insistence it made him feel quite shocked. He took a breath and leaned on the bar. The bartender, a man in his thirties wearing a smart tunic and a bored expression, came over to him.

"What can I get you?" the bartender said with a forced smile.

"Orange juice." After a few seconds he added, "Put a lemonade in there too, would you?"

"Bad night?"

"Yeah," Thomas said turning to look at the room.

The bartender placed Thomas' drink on the bar, the glass tumbler clicking against the tiles on the counter. Thomas went for his drink, but without warning a huge gale swept into the room, blasting open the doors leading to the upper levels, removing them from their brackets, and sending them into the crowd.

Two people were struck and went down, and all of the lights erupted in brilliant sparks that fizzed and sputtered before plunging the place into darkness.

During the maelstrom, Thomas managed to leap over the bar, much to the chagrin of the bartender, who he managed to catch in the shoulder with his foot, knocking him into the optics, and sending bottles of expensive liquor to explode on the floor.

As soon as the lights went out, high-pitched screams reverberated around the room, the wind dropped, and now the air was filled with hisses and snarls. From his position under the bar, Thomas watched the bartender as he looked across the room, his expression one of pure fear. The man began to back away, but he was already braced against the wall, instinct had him turning around, trying to avoid whatever was coming for him.

In horror, Thomas watched something dark and snake-like reach across the counter, grabbing the bartender by the collar of his tunic, dragging him back into the room as though he weighed nothing at all.

His scream joined the others for a second before his body came back over the bar, smashing into the wall, to land beside Thomas who clasped his hands across his mouth to suppress a cry of terror.

The hisses and growls were getting louder, shrieks and shouts continued amongst them. Glasses smashed, there were thuds and hideous sounds of something being ripped and torn, like wet, heavy material.

Thomas stayed where he was, numb with shock, but his mind was suddenly brought into focus when he thought about Beatrice. Despite his fear, he knew that he could not leave his sister, even if she had Claire, the greatest survivor of them all, at her side.

He saw a bottle in the gloom and dragged it to him, looking at the label. He unscrewed the top and grabbed the neck of the bottle and took a good slug, wincing at the taste.

"Man, lime juice is so gross,' he muttered, discarding the bottle after wiping his mouth on his sleeve.

Carefully, he came to all fours, listening to the sounds emanating from the room above him. The hisses and growls were as rhythmic as the sea at high tide. In fact, the sounds seemed to be getting quieter as though whatever made them was on the move.

Thomas thought about peering over the bar to see what was happening, and then decided to wait a little longer. He was no good to Beatrice if he was caught as soon as he stepped from cover.

That was when the bartender, who had remained still since being thrown into the wall, began to growl like an angry dog. By the time the man opened his eyes, and a terrible green light spilled out from his eye-sockets, Thomas decided it was time for an immediate change of plan.

Elmo rushed to the bedroom door and called out for Lucas several times. He was torn between heading downstairs in search of his errant friend and staying with Emily.

In the end, the obvious came to him and he went back into the bedroom, grabbing at his pockets for his cell phone. He yanked the device free, shouting in surprise as the tiny screen flickered to life before he could activate it, and the ghastly white face of Primrose sneered up at him.

Her eyes were encapsulated in dark sockets, fiery green orbs without pupils, staring out at him, her blue lips smeared with a dark substance, tendrils of which hung from her pale, pointed chin like ghastly spider webs. The strawberry birthmark was so dark it looked like an empty eye socket.

"There is no help," she said, throat thick with goo. "Not for any of us. We are all betrayed, some more than others."

Her tone was almost rueful, but any atonement was muted by the gurgle coating her words. For a second Elmo saw beyond the thing on the screen, a flicker of life in those empty eyes, a bright spark of nothing but absolute terror blinking back at him as clear tears trickled down pallid cheeks.

"Help me," a small, strangled voice came to him from the phone.

"Primrose?" he whispered.

No sooner had he said this when the face morphed into a mask of twisted hate and a hideous, mocking laughter filled the room. Elmo acted instinctively, hurling the phone at the nearest wall where it exploded, scattering its fractured carcass onto the bed and floor.

The laughing stopped as if a plug had been yanked from a socket, and in the silence Elmo looked at the shattered pieces of plastic on the duvet.

"Not the best idea I've ever had," he said miserably.

The room was suddenly plunged into darkness, and the hideous laughter began again.

At the first sounds of distress, Beatrice hesitated. Claire was behind her and placed a hand on her shoulder, trying to give a physical pause to her actions.

Then something struck the doors with an awful, sickening thud and the pane became a myriad of lightning streaks as it relented under the blow.

The doors hissed open, and there the broken figure of Clive Redfern lay on the carpet. His arms and legs were pointing the opposite direction to his head.

Dismayed, Beatrice took a step back. The inside of the room was dark for a brief second, and then many green orbs were flickering in the air. Beatrice immediately realised what they were, and gasped.

Eyes.

With the eyes came snarls and growls, and the foetid stink of something akin to spoiled meat. Oddly, the stench reminded Beatrice that she'd forgotten to put the beef back in the fridge after her supper.

An intense pain began to build in her right shoulder and Beatrice squealed. Nails began to dig into her bare shoulder.

"Ow, Claire, stop it! You're hurting me!"

Beatrice grasped the hand, but it was not Claire's at all. In fact the hand did not resemble that of a human being. It was gnarled, with yellowed nails and grey, flaky skin. She crushed the fingers and the owner snarled and yelped, and then she felt the hand yanked from her grip, as though pulled with great force.

Beatrice spun around, instinctively ducking low, gasping in surprise when she saw the scene behind her.

The figure skittering about the deck, was hideously malformed, a beast that had vaguely human features, but they were contorted, stretched or bent until it became nothing more than a grotesque parody of the person it had once been. Beatrice saw with despair that the creature was swathed in a dinner jacket, the white shirt soiled with dark fluids. This poor soul had come for a party, and had instead found horror.

Like the images in the room behind her, Beatrice could see that the beast also had green flames smouldering in its sockets.

Yet it was Claire who amazed Beatrice. The woman had managed to haul the creature away from her, and was now blocking its slow, menacing advance.

"What the hell is it?" Claire was breathing hard with exertion. She had somehow found a keel hook on deck, which she now brandished, and had kicked off her heeled shoes, bare feet braced and ready for attack.

"No idea," Beatrice muttered. She looked behind her as the things from the lounge crept forward, their shapes merging into each other, becoming one indefinable, seeping shadow of eyes and snaking limbs. "But it's got friends back here."

The things inside the room stalled at her voice, their hisses intensifying until they began to meld with the wind. Beatrice watched, her fear ebbing and flowing in time with the ocean beneath them.

"Why don't they attack?" Claire said. Her breathing was steady but hushed. The keel hook aimed directly at the creature in front of her.

It began pacing, growling as though impatient, she tracked its movements with the pole.

"It feels like they're waiting," Beatrice called to Claire.

"Waiting for what?"

Beatrice paused. "Okay, you got me on that one."

Even as she said this, Beatrice found her mind besieged by a series of images. They came as random entities, disjointed like a badly edited movie. There were people she recognised, Elmo and Emily, Patience and Skylar, Maud and Agnes, and her parents. With recognition came a great surge of love for these truly wonderful people.

No sooner had these faces registered before they were superseded by the ghastly face of Primrose, but the face was screaming as it was consumed in green, ethereal flames, and in the swirling embers rising into the air, she saw the callous face of Edward, eyes turned to jade fire. He also had a companion, a girl Beatrice recognised from her biology class, Alison Marston.

More images, now, as the scene opened out. Beatrice could see a boardroom turned to a sickening green hue as Primrose burned, display cases cracking open and contents falling to the floor, a cascade of glass and history hitting the carpet, some made dull by the light, and she saw in her mind's eye the plaque in the debris.

Then another flicker-flash image as she saw the plaque change to a strange disc that was encased behind a circular portal of glass on the upper deck. The gilded device sent arrows of white light towards her, and she felt powerfully drawn to it, the way a piece of iron is drawn to a magnet.

Beatrice realised that these insights were not imaginings conjured by fear, such things just did not happen in her Brave New World. The images came from The Light, doing its best to guide her.

"Beatrice?" Claire said with a high degree of concern. "Are you okay?"

"I've had better nights out," she replied. "Whatever has happened, someone intentionally did this, and these creatures are here for a reason."

"But what?"

A staggering thought hit Beatrice with such force she gasped.

Something was missing from her vision. Not something, but *someone*. Realisation put ice water into the pit of her stomach.

Out of all the people she'd been shown in her vision, Lucas was nowhere to be seen.

Elmo gently lifted Emily, his heart feeling heavier than the light frame of the girl in his arms.

As he carried her, Elmo looked down at her face, pale save for a livid scarlet bruise at her temple where her head had made contact with the arm of the chair. Her breathing was light but regular and, even as he watched, a small groan escaped her lips.

Elmo hated seeing her this way. She appeared frail and vulnerable even though he knew she was neither of these things. His stomach churned, he felt nauseous. When he thought of Emily too much, his heart actually ached. He cared for her so much.

As he placed Emily down on the bed something caught his eye, a glittering object that made him think he'd spotted some shrapnel from his ruined phone. His eyes sought it out and he saw the tiny button shimmering as though it had a power source all of its own.

He reached for it, held in in the palm of his hand just as he heard a dull thump come up through the floor.

He held onto his breath. The thud came again, and then the jangle of keys as they hit a work surface.

"Mrs Walker?" he called, but his voice was hesitant. He stood, and headed for the bedroom door, part of him eager to seek out help for Emily, part of him giving in to caution.

Just in case.

He stepped out onto the landing and peered down the stairs, his eyes straining to see through the gloom. As he focused, a dark shape edged up the stairs and he released a cry of fear. He fell backwards against the wall behind him, a picture frame clattered to the floor, the sound of breaking glass loud in the hush.

"Who is that?" the voice undulated with fear.

Elmo almost shouted with relief but instead he stumbled forward, just as Tamsin hit the torch on her Smartphone.

"Elmo," she declared. "You scared me to death. Are you okay? Why are all the lights out?"

"Power cut," Elmo said.

"I just walked back from work. The lights were on in the street all the way, though it's getting pretty foggy." Tamsin said. "Fuses must've blown in here."

Elmo considered this, but something began to distract him, warmth in the palm of his hand.

He looked down and his fingers were clenched into a tight fist, but a yellow light bled through, streaks of brilliance defining where each digit met, radiating through his skin, turning the blood vessels into scarlet tributaries.

He raised his hand, palm up, his fingers opening slowly like the petals of a flower during a time-lapse rerun, the button now a dazzling pillar of light.

Elmo tipped the object onto the landing carpet where it hit the ground with a thud, as though it were made of lead. A thin shaft of light emanated upwards, where a pool of gold spread across the ceiling.

Tamsin stepped up to the button, stopped, and without hesitation, picked it up with her thumb and forefinger. At her touch the radiance died and the landing was dark once more.

"What the hell is that?" he said in amazement.

Tamsin looked at him, her face serene in the stark light from her cell-torch.

"The past," she whispered. There were tears in her eyes.

A huge crash against the front door below startled them. She dropped the button and it bounced down the stairs.

The crash came again as Elmo and Tamsin saw the letterbox suddenly edged with green light. The flap lifted as something pushed against it, and through the hyphen, a face mocked them with glee.

"I see you," Edward growled.

Chapter Sixteen

Before the World changed, Lucas was thinking about Beatrice, his face screwed up with concern when Elmo presented his theory about Elizabeth and her quest for some relic on the yacht.

Lucas had been battling against waves of love and fear, admiration and tension, when he heard the lone, rolling toll of a bell. At the same time, he felt the sudden pulse in the back pocket of his cargo pants. Puzzled he scanned around for his phone, the vibration in his pocket continuing without apparent end.

It didn't help when he immediately noticed that his phone was where he left it, innocuous and silent on his bedside table. He shuffled forward and snuck his hand into his back pocket, almost letting go of the object as it thrummed against his fingers. Yet this rejection was fleeting, with the contact came a connection and all thoughts of what was going on around him seemed irrelevant as he pulled the token free of his pocket and looked down upon it.

The button was glimmering with a brilliant light, turning his palm and fingers to the colour of buttercups, and amongst the glow he could make out a pattern, a circle dissected into wedges, almost like the markings of a compass. He blinked several times as the light became almost too dazzling to behold.

It was the hideous noise from Emily, and the desperate cries from Elmo, that pulled his eyes away from the button. When he espied his friends, the edges of the world seemed to waver, like pennants in the breeze, and without any warning he found the light from the button tingeing the whole room with its glow before his vision was nothing but stark white.

In this blanched void, everything that gave reference was erased. Time appeared to have no meaning, there was nothing for his senses to detect, and his emotions also became redundant—no fear, no anger.

It was as though he was in-between worlds and, aided by his anaesthetised emotional state, he was not at all afraid.

The world beyond began to bleed through the white light. At first Lucas thought he was willing this to happen but it became apparent that, in this netherworld, he had no more influence than he had a compulsion to leave.

Though he was devoid of senses, he did feel something, and this made him sigh with its touch, a pervading feeling of peace washing over him like warm water, relaxing him, making him *belong*.

Colour returned to his vision as though a white curtain had been thrown open to reveal the splendours beyond.

He was on a road, the ground yellowed with sand and grit, a breeze he could not feel ruffling fields of barley, making them as though they were alive.

Overhead there was a huge, bloated sun, yet it gave off no heat.

Further down the track he could see a building in the distance, and he walked towards it, casting no shadow on the ground despite the sunlight.

As he neared, he saw the house; red-bricks made dull with age, the windows black and uninviting, and the uneven, tiled roof patched up with corrugated sheet metal.

His eyes were drawn to a figure sitting on a low, flagstone wall. A young boy, no older than five, was sobbing, his tiny legs swinging, as his training shoes hit grey flagstones.

He was dressed in a blue Star Wars tee-shirt, his unruly mop of brown hair ruffled in the soundless breeze.

"Hello," Lucas said as he approached. "Are you okay?"

The boy looked up, his big blue eyes streaked with tears. "No."

"What's the matter?"

"A nice man took something from me," the boy sniffed. He wiped his snotty nose on the sleeve of his tee-shirt.

"Where did he go?" Lucas asked.

The boy shrugged. "Don't know, but Mummy does."

"Where is your mum?"

"She's in the house," the boy said. "But she's deaf."

"I used to know someone who was deaf," Lucas said, though he couldn't remember who. "Maybe I could talk to your mum about the man?"

"That won't help at all," the boy whined. "That's when she becomes deafer than anything."

"When you talk to her?" Lucas said.

"No," the boy whispered. "When you talk about *the man*."

"Oh. Then how about I go and look for him?" Lucas offered. "Maybe you can come with me? Keep me company? You can point him out when we find him."

"Can't go anyplace but here," the boy said. "This is where I belong."

"Then how will I know it's him?" Lucas asked.

"That's *easy-peasy*," the boy said, leaning forward. "He whistles a tune only we know."

"I'd better keep an ear out, then," Lucas said. "So, which way did he go?"

The boy lifted a small, thin arm and pointed further up the road, where the ground began to incline. Beyond that, there was a hill dotted with trees, their canopies dark green smudges on the landscape.

"You'll need to be quick if you want to catch up with him," the boy said. "He's been gone a long time already."

Lucas acknowledged the boy with a small nod and waved him goodbye. "When I find the man, I will get him to give me back what he took," Lucas said. "What did he take, anyway?"

"Who?" the boy asked with confusion.

"The man?" Lucas urged.

"What man?"

"The *man* we've just been talking about?" Lucas said, slightly puzzled.

The boy jumped down off of the wall, and made his way down the small, overgrown path leading to the house, leaving Lucas to watch him go, his question unanswered.

Lucas headed up the hill, going only a few steps before turning to ask the boy his name. He was not surprised to find that when he did look back, the boy, the house, and the flagstone wall were no longer there.

Emily's body felt as if she had no substance at all, her clothing ruffled under the touch of a cool breeze, her movements feeling deft and unfettered by gravity. Peace pervaded her mind, a kind of serenity she'd not truly experienced, but in the pit of her stomach a churning sensation made her nauseous, making it quite clear that, although it appeared as if she was static, she was in fact travelling.

The destination was as incredible as the means, because one moment she was in Lucas' bedroom, the next she was drifting through, well, wherever this was. The nausea in her gut told her she was descending. She finally hit the ground and rolled unceremoniously until something barred her way.

When she opened her eyes to look up, she saw the ghastly green eyes of a shadowy, buckled figure gazing upon her. Emily realised that somewhere along the line, premonitions and reality had instantly become one and the same.

On the bridge of the yacht, Trevor scowled at Barker.

He'd just given an order and, as usual, the helmsman had merely sneered at him, as though the command held no water with him.

"Get that miserable face out of my sight, Barker,"

Trevor said. "And don't be looking at any dairy products on your way past the food cart, you'll be turning it sour."

Barker grumbled something under his breath as he made to exit the bridge, but Trevor sensed the man knew better than to backchat. The one thing Barker loved more than himself was money, and losing his job would mean he couldn't pretend to anyone he met that he was more than he actually was, a sad counter to his low self-esteem.

It was a mindset that Trevor never made any attempt to understand, for fear it tainted him in some way, like a disease caught whilst handling the sick. His upbringing in Trinidad had been one that fostered pride and honour, concepts Barker wouldn't comprehend if they were stapled to his forehead.

There had not been much money in the family home as Trevor was growing up. He was the second oldest amongst four other siblings, with Gemma his older sister, overseeing the younger children—two girls and a brother—as their father worked long shifts in the local cannery. Winston, Trevor's father, had always made sure his family came first, their mother having passed on from pneumonia when Trevor was only ten years old.

Where others would have been broken, Winston swore he would provide and keep the family safe. And he kept his vow. Trevor learned the value of honour along the way.

He'd left home when his father died in his sleep at the ripe old age of 90. By this time his brother and sisters had established families of their own. Trevor had always found himself succumbing to restlessness that, for a while, he was able to sate with working long hours in the family store.

Then, one day, a sailor happened into the store and regaled a restless Trevor with tales of the sea and the huge, fascinating world that lay beyond the shop shelves. At 30 years of age, Trevor had sold up, given his cut to his siblings, and joined the merchant navy, scrubbing decks and hauling crates.

It was hard, dirty work but he revelled in the freedom, walking out on deck each morning, a vast, endless ocean and the camaraderie of good, hardworking crewmates all around him.

Soon he was to see another side of life on the ocean. The huge ocean yachts moored in the harbours and ports around the world were like glittering jewels bobbing in the tide.

Trevor's nature wasn't a desire to own one, but to crew, sample a scaled down version of oceanic life in his later years. At 40 he joined Redfern's. By 45 he'd met Melville, and had served under him for the last 5 years on various outings. The voyage on *The Spirit of the Ocean* was their first together on a brand new vessel. Trevor finally felt a sense of peace that he'd not truly felt for a considerable time. It was odd, but he actually felt he'd found his place in the world, that he had finally found a home.

Trevor's attention turned to the monitors scattered around the bridge. The screens appeared to sputter, the images rolling for a couple of seconds before switching off completely. Next thing he knew, total darkness had followed.

A cry of frustration escaped his lips as he went for his cell phone, his intention to activate the torch. In the pitch black he heard the doors to the bridge hiss open and an eerie green hue washed over the bridge.

Trevor turned to see twin green orbs hovering a few feet away from him.

"Barker?" he whispered to the sickly gloom.

A terrible chuckle came back at him from the darkness. Trevor shivered with fear as he took an instinctive step backwards, and found the Comms desk blocking his way.

The chuckle came again, thick and wet. Trevor could feel cold breath on his cheek, and a rancid stench of sour milk made him gag.

I guess you did look at the dairy cart after all, he thought.

His trembling fingers found his cell phone, forcing his arm to lift the tiny device as his jittering thumb activated the torch. The beam cast its light into the face of the thing standing mere feet away.

Man and beast screamed as one.

Cotteridge stared blankly at Melville. The detective's mouth shimmied as he chewed his lip in thought. After a few palpable seconds, he spoke and his tone was laced with disbelief.

"Your uncle isn't a Professor Royston Kane of Keele University?" he said.

"I'm not a detective, but the surname kind of gives that away," Melville said looking very bemused.

"People change their names all the time," Cotteridge said. "For many different reasons, I hasten to add. Bad blood, for example. The info I received informs me that the professor is missing and you are his kin."

"Then your info is bad," Melville said, the first signs of impatience beginning to show in his voice. "My father was an only child, and when we get back to port, you can confirm that as a fact."

"As I intend to," Cotteridge said. "Though, I do question how local law enforcement could get something so wrong."

"Are you calling me a liar, detective?"

True justice in search of an unsound crime. The disembodied voice was loud enough to have Cotteridge open his mouth to speak when a distant crash and a piercing scream stalled the exchange.

"What the—?" he said.

"That came from the bridge," Melville said.

Both men were moving quickly soon thereafter, their discussion forgotten.

At Gull Cottage, the front door began to bow inwards. Elmo and Tamsin looked on helplessly from the first floor landing as streaks of jade light punched through the seam where door met frame. A loud snapping came to them as the frame gave out and the whole door flew inwards, the entire hallway suddenly awash with swirling green flame.

On the threshold, Edward stood with his feet planted apart, arms rammed at forty-five degrees, the fingers of each hand splayed and trembling with the energy flowing through him.

"Man, this feels good," he yelled. He laughed and

it was a cold and bitter thing. He aimed his terrible gaze at Elmo. "You need to try this sometime."

"Looks like you've got a handle on it," Elmo said. His face jittered with fear.

"Look what you've done to my front door, you vandal," Tamsin snapped. "When this is done, I'll be coming to your mother for compensation."

Edward appeared completely bemused as he studied her with the same indifference as a scientist would a lab rat.

"When this is all over, fixtures and fittings will be the least of your problems." He put his hands against the doorframe.

"Edward, wait!" Elmo said quickly. "You've got to fight this thing. This is about Primrose Meadowsweet, she's been possessed by a 16th Century witch, and she's using witchcraft to get even with someone on that superyacht. Somehow you're caught up in it, we all are."

Edward tilted his head as he regarded Elmo. "You know how stupid that sounds?"

"I was hoping the green fire and your sudden telekinetic abilities would soften it up a little?"

"This isn't about witches, you idiot," Edward said. "It's much bigger, and I can see it all. The natural, the supernatural, we are all devices in its plan to be free."

Edward stepped into the hallway and green puddles of light marked his passing as he came for the stairs. "Now, where is Lucas Walker?"

"You leave my boy alone," Tamsin cried.

She clutched Elmo's hand as Edward placed his foot on the first riser, his fierce green eyes never leaving them, the smile on his face an evil leer.

"That's *so* not gonna happen," he laughed.

As Edward mounted the staircase, a great wall of flame shot towards the ceiling, which made him cry out in fear. Orange and red plumes fanned out, and neither Elmo nor Tamsin felt any of its heat. Edward screamed as though seared, the flames wrapping around him until he fell backwards and landed in the hallway.

A bolt of yellow flew from the blaze catching Edward in the chest, shoving him back through the doorway and onto the street. The front door flew into its frame as soon as the boy was clear, where it fused into the jamb with a sizzle.

"What was that?" Elmo said, amazed yet grateful.

"Look," Tamsin said.

The sheet of flame remained at the foot of the stairs, yet its surface was now sheer and smooth, like that of a wall. It reminded Elmo of a force-field special effect in a low-budget space movie. As they both looked upon it, the flames lost their intensity and became a dull orange.

Elmo went down to it, again the wall gave out heat, but as he approached a great sense of peace came over him, his fear falling away like a discarded tee-shirt. He found his hand lifting and reaching out towards the light. At its touch, he felt a tingling sensation on his fingertips, and the surface yielded, allowing his digits to pass through for a few centimetres before they met resistance.

"It's protecting us," Elmo said. "But how?"

He scanned the edge of the wall, traced its perimeter across the ceiling, and as it overflowed down the side of the stairs, it sealed off access from the kitchen and back of the house, and effectively cut off any access to them.

As he looked at the base of the barrier, Elmo saw something, an intense circle of light, and he recognised it by shape rather than features.

"It's the button," Elmo said back to Tamsin. "Y'know, you're really going to have to tell me about that thing."

But Tamsin wasn't looking at him when he turned to seek her out. Instead she was looking behind him, up at their newfound barrier, and the look on her face was one of rapture.

Elmo turned back and saw what had garnered Tamsin's attention. His mouth hung open as he shook his head in disbelief.

On the barrier was an image—an orange and yellow landscape in relief, amber clouds crossed tangerine skies, buttercup trees lined honeydew roads. Ambling across this psychedelic vista was a figure, a boy with yellowed, spiked hair.

"Oh, my," Elmo breathed, his eyes blinking several times as he took it in.

"Lucas," Tamsin said with a smile not diminished by her tears.

Chapter Seventeen

BEATRICE'S EYES NEVER left the creatures lurking in the shadows. She took meagre comfort from the contact of Claire's back against hers, both braced and ready for any pending attack. But the nagging thought that Lucas was lost to her mind's eye was difficult to push aside.

Until the thump, thump, thump of something rolling across the deck brought her back to the here and now.

"That's weird," Claire said behind her.

Beatrice couldn't think of anything that could top the creatures in the ballroom, but she went with Claire's assessment.

"What was it?"

"A girl appeared out of nowhere and landed on the deck," Claire said.

Beatrice thought this met the standard. "Yeah, okay, that's pretty weird."

She risked taking a peek over Claire's shoulder. The malformed figure prowled the deck, green eyes glaring, and then to Beatrice's surprise, Emily jumped up and stood up to face the creature as it lunged.

Beatrice moved fast, circumventing Claire, and

reached out to grab the collar of Emily's jacket. Beatrice pulled hard, dragging her friend towards her as the figure came at them with its vicious talons.

Claire drove the boat hook hard into its abdomen, driving it back as she put her full weight behind the assault. The creature slipped over, grabbed at the pole to stay upright but succeeded only in yanking it from Claire's grasp.

"Dammit," she yelled in frustration.

The creature leapt, arms extended, claws slashing. Claire did her best to avoid the onslaught, lifting her hands to fend off the blows. She brought up a foot and caught the beast in the knee. The sound of snapping twigs followed, before the creature went down, howling in pain and anger.

Claire eyed the fallen keel hook and went for it, but the felled creature rallied and launched itself again, fingers splayed—talons at the ready—many finding their mark on Claire's forearms. She cried out as those terrible nails rented and gouged, each wound producing a searing agony.

She collapsed as Beatrice and Emily looked on helplessly, her eyes seeming to see them as if for the first time, before a shadowy figure blocked out everything.

Thomas watched in fascinated horror as the bartender crawled towards him. His back was against a wall and he had literally nowhere to go. The twisted face edged closer to him, drooled, and growled.

"Nice doggy," Thomas whispered as he brandished

the bottle of lime juice he'd sipped from earlier. He raised the bottle as if to throw it. "How about a game of 'fetch'?"

The bartender looked at the bottle and then back at Thomas. In this time the boy threw the bottle so fast that it hit the bartender hard on the forehead, dimming his eyes for a few seconds.

Thomas used this time to jump up, his feet landing on the bartender's back, flattening him out as he hissed and screeched with rage. Thomas cleared the bar.

On the other side he met a sea of bent and buckled shapes. They were crawling around the floor like skulking animals, men and women in dinner jackets and cocktail dresses, all with those livid green eyes, but their heads were not turned towards him, they looked beyond the set of double doors facing the foredeck. Through those doors, he saw a curious sight—Beatrice and Emily, clinging onto each other as another creature swiped at someone on the floor.

To his horror he realised it was Claire.

He began moving towards the foredeck, but he was grabbed around the neck by a thick forearm and lifted back onto the bar. The bartender's rancid breath was hot against Thomas' cheek, and he began to choke as the arm around his throat tightened. He fought furiously, but the constriction only worsened, making his vision fog.

Out of that fog, someone stepped up—a figure in a raincoat and headscarf.

Oh, that's just great, Thomas thought. *I'm about to die and the last person I'll ever see is Edna bleedin' Duffy!*

Despite this, Edna came into view, face grim and eyes fierce, and in her hands was a silver tray. She raised it and brought it down so hard on the bartender's head, it created a dome on its surface. The bartender toppled with a whimpering snarl, and then disappeared behind the bar with a sound of tinkling glass.

Thomas coughed and spluttered as he fought to regain his breath, and Edna grabbed his arm and pulled him towards her.

As Thomas' vision cleared, he could see Dorothy Arnold behind Edna. She was brandishing her umbrella like a sword, her eyes never leaving the throng of gnarled shapes massed by the foredeck doors.

"Come on, young Thomas," Edna said harshly. "We have to be getting topside."

Thomas pulled away from her clutching hands. "My sister is out there. We have to get to her."

Edna sniffed in disdain. "Yeah," she said eventually. "But we're not going to get to her that way. Follow me if you—"

"Want to live?" Thomas said in awe as Edna appeared to be reciting his favourite Arnold Schwarzenegger line.

"If you want to get to your sister," Edna said, pulling a puzzled face. "Come on, Dorothy."

Edna and Dorothy backed away from the throng, and filed out through the ballroom entrance at the back of the room. As Edna went into the darkness of the passageway beyond, Thomas could have sworn she'd uttered the words "stupid boy" under her breath.

As the creature that used to be Barker came for him, Trevor managed to roll backwards, feeling the bite of harsh plastic as monitors dug into his back. He heard the creak and snap as they yielded under his weight, momentum taking him over the desk.

He fell onto the floor on the other side of the console, using Barker's fiery eyes to track his assailant's movements as it stalked him.

Trevor scuttled away on his backside, hands grasping for anything that he could use to protect himself, but he knew the bridge was not a place abundant with loose items. The last thing a crew would need in an emergency was unsecured items flying around the bridge.

In an emergency.

The words came faster than Trevor ever figured possible given his fears, but he was grateful for the hope they gave. Somewhere in the confined space to his left was the emergency locker. And in the locker were items for the bridge-crew should disaster loom.

Trevor could picture the items now: life-jackets, rations, but his primary focus was the bright red flare pistol stowed in its equally vivid crimson case.

Opposite, Barker's glowing eyes began to move to his right, as the creature followed the run of the console. Trevor could hear the click-click of claws on the plastic surface, and the dull thud of the huge leather chairs rocking as he passed by.

Barker sidled around the console, and Trevor moved away from him, using his feet to push his way towards the gloom, where he knew the storage locker sat, flush with the walls, its steel door reflecting Barker's hideous stare.

Trevor moved with caution, his nerves stretched until they were screaming out warnings. Every time he saw those eyes he feared that Barker was almost ready to pounce.

He finally made it to the steel door, using his hands to probe for the rectangular handle in the smooth, cool surface. He found it after a few desperate seconds, and he pulled the mechanism downwards. A loud thud filled the bridge, making Barker hiss a warning.

Trevor pressed on. He fumbled inside the locker, his eyes never leaving Barker. He found the bulky life-jackets, he found a wooden stave and realised that it was a short handled fire axe, and suddenly he didn't feel as vulnerable to the oncoming creature. He held the axe firmly in one hand, ready to strike out if needs be, but his true aim was to keep plenty of distance between him and the Barker-thing. To this end, he continued to seek out the orange case that he knew housed the flare pistol.

He found it, and pulled it to him, desperately trying to open it with one hand as he held up the axe to ward off the approaching figure.

Barker turned the corner, only twenty feet away from him, and snarls came short and sharp.

"I can see you, Trevor," Barker hissed in a voice that didn't really sound like its owner at all. "I don't think you're going to be able to load that thing before I get to you and introduce you to my claws."

Trevor waved the axe as a reminder. "I still got this, Barker, and I'll bury it into that malicious skull of yours if you come any closer. Don't think that I won't!"

Barker chuckled. "Oh, I think you'll try, but it won't do you any good. You'll be dead before the axe falls. Then you'll become just like me, and we'll live forever. Won't that be great?"

Trevor's breath stalled in his throat as Barker's laughter filled the bridge. "I'd rather die than be what you are, and that was before you changed into whatever the hell you are now."

Barker gave out a roar and came at the fallen man, but Trevor had been busy while he taunted the creature. The flare gun was now in his hands and primed with a cylinder. The gun looked painfully small and insignificant but he knew it was all he had.

Barker charged him down, and Trevor gave out a strangled cry as he lifted the pistol, his hands shaking wildly. He discharged the flare, and it streaked towards Barker like some misguided firework, striking him in the face with a spectacular shower of red sparks.

One of the green orbs disappeared and Barker screamed out in pain, his corrupt shape staggering around the bridge as his clothes caught fire. The creature beat at the flames as it fell against the bulkhead, rolling along the walls in a frenzied attempt to douse the blaze. The gestures proved futile, and the figure eventually collapsed in a fiery heap on the console.

Trevor stood on legs that threatened to fail at any moment. Barker's conflagration was now ebbing away. Then Trevor looked down on him and, to his disbelief, saw nothing but a pile of ruined clothes where the man had once been.

Another sound came to him, a thin scream that rose from the foredeck. He rushed to the window and saw shapes below. For a moment, he thought it was Barker stalking some people on the deck, then he realised this creature was taller and wore a dinner jacket.

There was someone on the ground and the creature was strafing them with claws.

Without another thought, Trevor took the axe and frantically went to work on the window.

After yanking Emily out of the way of the creature, Beatrice moved without thought, charging at the beast as it clawed at Claire, who was desperately trying to fend it off.

Beatrice pulled up short, her right leg already drawn back, the pause was momentary, and then she delivered a significant kick to the malformed head, rocking it, sending it snapping sideways, and knocking the hideous body off balance.

As it fell, Beatrice and Emily took hold of Claire, and pulled her along the deck, the glistening teak slats making the process easier than Beatrice thought possible.

But the beast came again from the shadows, its whole body shuddered and Beatrice saw the fury in its eyes.

A cascade of glass fell from the sky, tinkling as it bounced on the deck. Beatrice looked upwards and saw the bizarre sight of an arm jutting through a hole in one the windows overlooking them. There was a loud pop then a sizzling hiss as a streak of light flew down, trailing thick acrid smoke. There was a blinding explosion of bloodshot sparks, cutting off the creature's advance, and making it shriek with fear, before scuttling off to the darkness.

The flare continued to fizz and sputter on the deck, keeping it at bay, while throwing bizarre light across the boat. Claire was sitting upright in the gaudy light, arms covered in a lattice of long, black gashes.

Beatrice looked around her, seeking out some way off the foredeck without having to go through the ballroom. Emily got her attention by tugging at her arm, and Beatrice found strength from seeing her friend. Beatrice and Emily went and helped Claire to her feet, each of them careful not to touch the vicious wounds.

"Don't believe we've met," Claire winced as she spoke to Emily. "I'm Claire."

"Emily. No time to chat, though. Busy, busy. Let's go that way."

She pointed to her left. Beatrice turned and saw the narrow walkway separating the exterior walls of the ballroom from the railings on the side of the boat. There was a thin chain fencing off access, but Beatrice nodded in agreement.

"Lead the way," Beatrice said to Emily, and gave her friend a grateful smile.

Yet Emily appeared suddenly confused making Beatrice peer at her.

"What's wrong?" she said carefully. "Are you okay?"

Emily closed her eyes as though clearing her thoughts. Beatrice put a hand on her shoulder to get her attention.

"Emily, you need to look at me," Beatrice said softly. "Otherwise you won't be able to read my lips."

Emily opened her eyes. "I don't need to read them. I can hear you."

Beatrice blinked. "Hear me?" She put a hand to her mouth in shock.

"It's not hearing exactly," she said. "It like the voice is in my head a few seconds after you've said it, like a badly streamed movie."

Beatrice shook her head in amazement. "I can't believe it."

"Neither can I," Emily said. "But for now I'll take it. Then wonder what it all means once we get out of here."

Beatrice nodded.

Out of all the incredible things happening, getting out of it all in one piece seemed the most far-fetched of all.

Beatrice carefully ushered Claire forward as Emily unfastened the chain link garland.

"What's happening?" Claire said.

They looked back and saw the brightness from the flare was sputtering out.

"Not sure yet," Beatrice said. "But we've got to get off this deck before those things in the ballroom decide to come outside and get some sea air."

They all looked towards the ballroom and the many, many green orbs looking back at them through the black windows. Bloated palms occasionally slapped against the glass, testing the barrier.

Claire nodded and Beatrice saw some of the strength return to the woman's eyes. "Let's go," she said.

Emily led the way, Claire followed, and Beatrice hung back, keeping an eye on the creature beyond the dying flare, and those following their path through the dark panes on their left.

Claire stumbled and groaned as she grabbed the rail at the side of the boat.

Beatrice went to her, dismayed at the wounds on Claire's pale arms. The slash marks were deep in places and blood oozed down her wrists and their touch dulled the glittering railings.

Claire slipped the bedraggled cream shawl from her shoulders and tore the material into two pieces, skilfully wrapping them around her forearms, as Beatrice supported her.

"Nice work," Beatrice said. "First aid course?"

Claire tested the movement in her arms and grimaced. "Girl Guides. You should see what I can do with bed sheets and a washing line. It'll be fine until I can get to a first aid kit. Thanks."

She looked behind Beatrice. Eyes pained yet alive with anger. "Damn things aren't even following."

"Then that's a good thing," Beatrice replied.

"Is it?" Claire said. "Experience tells me that wild animals wait until their prey is at its most vulnerable. Maybe that's what all this is about."

Beatrice thought this over. She turned to look back at the creature on the foredeck, which stood motionless, watching them from the chain link barrier.

"Let's keep moving," Beatrice whispered, nudging Claire forward, their steps uncertain against the rise and fall of the ocean. Beatrice clung to the rail, her hand touched a smear of blood left by Claire, and a jolt—akin to that of static—made her look down at her fingers. Droplets of blood were paused in mid-air, their fall to the water arrested by some strange magic.

Elizabeth's magic.

Then the droplets fell to the water, where they should have been lost to the waves. Beatrice could see that for every drop that fell, a green pool appeared on impact with the swell.

A great thunder clap echoed around the ship, so loud that both Beatrice and Claire slapped their hands to their ears, and Emily sensed the vibrations through the boat's infrastructure, and looked about her in fear.

By the time the rumbling din had faded, the ocean, the clouds and the very world around them had disappeared.

The silence was total.

Chapter Eighteen

THE OAK TREE was huge and from where Lucas stood, its shape reminded him of a piece of broccoli. The great trunk was thick and gnarled, the leaves spreading like a vast canopy of deep jade. This magnificent symbol of nature sat alone in a green field, an azure, cloudless sky as a backdrop. Lucas ambled up the hill. There was no such thing as urgency in a place such as this. His heart maintained the sense of peace he had carried since . . .

When?

He wasn't sure, and when he thought about it he realised the matter was not important. He stalled and looked back down the hill, his journey marked by the path he'd trampled into the deep, emerald grass.

At the bottom of the hill, the fields went on for as far as the eye could see, a writhing mass, making it difficult to focus. For some reason the image of a house with a patched roof and a small boy sitting on a wall came to mind but it drifted away before he could grasp at it.

He shook his head, a smile spreading across his face at the oddities going on around him, within him.

Lucas saw movement at the base of the tree. He

squinted to sharpen his vision and there, sitting with her back against the mighty trunk, was a young woman.

He figured she was in her twenties, and her hair was almost as blue as the sky. She wore lemon dungarees, with a white tee-shirt underneath. The woman looked up as Lucas neared, the smile on her face was at odds with the tears that rolled down her face.

"Are you okay?" Lucas asked.

"Oh, don't you worry about me," the woman chuckled. "This is the way we get through the tough times."

"Who is 'we'?"

"Parents," she explained. "It's called 'putting on a brave face', and makes sure we keep the kids from the bad stuff for just a little bit longer."

"I see," said Lucas. Somewhere far away, he didn't think he could 'see' anything at all.

He noticed a small box in the woman's lap. Her tears fell on the lid with small, intermittent taps.

"What's in the box?"

"Memories," she said. "It's all he leaves behind."

"He?"

"Would you like to see?" the woman said.

Before Lucas could respond, she tilted her head and the rivulets from her eyes changed direction, moving diagonally down her cheeks and neck where they seeped into the collar of her tee-shirt.

She opened the lid of the box, and there came a great light from within it. This brilliance did not stream out, though. It oozed like luminous milk escaping from the bottle, coursing over the sides, corporeal and dense. The woman scooped out the contents and Lucas looked upon a small pile of brass buttons, each with a wedged circle.

"It's what he leaves for us to follow," she explained, though Lucas didn't really need an explanation. This place didn't require him to fully understand its nuances.

"So why are you staying here?" Lucas asked.

"Everything has its place, and this is mine." She dropped the buttons back in the box, and then closed the lid, streaks of light remaining on the surface like silver scars. "Besides, he is always passing through these parts. Until he comes around again, I have my box of buttons to keep me company."

"Haven't you ever thought of going with him?" he said. "Then you wouldn't have to wait for him to come back?"

The woman appeared pensive, as though such a notion had never occurred to her. Eventually she shook her head.

"Everything has its place and mine is here," she repeated. "That is the way it is for me."

Lucas nodded. "I get that, but I'm thinking where does that leave me?"

"Some people stay put," the woman said. "Others choose to follow. Sometimes we can search forever when what we're looking for is never truly lost at all."

"Is that what the man is doing, searching for something?"

The woman sighed, the tears still flowing, the smile as radiant as the buttons in the box.

"The horizon hides our dreams," she said looking to her left, where the hill met the sky in an arc of writing green grass. "Maybe you should take a peek beyond it."

There was a dull *whooshing* noise as the wind ruffled the boughs overhead. Lucas looked up as small objects fell down from the tree and onto the grass like silent tears, and the ground became speckled with buttons, the tree spilling them from its branches like overripe fruit unfit for harvest.

He held out his hands and laughed as the tiny objects patted against his arms, shimmering raindrops that filled him with delight and wonder.

"Maybe this is why you stay here," he said. "It's amazing."

The woman did not reply and Lucas made no attempt to move his eyes away from the beautiful sight falling from the tree. Not because it was a mesmerising, but because he already knew if he did seek the woman out, he'd find that she would not be there.

"What the hell's happening?" Melville yelled as he marched onto the bridge. "Number One, report!"

Trevor stepped away from the ruined window, his arm hanging limply at his side still clutched the flare pistol. Smoke drifted up from the barrel, turned cream by the dying embers on the console.

"Trevor?" Melville snapped.

He looked up, face dazed. He saw his captain was with another man, wearing a heavy coat and glasses with yellow lenses. He couldn't help but feel the newcomer seemed out of place on the bridge.

But so did the smouldering remains of their navigator!

"Trevor?" Melville said again. This time his tone was softer. "What's going on?"

"Crazy things, Captain." Trevor's voice trembled. "Bad things."

Cotteridge approached the ruined clothing. "Is that a *man*?"

"His name was Barker," Trevor said.

"Are we saying there's been a death here?" Cotteridge's asserted.

Trevor looked at the man in the coat.

"It's okay, Trevor," Melville said. "He's a police officer."

"A *detective*. Cotteridge, in fact," he said firmly, peering at Trevor. "Did you kill this man?"

"It was no man when I shot it," Trevor said. "Neither were those things I saw below on the foredeck."

Melville went the window and peered out, his face going pale as he surveyed the seascape.

"This area is a crime scene," Cotteridge said. He looked at Trevor. "And I will ask you, sir, to put the weapon on the floor."

Melville gazed down at the foredeck, eyes widening. "Before you start reading my First Officer his rights, Cotteridge, I think you need to know we have bigger issues."

Cotteridge went over to him, his eyes watching Trevor with suspicion, but by the time he looked out and saw what was going on outside, all thoughts of crime and arrests left him.

The insistent buzz of a cell phone came from Lucas' room and Elmo rushed back inside, leaving Tamsin to stare at the image of her lost son as he walked across surreal landscapes.

No sooner had Elmo disappeared from view when a cry of anguish brought Tamsin to the here and now, and she ploughed through the door.

Elmo was staring down at the bed, hands clasped to his head, incredulous.

"She's gone," he said, his voice weak. "Emily's gone, too!"

He turned to Tamsin. She was staring, eyes bleary as though she'd only just woken.

The phone continued to buzz and Elmo sought it out, eventually finding it beneath the chair Emily had been sitting on before she'd collapsed. As he scanned the screen he saw several messages from Patience.

He hit the return call dial.

"Elmo? Where the hell have you guys been?" Patience sound both maddened and relieved in the same hit.

"Patience," Elmo breathed. "You need to be quiet for a few seconds. Can you do that?"

The silence from the phone told him that Patience really could do that. He took in air, held it, and then explained everything that had happened, right up until Lucas' image on the light barrier. Throughout his retelling, Elmo was looking down at the spot where he'd left Emily.

Tamsin was no longer with him. She had left the

room while he was bringing Patience up to speed, and he couldn't blame her. If he had the chance to see if Emily and Beatrice were okay he'd take it, too.

When he'd finished, Patience sounded exasperated. "So you're saying Lucas and Emily have disappeared, and you're being protected from a possessed Edward Chorley by a magical force field, which has Lucas inside it?"

"That's pretty much it," Elmo agreed. "Though, I'm not sure if Edward is actually that possessed, he still seems pretty much the same to me. Magic powers, aside, of course. But we have found Lucas. There could be a way of getting through to him. We need to find out if he can tell us where he is, how we can help him, maybe the others, too."

"We still don't know what's truly going on," Patience said. "The words I saw on the screen said it was a curse. That points to Elizabeth."

"But Edward said it was more than that," Elmo reminded her.

"So we believe sixteen-year-old sociopaths these days?"

"Sixteen-year-old sociopaths with green *fire eyes*," Elmo said. "It helps to *emphasise*."

"Then if it isn't about Elizabeth, then what are the alternatives?" Patience said. "This now involves all of our friends. How can that be?"

Elmo thought it over.

"You still there?" Patience said.

"Thinking."

"That's not your best skill set," she pointed out.

"Cute," he muttered. Then a small groan came from him.

"It's hurting that much?"

"The words you saw were from the Cryptic Crypt," Elmo said.

"Oh, now we're playing the 'let's-say-out-loud-what-we-already-bloody-know' game?"

Elmo pressed on. "What I'm saying is those words were meant to be found and meant to be said. Maybe they were meant to be said when the time was right. If this was about Elizabeth, surely she'd just evoke the curse and not need you to do it."

Patience acquiesced. "Okay. Go on."

"The script was old. Even you said that. I think older than Elizabeth Caldecott's era," Elmo said. "And based on our insider information from the sixteen-year-old sociopath, this is much bigger than witches."

"I don't understand," Patience said. "We know there are artefacts from The Raven on the superyacht. We know that Elizabeth thinks the captain is related to the man who executed her and her mother. It still points to her."

"And Edward?" Elmo asked.

"He's just under her influence," Patience offered but there was a lack of conviction in her voice. "The curse has been evoked and is now in play."

"It's time to get logical," Elmo said. "What is it the curse has done so far? Facts we know are: Lucas and Emily have disappeared, Edward has gone all Scooby-Doo, and we have a fireworks display on the stairway."

"Yes, but that's all we know about," Patience replied.

"We're missing something for sure," Elmo said. "Because all of this makes no sense if we go with the 'witch's revenge' angle. What else have we got?"

Patience clucked her tongue as she thought. The sounds seemed thick in the speaker. Eventually she came back,

"Remember the waiting room, when Beatrice saw Primrose as Lizzy?"

"Yes," Elmo said slowly.

"Primrose recited a poem. The same words that Thomas wrote out for Beatrice."

Patience recited it:

> *"Water and blood from the Amazon join,*
> *True justice in search of an unsound crime,*
> *Curses and blessings, one and the same,*
> *Places are taken at the heart of the game"*

"That's the one," he said. "No mention of revenge as far as I can see."

"Lucas already looked at this, right? There's no history or areas in the Amazon that had any meaning, just rivers and jungles. And online shopping, of course. That reminds me, I need to put this year's *Black Friday Sale* date in my calendar."

"You never quit, do you?" he said.

"It helps me think," Patience said with petulance. "One of us has to. Besides, you said be logical, I'm just going through different meanings of the word."

"I'll let you off this once," he said softly. "Only because it's an emergency."

Elmo rubbed his eyes, and blinked away fatigue. As his vision cleared he found himself looking at Lucas' bookshelf, and his heart sank as he surveyed the spines of books his friend loved so much. There were copies of The Hardy Boys and Nancy Drew, The Three

Investigators and The Secret Seven, as well as modern mystery thrillers by authors such as Lee Child and James Patterson. But there were also older novels that Elmo recalled as movies on TCM but had never read. He saw Treasure Island and Ivanhoe, Tom Sawyer and Robinson Crusoe.

He shook his head, trying to remove some of the negative thoughts rattling around in there. He had feared the worse for Lucas but the image on the flickering wall had given him some hope, as slim as that may have been. He paced the room, and happened across a small pile of comic books, Lucas' other passion, and when he saw the cover of a Justice League edition, his mouth fell open with a small gasp.

"At last," Patience said in his ear. "We have life."

"Amazon isn't talking about a place," he said in a hush. He stooped and picked up the comic. "Amazon's are warrior women, just like *Wonder Woman*."

"Wonder Woman?" Patience sounded sceptical.

"Well, not *exactly* like Wonder Woman," he corrected. "But like the Greek myth. Y'know, Apollo's race of warrior women?"

"Apollo," she repeated sounding increasingly vague. "I think I preferred it when you were being quiet."

"Rude. Let's get back to the poem," he said. "It talked about the Blood of the Amazon, right? Who do we know who is like, you know, a warrior?"

Patience started. "Beatrice!"

Elmo calmed her. "It can't be Beatrice, she's protected right?"

As he said this Elmo had a thought that rocked

him, and the thought he had was a catalyst for several others that came in quick succession.

"Claire Drill is the Amazon, Patience," he said with total conviction. "And you're right, Beatrice *is* protected. But now she's on the boat with Claire, and she was always meant to be on that boat, just like those words in the crypt were always meant to be said."

He paused to allow it all to sink in.

"This isn't a curse, Patience," he said. "It's a trap."

Melville and Cotteridge looked out on the emptiness beyond the window. Trevor was on the other side of the bridge watching the exit, flare pistol primed and ready.

"How did this happen?" Cotteridge said.

"You're the detective," Melville replied without taking his eyes away from the darkness outside.

"And you are the sailor, Captain. This is more your arena than mine."

"This boat is no longer on the ocean," Melville said. "I've never seen anything like this in my entire life."

Cotteridge wiped his brow with a sigh. "I doubt anyone ever has. Still, it is my experience that all things happened for a reason. They will have cause and motive, as would a crime."

"What the hell does that mean?" Trevor said, staring down the corridor beyond the exit.

"Who? How? And why," Cotteridge explained. "The ingredients for solving a transgression."

"Right now we have to focus on more immediate matters," Melville said.

"I'm wondering if there's anything more immediate than falling off of the world?" Cotteridge mused.

"The safety of everyone aboard this boat?" Melville offered.

Cotteridge acknowledged him with a nod. "Very well, Captain. What do you suggest?"

Melville was about to speak when something brushed against the detective's hand making Cotteridge shudder. He flailed his arm around and took an involuntary step backwards, almost stepping onto Trevor's plimsoll.

"Hey, I got enough on my plate without you breaking my foot," Trevor protested.

Cotteridge smiled with embarrassment but his eyes were alert and keeping an eye on the floor, even though it was too gloomy to see anything in detail.

"My apologies, I thought it may have been a spider. They are a pet fear of mine. The mere presence has me all of a dither."

Trevor gave him a firm look and then his face softened. "I guess we all have our fears," he said. "I'm not above such things. I hate bats, ever since I got one caught up in my jacket when I was on leave, and it scared me to death. Take our captain here—he's so terrified of pythons, he checks under his desk as if he's going to find one on a boat."

Melville scowled. "Thanks for that, Trevor. Now perhaps you could see your way to making sure that corridor is clear."

Trevor peered through the glass doors. Emergency lighting in the walls gave off a murky, cream light, and it hinted at nothing sinister lurking ahead.

"Clear," Trevor said. He forced open the doors and stepped through, pistol trained on the way ahead. "I'll go and check to see if the coast is clear."

Melville agreed. "You make sure you stay safe. No heroics, that's an order."

"You got it, Skipper."

Trevor made his way down the passageway, his eyes keeping close attention on the run of doors on the right. Three-quarters of the way in, he could see that the double doors of the boardroom were blasted outwards. The edges were ragged and splintered, one of them rested against the opposite wall.

With caution he edged forwards, the pistol shaking slightly in his hand. He took comfort from knowing the flares were effective against the things roaming the boat, but he was also aware he only had four of them left, one inside the pistol, and the others in his back pockets.

As he neared the broken doors, Trevor could see the floor was obscured with an undulating fog, turned dirty grey by the emergency lights embedded in the carpet runners. This thick smog seemed to pulsate as it moved, as though alive, and tendrils reached up as it made contact with the walls and ruined doors.

Trevor paused, reluctant to pass through it for fear it would grab him like some deep-sea creature he'd heard tales of on his travels across the oceans of the world. He'd once heard a story from a drunken fisherman of how a giant octopus had dragged a trawler and her crew down to their doom.

Cussing at his stupidity, he walked up to the edge of the fog's borders and gingerly nudged it with the toe of his plimsoll. His foot went through and the mist yielded at his touch.

Despite his puerile fears being unfounded, he still sighed, and found himself catching his breath. He turned to his right, peering into the boardroom and saw the damage within.

All the display cases were obliterated; the surface of the boardroom table was warped like a vinyl record left in the sun. It was an amazing yet unsettling sight. However, this didn't come close to the horror of the thin, charred arm rising from the fog further inside the room.

Its fingers were hooked, and in its palm was a glittering object he recognised as one of the items from the display cases.

A compass.

"Captain! You need to come see this!" Trevor called back to the bridge

Trevor watched as Melville and Cotteridge moved quickly down the corridor towards him, their slight pause as they saw the fog absolving him of his own initial misgivings.

Melville looked into the boardroom, his eyes settling on the arm as it rose from the fog like an ancient tree in the early morning mist.

Cotteridge's eyes widened, and without warning went into the room, striding through the fog, creating a wake that sent it lapping like water against the walls.

Melville looked at Trevor. "Keep watch."

With that Melville followed Cotteridge, and found him down on his haunches examining the body on the floor, his fingers absently rubbing his chin.

"Burnt to a crisp," he said at Melville's approach.

With a grim face, the captain looked down at the owner of the arm. The fog seemed to have washed away from this part of the room, and the ghastly image of a charred skeleton, its lower jaw askew, stared at the ceiling through empty sockets. Around the scrawny, charred neck was an oval pendant; remarkably untouched by the inferno that had consumed its owner.

"I recognise this pendant," Melville said. "This is Mayor Codd's aide, Primrose Meadowsweet."

Cotteridge looked down at the remains. "Yes, I've met her. Poor woman. Did she have free rein over the boat this evening?"

"No, and definitely not in here," Melville whispered. "Only Clive Redfern and I have access."

"The state of the doors suggest not," Cotteridge said.

Melville reached up to take the compass from the charred hand, his face pulled into a grimace.

Cotteridge placed his fingers on the captain's outstretched arm. "What are you doing?"

"Taking a closer look," Melville said. "It may mean something."

"It means that someone died for it, Captain," Cotteridge said. "And therefore it is evidence."

Melville's face flushed with anger and impatience. "Are you out of your mind, Cotteridge? We're in pretty bad shape here, in case you may not have noticed. Can I remind you that we're hanging in empty space or do you need to take another look out of the window? Normal rules do not apply here. Do you understand that?"

Cotteridge looked back, impassive. After a few seconds he nodded. "Very well, Captain. I shall follow your lead."

Melville grunted with impatience and carefully held the edges of the compass. He pulled gently, feeling resistance from the crisped fingers hooked around its circumference, one of them cracked and fell off as he finally lifted it free.

The compass was a perfect golden circle, the face white, and the needle black and fashioned into arrowheads on either end. He realised immediately it was not the compass from the display case in his cabin.

Fascinated, Melville turned the device over.

"There's an inscription on the back," he said. He held it up so that he could see it in the light from Cotteridge's torch. A small hiss of surprise came from his lips.

On the base of the compass was an inscription, engraved in spidery script:

The Raven, 1587—Let the past be your guide.

"This isn't possible," Melville said.

"Weren't you the one who just said the rules have changed?" Cotteridge said.

Melville accepted the criticism without comment. "This cannot be from the vessel it claims on the inscription. The Raven would have had a large compass made of card. Compasses of the size and design I'm holding here were not turned out until over a century later. However, The Raven most certainly had an astrolabe, a circular device designed to measure the latitude between the North Star—Polaris as it is known—and the horizon. It helped navigators guide the ship within a few degrees of true North."

"Fascinating," Cotteridge said with sincerity. "Then we are wrong to assume it has no significance. Logic dictates it would not be here unless it is important to events.”

The two men looked at each other and an understanding passed between them.

“Primrose was trying to guide us, even in death,” Cotteridge said.

“How so?” Cotteridge said.

“This compass is Fool’s Gold—it should not exist and points us to the true means to escape this void.”

Cotteridge appeared puzzled. “I don’t follow you.”

“The Raven’s astrolabe is on the top deck, embedded in the floor, behind a glass portal,” Melville explained. “Other than a wooden plaque, it is the only other item ever recovered from that fated vessel.”

“And what does this astrolabe look like?” Cotteridge asked.

“A brass disc made up of three concentric plates, and markings for plotting a course. Redfern said it came from an antiques faire. We saw the plaque and the astrolabe being on this vessel as a good omen. Now I say different. I say it is by design.”

“The compass and the astrolabe, they mean something,” Cotteridge said. “We must keep this in mind as more clues arise.”

Just then Trevor called into the room. “Skipper, I hear a ruckus from the aft-deck!”

With that Cotteridge and Melville jumped up and went to the shattered doors. Trevor looked back at them, his eyes seeking out guidance.

“What do we do, Skipper?” he said.

Cotteridge listened at the din coming from further down the corridor. It was a mix of screams and curses, and the sound of heavy thumps.

"Well, we are all public servants at this dreadful time," Melville said. "So I guess we must do our duty."

With that, the three men made for the aft-deck, and whatever horrors lay in wait for them.

Chapter Nineteen

FOR THE FIRST time in what seemed like forever, Beatrice felt genuinely terrified. Not scared, or afraid, not anxious or the many other nouns that she'd heard people describe how they felt when confronted with their worst fears. This was bone-chilling, brain-seizing fear, the kind that robbed rational thought, the kind that turned each chamber of her heart to ice water.

The land was gone. The sea was gone. Overhead the nebulous clouds and the stars in between were gone. All around the boat was an endless nothingness, so complete that it appeared both small and vast at the same time.

This was *The Darkness.* She knew this with a certainty that almost had her legs collapsing beneath her. Her arms were heavy, hanging at her sides like they were as useless as her situation.

"Well, I said I wanted to be in space but this isn't quite what I had in mind," Claire breathed beside her. "And here I thought this couldn't get any worse."

Beatrice tried to speak but nothing came except for an indiscernible squeak.

Emily was suddenly with them and she grabbed at Beatrice's wrist. "We have to go," she said.

Beatrice took this in and began to laugh, incredulous. "Go? Go where? Look around, there's no place *to* go! We're in the world of The Dark Heart, Emily! There's no going anywhere!"

Beatrice yanked her arm away and the look in Emily's eyes was one of both surprise and hurt. She turned from Beatrice, and held a hand out to Claire. "You coming or do you want to give up, too?"

At Emily's words, Beatrice became consumed with anger, she chased after her friend, footfalls heavy and dull. She reached out and grabbed Emily's shoulder, spinning her around, ignoring the yellow hair that slapped into her own face.

"Given up?" Beatrice yelled, tears of rage spangling her vision. "Why wouldn't I? This is for *me*, don't you get it? All of this is to get me here, so The Dark Heart can end me!"

Emily knocked Beatrice's hand away from her shoulder. "Maybe you should let it," she spat, her own tears falling. "Then all of *this* would end, and there would be no one left to care."

Beatrice slapped Emily hard, the action fast, giving the deaf girl no chance to prevent it. Her head snapped right, the force of the blow sending tears arching through the air, and Emily stumbled onto the aft-deck where she crashed into a seating area. In effect, it was a lounge exposed to the elements, complete with a fixed dining table under an awning.

"Hey! Beatrice, stop!" Claire said, voice firm but panic shaving the edges. She tried to reach out for Beatrice but her arms were batted away. She gasped in pain and fell against the railings.

Beatrice went after Emily—hands balled into fists—

and managed to corner her on a sofa, raining down punches as Emily fought desperately to fend them off. She took blows to the shoulders and rib cage, but managed to kick out, catching Beatrice in her stomach and winding her. Emily retaliated with her own assault, grabbing Beatrice's hair, dragging her to the floor where she began to claw and scratch at her exposed arms and neck.

Emily lifted her right foot in an attempt to deliver a blow to the ribs, and in desperation Beatrice clutched at her left leg, toppling her over. Emily hit the deck hard, her breath knocked from her, and Beatrice grasped the girl's flaxen hair and pulled hard with her left hand, nails seeking out her face as both of them rolled heavily around the deck.

"Stop it, hellcats," came a voice from above them. Several blows came down on them both from a rather battered umbrella, and Beatrice and Emily were distracted enough to separate and look up panting as Dorothy stood over them, her face pulled into a mask of disdain.

"With all that's going on here, you two go at it like hammer and tongs?" Edna said behind Dorothy.

"She started it," Beatrice said with venom.

"And we'll sure as Heaven's end it," Edna snapped back.

"This doesn't have anything to do with you," Emily spat. "It's between me and this bitch!"

"Listen to you," Edna said. "How many time have you been keen to tell us old uns how grown up you are, and now at the first sign of trouble we get kid's stuff? You ought to be ashamed, Beatrice Beecham. People have lost a lot to make sure you earn respect in this town."

The rage surged through Beatrice again. She eased herself up onto her feet, hair as wild as the look in her eyes.

"You better get away from me, Edna," Beatrice snarled. "Or I might not be responsible for what happens to you."

"How dare you threaten Edna, you young upstart," Dorothy said raising her umbrella.

"Yes," Edna said with equal disgust. "Show your elders some respect."

"Maybe our elders don't deserve respect," Emily said suddenly to Beatrice. "Maybe they should be put down like the useless dogs they are?"

Beatrice thought that this made sense, there was a fire in her belly and the heat made her feel powerful, it made her feel superior to anyone or anything in the world. She took a step forward and that was when Thomas came from the shadows and upended a silver bucket of iced water over his sister's head.

The shriek was long and hard, and then Beatrice flopped to the floor, Thomas managing to catch her before she caught her head on a handrail.

They all watched as Emily began to swoon too, and she toppled sideways, landing in a heap next to Beatrice, leaving the group of bewildered spectators to look down at them in silence.

Lucas looked down onto the meadow below, a sea of long green grass moving backwards and forwards like anemone in the gentle swirl of the ocean currents. He'd reached the brow of the hill without looking back on his progress. He had a dim recollection of meeting someone beneath a tree but he couldn't quite recall who it was and what he'd said to them.

He did, however, remember that buttons fell from the tree and that he should continue looking for a man who he needed to find. His heart felt lighter when he considered what it would be like to speak to the elusive wanderer once he'd caught up with him. Lucas had questions, but whenever he tried to formulate them, he found himself forgetting soon afterwards.

Instead, he decided to wait until he found the guy and wing it on the questions. Lucas heard the bell toll, and looked east. The sky was the colour of tangerines, and the clouds crawled like jaundiced balls of cotton wool. He smiled as one of the clouds appeared to look like a large boy waving frantically in the unfelt breeze.

Lucas shook his head, this place was *so* funny.

When he looked back towards the meadow, he found it was no longer there and his mind soon began to forget it ever was. In its place was an expanse of dark rocks and blackened trees. Here and there, swirling grey eddies crossed the ground, the dust spinning at such a rate, flecks of silver could be seen in the vortex.

The sky overhead had also become muted, as though reflecting the landscape below, the orange fading, the gun-metal clouds seeping through like a cheap stage set, the horizon becoming a black streak.

Lucas walked until the uneven ground became rugged boulders that became difficult to navigate. As he clambered over the boulders, thick bushes with vicious thorns did their best to snag his clothes while, draped over the rocks, thick, snake-like vines threatened to trip him up.

"Someone doesn't want to make his easy," he chuckled, not knowing or understanding just how close he was to the truth.

Agnes rifled through the paperwork that both her and Maud had compiled the previous evening. Her thoughts were turning to going up to her apartment and making a nice, big mug of cocoa when a small sound came to her from deep within the library.

At first she thought she was imagining it, putting it down to tiredness. Then it came again, a series of tiny clicks, until the unmistakable sound of a bell rang out.

She stood, her eyes going to one part of the library that was reserved for the staff. The sign on a plain door said as much and Agnes often wondered if the library had ever had such a thing as 'staff.'

Beyond the door was a small office, and on a small desk was an Underwood typewriter—an ancient thing made up of black paint and dull silver metal—that she still used to keep her records up to date. Yes, she enjoyed using the sophisticated referencing systems of her PC, but nothing could replace the visceral splendour of punching out the title of a reference book on an index card. She'd happened across it by chance in a charity shop a few years ago, not believing that someone could ever give up such a beautiful machine. She felt duty-bound to treat it with the respect its previous owner obviously had given it.

The Underwood was well-maintained and serviced in town every year. Parts were few and far between these days, but she always managed to find them online, somehow, somewhere. Part of her knew that someday she would run out of luck and the machine would be retired and redundant.

"A little like you, Clutterbuck," she whispered with a wry, sad smile.

The clickety-click of heavy keys hitting the platen came again and Agnes moved, her soft shoes barely making any sound.

She went up to the office door and put her hand on the handle.

The sound stopped.

"Your old ears are playing tricks on you again, old girl," she said.

But no sooner had she spoken when the unmistakable sound of typing began again, and with her heart fluttering in her chest she pushed open the door.

At the centre of the small room, the Underwood was frantically typing out, the keys depressing under their own volition. Amazed, the librarian tentatively approached the machine, and watched the type guide and the ribbon vibrator, lifting and shaking, the type bars hitting the cylindrical platen, the carriage moving until a small bell pinged, and to her amazement, the 'carriage return' activated without visible help, the cylinder flying back to the right where it began the process all over again.

There were no sheets of paper in situ, and Agnes went immediately over to a cabinet made from dark, scratched wood. She pulled out a pack of A4 vellum and thumped it down on the table.

The typewriter stopped instantly and Agnes feared

that she may have broken the spell. She continued, however, and used the time to place the sheet into the paper feed with a few twists of the roller on the side of the machine.

She had just managed to lock the paper in place when the typing started up again and Agnes looked down at the words as they appeared on the sheet. For a few seconds her eyes struggled to focus, the words were coming so fast, but then she was able to see exactly what was being written. She covered her mouth in total shock, the sound of the bell ringing over and over.

Soon the sheet filled and the paper was ejected, the Underwood's whole metal carcass shuddered and stalled, bringing a terrible silence to the room.

Agnes ignored this and picked up the piece of paper. She looked down at it.

On the sheets were two words printed out, first as one continuous sentence repeated over and over, until halfway down the page and the words separated, becoming legible from the endless blocks of text.

Two simple words, but their impact was staggering.

FORGIVE ME.

Agnes took another sheet of paper and fed it into the Underwood. She tried to ignore the fact that her hands were shaking.

On the clean sheet she typed three words.

WHO IS THIS?

She took a step back, as though her actions were likely to have the typewriter leaping off of the desk. Instead, the machine sat in a sobering silence.

Agnes stepped forward and, at that very moment,

the type-bars punched letters into the paper. She watched the print as it appeared, mouth open in disbelief, her hands digging inside her body warmer to call Maud.

As she hit the speed dial number, Agnes' pale eyes gazed down at the letters on the page.

PRIMROSE MEADOWSWEET.

Inside Beatrice a fierce rage burned. The focus was Emily, the mere presence of her made Beatrice want to strike out, to hurt her until the anger was quelled. She had woken from her faint, and saw her brother sitting beside her. The sight of him calmed her to a degree. All the time she was also aware of Emily on the other side of the deck. The girl was sitting on a storage box, glaring over at Beatrice. Emily's eyes blazed and livid scratches from their brawl strafed her right cheek.

"Why is she still here?" Beatrice said. "I don't want to see her."

"I'd have thought you'd have woken up in a better frame of mind," Edna said coolly. "We've nowhere else to go, or have you forgotten, child?"

Beatrice stood up, fury making her arms tremble. "I can't be with her, don't you get it?" she yelled.

Thomas stood up with her, his face a mask of concern. "Bea. Emily is your friend."

"No!" Beatrice screamed at him. Spittle flew from her lips, her hair still wet from the dowsing he'd given her, hung dark and lank. "She is dead to me."

For emphasis, Beatrice signed the words in bold shapes.

"You should be dead!" Emily shouted back at her. 'This is your fault, all of it. You don't deserve to have friends. You should be alone forever."

Beatrice was running again, feet pummelling the deck, gaining speed, the intensity of emotion exhilarating, the aim to get to Emily, to rip out her devious tongue, and throw it onto the deck.

Emily climbed to her feet, too, and braced for impact.

Claire tried to intercept, but her lack of strength made the attempt clumsy. Beatrice was easily able to dodge her. The collision with Emily was almost inevitable when, at the last moment, Beatrice surprised them all by veering slightly right.

Before anyone realised what was happening, Beatrice had jumped overboard.

All but Emily dashed to the spot where Beatrice had plunged from the boat, looking over the side into the total darkness.

Thomas was crying, his tears coming between great sobs, Claire draping her ruined arms about him, her own tears falling into his hair.

A single piercing scream came to them all. It did not rise from the darkness, though. Instead, it came from Emily as she once more, fell into unconsciousness.

Tamsin appeared drawn with concern. Elmo scrutinised her face, feeling generally uncomfortable having just told her the reason she saw Lucas on the wall was, perhaps, because he'd disappeared into thin air shortly before Emily.

They were sitting on the landing, backs against the walls, the flickering of the barrier splashing sputtering light on them. From time to time, Tamsin's eyes would drift to the image of her son walking across the tangerine landscape, and a sad smile played on her lips.

"What does all this mean?" she said.

Elmo shrugged but nodded towards the wall. "We don't know, but we do know that wherever Lucas is, he's safe."

For now, at least, his mind said, but he shoved the intrusive thought away.

When he began to think of where Emily and Beatrice could be at that moment, he felt panic rising and stood up, pretending to stretch his legs. In reality, he needed some distraction.

"This kind of thing seems to run in our family," Tamsin said.

"Eh?"

"Lucas' dad," she said with a sigh. "He disappeared when Lucas was very young. We never talk about it. I thought I was protecting him."

Elmo leaned his back against the wall and slid down until he was sitting again.

"It's something Lucas never wants to talk about," Elmo observed. "Maybe we need to, I mean, it might be relevant to what's happening here."

"I'm not sure." She looked at him, eyes tired as though recalling an event that she had visited many times before and found no resolution. "It was a long time ago, and we don't know what actually happened."

Elmo looked at the vibrant orange barrier.

"Maybe we do," he said quietly. "Maybe talking now will make a difference.

Tamsin took a breath. "Okay, it's not like we can go anywhere, right?"

"There is that," Elmo confirmed.

"Lucas' dad was called Alan," Tamsin began, "and he was in the army. Royal Artillery if we're getting down to the detail."

The button, Elmo thought as he looked down at the object at the base of the barrier. *Not a compass, but a canon-wheel, the emblem of the Royal Artillery.*

"Anyway," she continued. "I was always used to him being away a lot, came with the turf, you know? I had a chance to go with him, they had houses near to where he was stationed in peace-time. In those early days that's what I did, but we grew up here in this town. It was our home, and when Lucas was born we both made the decision he was to have some roots, not follow his dad all over the world."

Elmo remained quiet, sure he had questions but it didn't seem the right time to ask them. So he listened intently, learning the background of his best friend. Part of him felt privileged, another part felt as though he was a snoop, no better than Edna Duffy.

Either way, he didn't stop Tamsin telling her tale, and if she had any qualms they didn't show in her delivery, nor her desire to tell it.

"It was a joint decision," she emphasised. "Alan's more than mine, if I'm honest. He'd be away for long periods, but when he was home he'd dote on us. We were inseparable during his periods of leave.

"The plan was that he'd serve his time, use this to get skills so he could set up a small boat repair company here in Dorsal Finn. We saved hard and long and he only had a few more months before he was going to be discharged for good."

Tamsin paused as she collected her thoughts.

"So, what happened?" Elmo whispered.

"He came home on leave," she said. "He was meant to go back to barracks at the end of the three weeks for his final tour. He kissed us both goodbye, said he'd see us soon, and left. That was the last time I ever saw him."

"They looked for him, though, right?"

She smiled sadly. "Of course. The Military Police, the local police, then nationwide. Everyone said the same thing—the behaviour was out of character for him, he was a reliable man, loyal to all who knew him, especially his family. But after leaving this house, Alan vanished. Well, I always thought the word 'vanished' was a little dramatic." She looked at the barrier. "Now I'm not so sure."

A silence settled over them. Just as Elmo felt the tale was nearing its end, Tamsin began to talk again.

"It was an awful time," she said sniffing back tears. "So much uncertainty, so much false hope. There was CCTV footage from the edge of town that showed Alan walking up to the bus stop. Those were the last images anyone ever saw of him. From what the bus driver said, he never got on that bus. This means he never left this town. We were left in the dark, without reason, or hope."

Sometimes this town has its own reasons, Elmo thought sombrely.

"Lucas would sit on the wall at the front of the cottage and wait for hours and hours, hoping his dad would show up," she sniffed again. "No matter what I said to him, he was that way for several months. His way of grieving, I guess. We all do it differently."

As Tamsin finished her tale, she found her eyes drawn to the barrier once more, and her lids widened. Elmo followed her gaze to see that the image of Lucas had been replaced by a man sitting in an armchair beside a fireplace where flickering white flames danced in the hearth.

The man had a neat beard, his mouth pulled into a warm smile. He appeared to be talking to someone, a shadowy figure sitting in a chair opposite. Elmo couldn't make out the features. It was as if he was looking at the image through glasses smudged with sun cream.

"It's him," Tamsin said as tears welled. "It's Alan."

They both rose and descended the stairs to stand before the barrier. Tamsin reached up and gently touched the man's image.

"What happened to you?" she whispered. "Where did you go?"

Following Tamsin's lead, Elmo placed his finger on the smeared shape on the left of the barrier. Where his fingertip made contact, a ripple permeated the surface and, as it spread, the person came into focus.

Elmo's mouth dropped open with total incredulity. The person sitting in the chair engaging in conversation with Lucas' long lost father was none other than Beatrice Beecham.

Voice hoarse, Emily fell to her hands and knees, hair hanging over her face, obscuring her distraught features from those who stood around her. Claire went over to her, wincing at each movement as she placed a comforting hand to the girl's shoulder. Emily accepted the contact, out of need or lack of awareness, no one knew.

A sound came from above them and they all looked upwards, fear etched in their faces, as three figures emerged from a door on the next level.

Dorothy lifted her umbrella like a samurai warrior. "Keep back," she said with as much firmness as her voice could muster.

"It's all right, ladies, I'm captain of this vessel," said Melville as he went to the stairway leading down to them. "I can assure you that you are under our protection, and all is under control."

"I seriously doubt that of any man," Edna said flatly. "But we have people hurt here and one overboard."

Melville and Trevor hit the deck first, and they walked up to the group.

"Someone overboard, you say?" Melville said grimly. "Do we know who?"

"My sister," Thomas sniffed. He was trying to be brave; his face was jittering as he fought back emotion. "She went crazy, both of them did."

He indicated to Emily who was now allowing Claire to hug her.

"They had a huge fight, and then Beatrice just jumped," he began to cry then, and with his tears came anger. "Why'd she do that? It doesn't make sense."

"Well, your sister and I don't see eye to eye on most things, boy," Edna said quietly. "I'll say this of her: she's not one for doing things without reason."

"What about the girl on the deck?" This came from Cotteridge who was now descending the steps to them. "Is she still sound of mind?"

"What does a 'sound mind' look like these days," Claire said flatly. "She's upset and hurt, and that's all we need to focus on right now."

Edna looked back at the boat and then at the blackness around them. "If only that were true," she said.

Patience sat next to her parents. They were both lost to her at that moment, their slumbering forms had been her only company for what seemed like a lifetime. She'd turned her chair to face the doors, though she expected no one to come through them as there was no place for them to come to. The darkness beyond was as dense as oil.

The steady beep of the respirator kept its rhythm. Since her mother had drifted into her deep sleep, Patience had held vigil. She'd had no desire to eat, nor did she feel tired.

Instead, there were only the doors and the blackness beyond, and the deep-seated guilt that, no matter where they were or what was going on, this was all her fault.

Chapter Twenty

FALLING, THE SENSATION in her stomach was akin to going over the world's largest speed bump. Beatrice had no concept of time or place, no affiliation with the laws of normality. There was just the sensation of a hundred butterflies in her belly.

No sooner had she cleared the boat when the terrible rage that had consumed her vanished. The distance between her and Emily acted as a fire blanket, smothering the flames and leaving behind serenity, and the sensation of flight. She did not question it; she merely welcomed the innate, pervading peace.

As she fell, she began to see a change in the fabric of darkness, as though a distant light was somehow eating into the blackness. She made out shapes below her, structures that seemed both familiar and alien in the same instant. They also appeared to have symmetry, either lined or blocked. As these shapes came into view she found herself looking down on an ancient town, the buildings in ruins, the streets nothing but strips of cracked concrete, the foliage lining them overgrown with tangled weeds. The landscape was a blend of light and dark grey, as though the world had forgotten about the actuality of colour.

Beatrice felt herself upend, her feet now pointing towards the ground, which her feet touched as soft and light as a feather. She looked around her, at the buildings, at the trees, and she could see each structure was a shell, all the windows dark, all the doors thrown wide—a town where life no longer had any meaning, any place.

These things came to Beatrice as though they were a part of her, as though she had always known of the existence of this town from another time. And with this came acceptance of its place in the order of things.

She scanned both sides of the street. The houses were made of wooden slats—the lofty eaves undulated and warped against the gunmetal, featureless sky. A soft breeze drifted across her face, bringing with it the bitter taste of ash, yet despite this she took comfort from it because it showed her that she was still alive.

The breeze also brought with it a sound, the tiny toll of a bell. She sought out its direction, further up the street—four houses down—where a dingy lace curtain flapped lazily in one of the empty windows. Beatrice headed towards it, feet making no sound in this dead town, the tiny bell guiding her.

She stood before the house. There were two windows and the front door on the ground floor. The porch ran across the entire front of the house, supported by several balustrades. The second floor had three tall windows, all black and unremarkable, and toward the right aspect, a rectangular tower jutted from the roof, indicating an attic with a single window. The lawns were full of dark grey grass, ankle deep, and two sad looking acacia trees flanked the house.

Like all the other houses, Beatrice could see the

main entrance had its door thrown wide, and without fear she walked down the cracked path, and stepped up onto the porch, where the boards beneath her feet creaked and popped.

Something drew her forward, the inkling—a desire—she could not fathom. Whatever it was, she did not feel threatened. There was an air of familiarity in this place, and she sought not to question such notions, only to allow them to guide her.

The hallway beyond the front door was wide and long with a stairway separating it into two spaces. To the left there were wooden doors, all shut. To the left, however, a large rectangle with a timber frame, opened out and gave off a grey flickering light, like that of a sputtering candle.

Beatrice went to it and stood to peer around the jamb. In the sitting room, a man sat in an armchair facing a fireplace that gave off flames of light and dark greys, but did not put out any heat.

He was in his early twenties, his beard neat and dark, and his eyes flickered in time with the fire. He had a high forehead, and despite the blaze in the hearth he wore a heavy trench coat.

He looked up at her and smiled, and in the smile Beatrice saw something familiar. Her heart stirred as a feeling of great joy and sadness mixed into one moment.

"Come and sit," the man said to her. He gestured to a chair opposite him. It had a high back and heavy arms. "Make yourself comfortable."

"Do I know you?" she replied, walking into the room. She paused halfway to the chair. "I *feel* as if I know you."

The man smiled. "No, you don't, but that's fine. I

don't know you either. Yet here we are, in a place that should not exist."

Beatrice went over to the chair and perched on the edge of the seat. "And where is this place?"

"It is neither here nor there, it seems," the man replied. "Perhaps we should call it *The In-between.* But it is safe, of that I am certain."

"How can you be so sure?" Beatrice mused. "I mean, look at it."

"It's not about how it looks, it's about where it *is,*" he said.

"In-between?" she said.

"In-between," he confirmed.

Beatrice scrutinised the man in the half-light. His trench coat had many buttons, though on the heavy triangular lapel there were slivers of thread hanging like the legs of a spider.

"You've lost a button," she observed.

"I've lost a lot in this life," he said. "That button isn't part of it. It was given freely."

Beatrice screwed up her face in confusion. "You gave away a button? Why?"

"Why do we do anything? Because I saw the value in doing it," he chuckled. It was a warm sound. Beatrice liked it. She had a nagging feeling she'd heard the chuckle before, but the thought evaded her.

"Haven't you ever given anything away to protect what is important?" he asked.

Beatrice considered this and replied, "Yes. I have."

The man smiled.

"What?" Beatrice asked.

"I can see what you have given," he said. "You have given your heart and that is why we are both here."

"I don't understand what that means," she said. There was something surfacing inside her now, the first vestiges of emotion were starting to seep through her malaise. She suddenly felt panicked and instinctively stood.

"Someone holds us both, dear," the man said. "But we are dangerous. He must never find us. That is why there is *The In-between*. It is the place built to keep us safe."

"He?"

Emotion flooded back into Beatrice, surging through her like a torrent of a great river, almost knocking her back down into the chair. She gave out a cry at the intensity of it all.

The man in the chair merely looked at her, his smile never leaving his lips.

Tears coursed down Beatrice's cheeks. "Oh, God, no! You mean Lucas?"

"Where are the rest of the passengers and crew?" Trevor addressed them all. There were many sullen faces. Just as he feared no answer was coming, Claire spoke up.

"What's left of the guests were in the ballroom. They . . . " She shuddered, unable to finish.

"Changed?" Trevor offered.

She nodded.

Melville stepped forward. "Does anyone know what happened to Clive Redfern, the owner of this yacht?"

"He didn't make it," Claire said slowly. "I'm sorry."

Melville closed his eyes and put a hand to his brow, his lips moving silently for a few seconds. Cotteridge placed a comforting hand on his shoulder.

Trevor looked down at Claire's arms, still swathed in bloodied pieces of shawl.

"Can I dress that for you?" he asked softly.

"Yes," she said. "But we can't stay out here with those things. It's only a matter of time before they come for us. We need a place to defend, right?"

"What say you, Captain?" Cotteridge said. "Where is the best place we can hold out?"

Melville appeared grim. "Maybe some of the passengers made it out?" he said. "We should go and see to make sure."

"Those who made it out are standing in front of you, man," Edna said with irritation. "You go back into that ballroom and it'll be the last shindig you ever attend."

"This is hard to hear," Melville said. "All of those people were my responsibility."

"Then I guess we are, too," Dorothy said.

"Indeed," Edna added. "So, we going or what?"

"There's no going anywhere."

They all turned to look at Emily, who was now standing upright, her face puffy and scratched, yet her eyes were hard and determined.

"Beatrice is the only way we're getting out of here, don't you understand? She left this boat so we didn't hurt each other anymore." Fresh tears came to her eyes at the thought. "This is what it wanted, why it brought me here, to make all this happen. It's totally in control, calling all the shots and we're just its playthings."

"What is 'it'?" Cotteridge asked.

"You wouldn't understand," Emily replied.

Cotteridge stepped up to her and then knelt down so she could see him clearly.

"Help me to understand," he said. "Tell me everything."

Cotteridge listened intently as Emily articulated as best she could, the bizarre journey that had led them all to that point. At times he nodded, at others he shook his head, but not once did his bright eyes leave the girl's face, nor lose their intensity.

Time appeared to stand still as the tale was told. Melville kept watch on the deck just in case the creatures from the gala decided to make their move. But save for Emily's careful speech, the boat remained ominously quiet.

For men of the sea such as Melville and Trevor, the absence of the ocean roar was an unsettling concept.

As the story unfolded, Claire's arms were expertly dressed by Trevor using tablecloths found in storage lockers under the deck sofas. The wounds were carefully cleaned with bottled water, and most of the scratches had stopped bleeding. Antiseptic cream from a first aid kit was applied as Claire gritted her teeth against the pain.

Only a single tear escaped during the entire process. The material from the tablecloth was torn into strips and secured with a series of knots. Painkillers were gulped down with water to take the edge off the nagging throb of her injuries.

Edna and Dorothy were sitting on one of the sofas. At one point Dorothy fished around in the battered carrier bag and brought out a crumpled container that was so flat it looked as though someone had sat on it.

"Bon Bon?" she said.

No one took her up on the offer.

Cotteridge turned to Emily. "Is there anything else you can tell us that might help us get out of here?"

The detective fell silent as he considered his own query. After a few second a thought came to him. "Emily, have you ever seen a brass disc in your visions?"

"I've seen a circle of gold. I feel like its pulling me towards it. What is it?"

Cotteridge looked over at Melville who returned his gaze.

"It's an astrolabe," Melville said. "A navigation device."

"You mean like Sat-Nav?" she said.

"Yes," Melville said, smiling. "A 16th Century Sat-Nav."

"In each vision the astrolabe calls to me," she whispered.

"What does it say?" Cotteridge said.

"I feel that I have to be with it, hold it in my hands. The people I saw in my visions kept calling me The Oracle."

At this, Claire's intense gaze fell upon Emily's face. "I saw something," she said. "A vision like you saw. My dad—" She paused at the thought of her parents as they appeared in her hotel room, prompting Emily to place a comforting hand on hers. Claire continued after a moment. "My dad said the words 'The Oracle must seek out that which is lost.' This is all tied together somehow. *We* are all tied together. What can this mean?"

"There's only one way to find out," Melville said.

"The astrolabe is on this boat. I suggest we take Emily to it. You in?"

Emily nodded emphatically as she jumped to her feet. "Just show me where it is."

Beatrice turned, her intention was to exit the sitting room and go into the grey, desolate streets, and roam them, calling Lucas' name. She had taken a few steps when the man by the fire spoke again, his words quiet but insistent.

"Please don't leave."

Beatrice paused and looked back at him. "Is that a command?"

He sighed. "You're free to go at your own choosing. We both are. But just because we can, does not mean we *should*."

"Why not?" she said in frustration.

"Because The In-between is not meant to exist. It is the eye of the storm, Beatrice, the oasis in the desert. We're here to keep everyone we love safe. If we become contaminated, then Lucas will find me."

"And if he does find you?"

"Then he will never wish to leave me. He will be lost to the world. He will be lost to you, forever."

Beatrice felt her heart stall and then tear as though a hot knife had passed through it. She let out a stuttering breath.

The man watched and his face was morose. "This is what it wants. The Incorruptible Heart will be broken, her love lost, her resolve broken, she will be weak. Once this is done it will rise and claim the world as its own."

"What the hell is this thing?" she whispered.

"Hell?" the man queried. "The Darkness isn't defined by human beings, or the many faiths of this planet. It simply *is*. And anything that has happened right up to the point where you leapt from the boat and into its embrace is due to its designs on you, and what you represent."

Before Beatrice could question him, an image danced before her eyes, she was back on the boat, charging down Emily, the recollection made her voice hitch with horror. Then she was back there, living it, feeling every potent second.

Once more she felt herself moving through the air, her feet thumping the deck, the fingers on her raised hands creating pink prison bars from which there seemed no hope of escape. It felt like the right thing to do, made total and absolute sense. It would not be murder, it would be justice.

It would be sacrifice.

Her brain, she now realised, had also been at war, something malignant had burrowed into it, given credence by the climate it had created. Beatrice's thoughts had been suffocated by the intense fury coursing through it, blinding rational thought, and poisoning reason.

The Dark Heart, The Darkness, the thing that consumed and was itself consumed. The town known as Dorsal Finn had been there, making a play. The time was here but conditions were not quite right. The meddling of others had hampered the climate so painstakingly created to bring this girl to this point in time.

In that instant Beatrice could feel it, it ran through

her like slippery grease, making her entire body crawl with its malevolence. The Darkness was old, and it was adaptable.

She could sense its frustration. Unforeseen elements had been brought into the game, and now it was including them in the scheme. It had seen Emily as a threat. The deaf girl was a powerful ally, sister to the Incorruptible Heart, now she was a pawn in a new game, a distraction from the true nature of things.

Yet nothing could be done until the Incorruptible Heart was in its true domain, and Beatrice relived the moment when she was allowed an instant of insight, just enough for her to save her friend by leaping into the dark, where her nemesis waited like a hungry predator.

Then the huge, malicious roar of frustration as Beatrice was snatched from space before she could be consumed by The Darkness, and brought to The In-between.

"It manipulates everything," she said with quiet anger.

"Not everything," the man said. "Just the things affiliated with you, Bringer of Joy. It needs you impotent. Had you been drawn into its domain as it intended, it would have had the upper hand, and all would have been lost."

Beatrice's tears fell freely and her hands hung limply against her sides. "So what happens to Lucas?"

"He is in a dream where he has hope of finding something he has sought for many years," the man said. "He will forever be on the cusp of attaining this hope. It is a beautiful dream from which there is no waking. Not now. Not ever."

"What?" she cried. "You mean he's trapped there, forever?"

"To him, it will be an eternity of hope," the man said. "He will be at peace with it."

"You said that he would only be lost if he found his way here, found you," she said. "But now you're saying he's lost regardless?"

"If he finds me as The Darkness wants then Lucas will achieve his aim and have no other purpose in life," he said. "He will be as good as dead, Beatrice. To those who love him he *will* be dead."

Beatrice looked at the man, her eyes determined and stubborn. "I won't accept that, it's not—"

She stopped. The man's face remained expressionless but his eyes scrutinised her.

"Not 'fair', perhaps?" he interjected. "There is no fair here. He can be your love or your nemesis, a weapon to be used against you and the world. This is what it is to be The Incorruptible Heart. Your loss will bring hope to others. There is no distraction. There is only duty!"

He sounded as though he was reciting it from some unseen autocue. Beatrice felt the bitter anger of injustice building inside her.

"I never asked for this. I don't want it!"

"It isn't a plaything to pick and choose," the man said. "You are The Incorruptible Heart. There is no giving it away."

"I can't lose Lucas," she sobbed. "I can't."

"That is no longer your choice to make."

Standing at the spot where Beatrice had jumped from the boat, Thomas stared out into the dark. His mind was sluggish, thoughts slowed by the anxiety over what had happened to his sister. Sometimes it was not good to have an overactive imagination, and this was one of those times.

"She's quite the fighter, your sister," a voice said beside him.

Thomas turned to see Claire. She placed a hand on his arm, token comfort in the darkness.

"She's very bossy, and she hates Star Wars." His bottom lips trembled. "I want her to come back."

Claire watched his tears fall, and moved her hand to his shoulder, which bobbed in time with his sobs.

From their right, a sound came to them, a drawn-out hiss and the terribly familiar click-clicking of claws on the hull.

Trevor was suddenly with them, his face drawn with fear that pervaded them all.

"I'm sorry, Thomas," he said with sincerity. "We have to go. They're coming."

As he spoke they caught sight of movement. A waving black shape that began to creep from the foredeck, and down the side of the yacht. This creeping shadow had many, many eyes.

The lowly toll of a bell came to them, drifting from out of the oppressive, endless night all about them.

"I keep hearing that," Thomas said as they hurried to the others.

"Bells were a way of marking time on a sailor's watch-duty, every toll marked half an hour," Trevor said without stopping.

"What does eight bells mean?" Thomas asked from the steps.

"It has three meanings," Trevor said, stalling to look down at him. "The first is end of watch, the second is to mark a death at sea."

"And the third?"

Trevor looked down at the creatures swarming onto the deck.

"The third is to get your arse up these steps!"

"I think you made that last one up," said Thomas firmly.

"Beatrice?" Elmo whispered as he watched his friend in the flickering orange glow of the barrier.

He inspected the image by moving closer, the shimmering light responding to his gentle breath against its surface with a series of tiny ripples. Many things went through his mind, all of them distilled into three simple words: *what, how,* and *why*?

Beatrice remained engaged in conversation with Alan Walker. At one point she had stood up and walked towards the barrier and in that instant Elmo thought she was literally going to step through and join him on the staircase. Instead, she had stopped, her face pained, and Elmo wished he could have spoken to her, done something—anything—to remove the hopeless look from her eyes.

He was just considering if Emily was with Beatrice on the other side of the barrier, when a huge crash came from Lucas' bedroom.

Elmo turned and charged up the stairs, hoping that Emily or Lucas had returned and were now sitting on the floor in a heap, safe.

When he shoved open the door it was not either of his friends he saw. It was Edward Chorley and a girl he recognised from his year.

The window was blown in, the wooden frame now useless splinters that jutted like teeth in the sill. Glass was strewn across the room, the bed upended and broken, the bookshelf had collapsed and the precious tomes lay torn amid the chaos.

"First things first," Elmo said from the doorway. "That's no way to treat other people's property. Secondly, Eddie, your girlfriend is kinda hovering above the floor."

Alison's feet were indeed several inches above Lucas' carpet. Her head was tilted so far to one side that her cheek was lying almost flat to her shoulder. To Elmo, she looked broken, but her eyes were blazing with the all too familiar green embers of magic.

"Make your jokes," she hissed, "but I can taste your fear. Soon you will burn, along with the rest of this world."

"I see why you two get along so well," Elmo said to Edward. "I'll pass on the offer of eternal damnation, if it's all the same to you guys." He stepped back and slammed the bedroom door shut.

"Mrs W, we have to go." he said. "Now!"

Tamsin looked up at him from the stairs, and Elmo realised she had no intention of going anywhere. She was framed by the orange glow from the barrier behind her, a corona flared from the top of her head. Its intensity turned her face almost to shadow.

"Alan came to me the other night," she whispered. "He told me he was safe, but I was to stop looking for him. Strange when things come back to you, isn't it?"

"Some memories aren't under our control," he said. "Just like the situation we're in. He might be safe, but we certainly ain't!"

The bedroom door began to open, and the hideous green light oozed from the crack between door and jamb. Frantic, Elmo went down the stairs towards Tamsin.

As he reached Tamsin, the door to Lucas' room flew open and the sickly jade hue splashed out onto the landing, the hideous, hovering figure of Alison floating out with it. Elmo felt his back press against the barrier and it did not yield.

Alison was now turning in the air, facing them, head nearly bopping the ceiling like an escaped helium balloon at a toddler's party, and the smile on her face was pure and utter evil.

"Trapped like the vermin you truly are," she sneered. "Your precious defence is now your prison. Now it will become your crypt."

If Alison had any fear of the barrier, it did not show in her twisted face, though it was becoming clear to Elmo she was not coming down the stairs. She remained on the landing, Edward now beside her, below her, a standoff that showed very little sign of ending anytime soon.

Without warning, a series of bright jagged bolts, thick as vines, sizzled on the air and shot past Elmo and Tamsin. Around them, and up the stairs, both Edward and Alice cried out in anger and frustration.

The bolts seared towards Alison but she threw herself back into the bedroom, dragging Edward with her as though he weighed nothing at all.

As the light struck the back wall, it sent out several

tendrils, and in an instant, they had wrapped around the door handle and pulled it shut, fusing the wood to the frame with a crackling sound. A fiery branch slapped into the ceiling, and the loft hatch fell open. The ladder slammed into the landing, its aluminium frame crackling with white light.

"The stairway is not denied," Elmo whispered.

He grabbed at Tamsin's hand, and looked up at her. Her face was vague, as though waking from a deep sleep. "Come on, Mrs W. This is our chance."

"I can't leave," she whispered as the light bounced all around them. "I've only just found him again."

Elmo looked at the woman and then back to the barrier. There were no longer any images; its surface was just a writhing mass of orange swirls.

"I'm sorry, Mrs. W, but the wall is blank, and he's gone." He looked into her vacant face. "We're still here, right? We have to go."

Tamsin blinked a few times and then nodded, allowing him to steer her up to the ladders. The bedroom door to their right was blackened where it had fused with the doorframe, the paintwork webbed and peeling. Elmo encouraged Tamsin to go up the ladder first, his eyes staying fixed on the bedroom door which vibrated violently, and cracks began to show in the walls around the jamb.

Elmo didn't loiter. They charged up into the loft, the rungs clanking fiercely as he ascended, and then he pulled the ladders up after him, darkness swallowing him as he slammed the loft hatch shut.

"Mrs. W—you got any light in here?" he said to the blackness.

There was a terrible snapping and cracking noise

that filled the loft space, and suddenly a shaft of green light splashed onto him as the roof over his head was torn away.

"That wasn't quite what I had in mind," Elmo muttered.

Chapter Twenty-One

THE MAN BY the fire watched as a despondent Beatrice paced the sitting room. Twice she had appeared as though she intended to stomp out of the house, but the internal battle to go or remain always brought her back into the room where she would loudly air her frustrations.

"I have to get out of here," she said. "Surely I can't be expected to do nothing?"

"If you leave and Lucas finds this place, he will die," the man said. "You will have to live with the fact that your actions were to blame."

Beatrice stopped pacing. She eyed the man with contempt. "He's as good as dead now, though, right? I'll never be with him. He'll be gone forever."

The man offered her a forlorn smile. "The smallest of things can bring the greatest joys," he said. "Objects of desire are made so by what we ascribe to them."

He looked down at his coat, and plucked a button from it as though it were a berry from a burgeoning fruit bush.

He put it in his palm and held it out to her, and in the grey light the bright brass circle gave off a tiny incongruent golden flame.

In the flame, Beatrice could see Lucas.

She slowly walked up to the image now hovering above the man's outstretched hand. As her gaze fell upon it, witnessing Lucas as he sat on a grassy hill and stared up at the azure sky, she smiled. Lucas too gave out a big grin as though he could see her, and Beatrice blinked away her tears.

"This is the difference between life and death," the man said. "When you look upon him, to him it will be like a memory, a good memory that he will always treasure."

She stood transfixed on the mirage. "Is this real?"

"The place is as real as this," the man said. "This is Lucas' *In-between*. And this button will make sure he will always be with you. Safe. Alive."

Beatrice considered this, but she could not say she accepted it. Her heart was breaking, and if The Darkness wanted to see her vulnerable and beaten then she felt that it had got its wish.

The man reached forward and closed his fingers over the button, extinguishing Lucas' image. Beatrice began to cry.

"Oh, this hurts so much," she wept. The man gently took hold of her right hand and held his fist above it.

"Perhaps this will ease the suffering," he said and dropped the button into her open palm. Her fingers closed over it and she held her fist to her chest as a quiet warmth spread through her.

She sighed, suddenly at peace. With this peace came a begrudging acceptance, but it was distant, overshadowed by a powerful sense of duty. Her psyche absorbed it until it became part of her, shaping values and honing her perspective.

The man sat back in his seat, the smile on his face one of contentment, as though a good deed had been fulfilled.

Beatrice shuddered. She felt connected to so many things at that moment. Time and space were now shimmering tributaries that danced before her eyes. In the brilliance she saw things she did not understand because now was not the right time. But there was one notion that was immediately blatant.

"The Light did all of this." It was a statement because she knew it to be true. "Snatched both me and Lucas and put us here."

"Emily, too," he reminded her. "To make you stronger, to preserve all you hold dear. No distraction, no vulnerability," the man conceded. "It is not like The Darkness. It will manipulate moments, not the people who pass through them."

"Then it is as the poem said: it's all game," she said flatly.

"A game that has been in play for longer than recorded time," the man replied. "And, yes, everyone has their part to play, but no one will know how to move until their moment comes."

"So what must I do?"

"You must accept what is, and what is lost, and then do your duty."

"You mean Lucas?" she moaned.

"Yes. Then you can leave this place to protect those who need you."

Beatrice immediately saw other images she *could* recognise, places and faces, and the dilemmas faced by all. Immediate dangers screamed out at her, and there was no denying where she was needed the most.

"Are you ready to do your duty, Bringer of Joy?"

"Yes," she replied, her heart suddenly quelled. "I accept."

"Then it is time for you to leave."

"How will I find my way back?" she asked.

"Wait for your guide, of course," the man said.

"Up the steps! Now!"

Melville's voice rang out from the platform above, mobilising them all in an instant.

The shadow oozed across the aft-deck, a pulsating mass of creatures, too ill-defined to count, but all sporting claws and those hideous green eyes.

The first of the creatures scuttled up the steps and Trevor took aim with the flare pistol. The repulsive maw opened to let out a hiss, and he put a flare into it. The figure erupted into red flame, and toppled back down the steps, sending the others below screeching to the edges of the deck.

"We need to get to the next level," Cotteridge called. "We can gain advantage being on higher ground."

"Agreed," Melville said. "Follow me."

He raced further down the passageway, where another stairway lay in wait. As he made to take his first step, Melville saw a pair of hideous eyes looking down on them. He recoiled, almost knocking Edna to the floor.

"Damnation, man," she cursed. "I've got enough to be getting on with without an oaf like you almost squashing me flat!"

Melville ignored Edna and addressed them all. "They're above us!"

"Is there another way through?" Claire asked.

"There's internal access," Melville said. "It means going inside, through the galley, and the stairs are on the other side."

"The stairs leading up to the top of the boat?" Dorothy asked.

"Yes," Melville replied.

"Where those things might already be?" she clarified.

"Just because I saw one above us, doesn't mean they're on the roof deck," Melville said. "And given how they react to fire and flame, I'd say if there are only a few of them, we can drive them off it for the time being."

Dorothy was about to speak when Edna barged past her. "For goodness sake, Dorothy! If we don't get torn to pieces, we'll be bored to death waiting for you to come to a decision if it's safe or not."

"It's got to be safer than what is behind us," Trevor called back as the tide of twisted shapes stalked them from the stairwell they'd just vacated.

Cotteridge watched contorted limbs and lamp-like eyes oozing onto the concourse.

"Wish I could disagree," he muttered.

Maud shrugged off her coat and scarf as she hurried into the library. Agnes had told her an incredible tale over the phone, a tale she'd have never believed if this had been a different woman in a different town.

She'd moved through the town at a rapid pace, leaving her somewhat giddy with effort, but spurred on by the low lying fog that now flowed through the streets like a pulsating river. Even as she walked through it, she could feel the resistance, as if she was walking through snow and not mist. Determination kept her going, though she could see that in places the fog was becoming so dense, it was lapping and climbing the walls of the buildings it touched.

During that time, she thought about all of those she held dear. George and Maureen Beecham had gone down to the harbour to be part of proceedings, but of the others Maud had no real idea of what was happening or where they were. It left her unsettled to the core, and Agnes' news hadn't helped one bit.

By the time she got to the library, visibility was down to a few feet in every direction, and she was thankful of the clarity and warmth once she got inside the foyer.

She found Agnes still in the office, where the Underwood typewriter sat silent and imposing in the centre of the table, several sheets of paper in the librarian's hands. Agnes' face was dour as Maud stepped up to her.

"What ye got there, Agnes?"

"It's what we already know, and even more dreadful news," she said. "Primrose is dead, Maud. This is her tormented spirit reaching out to us."

"Through a typewriter?" Maud said.

"Primrose has told me it belonged to her mother and she gave it to a charity shop when she passed on," Agnes explained. "I bought it. This is the last emotional connection the poor girl has to this world. She's using it to tell all."

Maud's face reflected the brevity of the tale. "She was a sourpuss, to be sure, but her heart was stout and loyal. Did she shed any light on these dark times?"

Agnes shook her head, despondent. "She is crippled with guilt at what she has brought to this town. To this world. Elizabeth possessed her, but the witch was herself duped into setting free the climate for the yacht to be sucked into a netherworld, where the forces of The Dark Heart have greater power. Now she is crying out for forgiveness and salvation."

Maud nodded. "I can understand the poor lamb's need for such a thing. How do we stop what's happenin'?"

Agnes looked up at Maud, her eyes dull with sadness. "No matter how we do it, we can't do it alone."

Maud was already on her cell phone.

Back on *The Spirit of the Ocean*, the beleaguered group made their way through the murky glow thrown out by the emergency lamps. They crossed the lounge, a squared area where sofas followed the contours of the walls, and passed by high-tech entertainment equipment, including a huge TV and computer area. The once resplendent room was now a place of deep red light and pitch-dark shadow.

There was also a pool table from which Cotteridge lifted a cue, snapping it in half across his knee and keeping the handle as a make-shift baton. He did this again and handed another to Melville, and the captain took it with a nod of gratitude.

Trevor led the way, flare pistol reloaded and ready

to blast anything he saw with green eyes. Cotteridge was at the back of the group, brandishing the baton. The detective kept close watch on the surroundings, his keen eyes scouring every nook, every cranny.

In front of him, Edna and Dorothy shuffled along, their handbags and umbrellas at the ready. Thomas and Emily walked side by side, both with grim faces, their resolve motivated by a steely will to survive long enough to establish a way to find Beatrice. With them was Claire, her body taut with readiness, and her eyes alert and flitting from shadow to shadow, the axe Trevor had given her, ready to strike.

At the other end of the room they found a heavy set of double doors with twin oval windows through which a flickering light danced in the panes.

Trevor turned to them after peering through one of the windows. "The galley is behind these doors. We go straight through. There are doors on the far side, a dining area after that, and the stairs are in a corridor off of that room."

"This guy sounds like an estate agent," Thomas muttered. "Can we just get in there?"

Trevor smiled at Thomas' impatience. "Let's just make sure we aren't walking into trouble, okay?"

"Sure," Thomas replied, but it was with reservations attached.

Trevor pushed open one door and Melville the other. Through the gap they could make out the stainless steel work surfaces, laid out in rows and creating small aisles between them.

Butted up against the walls were squat chest freezers and tall fridges, interspersed with storage racks. In the centre of the room was a bank of gas hobs, most of which were alight, and the eerie sound of unattended pots of water bubbling away filled the galley.

"Looks clear," Melville said. "I'd suggest we move with caution but there are things we can use to defend ourselves in here, so I say keep a look out for something that will come in handy."

"Not sure what good a balloon whisk will be against a bloody spectre," Edna muttered.

They entered the galley, the heat meeting them like the warm breeze on a summer day. Their progress was tentative, all of them aware that the confined space was not the best place to be caught by the shadow-creatures.

Edna found a large rolling pin and tested its weight. "Aye, that'll do just fine."

The others helped themselves to different implements; Claire found a tenderising hammer, a vicious-looking thing with a square head and multiple raised blisters on its surface. She handed the axe on to Trevor as he passed a storage shelf, and spied several bottles. He paused and called Dorothy over.

"I'm going to need your bag," he said.

"As long as I get it back," she said, reluctantly handing it over. Trevor looked at the battered shopping bag and smiled.

"Might even get you a new one," he said.

"It's a bag for life," she said bluntly. "Paid ten pence for it."

He shrugged and proceeded to load the bottles into it. "No worries. I'll even carry it myself, how about that?"

Dorothy didn't seem sure. "What is that stuff?"

"Cooking oil," he said. "Might give us the edge when there's a lot of 'em."

"Are you mad, Number One?" Melville interjected. "We could end up burning the entire yacht. With us on it."

"It's just a contingency, Skipper," Trevor assured him.

"Think I'd rather be toast than left at the hands of what lies in the dark," Emily said ruefully.

"Let's make sure neither of those has to become an option," Melville said. "Keep moving."

"We don't even know if we're going to be safe when we reach the top of the boat," Thomas said.

"No," Emily said. "But we know that the astrolabe is important, and when we get there we can figure out what we're meant to do with it."

There was a loud thump nearby, startling them all.

"What was that?" Melville said.

"It came from one of those chest freezers," Cotteridge replied.

There was another dull thud. This time it was Claire who responded. "That came from the stand-up fridge."

A series of bangs and heavy blows came to them seemingly from all around the kitchen. Then, as one, the doors of the chest freezers and fridges flew open, the contents lifted in the air, or spilling out all over the galley.

"What are those?" Thomas said as something flopped and rolled across a nearby worktop.

It was pale pink and ovoid, no bigger than the size of a cat. Stumpy back legs and reedy, fingerless front limbs skittered for purchase on the smooth work-surface. Another object landed beside it and several others slapped down at other points in the galley.

"Dark-beasts," Thomas said in awe.

"Dark-beasts my arse," Edna said. "They're bloody chicken carcasses."

They all peered at the writhing creatures and, sure enough, considered in horror the carcasses of chickens, plucked and prepped for cooking. One of them slithered across one of the shelves, knocking foodstuff to the floor as it came. Dorothy looked up at the stump of its neck and grimaced.

"Think I'm going vegetarian after this evening," she said.

The carcass quivered, its goosed flesh rippling as convulsions took it. Before their eyes, a great cavern opened in its neck, and row upon row of tiny, needle-teeth protruded from this slavering maw.

In unison, the other creatures morphed, and their unsightly mouths became wide and threatening.

"See?" Thomas shouted. "Dark-beasts, just like I said."

The creatures lurched forward and the humans all moved as one, heading in the direction of the dining room exit. The creatures came for them, some airborne once again as the stumpy legs suddenly found enough power and proficiency to produce an effective leap.

Claire took one out of the air by swinging the tenderising hammer, catching it in mid-pounce with a sickening cracking sound before it flew into the hobs, bashing into a cooking pot on the stove. It crashed to the ground, scalding water splashing over another creature that was scuttling across the tiled floor. The tiny beasts gave out pitiful cries, but they were cut short by the hissing of steaming water.

Emily was moving fast when another of Thomas' dark-beasts struck her heavily in the shoulder. She went down hard, the wind knocked out of her, and a searing pain in her right forearm told her that the vile creature had found purchase by clamping its mouth over it.

She screamed in pain and dragged her arm towards her, the dark-beast coming with it. The bloated pink hide, still cold to the touch, its limbs flailing to get any kind of grip on the floor. She held the beast to her so it couldn't pull away, taking her arm with it, and in that time Thomas came in from the side and skewered it with a kitchen knife. The beast immediately opened its mouth to screech, and freed Emily's arm, which was running with blood.

Thomas hefted his leg and kicked the creature across the galley where it slammed into the storage shelves, sending cookery paraphernalia everywhere.

Cotteridge bashed a beast who was trying to sneak up on him from an overhead light, and the thing fell to the floor. The detective looked up at another freezer that was now shaking as though many living things were inside it, fighting to escape.

He called out to Melville. "I'd suggest it's time for that contingency, Captain!"

Trevor looked at Melville as the door to the last chest freezer bowed and buckled under the pressure of something inside. The hinges finally gave out and something rose from within. The carcass of some other, larger animal, Cotteridge suspected a roasting pig, but he genuinely did not want to know much more about it.

Melville espied the new dark-beast. "Do, it, Number One," he said.

Trevor grabbed a bottle of cooking oil from Dorothy's bag and opened it. "Everyone, get out now!"

They all ploughed past him, through the set of doors into the dining area.

As Cotteridge looked upon the body of the great carcass, there came a tremendous cracking sound and, to his absolute horror, eight hairy spiderlike appendages emerged.

Frozen in terror, Cotteridge could only watch as this malformed creature began to scuttle towards him, the clicking of those great legs filling the galley.

"Cotteridge, move!" Melville called out. The detective, however, was mesmerised by the ghastly animal as it made for him. One of the smaller darkbeasts leapt up from a low unit, though, and caught Cotteridge by the throat.

Melville watched him go down, and brushed Trevor aside.

The captain wrestled with the creature, which at this time had a strong grip on the detective, and even Trevor could see by the dullness in Cotteridge's eyes there was no hope for the man.

"Melville, he's gone," Trevor yelled. "Get out of there!"

Opposite, the dark-beasts rallied, clambering on work surfaces, the great meat-spider was now morphing into something with huge teeth and gnarled, clawed hands. The door through which they had entered the galley crashed open, and the shadow-creatures, excited by the din, took the opportunity to make their assault.

Melville punched and screamed at the creature secured to Cotteridge. It was a final protest, a realisation that his attempt at a rescue had failed. With bitter resignation he stood up, intending to head to where his first officer waited. Trevor had the cooking oil and flare pistol at the ready, and Melville drew comfort from it.

As he moved, the captain could see the oncoming horde of creatures, weighing up the odds of him getting out of the galley and giving Trevor enough time to quell the assault. The maths just did not add up in his favour. He knew that it was too late for him, and Trevor saw it in the captain's eyes too.

Melville ignored him and picked up Cotteridge's baton. "Lead them out, Number One," he said, and turned to face the advancing creatures. They met him with hisses and the click of their claws.

In despair, Trevor saw Melville launch himself into them, batons swinging, taking down three of them before he was overpowered. The great beast roared from the corner of the galley and began tearing the tiles from the floor as it came toward Trevor.

With tears in his eyes and anger in his heart, he threw the bottle of cooking oil into the galley, the bottle spinning, pumping out the gloopy contents as it went.

The plastic vessel hit the floor and exploded, disgorging oil, splashing it on the tiles, the walls. Trevor raised the pistol but something caught his eye before he could fire. A gout of bright blue flame flared over to his left and he realised that some of the oil had found its way onto one of the burners.

He drove himself backwards through the doors, which parted, and he landed on his back. As the door swung closed again he saw the flash as the rest of the oil ignited, and then a huge roar as the conflagration took hold. The hideous screech of dark-beasts as they were overcome by the flames followed shortly afterwards and, in the dining room, the group covered their ears at the horrendous sound.

Trevor found himself being dragged to his feet. Claire, Emily and Thomas all helped him up. When he was upright he realised that five expectant faces were looking directly at him.

"What?" he said with a sigh. "What do you want from me?"

"Where we go from here would be a start," Claire suggested.

"Where we go?" he scoffed bitterly. "To hell by the looks of it."

Edna shuffled up to him and prodded him in the chest with her rolling pin. "Best get your act together, lad," she sniffed. "Looks like you've just been promoted to captain."

The small black car raced down the dark and quiet road, headlamps highlighting the bushes and long grass. At the wheel, Albert sat grim-faced, his eyes never wavering from the road ahead. Beside him, the huge frame of Dennis wriggled trying to find some comfort in the ill-fitting seats.

"For God's sake, keep still, man," Albert said.

"Yer vehicle ain't big enough fer a gnome, let alone me. Why not get yerself a peddle car an' be done with it?"

"Comedian," Albert muttered. "Just stop shimmying around. You'll have us over the edge."

Their journey from Bramwell Hall to Monument Point had been rapid. When Albert had first received the call from Maud, his immediate response was to tell them to stay put and he'd meet them at the library. His intention had been to go alone, but just as Maud was about to explain further, the line went dead, which he didn't consider a good sign.

He'd raced to the car, calling Dennis on the internal phone at the hall, and asked him if he could meet him in the garage, where he explained what had happened up to now.

"Trust ol' Maud and Agnes to be gettin' us involved after the event," Dennis griped. "An' as I was just off down to the Salty Sailor fer a night on the Cinder's Cider."

"Your head will thank them for it in the morning," Albert replied. "Besides, Maud doesn't involve us unless she really has no other choice. This must be important, Dennis. You know it."

"Aye," he conceded. "There's no hysterics in ol' Maud or Agnes. If they say there's trouble then I ain't ever gonna doubt it. Just wish they'd get in touch sooner is all I'm askin'. Mebbe we blokes could help out headin' this stuff off before it goes bouncin' off into the dark."

"If you're saying this would be sorted out if men had been involved from the start I'd keep that piece of advice to yourself," Albert said with a grim chuckle. "Or at least say it when I'm standing well clear of Maud Postlethwaite."

Both men laughed, but their mirth was brief as they came over the bluff. Albert slowed the car until it came to a halt.

They climbed out and looked down upon the town below. It was covered in a fine mist, the colour of freshly cut grass that appeared to throb as though alive.

"Adds a whole new meanin' to a pea-souper," Dennis muttered. "I'm guessin' it ain't just Maud and Agnes that need us. Best get movin'."

Albert was already heading for the car.

Trevor stepped into the access corridor, the rest of the group hanging back in the dining area until given the heads up that the way was clear. The corridor stretched off, the smooth walls turned to rust by the emergency lighting.

At the far end, he could make out the stairway that would ultimately take them to the roof terrace, where the astrolabe was embedded in the floor.

Trevor didn't pretend to understand what was going on, until tonight he had no idea the astrolabe existed. Emily had been insistent that they needed to get to the ancient navigation device. This had been supported by his Captain, and was enough for him, the final order of a great man. When he thought of Melville, a lump came to his throat and he had to swallow it back down.

At some point, if they ever got out of there, he would get a chance to rue the loss of his friend and, for that matter, the detective he barely knew.

Inwardly cursing himself, Trevor forced the immediacy of their predicament to the forefront of his mind. As much as he didn't like the idea, he was now responsible for those left alive on the yacht, and if it meant getting them to the top of the boat where Emily could literally work her magic then so be it.

Either that or die trying.

"We moving on or what?" Edna grumbled behind him.

"The way looks clear," he said.

"Is that a yes?" she said.

"I guess it is," he replied.

The group moved with caution down the corridor. This time it was Thomas and Emily who hung back to make sure nothing shadowy was following them.

Thomas chewed his lower lip as he pondered on a question.

"What is it?" Emily asked when she got tired of waiting.

"*Can* you get my sister back?"

"I don't think it works that way," she said.

"So how does it work?"

"It'll be Beatrice who has the power to get back to this place," she explained. "I think I'm meant to show her where we actually are."

"You mean guide her home?"

Emily started as she recalled the dream of Captain Crane eating gold because there was no one to show him a way out of his penance. So it was he was to be doomed to live out his punishment forever, lost to his guilt. And had he not asked her if she was The Oracle— the only way he could find a way back to righteousness?

"Yes," she said eventually. "Yes, that's exactly what I mean."

"Good," he said.

They carried on walking in order to keep up with the others.

Ahead, Trevor went through the oval hatch that gave access to a wide, spacious stairway. He ducked through, keeping the pistol aimed up the stairs, the cylindrical rails bolted to the walls acted as a guide in the rouge half-light.

He signalled the others to follow him, and climbed the stairs. The footfalls on the plush carpets were as light as they could make them, but still raised a series of soft thumps as they went.

At the top of the steps was a small landing that gave out onto the top deck. Here Trevor paused and turned back to the others. He saw Emily looking back at him and her eyes were keen yet distant.

"There's a large deck out there, seats skirted around the edges. The company logo is carved into the deck at the centre," he said. "I've not seen any astrolabe."

"I know where it is," Emily replied. "It is at the centre of the logo. It is covered over with a wooden lid, but I can see it."

Thomas looked at her in awe. "You mean you've got X-ray vision now?"

Emily smiled and tapped her temple with a finger. "I mean in *here*, Numpty."

"What do you have to do?" Claire asked her.

"No idea. I just feel as though I have to have contact with it."

"Mental or physical?" Claire pressed.

Emily pondered. "Physical, but beneath the wooden cover it's behind safety glass," she finally said.

Trevor's face became an anxious mask. "The

wooden cover was to keep it secret until it was unveiled, so should be easy to take off. The safety glass will be a different story."

Claire brandished the tenderiser. "Between this and your axe, I'd say we have choices."

"They might work," Trevor said.

"They're going to have to," Edna said. "I don't intend to stay on this damn piece of driftwood any longer than needs be."

They went out onto the deck, after the confines below, the emptiness all about them created an oppressive edge in all but Emily.

Her mind was incredibly focused, consumed by the image of the astrolabe. A low hum took up residence in her brain, and although she did not know how or why, she understood that the sound was a calling, the device she sought to guide Beatrice home was in turn steering her towards it.

Emily pulled ahead of the others, the urgency driving her on despite Trevor's calls for her to slow down. She made her way to the centre of the company logo, and at its centre was a raised circle of blue wood. She found the edges and prised the veil free with ease, discarding it immediately.

Eyes cast down to the deck, Emily saw a circular glass portal, and then the astrolabe, beneath; it's golden, circular structure glittering despite the meagre light. Its surface was an intricate pattern of vines and leaves of raised gold that edged a series of concentric circles.

Finally seeing the device of her visions was almost as dizzying as the sudden vibration she found in her sternum as she looked down at the portal.

Trevor was suddenly beside her, shattering the moment. He gestured for her to step back and as she moved clear, he brought the axe down, hard and true. A diagonal crack appeared in the glass, but it did not shatter.

The axe was lifted high and came down again, the head burying deeply into the portal.

"Don't damage it!" Emily warned.

Trevor pulled on the handle to find the implement was stuck in the pane. He grunted as he tried to prise it out.

"Damn thing is stuck!" Trevor said.

A protracted hiss made them all freeze.

Then another, and another, these accompanied by the click-clicking claws of Thomas' so called dark-beasts.

The creatures skulked from the stairwell at the far end of the deck, at least ten of them. Over twenty yards away shadows emerged from the foredeck below, bodies low and stalking them.

Claire heard movement behind her. At the base of the stairs that led from the dining room, the green eyes of those who had survived the kitchen fire looked back at her.

"They're back here, too," she called out. "We're trapped."

Thomas stood with her, his body tense.

"I'm pretty scared right now," he said.

"Me too," Claire whispered. "But we've got to be strong, Tom. We've got to hold them off so Emily can do her thing."

"What if we can't?" Edna interjected from nearby.

"Then the world will become so miserable you'll feel right at home," Thomas said.

If Edna had any intention of replying to the jibe, she never got the chance.

The dark-beasts launched their attack.

Rough hands grabbed at Elmo's collar, and yanked him upright, lifting him through the jagged opening in the tiles, and he was suddenly airborne, the night air around him, the sky bellowing with ominous grey clouds.

His vision was suddenly filled with the malevolent face of Alison, her green eyes broiling and devoid of mercy.

"Lost for words?" she gloated. "Well, that makes a change. Perhaps you'll find your voice where I drop your useless carcass to the cobblestones."

Elmo instinctively reached out and tried to grab hold of her shoulders, but his hands froze in the air, held firm by some strange magic.

Alison laughed, and they both ascended until the roof of Gull Cottage was over twenty feet below them. Elmo's breath came in short, sharp gasps as fear kicked in.

He was aware of movement beside him and he saw Edward floating on the air as though it was the most natural thing in the world.

"If you drop this tub of lard, I think he'll bounce," Edward laughed.

Struggling to move his arms, Elmo's legs flailed in the air. "Don't do this," he whispered. "Please don't do this."

Alison spun him around and he cried out in

surprise and terror. Now facing the ocean, the breeze hit his face. Even through his panic he could see the harbour, and the many, many people—the entire town, it seemed—standing on the edge, facing out to sea.

From these people, hundreds of thin beams of green streaked out to a single point on the ocean.

"Look at them," Alison said in awe. "So jealous, so consumed. If it wasn't for them none of this would be possible. Desire is a powerful tool in dominion."

Elmo realised the focal point, an object out on the water, turned to writhing mist by the luminous gazes of those in the harbour.

"The yacht," he breathed. "Beatrice."

"And Emily," Alison said. "Just so you know."

"Why?" Elmo asked. But it was a stall, an attempt to delay what was fast becoming inevitable.

"Because we can." Alison smiled.

Then she let go.

Chapter Twenty-Two

THE FOG IN the streets made the drive to the library slow going, the density reflecting the headlamps to such a degree that Albert turned them off and used only sidelights.

Sitting forward, he peered through the windscreen.

"This isn't normal," he muttered.

"Damn right," said Dennis. "Normal is a night in the Salty Sailor drinkin' pints of Cinder's Cider until ye can't tell difference between the landlord and a coat stand."

"How did we ever become friends?" Albert said.

Before Dennis could reply, a shadow crossed in front of the car, forcing Albert to stamp on the brakes. Dennis whacked his head off the windscreen and cursed profusely as he rubbed his forehead.

"Another piece of drivin' like that an' we ain't goin' to be friends much long after," he grumbled.

"I almost hit someone," Albert said. His hands were gripping the wheel, and he'd stalled the engine. "Guess I'd fail if this was my driving test."

"That's assumin' ye ever took a test in the first place."

Albert ignored him. "This is hopeless. I'm guessing

we can't be that far, we passed the museum before hitting this thick patch, which means the library can't be any more than a few hundred yards ahead."

"Ye suggestin' we walk?" Dennis said with distaste.

Albert popped his seatbelt and opened the car door. He climbed out without a word.

"Damnation," said Dennis.

The two men stood in the street, the green mist rolling around them.

"It's colder than a pub-widow's welcome out here," Dennis said.

Albert squinted into the gloom. There was no sign of the shadow that he'd almost hit. He sought out Dennis.

"The library is up ahead. If we stay to the kerb we can't miss it."

"Don't be sure," Dennis chuckled. "I've missed the kerb many a time."

"Well, tonight might not be the best night to get lost," Albert said as though Dennis needed any more of a warning.

They edged forward, keeping the kerb to their left, following the angle it took, each of them aware that to dally would mean getting lost in the eerie mist.

Every few yards the fog would oscillate as currents of chilly, cloying air wafted through, and as the mass shifted, they could see the ghostly, dark shapes of buildings. Then the structures were gone as the fog closed them off once more.

Vision was now down to a mere foot and Dennis tugged on Albert's sleeve.

"We need to be gettin' where we're headin' soon, old fella," he said. "Or we could be walkin' into the bay an' wouldn't know it until we were spottin' the fish."

Albert was about to respond when a hand shot toward him and grabbed hold of his shoulder, making him cry out.

Dennis pulled back an arm, his hand balled into a fist ready to deliver a blow, but a small voice came to them.

"Now, now, Dennis Hodges. Ye're ain't taken up fightin' old women now, have ye?"

"Maud," Albert said embracing her. She hugged him back and gave him a peck on the cheek.

"Think ye're pleased to see me then, Albert?" she grinned.

"Of course," he said. "We thought something had happened."

"Somethin' has happened," Maud said. "An' this damn fog is part of it all."

"Then let's get inside and you can fill us in," Albert said in a dour tone.

Maud ushered both of them up the kerb and there they found the library steps which they carefully climbed, each holding the hem of a cardigan or jacket so as not to get lost *en route*.

"Ye're a sight for sore eyes, Maud," Dennis admitted behind Maud. "There could be worse things out here in this damn soup."

"Ye're a sweet talker, Dennis," Maud laughed. "Don't let anyone tell ye otherwise."

The doors emerged through the mire and they got into the reception area where Agnes was waiting anxiously for them. She hugged the two men and they went into the main reading area, where they all sat down with sheets of typewritten vellum.

"Have you gone back to night school, Agnes?" Albert mused.

"These aren't mine," Agnes said. "They belong to Primrose."

Albert looked about him. "So where is she?"

The two women exchanged glances and Agnes passed several sheets of paper to Albert and Dennis, who read them with grim faces. From her tormented, unspecified prison, the spirit of Primrose Meadowsweet had told all. From the resurrection of Elizabeth Caldecott by hapless archaeologists in search of another witch in Cooper's Cove, the evoking of the ancient curse, and the way she, and many others had been used by the entity at the heart of the town. The combined jealousy of the town was holding the yacht in an eternal grip, fuelled by what she called *The Green Man*, a current real-life representation of the governor who had murdered Elizabeth's mother.

There were gaps in the tale. Both Primrose and Elizabeth had not been party to the real designs in play, but Primrose did write that before her demise she had been able to leave a few clues for those on the yacht to fathom, if such minds were as acute as The Dark Heart feared. The guilt on the pages was palpable, her attempts to communicate her only way to redeem her terrible actions.

After considering the text and its implications, Albert put the papers down in front of him. "So where the hell is the yacht?"

"We think it's between this world and whatever place The Darkness inhabits," Agnes replied. "And Primrose tells us what's keeping it there is the curse evoked by Elizabeth. It causes jealousy to consume the host, and in turn that is converted into a powerful binding spell. The town is bewitched; those not affected are trapped indoors by this accursed fog."

"So how do we break the spell and get those kids out o' there?" Dennis said. His voice was gruff with anger.

"We have to wake *The Green Man* of Elizabeth's curse," Agnes said. "The physical totem of the governor from Elizabeth's past."

Dennis sighed. "There used to be a time when fightin' with fists was good enough."

"Aye, lad," Maud said flatly. "But it ain't about the means; it's the will to do it. Who can be this totem, Agnes?"

They thought for a moment. Then Albert slapped his forehead in annoyance.

"It's obvious!" he said, exasperated. "Khaldun Userkaf! The poor chap has been in a coma since all this started, and Primrose was with him on the day he winked out."

Agnes thought this over. "Well, if this is about totems, then Khaldun would fit. His current state could be a representation of Elizabeth's original curse."

"So this is Khaldun's fault?" Dennis quizzed.

"This ain't anyone's fault but the thing in this town," Maud said. "An' from what I reckon the governor in Lizzie's tale was a man who was already jealous, an' would do anythin' to keep his power. Khaldun has a good heart. It ain't fittin' for ol' Maud."

The silence that followed made it clear everyone was in agreement.

"But who do we know who is so self-absorbed and wants everything they haven't got?" Albert said.

Maud eyed everyone in turn. "Anyone seen anythin' of Gideon Codd these past few days?"

At the moment Maud queried the whereabouts of Gideon Codd, Dorsal Finn's local civil servant was still in his sitting room, lying on the sofa upon which he'd collapsed a few days before. The flames in the hearth were no longer crackling with orange embers, they were a pulsating green glow, sending out vines of green mist.

Codd's mind was, of course, elsewhere. And in this elsewhere he found himself in a dusty street, dressed in rags, shivering in the cold breeze as it crossed his exposed skin.

In his belly was a gnawing hunger that almost drove him insane. He had no idea when he'd last eaten; a steady growl came from his empty stomach as he watched, through the plate glass window of a restaurant, a man eating a lavish feast.

To him, this meal had appeared to go on for over an hour, course after course landing on the table to be devoured by the single occupant. The man was vaguely familiar, he wore a white suit and Panama hat, his trim goatee beard was also white, flecked with food.

Once or twice the man had wilfully turned to look at him as he placed a forkful of chicken or beef or lamb into his mouth, and every time, Codd's mouth had opened, mimicking the movement perfectly.

With every mouthful Codd watched pass the man's lips, so the envy grew, the yearning—the desire—to live as this man lived, to have a seat at that table, to be the one looking out at the miscreants on the street.

This feeling was incredibly potent and it almost drove him to distraction.

He watched the endless meal for what seemed a lifetime, tears of want streaming down his cheeks as his mouth grinned with the thought of possessing it all.

The dark-beasts moved as one, maligned pack, their terrible hisses marking their approach.

Thomas and Claire made their way towards the astrolabe, where Trevor and Emily pulled frantically to free the axe from the portal.

A dark-beast leapt and landed between the two groups. Their pathway blocked, Claire yelled out to Trevor who loosed the axe for long enough to pull the flare pistol from his belt, and discharged it towards the creature barring their exit. The flare embedded in the body of the beast, setting it aflame.

Claire brought the tenderiser up and smashed the creature aside with a huge, animalistic grunt, sending the entire carcass towards its comrades who immediately withdrew from the heat with loud cries. They fell back through the oval door and into the stairway where they skulked as their kin lay on the deck, burning brightly.

Their way now clear, Claire and Thomas approached Trevor who had managed to free the axe, and was getting ready to take another swing. The dark-beasts on the other side of the deck were now looming closer.

"They're almost on you," Claire called out to him. Distracted, Trevor mistimed the swing. The axe came down again and instead of hitting the glass, it caught the metal frame. The recoil jarred Trevor's arm enough to cause him to lose his grip and it went spinning off into the darkness.

"Damn it!" he cried out.

A loud snarl brought his attention back immediately. A dark-beast came at him and he primed another flare, the pistol trembling in his hands. He moved swiftly, the creature closing the space between them quickly, its limbs long and its frame emaciated, but the twisted face was snarling, and its mouth a place of needle-sharp teeth.

The dark-beast pounced, crossing the dead-air like a panther. Emily went onto her knees, splayed fingers making contact with the portal. Trevor unleashed the flare, but it went wild, streaking off into the endless night. The creature landed upon him, claws going to work as he cried out in frustration and pain.

The flare pistol fell from him and skittered towards Thomas who picked it up, but without the flares it was just useless metal.

Heartened by the successful assault the other dark-beasts gained confidence, and emerged from the shadows, eyes gleaming and claws eager.

Claire beat at the creature attacking Trevor, but it somehow managed to take the blows. Trevor was doing his best to stave off the attack, but he already had several slashes across his white tunic, and Claire empathised as she saw the weals beneath.

Then something flashed to her right, the glimmer of metal as an axe came through the air, and struck the dark-beast on the side of the head, sending it rolling away in agony. Thomas stood gasping with exertion as the beast found its footing and glared at him, its gait unsteady after the blow it had just sustained.

Edna and Dorothy stood close by, fending off a sly counter-attack. Edna had caved in the head of a shadow-creature with her rolling pin, as her friend managed to blind another with the tip of her umbrella. The two women appeared lost amongst the tide of shapes near them, yet their determination to join the others was remarkable to all who looked on.

Claire helped Trevor to his feet and Thomas handed him the flare pistol. Trevor looked back at them both and shook his head.

"I got one more left and that's it," he said.

"There's too many of them," Claire said. Her face was etched with anger, not fear.

"You've got one flare but a bag of stuff," Edna said from their left. "Maybe we need to circle the wagons."

"That probably means something to someone over the age of eighty," Thomas said.

"I know what she means," Trevor said and there was hope in his voice.

He grabbed Dorothy's shopping bag and pulled free the cooking oil. He threw a bottle to both Claire and Thomas.

"Slop it out onto the deck. Create a circle, and everyone else gets in the middle!"

Claire nodded with understanding, and opened the bottle. She began pouring, moving in a cumbersome semi-circle as the creatures came forward. Thomas did the same, until the grease glistened all around them.

A great shape bowled into the group, scattering them. Claire was knocked backwards and landed heavily on her backside. Thomas and Edna were sent beyond the circle, the grease giving their trajectory momentum. Trevor collapsed as a great weight landed on him, and as he looked up he saw a wriggling black creature with many legs, and great, writhing tentacles that were made of snakes, their heads hissing like heavy rain upon Tarmac.

The creature had two heads—two faces—each a one a twisted parody of Cotteridge and Melville.

Trevor's horror did nothing to stop the realisation dawning on him as he saw the spider legs and snake tentacles. *They become our worst fear*, his terrified mind told him. *Once it devours me, I shall have bats crawling inside me forever.*

With rage, he lifted his hand to fire the pistol directly into his assailant, but it was no longer in his grasp.

The Cotteridge-beast leered, Trevor could see that it was taking its time, enjoying the moment, relishing the fear it could no doubt see in his eyes.

Claire came to Trevor's aid. Her fists and feet brought about many blows, but she was swiped aside and landed on the deck. She did not stir.

From his place beyond the circle, Thomas saw Claire go down and he cried out in rage. He grabbed at the axe and hefted it, a dark-beast came for him and he cleaved its head, and it fell down without a sound.

Thomas charged to Claire's aid, but en route a small moan of pain came to him, and he saw Edna staggering towards him. A bloody smear ran from under her headscarf.

Seeing the old woman in discomfort reminded him about how he'd feel if the same happened to Maud or Agnes, and he knew he could not leave her at the mercy of the dark-beasts which, even now, he could see stalking her. He went over to her and tried to offer assistance, but to his surprise she resisted him.

"Get your hands off me, Thomas Beecham!" she yelled, and dragged her arms away from his reach. He saw that her right hand clutched at something.

The flare pistol.

"Today is for the young," Edna whispered to him.

At first Thomas thought that the old woman had tripped, she ploughed into him, sending him backwards where the grease took him back into the circle. Then, as he crashed into Trevor and the Cotteridge-beast, he saw Edna raise the pistol and aim at the deck to his left.

The flare spat towards the circle and suddenly an immense wall of flame shot skywards, and a great roar went up from every dark-beast on the yacht.

The last thing Thomas could see before the flames obscured his view was the lonely sight of Edna Duffy, surrounded by countless green eyes.

The chilly breeze swept across a plaza made of marble and limestone. Balustrades as thick as tree trunks lined either side of an immense space, and the floor was covered in mosaics of cavorting, fire-breathing creatures. Codd leaned against a large gate, fashioned in gold, each slat a twisted, ornate vine. In his grey rags, he looked so out of place, two differing worlds defined by beggar and surroundings.

On the other side of the plaza was the palace. Like the gate giving access to it, the building was a thing of ornate beauty, a place of kings and queens, of wealth and power.

Codd looked upon walls of solid gold, windows

with silver frames, doors of ivory and decorated with precious stones. He rested his head upon the gate, relishing the coolness of the gold against his brow, craving access to the building beyond.

His eyes watched the people moving to and fro across the plaza, their clothes vibrant, and regalia glittering under a pale sun.

In his belly, the desire to be on the other side of the gate, to join those enjoying this lavish and omnipotent lifestyle was overwhelming. Still, he revelled in the pain it brought to him, the feeling should have left him crushed, but instead it merely perpetuated his desire to have such things, to claim them as his own.

His hands clutched the bars of the gate and he wept, not with hopelessness or pity, but the power that he found in envy.

"This infernal fog has gotten worse," Albert said as he peered through the glass panels in the library doors. The mist lapped idly against the panes, a seemingly solid wall of pale jade. "We've not a hope of finding our way safely back to the car, let alone Codd's house."

"Then we're stuck here," Agnes said with a dejected refrain. "It's hopeless."

"Sewers," Dennis said loudly.

"There's no need fer that Dennis Hodges," Maud warned. "Agnes was only expressin' the obvious."

"I mean if we can't go through the damn streets, we'll go under 'em."

Albert turned to Agnes. "Do you have schematics of the town?"

"This is the best library in the district," Agnes said proudly. "Of course it does."

She headed off to the resource section and pulled out the town plans. Opening the ledger, she searched the index, before turning to the respective section in the beaten book.

"These are a few years old," she said, laying the pages open for all to see. "But I doubt anything has changed in that time."

"Not with Codd's nose in the coffers," Maud sniffed. "Town's been thinkin' itself lucky to get a new bus shelter."

"Aye," Dennis said. "The mayor is a rum un fer sure. But right now he's the key to stoppin' the shenanigans goin' on in this town. So, we better go an' get him."

Albert scrutinised the schematics, his finger tracing a route on the page. "I figure we have a ten-minute walk below ground at best. Nearest manhole is just beyond the library steps."

"How do we find the cover?" Agnes said. "You three barely made it back in here."

Albert thought this over. "During the war I recall RAF pilots cleared fog by putting burners on the runway. If we create heat then maybe we'll be able to see enough to get to the manhole cover."

"Ye got a paraffin lamp?" Dennis asked Agnes.

"Yes," she replied.

Dennis grinned. "Then I guess we're in business."

Chapter Twenty-Three

GNES WRINKLED HER nose despite the heavy scarf wrapped around her face.

"Just when I thought we couldn't sink any lower," she said. Even though her voice was muffled, it bounced around the sewer tunnel, a narrow passageway of red bricks that stretched off into a seemingly infinite gloom.

"I dunno," said Dennis. He was up ahead, a handkerchief tied around his face, which made him look like a cowboy from an old movie. "I've drunk in worse places than this."

"You're aware that fact surprises no one?" Albert said from in front of Dennis. He had his own mask, a heavy towel draped over his head and around his mouth like some flannel balaclava.

"Let's keep goin'," Maud said from behind Agnes. The hideous wheeze of a gas mask respirator punctuated her words. "I ain't sure if what's niffin' out there can be worse than the smell of rubber in this here headpiece."

Albert rubbed at his face. "Believe me, Maud, what's out here is *worse*."

He had used the paraffin lamp to heat the air as

they all stepped from the library. The reaction from the fog to the heat had been mercifully predictable, but none of the group would have described it as natural. Rather than evaporate, the fog appeared to recoil from the touch of the lamplight.

As they made their way from the library to the circular manhole cover, they had kept close, watching as Dennis used his might—and a crowbar he'd produced from inside his coat—to gain access.

Now, as they walked carefully through the passageway, the lamp sputtered, throwing crazy shapes around them. The walls were coated in thick, brown-green slurry, not dissimilar to the pungent ankle-deep black water they were wading through.

The ceiling was arched and at various points they came to intersections with ladders screwed into the slimy walls. At the apex of these wrought iron rungs were manhole covers leading to the street above.

At one such intersection Albert paused and checked the map he held under the lamplight.

"What's with the dawdlin'?" Dennis said over Albert's shoulder.

"We're here."

They all looked up. The manhole overhead was edged in the eerie green light from the fog beyond.

"I'll go up and get that cover open," Dennis said, crowbar at the ready.

A low, thin screech came to them from further down the tunnel. The sound was haunting—mournful—yet accompanied with an underlying, sinister hiss.

"What on Earth is that?" Agnes said.

"Dunno, but at this point it's about as welcome as a skunk at a weddin'," Maud observed.

"Let's get up these steps," Albert said, ushering Maud and Agnes to the rungs.

Dennis was already at the manhole, feet planted on the rungs, back pressed against the metal cover. He pushed up with his legs and gave out a huge groan of effort, then eased off, gasping.

"Damn thing won't budge," he breathed.

Maud and Agnes looked anxiously towards the oncoming din; the hiss now seemed to resemble many scratching claws.

"*Make* it budge, Dennis," Maud said. "We ain't wantin' to make acquaintance with whatever's comin'."

Dennis resumed trying to move the hatch. Grunts and expletives came in quick succession. Then a loud screech rang out in the tunnel.

"Thank God!" Albert said. "Knew you could do it, Dennis!"

"That wasn't the hatch," Dennis said grimly.

A writhing mass of scrabbling shapes came at them, tumbling through the tunnel, splashing through the filthy water, bristling with tiny green eyes.

"Rats," Albert said.

"Ye need stronger swear words," Maud muttered.

On board *The Spirit of the Ocean*, bedlam had taken hold. The deck was ablaze, a flickering yellow circle, in the centre of which was Thomas and the remnants of the group.

Dorothy was wailing for the lost Edna, Trevor

yelled in pain as the spider-beast, startled by the sudden gout of fire, used him as a springboard to leap away—over the blinding flames.

Outside the circle, the dark-beasts yelled and spat, frustrated that they were unable to get at their prey, at least for the time being.

Claire crawled over to Trevor. "Are you okay?"

"Feels like that thing used me as a doormat, but I'm still breathing," he said through gritted teeth.

Claire looked through the flickering flames and saw the arachnid shape as it scuttled to and fro, testing the burning perimeter, the actions a clear demonstration it was neither gone nor any less determined to get to them.

"The thing is still here," Claire said.

"Fire is going to die down soon," Trevor said. "We've nothing left to fight them but an arsenal of kitchen equipment. The odds are not good."

Claire turned and saw that Dorothy was sitting with her face in her hands, shoulders shivering with grief. Thomas was looking out beyond the flames, the axe hanging limply in his hand. He looked drawn, and so very young.

"What a mess," she whispered.

She looked around her and saw that, as Trevor predicted, the flames were beginning to dampen as the cooking oil burned off, and beyond the shadowy figures of the dark-beasts scurried backwards and forwards, eager for opportunity.

It was hard not to allow a sense of hopelessness to nudge at her, but any kind of terrible wonder Claire had ascribed to the beasts paled when she saw Emily beside her. She came through the smoke and flame, the girl's eyes were now twin white orbs and the smile on her face was instantly both terrible and beautiful.

"Come, Sister," Emily said to something unseen ahead of her. "It is time to guide you home."

"Here they come," Albert yelled.

The rats sped towards them, no more than a few hundred yards away, and sheer numbers thrashing through the water. Despite the apparently slick surface, others were somehow able to skitter up the walls. Whether in the water or over the brickwork they came as one impenetrable mass.

Dennis was frantic as he pushed and shoved against the metal disc. "This damn thing is as stubborn as Maud." He grimaced and continued to press his broad back forcefully upwards.

"Can't you use that crowbar you've got?" Albert said.

"Think I ain't thought of that?" Dennis said between shoves. "There ain't room to swing a cat up here, let alone a bloody crowbar."

Nodding, Albert ushered the women towards the ladders, his eyes never leaving the oncoming horror.

"Get climbing," he insisted. "Let's not make it easy for them."

With exertion, Agnes and Maud began climbing up the ladders, moans and groans matching those of Dennis several feet above them.

"Get yer backside up here, Albert Smythe," Maud called down. There was tightness to her voice, fear making its mark.

Albert watched the rodents, who were now only twenty feet away, their tiny voices morphing into one huge squeal. The green eyes bobbed and glistened like jewels as they ran, adding to the surreal horror of it all. Albert looked up at them, and then down to the lamp.

He loosened the fuel cap, hefted the lamp and threw it at the oncoming wave of slick fur. As the lamp landed, it sent up a plume of flame, the paraffin creating fiery islands on the surface of the water, and the rodents were moving too fast to avoid them.

The hideous sound of maimed creatures came at him before a wall of heat. He grasped the rung as several rats launched at him, regardless of the flames, most of them missed, but two managed to find him. One locked its jaws on his lower arm where it swung, frenzied, from the material of his sleeve.

The second rodent found its mark, sinking its vicious incisors into his shoulder, the tiny claws raking his coat. He cried out and almost lost his footing as he tried desperately to dislodge his attackers.

Above him Maud was calling out, and Albert managed to use her angst to motivate him against the pain in his shoulder. He smashed the rat hanging off his sleeve against the wall, where it squeaked in pain and fell to its comrades below.

Fighting for support, he hooked a rung in the crook of his arm and grasped the flailing rodent with his left hand. It squirmed under his grasp, the soaking wet fur slippery, making purchase difficult. He closed his hand over it and dragged it away from him, feeling a sharp pain at the wound's site, but this was nothing compared to his desire to be rid of the infernal creature.

The tail slapped across his face, vile droplets of water hitting his lips and eyes. Albert threw the rat into space where it disappeared into the flickering light below.

As he fought for breath, Albert could see the light below fade as the flames diminished, and the screeches came up to them as the remaining colony of rodents reasserted themselves for a second assault.

"Ye all right, Albert?" Maud called to him.

"Got bitten," he said, wincing. His shoulder felt tender but he could feel no wetness to indicate the rat's teeth had broken skin through the material of his coat. "That's not the problem right now. The fire is dying and the things are getting brave again."

A deafening sound filled the tunnel, startling them, a roar like an angry tiger. This time the direction of the noise came from overhead.

"What now?" Agnes said, voice juddering with fear. "I'm far too old for all this excitement."

The heavy thud accompanied a loud cry of triumph. They looked up to see a circle of green mist above them, the manhole cover nowhere to be seen.

"Well done, man," Agnes said, relief evident in her tone.

"Well, ye've either got it or ye ain't." Dennis grinned before climbing out of the hole.

Albert took a moment to glance below. The rats were leaping up at his feet, missing by mere inches. One of them found a lower rung and, clinging to it, found enough momentum to reach for another above it.

"Keep moving," Albert called out. "The vermin aren't looking like they're giving up either."

They exited the tunnel as fast as they were able, Dennis helping them all as they reached the hole in the road.

When Albert was clear, the two men dragged the cover across the wet cobblestones and shoved it back in place, cutting out the hideous squeals below.

Even as they all stood looking down at the metal cover that had almost sealed their fate, they could hear tiny thuds as determined rodents tried to get to them.

After a few seconds they all turned away, no one inclined to say a word.

The commotion had become irrelevant to Emily as soon as her hands had made contact with the portal. Her delicate fingers had inadvertently made contact with the glass, and at her touch, the pane rippled as it turned to liquid.

Emily's mind seemed to have an incredible sense of clarity. The astrolabe was hers, it was her tool in the war ahead, a weapon to ensure that The Darkness could hide nothing more from them, and in her hands—and only her hands—it would make clear all that sought to confound them.

She reached into the pool of water, and retrieved the device. In an instant, everything felt right, the pieces of a great puzzle were in place, and she was now a player in the greatest game of all.

Emily stood, clutching the astrolabe in both hands, and lifted her arms, looking upon its design as the surface thrummed against her palms.

She thought of only two things.

A split second later, both appeared on the deck.

Dennis looked up at Codd's house. "Well, this is where real rats hide out these days, is it?" he growled.

Agnes shuddered. "Please, no more talk about rats."

Once out of the sewer, they had all been taken aback to find the fog in the street was low, a mere lake of mist swirling about their boots. The houses remained dark, no signs of life in the windows, save for one on the second floor of Codd's house which was illuminated as a lime-green square. To their amazement, a jade cataract of smog flowed from the sill and down onto the street.

"X marks the spot," Maud said.

They made their way up the short run of steps to Codd's front door. Albert tried the door handle and found it unlocked.

"Not very security minded," Albert observed.

"Codd's a lot of things but he ain't for lettin' people just walk into what belongs to him," Maud said. "Somethin' definitely sniffs in this larder for sure."

Albert nodded. "Then we must be cautious."

"Ye can bet on that, fella."

Dennis hefted the crowbar and went into the house. The others followed, looking into the gloom as they went. Agnes found a light switch in the hall and clicked it a few times, her efforts making no difference.

Dennis led the way, their footfalls on the stone steps echoing about the reception hall. Maud stopped halfway to look upon a large painting of a clipper riding on a stormy ocean, recognising it as *Charlotte*

Elizabeth, the vessel that had succumbed to a false light before being wrecked on the rocks of Monument Point.

She sighed at this thought and carried on up the steps.

On the first floor landing they saw luminosity coming from their right, where a corridor led to Codd's sitting room. A slab of green light lay on the carpet ahead. Cautiously they went, taking care not to make too much noise, their ears tuning in to the strange clicking noise coming from within the room.

Dennis peered into the room and saw that it was awash with a flickering green fire. The flames swirled but gave off no heat. Such was the strength of the gaudy light within that Dennis was forced to take a step back. He bumped into Albert who looked over his shoulder in shock.

"Where's Codd?" he breathed into Dennis' ear.

The two men scanned the room and found the mayor a few seconds later. They saw a leg poking out from behind a large Chesterfield sofa, a twitching, chubby foot pointing to the ceiling. There was no sign of his loafer.

"We need to get in there," Agnes said, moving forward.

Dennis held up a wary arm. "We don't know what that stuff will do to us."

"And I cannot just stand by and watch a man die," Agnes said, brushing his arm aside and stepping into the sitting room.

Maud followed Agnes at speed. "I'm with her," she said in passing.

The two men shrugged and followed the two women, who had now raced to the fallen mayor's side.

They all stood looking down, their mouths gaping as they studied Codd.

"Oh, dear Lord," Agnes said.

Codd was lying supine, head tilted back as though fast asleep, yet his eyes were wide open. Also agape were his fat, red lips and from both his sockets and his mouth the billowing green flames flew into the air, writhing on the ceiling, flowing out through the open window.

"We've found The Green Man," Maud said.

Dennis shook his head, his face grim. "How'd we stop it?"

Agnes looked around the room.

"There's no on-off switch this time, Agnes," Albert said.

"We'll see about that," Maud said.

She went over to the drinks table. She picked up the soda siphon, and shook it. Satisfied she went over to Codd.

Standing over him she blasted his face with tonic water. The green flames sputtered as Codd seemed to stir, but intensified again within an instant. The walls began to tremble, cracks snaking across the plaster.

The siphon fired again, a longer blast, the flames dimming, and this time Maud paused only to prime the mechanism before letting go another jet of soda. Codd's face became animated, his hands coming up to ward off the water.

As he did so, a pulse of jade pushed the group backwards, almost knocking them down. The room creaked as the building's infrastructure shifted. Ornaments crashed to the floor, bottles and glasses tumbled from the table as it tipped over, and the window blew outwards with a terrific crack and the tinkling of glass.

Codd rolled onto his side and spluttered, hands pawing the water away from his face. Albert and Dennis went to him and began dragging him to his feet.

"What are you doing?" Codd protested. "Unhand me you buffoons!"

The floor beneath them seemed to lift and a great cracking noise filled the air.

"For God's sake," Codd said as he watched the destruction going on around them. "Help me get out of here!"

"Changin' yer tune like a tone-deaf piano player as usual, Mayor?" Dennis said as he hefted Codd towards the door.

Maud and Agnes steadied each other as the carpet rumpled, the floorboards pushing upwards like giant, probing fingers. They all made it into the corridor, alarmed by the way the walls were out of alignment, making the passage ahead appear like something from a fairground funhouse.

Disorientated, the group made for the stairs, plaster falling from the ceiling, peppering their hair like snowflakes. A murky light came from streetlamps outside, diffused by distance and the powdery plaster showering down, but it was enough to navigate their way down the stairs. Maud let go of one of the stone banisters as it sheared off, and went tumbling to the reception hall where it broke, sending large chunky pieces skittering across the expensive marble tiles.

In the ceiling, the large chandelier danced wildly,

crystal bulbs falling like fat teardrops that exploded on the harsh floor like small bombs.

At the bottom of the stairs, Dennis shoved Codd forwards, the mayor struggling to stay on his feet as he tried to weave through the broken chunks of banister. The chandelier landed only a few feet away. Codd shrieked in fright.

Albert lingered so that he could make sure Maud and Agnes weren't left behind, and then they were all outside, moving down the run of steps, leaving behind crashes and bangs as the house died.

When they were clear, they all turned to the house. Codd looked aghast as the roof fell inwards and clouds of white dust pumped out of the windows and front door.

"Look what you idiots have done to my house!"

"Let's make a deal," Dennis said as he slapped a hand down onto the mayor's left shoulder. It was hard enough to send a puff of plaster dust into the air. "How about ye shut yer mouth and I won't be throwin' yer ungrateful carcass back inside that pile o' rubble?"

Codd's silence told them he'd already decided to accept the deal.

Across town, the crowd of people who were standing in the harbour looking out at a single point on the ocean didn't feel the need to do so anymore. In fact, the awful feeling of resentment and envy possessing them slipped away as though they were shrugging off a bad cold.

Many of them looked blankly at each other as

though waking from a long sleep. Others, George and Maureen Beecham amongst them, broke into smiles when they saw people they recognised.

Conversations followed; chit-chat about how wonderful the launch had been, as though no memory of events lingered in their psyche. There were no prompts or reminders to keep them on-topic, either. Starved of its power source, the fog sank back into the ground, the sickly tide absorbed by the cobblestones and concrete, leaving no trace.

Just like the fog, the crowd began to disperse. Tonight, after all, was about the lucky few on the yacht, and the fun they'd no doubt be having as the night progressed.

That would be if 'fun' was now defined by a battle to survive.

Elmo tried to scream but his lungs were seized in his chest. The ground seemed to come up at him in super-slow motion, and he closed his eyes, not wanting to see his doom when it finally came.

Lots of thoughts ran through his mind, but the one that was strongest was the image of Emily and how he'd never see her again.

There was a sudden piercing scream and Elmo thought that he'd somehow found his voice.

It was enough for him to open his eyes. To his surprise Alison was falling with him, her hair tangled, her clothing rippling in the wind like the wings of a stricken crow.

He saw despair in her eyes, the corneas no longer

jade but blue, and horror on her face as it contorted with grief.

"I can't save myself," a voice said inside Elmo's head. He recognised it as Alison's, and it was crackling with guilt. "I don't deserve to be saved."

She held out a trembling hand towards Elmo. He reached for it, the world around them now almost standing still. Instead of grasping his hand, Alison withdrew hers and shoved it forwards at speed.

A streak of pale white light escaped her palm and struck Elmo in the chest, blasting him backwards. He felt no pain, just a change in trajectory and he landed on a car, his backside putting a sizeable dent in the roof.

He turned away at the last minute as Alison hit the cobblestones, and he put a hand to his mouth, his whole body numb with shock.

The girl's inert form lay still, the realisation that her last act was one of atonement, making it clear that something in the town had changed.

He slid from the roof, over the windshield, and onto the bonnet, bruised but alive. Looking sadly at Alison, he realised that these days, such things were small mercies.

Elmo planted both feet on the ground and stood. He heard the sound of someone cursing, and followed the familiar voice. He saw Edward in a nearby tree, his coat caught in one of the branches, his collar hoisted as he dangled like some ungainly marionette, his heels bouncing against the trunk several feet in the air.

"Hey, Elmo," he called. "Help me out, would you?"

Elmo shook his head, incredulous at the others boy's gall. "A few minutes ago you'd have seen me splattered on the pavement. Just like poor Alice."

"Poor Alice?" Edward said as he struggled against his coat. "Evil bitch was going to kill us all."

Elmo wiped his mouth with the back of his hand as the heat of anger began to warm in his stomach. "Well, Alice is dead, Eddie. And even after all this is done, you'll still be bad to the bone. I think I'd like you to hang around for a while. It would be safer. For you."

He turned away, hand so tightly balled his fingers hurt.

He left Edward yelling and cussing in the tree, but Elmo had other things on his mind, things that were far more important than doling out retribution to the likes of Edward Chorley.

Somehow, some way, he had to get his friends back.

It was a noble mission and there was no way he could not have understood the enormity associated with such a task, nor the fact that, at that very moment, the process was in motion.

The first thing that appeared when Emily focused on the astrolabe was a door. It hovered six feet above deck, a rectangle edged in light, giving way to a hallway beyond. Inside the doorway was the second thing.

It was Beatrice, her face a mask of anger as she looked at the scene below.

As they became aware of her, the dark-beasts surprised all of those watching by recoiling in fear. Some of them even ran to the side of the yacht and jumped into the darkness. Others were resilient. They swallowed their fear and rallied to the arachnid.

The great creature reared up, four of its legs thrashed in the air like a startled stallion. It let out a harsh scream of defiance and spittle flew as a fine mist from Cotteridge and Melville's distorted blue lips.

Beatrice was beyond alarm and intimidation. Without a word, she stepped from the radiant doorway and hung in the air as though standing on an invisible platform. Her body was outlined by a warm white glow, and her eyes were distant, as though she was seeing something altogether different.

She looked upon the creature, and within her stare was a searing heat which made the very air between her and the arachnid swell like the incoming tide.

Without warning, the creature exploded, not with fire or brilliance, it merely shattered as though made from ice. Wherever the tiny pieces landed they turned the deck to smoke as the scorched embers passed through the planks as though they were not there at all.

Upon seeing the demise of their leader, the other dark-beasts scattered in terror.

Beatrice's eyes followed them and whenever her stare fell upon one of them, the bodies of these creatures would obliterate, their remains dispersed across the ship, searing wood and melting fibreglass and plastic, with small crackles and pops.

Beatrice closed her eyes, and everyone below looked on with amazement as an intense, inner glow turned her exposed skin translucent, and the air around them changed with a hideous ripping sound.

Gone was the emptiness they'd grown accustomed to, and the stark silence. The ocean's roar was all around them, and the sky was full of twinkling stars.

Claire laughed at the sight of it and hugged Trevor who smiled despite his wounds.

With the stars above her, Beatrice floated down to the deck, her bare feet making no sound as she walked across to the dying circle of flame. She stared at the blaze and it winked out. The next thing she knew, Thomas slammed into her and held her tightly.

She looked down at him, for a moment her face was bemused, as though she did not recognise him at all, and then life came back to her eyes and she embraced him.

Deep within the yacht there was a low rumble. They all felt the ground beneath them shudder, and somewhere to their left a bright flash illuminated the water. The blast came a few seconds later, debris smattering into the water.

Emily came to Beatrice and Thomas, her face serene. Beatrice reached up and placed her palm to Emily's cheek, and held it there.

"Sister," Beatrice said simply.

Emily put her hand over Beatrice's and nodded in accord. "Yes."

The yacht began to list, the chairs and loose objects slid across the deck. A long creak filled their ears.

"We're sinking," Trevor shouted.

"Are there any lifeboats?" Claire asked.

"Aft-deck," he said. "But we need to move while there's still time to launch it."

Another huge explosion ripped through the yacht, and this time all but Beatrice and Emily were knocked off balance. Thomas still clung to his sister, who appeared to be defying gravity as the aft-deck collapsed and a spout of water gushed skywards, soaking them all.

"It's too late," Trevor said. "She's going under with us on board."

The bow began to lift, and Trevor and Claire began to slide towards the railing that overlooked the rapidly disappearing aft-deck. Trevor grabbed onto Dorothy who was rolling towards them with small whimpers coming from her lips.

They rested against the rails, watching the roaring sea as it came up for them. Claire looked desperately at Beatrice, Thomas, and Emily.

"Help us," she cried.

The world became a blur as bracing seawater washed over her legs, taking her breath away. Claire's eyes met Beatrice's and she could see the red hair was almost as fire.

The next thing she knew, Claire was lying on the cobblestone streets of Dorsal Finn promenade, and *The Spirit of the Ocean* was nowhere to be seen.

Patience felt the floor tiles shake beneath her feet. At first she'd thought it was her imagination, and then the drip stand connected to her father's inert form jiggered with a barely perceptible rattle.

Outside the window the blackness was fading, and the sight of magnolia walls bleeding through the greyness made Patience gasp with delight. She stood, and went to peer through the glass pane. Sure enough, the hospital corridor was back, all trace of the omnipotent darkness, gone.

"Patience?"

The quiet voice of her mother was infused with a yawn, and Patience spun round, the smile on her face huge with relief. She went over to Skylar, who by that point was engaged in a post-slumber stretch.

A sudden alarm started up from the machine attached to Khaldun, and both Patience and Skylar rushed to him, panic in their eyes.

"Get the nurse!" Skylar said in a wavering voice.

Dejected, Patience went to the doors that, for an age, she had no desire to open. As she approached them, she could hear the oncoming footsteps as medical staff hurried towards their room.

A great cry came from her mother and Patience turned quickly, fear almost seizing her heart. When she saw that Skylar was draped over her father's body, racked with sobs, Patience felt an emptiness wash over her.

Tears fell, splashing the linoleum, the image of her mother crying and her father's arm lying still above the bed sheets becoming so blurred she could almost imagine her father's hand lifting from the bed, and going to the small of Skylar's back to give her a weak hug.

It was only when that same hand gave Patience a thumbs up sign, she realised that her tears played no part in this at all.

Within seconds she was rushing to the bed and joining her mother, tears and joy intermingling into a potent welcoming committee.

"Can anyone tell us what just happened?" Trevor looked around him, shocked by the empty streets where only seconds before there were the churning waters of the Atlantic.

"Well, you just had the world's shortest commission," Dorothy said flatly.

Trevor saw Beatrice and Emily staring at him. Their faces were equally as bemused.

"I guess I thought about us being safe and here we are," said Beatrice.

Trevor's face remained dissatisfied. "What happened tonight?"

Beatrice did not hesitate. "We stopped something bad from happening."

"Yes, but what?" Trevor asked with urgency.

"A *bad* thing," she said, and placed her hands on her hips, refusing to be drawn.

"And is it over?" Claire asked beside him.

This time Beatrice had no answer. She held out her hand to Thomas and Emily.

"Come on," she said.

"Where are we going?" Thomas replied.

"Home," Beatrice said.

The three of them walked up the cobblestone street. They had gone only a few yards when Beatrice turned to the others.

"Well?" she said. "Are you lot coming or not?"

A bell tolled and, once again, Lucas looked in the direction from which it came.

Failing to pinpoint the source, he turned back and

found himself standing in front of a house in a long street.

All the hedges were neatly trimmed and the trees pruned to such precision they all appeared the same. There were no cars on the drives or vehicles on the street. The whole area looked pristine, a place of fresh paint and polished timber.

The path to the house was lined with neat bushes, and wound through lawns of emerald green. Lucas walked up to the front door, which was wide open and saw a welcoming hallway within.

Lucas mounted the porch steps; the balustrades supporting the slats overhead threw dark stripes against the wooden blue fascia. He smiled. The whole house made him feel peaceful and he found quiet excitement, an expectation, building in his chest.

He entered the house and the anticipation increased, making him feel like a child on Christmas Eve. There was a sitting room to his left, accessed through a large rectangular space. A fire roared in the fireplace, two chairs either side of the hearth.

He went into the room and felt drawn to the chair on the right. He traced his fingers on the aged brown leather and chuckled as the tingling in his sternum left him dizzy with anticipation.

He sat down, pushed himself back in the seat, and closed his eyes. Every sense told him his search was at an end. He should wait there in the chair and all he sought would come to him.

He smiled and waited, the fire roaring and spreading its warmth, his heart full and content.

Chapter Twenty-Four

IN THE FOLLOWING days, the town of Dorsal Finn did what it did best, it healed. Part of this process involved embracing the nuances that came with living in the town, whilst on another level it meant denying a fair few things too.

Some things were hard to deny, the tragedy of the many lives lost on the night *The Spirit of the Ocean* was claimed by the sea. The reasons for its loss were compiled by Trevor, the only surviving crew member, and supported by his adamant witnesses, that for reasons unknown, a great explosion occurred in the lower decks, sinking the vessel within minutes.

In claiming ignorance, Trevor was able to fudge the detail, and while he was never able to return to the sea as a crewman, he did have more adventures, thanks to his friendship with Claire, and a new TV show called 'Perils of the Sea' where he acted as a consultant, and her co-presenter. Before she left town, Claire had made Thomas a promise to return once a year and they would sit on the beach and have a cookout, in memory of those lost.

There was loss closer to home of course. Funerals were held for Alice, Erica, and the latter girl's parents who were found drowned in Cooper's Cove. There was a huge turnout, and many tears were shed, as well as questions asked why such terrible things happened to the innocents of the world.

Primrose's funeral was a quiet affair that was attended by staff at the town hall and the very few people who knew her. The bill was paid for from the community coffers, though there was a rumour that the bulk of the payment came from Gideon Codd. No one dared ask him whether the rumour was true.

Lucas had a memorial too, attended by all who held him dear. Beatrice and Tamsin held hands throughout the service, the coffin filled with nothing but Lucas' favourite books and his laptop. It was painful and difficult to comprehend that he was gone-but-not-gone, and the tears they gave to the moment were a blend of grief and relief he was at least safe in The In-between.

Neither of them truly understood it, both only just accepted it. Surprisingly, Elmo struggled with the concept more than either Tamsin or Beatrice. The absence of his best friend cut deep, only marginally dulled by a fledgling relationship with Emily. Their connection had been apparent to Beatrice, yet she'd not been sure enough to ask Emily how she felt about Elmo. This was to change when, after reuniting, Beatrice saw them hug a little too long, and the kiss when they finally separated sealed the deal.

Beatrice was happy for them both, they deserved each other, deserved the happiness *togetherness* brought.

The thought had made her sigh. The ache in her heart had been intense but short-lived. The ordeal in

The In-between had left her changed in so many ways. The Darkness had duped them all with its spurious ruse of witches and retribution. That Beatrice had been the true target all along had not surprised her in the end, but the determination of her foe certainly had. It also showed her something else, that The Dark Heart was still weak and required others to do its work, or needed Beatrice in its own realm before it had any chance of defeating her.

It also made it impossible for her to ignore just how powerful she was in this war against this irrepressible foe, and where her weaknesses lay.

Yet Emily had become a true sister, bestowed with the gift to guide and, as The Oracle, the power of foresight. She'd retained these powers too, having to return to signing and lip reading in order to maintain her secret from all but The Newshounds. As selfish as it felt, Beatrice was uncomfortable with this because it meant Emily's powers were still needed, that the danger was still real.

Based on the issues they had finding the details of Elizabeth's past, Agnes and Maud made a decision to learn a lesson and dedicating time to keeping records of events, documenting the chronology relating to Dorsal Finn and its dark heritage, storing it on hard drives, yet still printed off and kept in a ledger hidden deep in the library reference section.

Agnes also delved deeper, going back through local folklore, becoming versed in it and its implications. Next time, they needed to be prepared. They needed to be ready.

Elsewhere, other changes had occurred. Khaldun had woken and made a full recovery, much to the relief of Patience and her mother. He had no recollection of events leading up to the accident, as though such things were now redundant, and in many ways they were. Beatrice and the others comforted Patience and made it clear that she was not to blame for evoking the curse that had paralysed the town. Patience accepted their platitudes, though Beatrice was not quite sure if her friend truly felt absolved.

Edward pleaded ignorance, of course. This was of no surprise to The Newshounds, yet after Elmo had explained the events at Gull Cottage, and the impact The Green Man had on the overall township, even Beatrice had to admit that perhaps Edward had not been entirely responsible for his actions. This conclusion was made with the kind of caution reserved for a dangerous predator, and there was no doubt Edward met the criteria for this definition with ease.

Not everything was lost. A day after *The Spirit of the Ocean* went down, the coast guard found Edna Duffy. Their attention had been drawn to a rather large piece of decking, upon which a delirious Edna sat singing *My Heart will Go On* at the top of her voice. The first thing that happened was Dorothy was taken to Edna in Ashby-on-Sea general hospital. She brought along a brand new headscarf and beard trimmer, though Edna sent her back home with the latter after a harsh tongue-lashing.

Evil entities and apocalyptic power plays aside, some things in Dorsal Finn would never change.

The pale sun washed the streets and cobblestones in sallow light. There had been a recent shower and the undulating streets were still glistening with rainwater. As the clouds moved on, the gulls returned to the sky and gave out their cries, which drifted over the town below.

Beatrice walked on the beach, the shale crunching underfoot, the tide lapping against the shore, a combination of sounds that always left her feeling at ease with the world.

Despite the watery sun and the whispering tide, some of the sparkle had been removed from her eyes. Her face was still young and pretty but her pale blue irises held something within them that was usually only seen in the sage or the experienced, it came from *knowing* things that no one else ever could.

Ahead, Beatrice could see Seer's Rock, the place that she and Lucas always wanted to be when they needed time alone. It was Lucas' favourite place, and when she needed to be with him, close to him, instinct always brought her here.

She climbed the worn steps that took her to the summit, the ocean below sending water into the air as it collided with the base of the rocks, moistening her face with its cool spray.

Beatrice stared out to sea for a while, the horizon surging under her gaze, a shimmering ribbon of light that looked as though the world had been torn and The Light was bleeding through. The simile made her smile, though a tugging on her heart reminded her that dark things were never too far away.

She tutted and ignored the negativity such a thing threatened. She placed her hand into the pockets of her jeans, and pulled out a small object. She carefully held the button in the palm of her hand, and was mesmerised by the power it held over her.

This was the most precious gift. An acknowledgment of the sacrifice they had all made to thwart a great evil. The button represented stolen moments, borrowed time in which she could remember what it had taken to give something back to the world.

Placing the button on the rocks, Beatrice watched as it gave off more lustre than the pale sun overhead really afforded. A 'V' of orange light was suddenly carved into the air and Beatrice found herself looking upon Lucas, his relaxed form sitting in the armchair where she herself had sat, legs resting on a footstool, feet toasting by a roaring fireplace. His face spoke of nothing but contentment and hope, the smile easy and infectious, Beatrice mirroring it as soon as it appeared.

She reached up, and touched the image, her fingers tracing Lucas' cheek, and on the wall of light his own hands went to the very spot where she'd made contact. He nodded and the smile on his lips grew, as though he was recalling the best memory ever.

Tears ran down Beatrice's face, yet the true impact of raw emotion was held in check, such was the nature of things, a layer of armour shielding *The Incorruptible Heart* from the pain of loss, or grief and suffering, even her own.

Just like the boy she loved, any sense of peace and acceptance of what was could only ever be achieved by holding on to the very thing The Darkness sought to remove from everyone.

Hope.

The End?

Not quite . . .

Have you tried *Beatrice Beecham's Cryptic Crypt: A Supernatural Adventure/Mystery Novel* by Dave Jeffery?

Or dive into more Tales from the Darkest Depths:

Novels:
The Mourner's Cradle: A Widow's Journey by Tommy B. Smith
House of Sighs (with sequel novella) by Aaron Dries
Beyond Night by Eric S. Brown and Steven L. Shrewsbury
The Third Twin: A Dark Psychological Thriller by Darren Speegle
Aletheia: A Supernatural Thriller by J.S. Breukelaar
Where the Dead Go to Die by Mark Allan Gunnells and Aaron Dries
Sarah Killian: Serial Killer (For Hire!) by Mark Sheldon
The Final Cut by Jasper Bark
Blackwater Val by William Gorman
Pretty Little Dead Girls: A Novel of Murder and Whimsy by Mercedes M. Yardley
Nameless: The Darkness Comes by Mercedes M. Yardley

Novellas:
A Season in Hell by Kenneth W. Cain
Quiet Places: A Novella of Cosmic Folk Horror by
Jasper Bark
The Final Reconciliation by Todd Keisling
Run to Ground by Jasper Bark
Devourer of Souls by Kevin Lucia
*Apocalyptic Montessa and Nuclear Lulu: A Tale of
Atomic Love* by Mercedes M. Yardley
Wind Chill by Patrick Rutigliano
Little Dead Red by Mercedes M. Yardley
Sleeper(s) by Paul Kane
Stuck On You by Jasper Bark

Anthologies:
Tales from The Lake Vol.5, edited by Kenneth W. Cain
Fantastic Tales of Terror: History's Darkest Secrets,
edited by Eugene Johnson
Welcome to The Show, edited by Doug Murano
Lost Highways: Dark Fictions From the Road,
edited by D. Alexander Ward
C.H.U.D. Lives!—A Tribute Anthology
Tales from The Lake Vol.4: The Horror Anthology,
edited by Ben Eads
*Behold! Oddities, Curiosities and Undefinable
Wonders*, edited by Doug Murano
*Twice Upon an Apocalypse: Lovecraftian Fairy
Tales*, edited by Rachel Kenley and Scott T.
Goudsward
Tales from The Lake Vol.3, edited by Monique
Snyman
Gutted: Beautiful Horror Stories, edited by Doug
Murano and D. Alexander Ward

Tales from The Lake Vol.2, edited by Joe Mynhardt,
Emma Audsley, and RJ Cavender
Children of the Grave
The Outsiders
Tales from The Lake Vol.1, edited by Joe Mynhardt
Fear the Reaper, edited by Joe Mynhardt
For the Night is Dark, edited by Ross Warren

Short story collections:
Dead Reckoning and Other Stories by Dino Parenti
Things You Need by Kevin Lucia
Frozen Shadows and Other Chilling Stories by Gene
O'Neill
Varying Distances by Darren Speegle
*The Ghost Club: Newly Found Tales of Victorian
Terror* by William Meikle
Ugly Little Things: Collected Horrors by Todd
Keisling
Whispered Echoes by Paul F. Olson
Embers: A Collection of Dark Fiction by Kenneth W.
Cain
Visions of the Mutant Rain Forest, by Bruce Boston
and Robert Frazier
Tribulations by Richard Thomas
Eidolon Avenue: The First Feast by Jonathan Winn
Flowers in a Dumpster by Mark Allan Gunnells
The Dark at the End of the Tunnel by Taylor Grant
Through a Mirror, Darkly by Kevin Lucia
Things Slip Through by Kevin Lucia
Where You Live by Gary McMahon
Tricks, Mischief and Mayhem by Daniel I. Russell
Samurai and Other Stories by William Meikle
Stuck On You and Other Prime Cuts by Jasper Bark

Poetry collections:
WAR by Alessandro Manzetti and Marge Simon
Brief Encounters with My Third Eye by Bruce Boston
No Mercy: Dark Poems by Alessandro Manzetti
Eden Underground: Poetry of Darkness by Alessandro Manzetti

If you've ever thought of becoming an author, we'd also like to recommend these non-fiction titles:

The Dead Stage: The Journey from Page to Stage by Dan Weatherer
Where Nightmares Come From: The Art of Storytelling in the Horror Genre, edited by Joe Mynhardt and Eugene Johnson
Horror 101: The Way Forward, edited by Joe Mynhardt and Emma Audsley
Horror 201: The Silver Scream Vol.1 and *Vol.2*, edited by Joe Mynhardt and Emma Audsley
Modern Mythmakers: 35 interviews with Horror and Science Fiction Writers and Filmmakers by Michael McCarty
Writers On Writing: An Author's Guide Volumes 1,2,3, and 4, edited by Joe Mynhardt. Now also available in a Kindle and paperback omnibus.

Or check out other Crystal Lake Publishing books for more Tales from the Darkest Depths.

About the Author

Dave Jeffery is author of 12 novels, two collections and numerous short stories. His Necropolis Rising series and yeti adventure *Frostbite* have both featured on the Amazon #1 bestseller list. His YA work features critically acclaimed Beatrice Beecham series and *Finding Jericho*, a contemporary mental health novel which has featured on the BBC Health and the Independent Schools Entrance Examination Board's recommended reading lists. Jeffery is a member of the Society of Authors, British Fantasy Society (where he is a regular book reviewer), and the Horror Writers Association. He is also a registered mental health professional with a BSc (Hons) in Mental Health Studies and a Master's Degree in Health Studies. Jeffery is married with two children and lives in Worcestershire, UK.

Hi readers,

It makes our day to know you reached the end of our book. Thank you so much. This is why we do what we do every single day.

Whether you found the book good or great, we'd love to hear what you thought. Please take a moment to leave a review on Amazon, Goodreads, or anywhere else readers visit. Reviews go a long way to helping a book sell, and will help us to continue publishing quality books. You can also share a photo of yourself holding this book with the hashtag #IGotMyCLPBook!

Thank you again for taking the time to journey with Crystal Lake Publishing.

We are also on . . .

Website:
www.crystallakepub.com

Be sure to sign up for our newsletter and receive two free eBooks: http://eepurl.com/xfuKP

Books:
http://www.crystallakepub.com/book-table/

Twitter:
https://twitter.com/crystallakepub

Facebook:
https://www.facebook.com/Crystallakepublishing/

Instagram:
https://www.instagram.com/crystal_lake_publishing/

Patreon:
https://www.patreon.com/CLP

Or check out other Crystal Lake Publishing books for more Tales from the Darkest Depths. You can also subscribe to Crystal Lake Classics where you'll receive fortnightly info on all our books, starting all the way back at the beginning, with personal notes on every release. Or follow us on Patreon for behind the scenes access.

With unmatched success since 2012, Crystal Lake Publishing has quickly become one of the world's leading indie publishers of Mystery, Thriller, and Suspense books with a Dark Fiction edge.

Crystal Lake Publishing puts integrity, honor, and respect at the forefront of our operations.

We strive for each book and outreach program that's launched to not only entertain and touch or comment on issues that affect our readers, but also to strengthen and support the Dark Fiction field and its authors.

Not only do we publish authors who are legends in the field and as hardworking as us, but we look for men and women who care about their readers and fellow human beings. We only publish the very best Dark Fiction, and look forward to launching many new careers.

We strive to know each and every one of our

readers while building personal relationships with our authors, reviewers, bloggers, podcasters, bookstores, and libraries.

Crystal Lake Publishing is and will always be a beacon of what passion and dedication, combined with overwhelming teamwork and respect, can accomplish: unique fiction you can't find anywhere else.

We do not just publish books, we present you worlds within your world, doors within your mind from talented authors who sacrifice so much for a moment of your time.

This is what we believe in. What we stand for. This will be our legacy.

Welcome to Crystal Lake Publishing.

THANK YOU FOR PURCHASING THIS BOOK